DREAMS AND SECRETS BOOK FIVE

THE RISEN QUEEN

LINN COLDIRON

Cover Design by Jules Designs
(www. coversbyjules.crd.co)
Book Layout by Linn Coldiron

The Risen Queen / Linn Coldiron ~ Second Edition 2025
ISBN: 978-1-955200-35-6

10 9 8 7 6 5 4 3 2

To Mom. I love you.

A Note from the Author

In the process of creating this story, world, and characters, I've spent hundreds of hours researching the cultures involved, including learning Mandarin and living in China for a period of about a year. However, research does not replace lived experience and I, in no way, claim that the experiences of my characters represent the entirety of the Asian American community. The same goes for the indigenous tribe I created for the sake of the story and clans. I created the culture based on my own readings and understandings of Native American tribes, particularly the Shoshone tribe which much inspiration was taken. For lived experience representation, please seek out books by authors of any culture you wish to read about. There is a list of some of my favorites on my website, linncoldiron.com.

Content Warnings

While a work of fiction intended for entertainment, there are darker elements and themes in *The Risen Queen*. This book contains the following content warnings: violence using fantasy magic, PTSD, discussions of genocide and colonialism/imperialism, swears and cursing, suicide, death, grief, regret, and loss of loved ones.

Derek

Chapter One

Derek gripped the handle of Mia's suitcase, watching her as she searched through her purse for her passport.

She muttered to herself, something inaudible, but her tone was harsh. Snappy. Frustration tickled his skin and he shuddered before looking away.

It was surprisingly busy for five in the morning, but still, the security line had so few people that Derek wondered if Mia had an ulterior motive for getting to the airport this early. Her flight wasn't for four hours. He understood the anxiety that came with international travel, but this was ridiculous. Still, he'd forced himself to wake up and take her to the airport, afraid that she would have left without saying goodbye if he hadn't.

"You could always stay," Derek said, not for the first time. "Finish high school here. Go to college. Start over."

A small grin spread across Mia's face and she pulled her passport out of her purse with a sigh. "Found it. I knew it was in here somewhere."

"Mia, come on." He shifted at the change in her emotions.

Anxiety to relief. He should have been happy that going to China brought her relief, but underneath it all was a current of absolute heartbreak he couldn't fix for her. Even his powers weren't enough to take away her grief.

"Passport, boarding pass, bags are checked in, got my phone fully charged…." She looked up at Derek with the smile she'd been sporting since announcing her move. It didn't look like her. Even though her lips were turned up in a smile, her eyes remained hollow. "That's everything."

"Mia. Let's think about this for a second." Derek's desperation flooded every word. Sure, she'd already enrolled in a school in Beijing. Sure, she had her tickets. Sure, their grandparents waited for her, eager to welcome her back to their homeland. But Derek wanted her to stay. Colorado without his twin? That wasn't how life was supposed to go.

She ignored him, focused on her phone. "Nainai wants you to visit soon. Maybe when school is over? We can wander around Beijing. Like old times."

Old times? The old times were gone. He couldn't go back to China and pretend like the past two years hadn't happened. There was too much to do. Too much to fix.

He let go of Mia's suitcase and placed his hands on her shoulders. Her smile faded as she looked into his eyes. How could he explain? How could he convince her to stay and help him? "This isn't right."

She took a deep breath. "I'll text you when I'm at my gate."

"Why are you leaving?" he asked.

Emotions flickered into Mia's eyes. They coated his skin. A barrage of textures fighting for control. Anxiety. Fear. Heartache. Grief. She placed a hand on his, and her breath came out shaky. "I don't want to talk about it."

But Derek did. Mia's emotions may not be a mystery to him, but her mind was, and he hated it. He hated not knowing what her thought process was. He hated fighting to get any information out of her. She'd gone quiet after the mage attack, but when Enya had set Willow Creek ablaze, the rest of the fight left her. Every moment since Blair's disappearance had broken her further.

"Mia, please. Talk to me." Derek gripped her shoulders tighter and she looked at the floor again. "Let's go home and talk about what happened."

Tears pricked her eyes. "I am going home."

She pulled away and grabbed her suitcase. Derek floundered, searching for the words to tell her that she wasn't. This was her home. This was where she needed to be. He wanted to tell her, again, that Blair wasn't dead. That they needed to work together—with Cody too—to find her. But anything he came up with faltered on his tongue. She wouldn't hear it. She'd seen Enya set Blair on fire. As far as she was concerned, Blair was gone forever.

Even though she wasn't.

"I love you," she said, placing a hand on his cheek, "but I can't stay. I promise I'll be all right."

He didn't believe her. She was running away from everything. She wasn't facing her grief or her assumptions. When she had a moment to relax, when she was alone with people who didn't understand, she would break down. She needed to be with family.

But what could he do? He needed her to stay, but maybe what she needed was to go. For a year. He'd let her go for a year. Taking a deep breath, he nodded. "Fly safe."

Her sorrow coated smile tore at his heart, but he didn't stop her. He didn't pull her into a tight hug. He didn't push happiness and relief onto her emotions. No matter what he did, he couldn't make her feel safe again because he didn't know if they *would* ever be safe again. The mage clans, while quiet, hadn't resolved anything. As far as Mrs. Arbour had told him, things were tense after Enola's death. But that was nothing compared to the other issues: Jae had the knife, and Enya was still out there, plotting.

They said nothing else. Mia didn't hug him. He didn't say goodbye. He watched her weave her way through the stanchions toward the front of the line. She looked like she was withering away. For the week they'd lived in his tiny apartment in Denver, he'd had to force her to eat. He'd suggested running. Lifting weights. Going to a nearby gym. She'd sat in the living room, scouring the internet for the best plane tickets.

He stayed in the security area until Mia finished and headed down to the trains. She never looked back. He was going to give her a year, but deep down he knew that she was never going to come back here again. Letting her go now meant letting her go forever.

A flush of anger burned his soul. Jae had this obsession with protecting Mia. Bringing her happiness. He'd taken her to protect her from pain, he'd said.

What bullshit.

Jae hadn't protected her. He'd *caused* this. He kept calling her his angel, but then he turned around and tormented her.

Had he known that his mother was going to try and kill Blair?

Had he known, when he spared Blair and took Enola's life instead, that Enya wouldn't let that stand?

Why, if he cared about Mia so much, did he keep destroying her?

In a few hours, Mia would be on a plane. America held so much pain for her. Too much. It'd broken her into a million pieces, and Jae had ground those into dust before Enya set them on fire when she set the mountains ablaze.

Derek took in a shuddering breath. With Mia gone and Cody leaving Denver for college after high school, he would be alone to do what he needed to. It was his job to stay strong. To keep a level head. He couldn't break down, no matter how much he wanted to, because Blair needed him.

It wouldn't be easy. There was no saying how long it would take, or how miserable his life would be. No matter what happened, he was going to find Blair, and he was going to bring her home.

Five Years Later

Chapter Two

By the time Derek was ten, he'd learned how to write research papers in both Mandarin and English. By fifteen, he was both proficient and fluent in three languages, bordering on four. By eighteen, he'd pushed himself to the brink, doing his best not to disappoint his academically-driven parents. He'd grown up in the academic world. He'd lived, breathed, and ate education, believing that if he'd learned enough, he could change the world.

Then nineteen hit and he'd decided none of it mattered. At that point, he'd had multiple attempts on his life, destroyed his relationship with Mia, watched his home burn to the ground, and lost the girl he loved to a fate worse than death. He'd given up trying to please his parents. He gave up on traditional education. No college. No grad school. No PhD. By the time he was nineteen, he knew better. He knew that his parents' reality, the one they'd pushed on him, didn't account for so many things. Papers and academic research wouldn't change the world. At least, not in his world.

Still, that energy had to go *somewhere*. It wasn't enough to sit around and hope for the best. So, for five years, he researched. Not human history, not modern day politics, and definitely not science of any kind, but instead he researched anything and everything relating to the world of magic. If he was going to find Blair Arbour, if he was going to bring her home, then he needed to know *everything*.

It'd taken the first year to figure out where she was. While fighting off calls from his parents and worrying endlessly about Mia, whom he heard from maybe once a month, he'd spent all of his time either at the mage library in Denver or wandering around the world collecting books that non-mages thought were trash. He'd learned to read multiple languages—though he could barely speak them—and communicated with any mage willing to risk talking to him. He was, by all means, an expert on magic. The languages, the history, the nuances. Mrs. Arbour thought he was overdoing it. Cody often told him he was ruining his life.

He didn't care. Because he'd found her.

He'd stumbled on the information quite by accident, thumbing through some ancient Chinese text one day. He wasn't sure why he'd stopped on that specific page, when nothing else had caught his eye, but he'd found it. A story, a myth, whose title translated roughly into, "Living in the World of the Dead."

In that moment, everything snapped into place. The story spoke of a young mage searching for his older brother, who'd vanished during war. The young mage had brokered a deal with Death to enter the world of death and search. That's when Derek had realized where he needed to go. The rest of the story—how the mage managed to enter the world, what happened there, and if he returned home—had been ripped out. Derek had yet to find the rest, but it was a start. All of his focus from then on went into finding out what happened when Death reaped someone's soul. He researched every religion he could find, both non-mage and mage, and realized that what he'd been looking for had been under his nose the whole time. Everyone called it something different. The

World of the Dead, Heaven, Death's Hold, whatever.

Derek called it the Realm of Death.

For the next four years, he'd honed his research. There were stories of mages who had entered the realm. Stories of mages who had never returned. He found rituals that had succeeded. Rituals that had failed. Some were in languages long dead to the world, but he didn't let that stop him.

He was going to save Blair and fix everything that Jae and Enya had destroyed five years ago.

Which is why he sat in the living room of his very messy apartment, books piled high around him, while he flipped through an ancient Arabic book that focused on the Realm of Death. Next to him, an Arabic to English dictionary sat, spine cracked, open to a page that wasn't helping him as much as he'd hoped. His Arabic was shaky at best when it was modern. Ancient Arabic? Even worse.

"You might as well give up," a deep, annoyed voice said.

Derek glanced up from the book and into the familiar green eyes of the man he despised more than anyone in the world. Niran sat on the couch, watching him with an ever present and judgmental smirk.

Rolling his eyes, Derek went back to his book, struggling over one word in particular. He flipped through the dictionary, searching for it, but he had a feeling it was an archaic word. He was going to have to find a different source.

A heavy sigh escaped Niran's lips. "I cannot wait until I'm in control. There's so much I'm going to do once I'm not a fractured soul. Starting with cleaning up this disgusting place."

Derek didn't acknowledge him. It'd been about two years since Niran had shown up and stayed. About six months since he'd started talking. With each passing day, Niran grew stronger. His form took on a more corporeal state. Sometimes, he could even touch things. Push a glass off a table like some attention starved cat. One day, when Niran became sturdy enough, Derek would take great pleasure in punching him in the jaw.

The book wasn't getting him anywhere. Annoyance built in his gut. He almost had it. His notes, while a disaster, had so much information. He just needed one more piece. If only he had any idea what that piece was or where to obtain it. Everything had been a shot in the dark. Luck. Five long years of luck.

"You could at least acknowledge me. I know you won't talk. You don't talk to anyone."

Derek ignored him, and before Niran could continue pitching a fit, a knock at the door interrupted him. Derek knew who it was without looking up. From his pathetic knock, to his range of concerned emotions, to his overwhelming power pressing against Derek's chest, Cody was easy to spot from a mile away.

Resisting the urge to glare at Niran, Derek marked his place in the book and stumbled to the front door. He stepped over dirty dishes, books, clothes, and trash. Niran had every reason to desire cleaning this place. But Derek didn't care. He had a place to sleep and work-out, both of which he took seriously. The last thing Blair would need when he showed up was an exhausted wimp who hadn't taken care of his body. Cleaning was the last thing on his mind.

Once he reached the door, he yanked it open, not bothering to greet Cody, and then headed back to his book. He pushed a lock of long, greasy hair out of his face. He needed to figure out this passage. Even if it destroyed his brain, he was going to understand.

Cody let out a long, dramatic sigh. "You're disgusting."

Derek waved him off. "What do you want?"

Cody had changed in the past five years. College and a stable job had been good for him. He wore nicer clothes, hair longer than before, but managed nicely, and he'd lost the anxiety that used to fill a room when he walked in. Well, not lost entirely. It was still there. He was still Cody Velt, certified ball of anxious. But it no longer overwhelmed every other emotion. It was a stream, digging away at his self-confidence, but not flooding his life.

What did flood his life, however, was his ever growing power. Every time he came to visit—mostly likely in part due to Intira's insistence—Cody's magic had grown a fraction. But a fraction of a million was still a hell of a lot.

Derek shuddered. What would Cody's magic be like in another five years? What if Cody decided to start training again? What would become of him? Would he even be able to handle it?

"Your mom called and asked me to check on you," Cody said. The door clicked shut and Derek glanced at Cody over his shoulder. "She hasn't heard from you in a couple of weeks. *I* haven't heard from you in a couple of weeks. Wanted to make sure you didn't die in this shit hole."

"Nope, not dead." Derek kicked some dirty clothes aside. "Couch is free."

"It is not!" Niran protested, but it wasn't like Niran could do anything about it. He could touch objects. Not people.

"Glad you're not dead." Cody didn't sit and instead walked over to the table where Derek had stacked so many books the table groaned. "I see you've been doing some light reading in…what language is this?"

He held up one of the books and Derek rolled his eyes. "Greek. Learn your languages, dammit."

"Like I could keep that many straight. How many are you up to?"

"No idea." Derek had no interest in a conversation with Cody. He didn't have time. Every second he wasted talking pleasantries with his only remaining friend was a second longer Blair had to spend in the Realm of Death doing who knows what. But, at least it was better than talking to Niran.

"So, what do I tell your mom?" Cody asked.

"That I'm fine."

"Uh huh. Sure. Fine." Cody pointed at a pile of dirty dishes. "You're going to die of mold exposure."

"So clean." Derek didn't have time for this. "I don't care. I'm close, and you're bothering me."

Cody sighed and leaned against the table, arms crossed. Niran appeared next to him, getting up and personal in Cody's space. Derek had no idea what the priest was up to as he examined Cody's face.

"So weird," Niran said. "You never see half-mage half-Vilaim children. Can't wait to pick his brain and challenge his magic when I'm me again."

Derek narrowed his eyes and focused on Cody, who watched him with a raised brow.

"What?" Derek asked.

Cody frowned. "Fine. I'll clean."

"Neat freak," Derek said.

"No, I'm just not a slob."

Derek returned to his translation. And as Cody went around his apartment, organizing books, throwing out trash, and running a load of dishes, Derek struggled, desperate to know what the book said and if it could help him. So far, it was a bunch of gibberish. Talking about the Realm of Death's beauty and how the spirits gathered together with their loved ones. At least, that's what Derek figured it was saying. Other books had spoken in great detail of the beauty of the afterlife, so why wouldn't this one?

Again, his Arabic, not so great.

After an hour, frustration got the better of him. He slammed the book shut, leaning his head against the wall, and closed his tired eyes.

"Giving up?" Cody asked.

"No," Derek snapped. Cody leaned against the frame that marked the entrance of the kitchen, arms once more crossed. Niran stood next to him, still examining him like he was a diamond amidst shit. The apartment, while still a mess, looked like humans lived there. Turns out, Derek had a floor.

Mia would have been *so* proud of Derek. Living in squalor. Speaking to no one. Reading books. Learning new languages to read more books. If she ever bothered to leave China, she'd lecture him worse than Cody. Well, maybe. Mia hadn't exactly been Mia since everything.

Cody let out an exasperated sigh before walking over to the couch and collapsing on it. "I know you think Blair is in this Realm of Death place, but you have no proof it even exists. And even if it does, you have no proof she's there. Alive. You keep saying you can feel her, but if she were alive, shouldn't I be able to as well?"

"You'd think that, but no." Derek shrugged. "Living people in the Realm of Death lose their connection to their souls. They can use magic at a cost, and they can still think and feel, but they don't have souls. It's why it's called the Realm of Death."

Cody raised an eyebrow. "That makes no sense."

"It does."

After a minute of silence, Cody examining Derek and Niran examining Cody, Cody asked, "When was the last time you slept?"

Derek sighed. "Irrelevant. The point is, my powers are different, even if they seem similar. I feel her emotions. You feel her soul."

"I didn't ask for a lecture on our gifts," Cody said.

Derek waved him off. "But if she's in the Realm of Death, then she isn't connected to her soul. Because theoretically she's dead."

"You can't bring the dead back to life. Not even Death can do that."

"No, but Blair is *theoretically* dead. She isn't actually dead. I can bring her back. I just need to figure out the last piece of the puzzle."

The impossible last piece of the puzzle. The one that evaded him, just out of reach.

15

Cody sighed. He sighed a lot when visiting, Derek noticed. He must have been so fed up with Derek's obsession. Like everyone else, he didn't believe Derek. Why should he? Besides Derek's empathy, there was no proof Blair was alive. Derek had half a mind to ask Cody why he kept coming over. He had a degree. A job. A condo. Savings. A nice car. A…okay, he didn't have a girlfriend, but he did well enough on the hookup market. So why? Was it pity? Was it obligation? Was it curiosity about Mia? Was it something else entirely?

Did Derek actually care?

"If you're going to judge me, leave." Derek grabbed a different book from a new stack. One in Latin. Latin was easier than Arabic.

While he read, he could feel Cody's eyes on him. The man's annoyance prickled at Derek's skin, but he ignored it. And after a minute, Cody's footsteps thudded against the wooden ground. The door opened. The door slammed shut. And Derek was alone.

Mostly.

"You push him away enough and he won't come back," Niran said.

Derek didn't care. It was his last year of life anyway. Besides, he had a puzzle to solve. He settled into the couch and flipped through the new book, scanning for familiar words, as the sun set behind the distant mountains.

Chapter Three

Reading books wasn't enough. After Cody left, Derek decided that he was sick of literature. He needed to *see* what was missing. He needed to *feel* the ritual he'd developed. It was time to move out of the theoretical and into the practical.

It took three days. Three days of little sleep. Three days of chalk and trips to find rocks from rivers, sand from fresh oceans, and mist from mountains in the clouds. He collected everything he needed, mostly at night, and set up the ritualistic circle that looked like something out of a damn horror movie. If anyone came in, they might think he was trying to summon a devil.

They wouldn't be entirely off base.

With chalk, he traced a circle on the wooden floors, trying over and over to get it right. The symbols in the circle looked made up, but they were from every ancient language he could find. A mishmash of everything he'd learned. There was no guarantee it would work. In fact, he was almost certain it wouldn't.

He checked. Double checked. Triple checked. All of his notes, written in various languages and varying degrees of legibility, were cobbled together in a mess of papers only he knew how to decipher. He had a feeling if anyone else tried, they'd go insane trying to figure out what madman had put all of this together. He didn't care. Let them call him mad. Let them brush him off and assume he had no idea what he was doing.

If anyone could open the door to the Realm of Death, it would be Derek.

After three days, he finished the sigil. Shuffling through his notes, he sat on his floor and glanced up at the circle now and then to see what he was missing. His butt hurt, and his legs complained, but he stayed put. As he obsessed over his design, the only thing keeping his determination from faltering was a memory from seven years ago. Back in the days when he knew nothing about the Iravata. When Death was nothing more than a man with a cloak and a scythe. Sitting in Blair's kitchen with Mrs. Arbour as she said the words he repeated over and over again:

"Anything is possible when it comes to magic."

Breathing in, he focused on the light coat of emotions that forever lingered on his skin. On days he needed to focus, he was perfectly capable of blocking them out, but when he needed motivation, he let them in. They were gentle today. Contentment. Peace. They often were in recent months. At first, she felt only fear mixed with rage. Sometimes uncertainty. But in the past two years, she'd adjusted to her life. Whatever it was. However it worked. She'd come to terms with her imprisonment, and Derek wondered if she'd want to leave.

"Of course she wants to leave." Niran sat across the circle from Derek with crossed legs and a hand in his chin. "No one *wants* to be in the Realm of Death. Dead or not. She wants to escape. Being used to a place doesn't make it home."

But what did make a home? Derek had, for most of his life, thought of Willow Creek as home. Blair had lived there her entire

18

life. As had Cody. It was comfort. It was safe. It was *home*.

It was gone.

No one had gone to rebuild it. There'd been talks, sure. The wasteland of Willow Creek couldn't exist forever, or so the governor said. But no one wanted to take on the task of actually doing it. Everyone who had lived there before—and had survived the fire— spoke of a curse on the land. Even those who didn't believe in curses had become wary of the mountains.

Focus.

He didn't have time to think about Willow Creek or what made a home. Niran was, annoyingly, right. Blair would want to escape. He had to keep that thought afloat because otherwise the past five years would be pointless. This would work. He'd make sure it worked.

"Your obsession with Blair is borderline disgusting," Niran said.

"It is not," Derek muttered.

"Oh? He speaks?" Niran clapped his hands together, letting out a cackle. "This has to be the first time you've talked to me. I feel *oh* so special."

Derek ignored him. He bit his lip and flipped through his notes. If only he could *see* it. The thing that he was missing. He had all of the physical items he needed. It was something spiritual. Something personal. Something that wouldn't be easy to obtain.

-The blood of the anchor.

Derek started. He looked up from his notes, glancing around his apartment in search of the voice. Had he imagined it? Niran watched him like he was insane, so it was very possible. Still, the words repeated themselves on the wind, a voice so obscure he couldn't place it. But he'd heard it before. A long time ago. Back in the days when someone was trying to kill him.

He glanced back down at his notes. Flipped through the pages. Nothing. He threw the notebook to the side and grabbed a stack of papers. At first, he found nothing, but after a few minutes of scanning, in the top right corner of a page of mostly Chinese, were those exact words in English.

"The Blood of the Anchor????"

Mind going a million miles a minute, he tried to recall where he'd found that phrase. The date on his notes indicated they were from three years ago. Why had he written it in English? Why hadn't he done anything with those words since?

What was going on?

"It can't be…."

With a flurry, he scrambled to his giant stack of notes on the table and almost dove into them. Searching. Searching. Searching for the words that now haunted his mind. Every now and then, regardless of the language of his notes, he found the same phrase written in English. Sometimes with more information. Sometimes with less.

This was it. What he was missing.

He glanced at the ceiling with a furrowed brow. The voice had helped him. But why?

"Figure it out?"

Derek glared at Niran before scrambling to find his phone. As luck would have it, he'd plugged it in to charge, so it was easy to find in the mess. From the beginning of his research, he'd always known he'd need to use his own blood. Not much. Just a few drops. But now? Now he knew it wasn't just *his* blood. He needed an anchor. Someone with powerful magic.

Like Cody.

He hit send on his message and collapsed on the couch, breathing deep. It'd been there. All along. For *years* he'd had all the parts. If only he'd figured it out earlier.

The phone buzzed.

<<I'll come after work.>>

Derek grimaced. He almost responded with an angry "now," but refrained. No matter what he did, Cody wouldn't leave work. Back in the first year, when everything was raw for everyone, Derek had tried to get Cody to help him. To leave school. Cody always refused. He didn't believe in Derek's mission. He just wanted to move on with his life. Mia had messed with his head. Sure, he used to ask about her daily. Sure, he used to obsess about her to Derek. But he'd always said it was time to let go of the past.

In the end, Derek had decided he didn't need anyone's help. He'd do this on his own.

"But you do need help," Niran said. "Don't worry. He'll help you. Cody is a good boy who does whatever he's told."

Derek's eyes flickered up to Niran, a frown etched onto his face. Niran smirked at him, and not for the first time, Derek couldn't imagine what Lady Shion ever saw in this man. This cocky, arrogant, asshole of a man.

Niran chuckled. "I didn't used to be this way, Derek. It's amazing how much death changes you. You see everything differently. Which, I suppose, you'll find out soon enough."

With a deep breath, Derek settled back on the ground, examining every inch of his circle to make sure it was perfect. Niran was wrong. He wouldn't find out the effects of death for a long time to come. Even if Niran kept insisting Derek didn't have much time left, and even if the shithead grew more and more stable every day, Derek refused to believe it. He had too much to do. Too much to complete. Starting with making sure that Blair was safe.

Derek grabbed Cody's arm the moment he opened the door and dragged the poor guy into the apartment so hard he almost tripped.

"Hey!" Cody yanked his arm out of Derek's grasp. He stumbled, catching himself on the wall. "What the hell?"

"I figured it out," Derek said. He reached for Cody's arm again, but the man jerked back with the nastiest glare Derek had seen in a long time. Derek rolled his eyes. "Come on. We don't have a lot of time."

Cody eyed him, then closed the door with a heavy sigh. "Have a lot of time for what?"

"The ritual. Pay attention." Derek stepped around the chalk circle, careful not to disturb anything. From the kitchen doorway, Niran watched with interest, and Derek shot him a glare before focusing on Cody again. "I need your help."

Cody scoffed. "No. Screw that. I'm not helping you with anything. I'm done with magic. You know that."

"*You* can't be done with magic," Derek said. Anxiety rushed into his stomach, turning it like a pirouetting ballerina. He didn't have time to argue. "Just give me three days. After that, Blair will be safe and we never have to speak again."

Cody shifted. "I don't want to not speak. I just–"

"Just what?" Derek flipped through his notes about the anchor before he rushed toward Cody, shoving the papers into his hands. "Never mind. Come on. I need you to act as an anchor. You have more magic than pretty much anyone, so it should be simple. All you have to do is stay put until I can get Blair out."

"Excuse me?" Cody laughed. "I can't do that. I have work. I have a life."

Derek desperately wanted to point out that, no, Cody didn't have a life. He worked, he ate, and he slept. He didn't have friends, he didn't have a girlfriend, and he barely spoke to his parents. But pointing out any of that wouldn't get him anywhere, so instead he said, "You owe me."

Cody scoffed with the most obvious eye roll Derek had ever seen. "Owe you? You haven't done shit for me. I don't owe you anything."

"I keep you updated on my sister." Derek knew that it was a low blow. Cody's emotions battered against him, fluctuating between the embarrassment and romantic interest that always popped up when he thought of Mia.

Cody bowed his head. "I don't need you—"

"Save it. She doesn't want to talk to you, you want to know how she is. I'm doing you a favor, and now you owe me."

"I don't owe you. I will not let you drag me back into the world of magic. It's done nothing but destroy my life."

"It's just for a few days!"

"No."

"So, you're going to punish Blair because you're a coward?"

Cody had almost made it out the door when he stopped, hand on the doorknob. Frustration clawed at Derek's skin. Cody let go of the doorknob and faced Derek with his head held high, expression empty. But he couldn't hide his emotions from Derek. Regret. Anger. Distress. Depression. Grief. Guilt.

From the kitchen, Niran laughed. "Low blow."

Derek didn't tell Niran to shut it, but it took effort to resist. Instead, he glared at Cody. Stared him down in the hopes that he could capitalize on Cody's guilt and force him to help.

The thing was, Cody wasn't wrong for wanting out. He wasn't wrong for wanting to go about his life without fearing for it, or his sanity. He'd done it for the past five years. Mia had done it for the past five years. The two of them had gone through their adult lives pretending magic didn't exist.

But Cody couldn't pretend like magic didn't exist. It *did* exist. As long as Cody was a Natara, as long as Derek was a mage, and as long as the Iravata haunted them, there was no running from the magic world. Yes, things had been quiet for years, but there was no saying when it would start up again. Derek was going to be prepared when that happened. He wanted to be strong. He wanted to be agile. He wanted to be standing next to Blair when it all fell to hell.

Cody breathed in deep. "I don't want to be part of this world."

"I know." Derek stepped toward him, extending a hand. "I wouldn't be asking if I had any other choice."

Staring at Derek's hand, Cody took in another breath "All I have to do is stay here for a few days? Nothing else?"

"Nothing else." Once Derek came back with Blair, Cody could go back to his day job and pretend like he wasn't involved in the brewing war. He could pretend like his father wasn't a major player. That he wasn't only half-human. He couldn't pretend like the Iravata had always been, and would always be, a part of their lives. Sure, it was easy to forget sometimes, especially for Cody, who hid away in his job. The Iravata had disappeared for the past five years. Sometimes, Derek felt them wandering around Denver—stalking him—but mostly they were off doing their own thing.

Derek knew for a fact that they wouldn't stay away once Blair was back. Blair vanishing had stopped the clock, but it was a compressed spring waiting for a release. Blair's return would start everything again, and while Derek wanted things to remain quiet, he couldn't let it happen. He couldn't let Blair suffer any longer, and that meant becoming involved with the assholes known as the Iravata.

"I like the Iravata," Niran said. "They're all very damaged people. Well, not people. But you know what I mean."

"Cody, I need an answer," Derek said. "Are you in or out?"

Derek knew the expression that slithered onto Cody's face. Cody wanted to leave and never look back, but he also couldn't say no. Derek knew that he couldn't say no because Cody was a good guy. He wouldn't let Blair live in the Realm of Death forever. Even if he hated magic. Even if he hated everything to do with the world he'd been born a part of.

Cody sighed. For a second, Derek thought his heart might stop in anticipation, but then Cody pushed away from the door. "Fine. But you owe me."

"If this works, you can have whatever you want." Derek grinned.

"Be careful what you offer him," Niran said. "You don't have much time left."

Derek didn't care. He was going to get Blair back.

"All right. Let's do this." Derek faced the circle, grinning.

"You might want to take a shower first," Cody said as he stepped around the chalk to the other side. "Pretty sure you want Blair to want to go home with you. She might do it if you look like shit, but you have a better chance if you don't."

Derek glowered at him. But he wasn't wrong. It'd been a while since Derek had showered. Or shaved. He probably looked like a crazed mess. "Fine. But after that, we're doing this. No running away. If you try, I will hunt you down."

Cody raised his hands. "I won't run away."

"Good."

From the other side of the room, Niran laughed. "Well, I'm certainly eager to see what this Realm of Death looks like. Aren't you?"

Derek didn't respond.

Derek squeezed water out of his hair before shoving it into a low ponytail. It wasn't the longest it'd ever been, since he'd taken scissors to it about a year ago, but at the moment it came down to his shoulders, and he had no intention of letting it fall into his face while traversing the Realm of Death. He thought, for a second, about asking Cody to cut it. He'd tried to go to professional barbers in the past, but looking in the mirror at Niran's face had been too much for him. Besides, he didn't have the hour it took.

Cleanly shaven—which took longer than he'd liked thanks to his hygiene neglect over the past…years—and with his hair at least tamed, he stormed out of the bathroom and grabbed what he needed. He'd already packed a backpack with two bottles of water and a change of clothes, but he also wanted food. His fridge was pretty much empty of anything but tofu and raw carrots, so he closed that and went to his pathetic pantry instead. Crackers. All he could find were stupid rice crackers. Still, he grabbed them.

It was better than nothing.

Cody was in the living room, flipping through Derek's notes, as Derek grabbed a pair of tennis shoes from the closet. They weren't brand new. He'd gone running and walking in them a few times to break them in, but they also weren't his old pair. The pair he'd bought to go running with Mia back in Willow Creek.

He hesitated. Longing tugged at his heart. He wanted her to come with him, honestly. There were two parts to it. One was that he didn't want to be apart from his twin anymore, and the other was that he needed to *prove* to her that he wasn't crazy. She didn't believe Blair was alive. No one believed Blair was alive. Maybe, if he got her to see everything, she'd understand and come out of her shell.

No. He couldn't fix her. He wasn't sure if anything could, but she had to want to heal, and the last time he'd seen her, a few months ago, he wasn't sure she was ready for that. Ready to face reality instead of slowly killing herself. She didn't want to leave China. She didn't want to leave safety.

It wasn't his job to make her.

Yet, he found himself grabbing his phone. He didn't know her life anymore. Maybe she'd delete it. Maybe she'd ignore him. But he had something he wanted to say.

It took him a minute to compose it. A minute to edit it. A second to send it. It was early in China. She wouldn't get it for a while. And he didn't have time to wait.

He breathed in and pulled on his shoes. Niran watched him from the bedroom, arms crossed, but with a grin on his face that Derek didn't like. Derek narrowed his eyes at him and pushed past. Their shoulders brushed. A first. Derek's stomach sunk into his gut, but he kept going. Cody had moved on from Derek's notes to a book Derek recognized as *An English History of Magic*. Boring. Not informative. Clearly biased.

"You ready to do this?" Derek asked.

Cody snapped the book shut and replaced it on the shelf. "Frankly? No. But if this works, you're going to make a lot of people happy."

He didn't need to say "Mia" for Derek to know that's who he meant. Cody's emotions flared to life, switching between all the ones he felt when he thought of her. Derek rubbed his arm, wanting the textures gone. He didn't like thinking about what happened between Mia and Cody five years ago. He didn't like knowing that his sister had done something so shitty. And he especially didn't like that Cody couldn't let it go.

"Then let's do it." Derek grabbed his knife from the table. Cody stared at it, but Derek ignored him. He'd bought it years ago, feeling the missing weight of *the* knife. He took it with him everywhere, hiding it with his magic when he needed to. It was stupid. He knew it was stupid. But it helped him feel better.

He walked around to the other side of the circle, where the bowl of seawater waited for his and Cody's blood. Without looking at either Cody or Niran, he pricked his finger. Pain shot through his hand. He grimaced, but didn't fight the pain as a trail of blood dripped into the bowl. The water hissed. Then, without a word, he handed the knife to Cody.

Cody grimaced. "Are you–"

"Just do it."

Cody scowled, then did as he was told. The moment their blood intermixed, every object in the circle exploded with it. With magic. With energy. With *life*.

This was it.

Breathing in deep, Derek focused. The words left his lips as if the magic dragged them out. A string of Latin filled the air, and a gust of wind kicked up at his feet. It pulled him toward the center of the glowing chalk circle. His heart raced.

"Well I'll be damned," Niran muttered.

Derek ignored him, even if he did look sturdier than this morning.

In the center of the circle, a glowing, beckoning oval swirled into existence. It tugged at Derek. Not at his body, but his soul. Without taking his eyes off of it, he said to Cody, "Whatever happens, don't leave this apartment."

"I won't."

An emptiness waited for him on the other side. Possible danger. The unknown. Many scholars had theorized about the Realm of Death. None had confirmed their suspicions. He would be the first.

Well, him and Blair.

He stepped forward. It was easier than breathing. He didn't want to admit it, but the Realm of Death called to him. Niran appeared next to him, and Derek glanced his way. The phantom's eyes were alive in a way Derek had never seen them before, and a shudder ran up his spine.

This was probably a mistake. He didn't care. It was something he needed to do. Something he would do.

He could do this.

A smile flickering onto his lips, he ignored Cody watching him, ignored Niran breathing heavily, anticipating, and walked into the consuming, glowing, oval portal.

Chapter Four

Derek expected to fall on his face. He tensed, prepared to stumble through the magic and fight against the realm that wanted his soul, not his body.

He did not stumble.

He did not fall on his face.

His foot pressed into soft ground. It trampled long grass in its wake, and he came to a stop. Around him, the white world exploded into color. It bled through the cracks, swirling like paint on van Gogh's brush. He could only watch, mesmerized at the crystal blue sky, the stretching fields of waving grass, and the massive trees off in the distance. Behind him, the sound of gurgling came into existence. He didn't dare look back. The oval of magic continued to glow, casting his shadow against the ground. If he looked back, what would he see? Would he see Cody? Would he see his mistakes? Would it all tempt him to abandon his journey?

Would Cody try and pull him back?

Then, the magic vanished, leaving his back cold and his shadow gone. A heavy breath escaped his lips. There was no turning back.

Not until he found Blair. Not until he'd conquered the quest no one had before.

He turned.

The rushing river brought him back to his dreams. The ones he'd had before Niran appeared as a phantom. Standing at the edge of the Mekong River with a vision that wasn't his, for a future that wasn't his. Back in the days before he knew too much.

Had he made a mistake? Had the portal taken him to Thailand? Why would it do that? He could visit the clearing by the river whenever he wanted, with his powers.

Glittering lights floated past him. One brushed his hand, sending a string of warmth into his body. Warmth like he'd never experienced. It burned him. It consumed his being. He gasped and jerked around. The orbs drifted past, lifting gently into the sky until they vanished under the sun's rays.

Okay, so maybe he wasn't in Thailand.

His body cooled to its normal temperature, and he shivered. He didn't know what those orbs were, and he had a feeling he didn't want to find out. There wasn't time to, anyway. Being here meant he was on borrowed time. There was a chance he could spend years exploring the Realm of Death and all its facets.

But he had a mission, and he'd be damned if he ignored it for curiosity.

He straightened his back, rolling his shoulders as determination settled over him. It was time to move. He'd read somewhere that the Realm of Death showed you what you wanted to see. Did he want to see Thailand? He couldn't imagine why. Blair wouldn't be here. Would she? If this place showed him what he wanted to see, then why wasn't he seeing Blair?

He scowled, then turned away from the river. His eyes scanned the world laid bare in front of him, searching for Niran. If Derek had come through, then Niran would too, wouldn't he?

Except, it seemed that Niran hadn't joined him.

A smile spread across his lips, and he threw his head back with laughter. Was he finally free from that prick?

Instead of Niran, a wall caught his eye. One that extended high into the air, making it impossible to see the top. One that stretched out on either side, disappearing into the horizon. One that called to him. Pulled at his chest until he could barely breathe. He waited, warily, in case this was the wrong choice. In his experience, things that called to him weren't always friendly. But what did he have to lose? It's not like he had other options.

He stepped forward. At first, his foot sunk into the ground. It wasn't as though he were walking on sand, but more like a trampoline. He jerked his foot back, staring at the dirt, and it bounced back at him, nearly sending him flying. He grimaced. If it was all going to be like this, he was going to have to be careful.

Another step. The ground didn't flex as much. Another step. More sturdy. Another. Solid ground. Derek frowned and glared at the dirt. It was messing with him. It had to be messing with him. Could a realm mess with someone? He had a feeling it didn't want him here. It settled deep in his gut. He wasn't welcome. He was alive, and the world around him wasn't.

He continued on. As he neared the wall, he considered what he needed to do when he got there. If he ran into any dead. His reports had indicated that the dead weren't friendly. To avoid them if he could. Some of those reports came from mediums. Others came from philosophy. He didn't know how accurate they were, but if there was any chance to avoid the dead, he was going to.

Taking a deep breath, he focused on his body. He couldn't disappear himself the way that Cody could. No, that was reserved for those with the power of souls. What he could do was create a prism around him. One that reflected light enough so it would be harder to notice him.

He tried.

He really, honestly, tried.

Nothing happened.

A scowl etched itself onto his face and he kicked at the ground. He'd known there was a risk, but he hadn't been one hundred percent certain that he couldn't use magic here. He was going to have to remain visible. An idea that made his stomach turn. But he'd prepared for this. Sort of. He knew enough about fighting and running, at least, to try and make this work.

Even without magic.

The closer he got to the wall, the stronger the tug became, and worry pricked at his mind. What behind it called to him? Why would it call to him? Should he answer it?

Did he have a choice?

He swallowed thickly before coming to stand in front of the wall. Just as he was wondering how to cross, a door shimmered into view. Small and wooden with metal rings as handles. He stared at them. They looked like they belonged in a Chinese temple, not one in Thailand.

Did this lead to another country?

He glanced around, before grabbing hold of the handle. It was cool beneath his fingers, chilling him to the bone, but he didn't let go and instead yanked as hard as he could. The door swung open. He stumbled back, landing flat on his ass, and groaned. That was unexpected.

Butt sore, he pushed himself to his feet and stumbled forward. The door remained open until he crossed the threshold. Then, it slammed shut behind him, nearly smacking him in the head. He spun around, only to find no door. No wall. Just an expanse of grass.

A shudder ran up his spine.

What was this place?

Still, the tug pulled at his arms, so he turned and continued on.

It must have been a while before he saw one of the dead, but he found he couldn't tell time. The sun remained overhead, unmoving. He didn't have a watch. His phone's clock had stopped at the exact time he'd entered. Sixteen-thirty. Had he been walking for ten minutes? Twenty? Thirty? Or maybe it'd been an entire day and he hadn't realized.

His body didn't tire. His throat didn't scream for water. His stomach didn't beg for food. His backpack weighed down his back, a reminder of the supplies he'd brought. But did he need them?

This was on his mind when he saw the first person. They drifted by, almost invisible. Derek wouldn't have noticed them at all if he hadn't almost walked through them.

He started, jumping to the side. The man—and it was a very old man—muttered something under his breath in what sounded like Thai, but *really* old Thai. Older than Derek had ever managed to read. He couldn't understand the man, but he did watch him drift aimlessly until the sunlight shone through him and he vanished altogether.

Goosebumps rose on Derek's arms.

"What the hell?" he asked the air. The air did not respond.

He shook his head before continuing on, this time paying more attention to the world around him. More dead floated past. More than he could count. They ignored him. He ignored them. They all muttered, not interacting with one another, but the further on he went, the more corporeal they became. Some didn't wander aimlessly. Some touched the ground. Others spoke in Thai he knew, though not from his studies.

He knew the words from Niran.

He waited patiently for understanding to befall him. When it didn't, he kept walking until he realized that the dead...weren't just floating into the abyss. They formed groups. Families. Some of them laughed, chasing children between the ghosts. Others cooked over false fire. They gained color. Stability. They had community.

Derek bit his lip. This had *not* been in any of his research. What was this place? Was he witnessing a world where people didn't come to die, but to live?

Each step brought him further into a living village. People of all ages and genders gathered. They wore clothes from all different generations of people. And all of them, every single one, looked alike.

He didn't think it was possible. At first, he thought he was hallucinating. They didn't look the same. They weren't clones of one another. But there was a resemblance only familial relation could explain. And when he looked closer, he noticed that there were no fathers. Only mothers. Oh, there were men. But they didn't have their children or wives with them.

They had their siblings.

They had their mothers.

They had their grandmothers.

And when Derek came face to face with a man he recognized, he halted. The man smiled at him, and then went on his way, but Derek knew who he was. He knew the bone structure. The bright, brown eyes. The crooked smile. They were the same ones his mother had. The same ones his grandmother had. The same ones as the man in the photo. His great-great-uncle.

Derek stared after the man. All of these people were family.

His family.

Understanding hit him like a brick. He wasn't seeing what he wanted. He was seeing his family. Through his mother. This was the place *he* would go when he died.

His stomach turned. He gripped the straps of his backpack and swallowed down the bile threatening to come up.

And he kept walking.

"Niran?"

At the sound of the priest's name, Derek froze. His great-great-uncle hadn't recognized him. No one had recognized him. But the woman's voice stopped him in his tracks as recognition, as confused glee, trickled in that name. He turned, finding himself staring into the brown eyes of the most beautiful woman he'd ever seen. Yes, more beautiful than Flora. Maybe it was because of the light glow on her skin, or the joy spreading across her face. Or, maybe, he saw her the way that Niran had always seen her, always admired her, three thousand years ago.

"Niran, it's you!"

Derek had never learned her name, and he was too frightened to ask now. But he knew who she was.

"I've been wondering," she said. If the dead could cry—and maybe they could—she would have. Her eyes crinkled at the sides, showing that she was no longer a young woman in her twenties, and she tilted her head. A hand reached out. Small and tanned. It brushed Derek's cheek, and his entire body blasted with heat before icing over.

He smacked her hand away, stumbling back.

A frown replaced her smile. "What's wrong? Don't you recognize me? I know it's been years, but you should recognize your own sister's face."

Derek's heart thudded. The pounding of blood overtook his ears, and he panted. That brief touch. What had she done to him?

"I'm not Niran," Derek stuttered out.

For a heartbeat, he thought she might leave him alone. He thought she might come to the conclusion that she'd mistaken him for someone else.

Only for a heartbeat.

Her face screwed up. Rage.

"You're not Niran?" she asked. The dead around them vanished. The world twisted and turned, and her body bubbled beneath the skin. Derek choked back words. Now wasn't the time to speak. "You took his body, then? I knew him crossing the river was a mistake. I knew someone would possess him. Would take his soul. He gave his real name to someone, didn't he?"

Derek backed up, tripping over his own feet and the stones on the path beneath them.

"You're an imposter!" the woman screeched.

Derek's eyes widened. He'd read *nothing* about this.

"An imposter!" Her voice rose an octave, piercing his eardrums and rattling his bones.

He didn't waste another second. Fear drove his legs. Each step was a miscalculation. He was used to running on smooth dirt or paved roads. Not cobblestone. It was a miracle he didn't fall flat on his face.

"Imposter!" Her screech was no further behind than before. He chanced a glance over his shoulder and found her flying—literally flying—toward him. Black wings stretched from her back, face screwed up with fangs peering out from beneath her lips.

"Oh *shit.*" Derek couldn't outrun her. If one touch had taken energy from him, what would she do if she got her hands—claws—on him?

He had to use magic. He couldn't, but he had to. He couldn't die here, in the Realm of Death. Who knew what would happen to him if he did?

"Come on, come on," he panted. He focused on the energy inside of him. Not just the magic, but his soul. It had a force here. He needed to use it. Needed it to live.

Warmth spread to his hands. He came to a halt. He didn't think.

He turned. He held out his hands. A burst of light exploded from them and shot through the air. Niran's sister collided with it. The light engulfed her, wrapping around her disfigured features. It sunk into her skin and she fell to the ground, wingless, fangless, and clawless. For a second, she stared at Derek, blinking, and then she vanished into a puff of glittering smoke. In her place, a glowing orb that floated toward the sky and disappeared into rays of sunlight.

Derek's stomach twisted on itself, and he placed a hand over his thudding heart. As it calmed, as the adrenaline receded, he tripped toward the nearest tree. His energy lasted just long enough for him to reach it. To slide down against it. Then, he closed his eyes. His lids dropped like stones, limbs heavy and unmovable, and sleep claimed him.

The sun burned through his eyelids, forcing him awake. He squinted, staring up at the still blue sky. Everything hurt. His body felt like it was under a weighted blanket. His arms wouldn't raise. His legs wouldn't shift. Breathing became difficult, and his eyes burned from exhaustion. Somehow, he managed to lift a hand to shield his eyes from the bright sun, and he breathed out.

"Have a nice nap?"

Derek flinched. His body didn't want to, but it did. He lowered his hand—or, more like it dropped to the ground—and stared at the man sitting cross legged across from him. He didn't wear modern clothing. In his colorful garb, he looked exactly as he had the first time Derek had ever *seen* him. The first time Derek had existed as him.

"Might be time to speak to me," Niran said. "I know I'm not your favorite person in the world, but it's just us. Might as well have *someone* to talk to."

Niran, unfortunately, made a good point. Derek was more than displeased that the man was back, and looking even more sturdy than in the Realm of the Living. But what could he do? He was Niran. Niran was him. There was no escaping. Even if Derek wanted nothing more than to pretend like Niran couldn't harass him, he had no one else to talk to. Niran knew all the same research that Derek did. If there was a chance, why not take it?

"Fine," Derek said. "I'll talk to you."

A smile split Niran's face and he threw his hands into the air. "The prodigal son speaks."

"Shut up." Derek had wanted to say that for years.

Niran merely smirked.

Derek groaned, pushing himself away from the tree. Everything ached. He ached in places he didn't know *could* ache. Still, he managed to get to his feet, glaring at Niran with all the annoyance he could muster. "You're dead. What can you tell me about this place?"

The smirk vanished from Niran's face. "To call me dead wouldn't be an accurate description. I'm more stuck. Suspended in space. At least, I was. For three thousand years I waited in the void for the right conditions to *become* again. The rest you know."

Not what Derek had wanted to hear. "So, you're no help?"

"No, but I'm *excellent* company."

Derek flipped Niran off, who howled with laughter, before he adjusted his bag and trudged through the grass. Away from where he'd found Niran's sister. This was supposed to be easy. He'd come in, find Blair's emotions, and get the hell out of dodge. Apparently, he'd overestimated his luck. For starters, he felt no emotions. Not even Blair's lingering in the back of his mind. He had no idea where to find her, or how he was going to start. Everyone here was related to him, apparently. Blair was not. Did that mean he had to go somewhere else?

As he continued on, Niran following him, he went through the most important notes in his head. Nothing helped. Most of his knowledge was about how to get into the Realm of Death, not what to do once he was here. Of course, it'd be easier to figure out what he needed to do if *someone* would shut up for two seconds.

Niran, however, had turned into a chatterbox.

"This place is so much like home, it's chilling. It must be comforting to those who have died, but for me? I'd rather go back to Earth and live there. In my *real* home."

"I can't believe you attacked my sister. I mean, sure, she wanted to kill you, but she didn't know what she was doing. What did you do to her anyway? Where did she go? What was that ball of light?"

"You're doing a great job of ignoring me. I get it. I've learned my lesson. Whatever it is. Just *talk* to me."

"You've got to acknowledge me sometime, Derek. I am you."

Frustration boiled in Derek's stomach. He wasn't getting anywhere. No matter how long they walked, Niran following him as a shadow, the scenery didn't change. The world around them didn't shift or adjust. Was he going to have to walk to America? If his family was in Thailand, then wouldn't Blair's be in the middle of nowhere Wyoming? He really didn't want to walk all that way. He really didn't have time to do so.

"Can you tell me what you plan to do once you have Blair? I'm curious—"

Derek spun around, eyes shooting flames. "Will you please shut up? I'm trying to think."

Niran's jaw slackened, and he took a step away from Derek. No longer his shadow. Derek expected a rebuttal, but Niran shut his mouth and tilted his head. More words formed on Derek's tongue—a verbal lashing to put Niran in his place once and for all—when Derek noticed it.

It wasn't obvious at first. Maybe it was the way the light reflected against it, or the angle Derek faced, or the fact that he was looking back, not forward, but he saw the shimmering line in the middle of reality. Every word in every language in his vocabulary vanished. The tug grew stronger, beckoning him forward. It called to him. Almost whispering.

Enter.

Without thinking, he placed a hand on Niran's sturdy shoulder—a first—and pushed past the man. The tear was only a few meters back. It took no time at all to reach it. When he did, he found that he couldn't look away.

"What the hell?"

Niran appeared at his side, crossing his arms. "It looks like a tear."

It did. A tear in reality, maybe?

"You gonna touch it?" Niran asked.

He wanted to. The tear wanted him to. It begged for him to touch it. To rip it open and step inside. He would have in a heartbeat, if not for the jolt of anxiety. The one that reminded him that he didn't know where it led. That none of his research had spoken of this. That this could easily be the way home. After all, why would it want him to go through it so much if it wasn't to kick him out of a place he didn't belong?

"It might be a trap," Derek said.

"Who the hell is trying to trap you?" Niran shook his head. "I've never met anyone as paranoid as you. Except possibly Tori. What? Are you still traumatized over the Natara stuff?"

No, he wasn't *traumatized*. In fact, he barely thought about Steven or Kathleen or the attempts on his life. Just in his dreams. And when he was alone doing nothing for too long. Or when he spoke to his sister.

So, not that often.

Niran snorted. "You're pathetic."

"Says the man who killed himself," Derek muttered. Niran snarled. Derek ignored him. He reached up to the tear, to rip it open further, but to his surprise, it reacted on its own. The opening widened, engulfing his hand in warm, glowing light. He gasped and tried to pull his hand back, only for the opening to suck in his arm. Then his shoulder. He pushed, trying to get out.

The light engulfed him completely.

Chapter Five

White light encased his vision as some mysterious force ripped him limb from limb. At least, he assumed that's what the pain was. An incomprehensible scream fled his lips as he tried to block out the torment, but it did no good. The light grabbed his body with little, probing hands and *pulled* until there was nowhere else for him to go. Each second that passed was another he wished that he hadn't touched the tear. That he hadn't gone anywhere near it. It was a trap. The end of everything. He'd failed. Barely in and he'd failed.

Then, like it'd never happened, the pain vanished. His scream disappeared, caught in his throat, and he stumbled atop cobblestone.

Panting, he placed a hand on the nearest wall, ignoring his shock that there was a wall in the first place. White continued to plague his vision, blinding him, keeping him immobile and pressed against brick. The rough texture scraped his hand. He flinched but stayed put while the light crept away from the edges of his vision. Before long, he was able to make out shapes. Then colors. Everything blurry came into focus.

Tall buildings rose into the sky, brick with iron, and the streets teemed with life. People, horses, barking dogs and twittering birds. Derek breathed in, trying to catch his breath, and ducked into the alley he stood in front of. No one stopped to talk to him. They were too busy rushing along, chattering away.

"What the hell?" he asked no one in particular. Maybe had hadn't been paying attention, or maybe he'd been too caught off guard by the familiarity of the landscape around him, but wherever he'd been before hadn't seemed quite as lively, nor quite as modern. There was no reason why they should be different. At least, that's what his mind told him.

"Where are we?" Niran stood next to him, staring out of the alley at the dead—at least Derek hoped they were dead. Otherwise he'd really messed up.

Derek frowned at him. The ghost wasn't exactly a ghost anymore. His body was solid, cheeks flush with life. For a moment—a brief moment—Derek saw Niran as a powerful mage. A man from thousands of years ago who was at the prime of his life. The lover of Queen Shion. Not an annoyance who made fun of Derek every chance he got. He wasn't bitter, but excited about the future.

The Realm of Death was making Niran stronger. Derek didn't feel any weaker, but there was no saying when that would start. When Niran would start being in charge and Derek would be swept away by his whims.

Niran sighed. "Please answer my question. I don't know where we are."

"I don't know." Derek peeked around the corner again. "Maybe Victorian England? It's hard to tell. I'm not great with Western history."

"Fascinating." Niran paused for a moment before stepping out into the street, sun gleaming against his black hair.

"What are you doing?" Derek whispered in as loud a voice as he dared. "Get back here!"

"Why?" Niran examined the young woman in front of him. She didn't pay him any attention, instead adjusting her gloves. "I'm dead. Not like they can hurt me."

But there was no saying in the Realm of Death. What if they could hurt him? What if they could hurt Derek through him? What if he got them in trouble? Derek had a feeling he shouldn't use his magic again, and the idea of escaping this place through another tear terrified him.

When the woman looked up, directly at Niran, Derek tensed, expecting the worst.

She didn't acknowledge him.

Instead, she tugged at her gloves one more time and smiled with a heavy breath. Like a young woman preparing for an important meeting. Like she had somewhere to be and nothing was going to stop her. She had plans. She had a life. Even if she was dead.

In that moment, when she smiled, when she looked up, Derek realized that he knew her.

The last time he'd seen her, she'd been in a very different dress. A prom dress. Low cut, maybe a little slutty, but not so tasteless that it was out of place from the other girls in their dresses. She'd had the same smile on her face, having been invited to prom with her senior boyfriend.

A stone the size of China dropped in Derek's stomach. He stumbled away from the street, disappearing further into the shadows. The stone grew heavier and heavier, his heart racing as his breathing shortened. She shouldn't be here. She was so young. So filled with life and joy. At least, that's how Mia had always described her.

When the fire ravaged Willow Creek, the Iravata had saved Derek, his friends, and their families. But no one else had known about them. Had known about magic. Probably still didn't know about magic. He'd thought—maybe he'd prayed a little bit, though he didn't know who to or why—that everyone had made it out. All of the people he knew. And while he didn't know her very well, she'd always been in his periphery. One of Mia's basketball friends.

Had Kaylee died in the fire? Or had something else taken her life?

"Why so pale?"

Derek jerked his attention away from Kaylee. She walked away, muttering something to herself, which left Derek in the shadows and Niran watching him with a tilted head.

"Nothing," Derek said. "I just…know…knew…I went to school with her. She was one of Mia's friends."

Niran nodded. "I'm sure that's bound to happen. It's been five years, and you've been a shut in since Mia left. Who knows how many of your friends are dead."

Derek's shock morphed into disbelief, and then anger. "You're pretty cavalier. She was Mia's friend!"

Niran dropped all friendly pretenses. His voice, normally filled with amusement, turned into ice. "I watched my entire family die from the ether." He stepped toward Derek, who stumbled away. "I spent three thousand years watching the world develop and change. People lived and died. Some when they didn't deserve it. Others when they did. While I waited for you to be born, I witnessed so much of history. Of humanity. Of plagues and colonization and imperialism. Wars. Genocides. Death doesn't scare me, Derek. Death is normal. Death is what comes for us all in the end. When you experience what I have experienced, a few dead friends is nothing."

"Yeah?" Derek snapped with a trembling voice. "Well this isn't nothing to me. I'm not used to this."

"You should be. You've killed before."

Derek flinched and reached for the knife at his belt. It was a reminder of everything. It was a reminder that he'd lost the artifact to Jae, failing Blair and Enola. And more than that, it reminded him that he'd made mistakes long before Jae had forced him to give up the artifact. That Shubishi had put him in an impossible situation and it had ended with Derek taking a life. Steven's life.

What for? Shubishi had said it was to prepare him, but for what? For this? Had Shubishi known that Derek would face the impossible? He'd always known more than he let on. This wasn't that far of a stretch.

Pulling out the knife, Derek examined the blade. It looked like the artifact in shape, but that's where the similarities ended. It didn't hold the same weight. It didn't have the writing on the side. The words didn't glow blue as the magic exuded from every inch of the metal. It didn't bring him warmth.

"You miss it," Niran said.

Derek breathed out before sliding the knife back into its sheath. "No. I don't."

"You do." Niran leaned against the wall next to Derek. Derek made to argue, but Niran held up a hand. "Look, I understand. I miss it too. It's dangerous and there's a lot of negative history associated with it. I'm sure that won't change anytime soon. But–"

He sighed. "But there's something about the power that is intoxicating. I felt it the moment it was in my hands, and I'm sure you did as well. It's nice to be important."

Derek wasn't sure that had anything to do with it. Whenever he let himself think of that day in the forest, when everything fell to hell for the third time in two years, the only emotion he felt was regret. Regret at losing his security. Regret at failing Mia's trust in him to keep the knife safe. Regret that because he hadn't been strong enough, Jae had won and taken Blair's grandmother with him. While he felt no love for the old woman, Blair had. Did. Blair did.

He would give anything to go back and relive that day, making different decisions. No, he hadn't taken the knife and stabbed Enola in the back. But he felt like he had.

46

Pushing himself away from the wall, he took a deep breath and forced his thoughts away from Enola. Away from the Jae and the knife. He instead focused on the world around him. Kaylee was here. He knew her. If everyone before going through the tear had been his family, then this must have been hers. He didn't know what they were, exactly, but these spaces between tears were related to family.

So, he dubbed them Family Trees.

There was no reason to stay here. Blair, despite her dad's family history, had no relation to England as far as he knew. Her dad's family had immigrated from Ukraine after World War II. If he was going to find her, assuming she was in her family tree and hadn't traveled like he had, then it was going to be some weird version of Ukraine, or possibly Wyoming.

He closed his eyes and focused. Her emotions were stronger than before. Still muted, but stronger. Contentment. Sorrow. Her usual emotions.

"What are we going to do?" Niran asked. "If Blair's not here, then–"

Derek knew what he needed to do before Niran finished his sentence. Niran fell silent, eyes going wide.

"Are you insane? You thought you were dying when you went through the last tear."

"But I didn't." Derek shrugged. "Look, it's the only option I have. If you have a better suggestion, I'm all ears." He waited, but Niran said nothing. "Thought so. Now, come on. Now that I know what they feel like, I think I can find another one."

"You *are* insane," Niran muttered.

Derek ignored him and headed out of the alley. Members of his family hadn't noticed him before Niran's sister, so maybe Kaylee's family wouldn't either. They moved around him as though he weren't there, and he grinned. Finally something was going right.

Closing his eyes, he felt for the shimmering feeling. The slight glint that marked a change in reality. It didn't take long for him to locate one. Two. Three. He hesitated. Okay, maybe things weren't going right. Three tears, three options.

"Which one are you going to take?" Niran asked.

Derek opened his eyes, turning toward the direction of the nearest one. "It's going to be a guessing game. Might as well get through as many as possible."

"You're insane."

"So you've said."

"I'm not wrong."

Derek didn't dignify that with a response before he took off running, passing an unobservant Kaylee in the process as she once more adjusted her gloves.

Each tear he passed through hurt less and less. By the fifth, he felt almost nothing at all.

While he was beyond grateful for the lessening pain, it also brought about a whole other set of concerns. Why was the pain getting better? What was it doing to him? What were the consequences of traveling between Family Trees?

As the questions plagued him, he kept going. In every tree, there were multiple tears. It took some time for him to decide which to travel through, and Niran was no help. He kept reminding Derek that they didn't know anything about this realm. The last thing Derek needed was to walk around in circles.

Derek, pointedly, ignored him. Even if Niran was right and Derek was making the wrong choices, he had no other option. Each Family Tree was wrong. None of them belonged to Blair's family, which he could be certain of because in each one, no matter how fast he got out of there, he always ran into someone he knew.

Sometimes it was someone from high school.

Once it was a person who had served him at a bar. A young woman who had chatted him up, flirting to get more tips even though he wasn't interested. In fact, he couldn't remember why he'd gone to that bar in the first place. Frustration? Anger? The need to drink? Was it around the time Niran had started talking to him? Appearing in more than just his periphery?

It didn't matter. These people, some he barely knew, some who he'd considered good friends in high school, never saw him. They never acknowledged his presence, and for that he was grateful.

Blair's emotions got stronger with each passing tear. He kept going, trudging along even as his legs screamed at him to sit down, and his limbs weakened. Niran told him more than once to sit down and wait. Derek could not wait. He'd already made Blair wait for five years. He wasn't going to pause.

After a time, having lost count of tears, he struggled through a barren wasteland of snow. There were no mountains. What was snow without mountains? What was the point?

"I've never liked snow," Niran said, drawing Derek's attention away from his destination. The tear was further away than some of the others had been, giving Niran ample time to talk his ear off. Even though Derek shivered, the cold settling deep into his bones, Niran didn't react to it. "I saw it once or twice when I was alive, but mostly I've experienced it through your eyes and I can't say I'm a fan. I much prefer the warmth of summer. The heat of home."

Derek rolled his eyes.

"You like snow?" Niran asked.

"It's fine." Derek had no real opinion on snow. Yes, it was annoying, especially at the moment, but when he was inside, wrapped in a blanket with a cup of steaming tea and a book, he didn't mind it. It was pretty.

Niran chuckled. "Even though I've seen the world through your eyes, it still amazes me how *different* our lives have been. Even our homes. But the world you were born into is nothing like the one I was. It's amazing. There's so much to do. So many people to meet. You squander it away in your hidey hole, but I wouldn't. I'd see everything. Experience everything. You waste away in the middle of a silly country. It's pathetic."

"You would think that," Derek muttered. He had no interest in debating the patheticness of his existence. Yes, he was pathetic. So what? He had a job to do. There was plenty of time after he rescued Blair to see the world. There was no point in seeing it if she wasn't right there with him.

A hand grabbed his shoulder, yanking him back a step. Derek didn't fight it, in part because he wasn't expecting it, and in part because Niran had *grabbed him*.

Shock flooded his system, and his jaw dropped. Niran stood there, no amusement in his expression.

"You won't have time, Derek. You're already getting weaker, and I'm getting stronger. You think you can stop it. *I* thought I could stop it. But I couldn't, and you can't. Either you will die and the cycle will continue, or I'll take over your body. There is no stopping your destiny."

Derek narrowed his eyes. "Screw destiny. I'm not going to let it win."

"You have no choice."

"I always have a choice." He yanked his shoulder from Niran's first grasp. "You might have failed, but I'm not going to. I'm not leaving Blair the way you left Shion."

Niran flinched, then scowled. "That's not how it works."

"Then how does it work?" Derek crossed his arms. "Since you know so much, tell me how it works. How did we get stuck in this cycle?"

"The knife."

Derek dropped his arms, eyes widening. "Excuse me?"

Niran let out a heavy sigh before turning away from Derek. The snow lessened, but didn't let up completely. In that moment, standing in the snow with flushed cheeks and a faraway look, Derek felt a moment of camaraderie. The snow drifted down, flakes dusting Niran's hair.

"When I was growing up, I went through the same thing you did. I saw a man. He never told me his name, and unlike with me, he'd never been important. But what I did know is that he was me. I was him. He is us, Derek. We are the same person. He lived a hundred years before I was born, and he died because of the knife, just like I did."

"The knife takes your soul, it doesn't make it reincarnate," Derek said.

"For most people, yes. But for those people, someone else killed them. For us…."

Derek's jaw dropped. In a quiet whisper, he said, "You killed yourself."

"And the man before me did the same." Niran faced Derek, eyes alight with anger and frustration. A hint of those emotions brushed at Derek's skin, but they could have been his imagination. "That knife is attracted to us. I don't know how it was made, when it was made, or why it can do what it does, but a thousand years before I was born, a man killed himself with that knife and started the cycle. Each one of us has died the same way, always before the reincarnated soul can take over. It doesn't matter what we do with the knife. It will *always* find us again."

"Then how could Jae have taken it from me?"

"Don't know. But just because he has it now doesn't mean it won't be back. Our destiny is intertwined with the knife, whether

51

we like it or not. I'm guessing Jae hasn't done anything because the knife is throwing a fit. He killed two with it before, but that doesn't mean it'll let him kill more."

"You talk about it like it's alive."

"It's the Knife of Souls. Of course it's alive."

A shudder ran up Derek's spine at those words. He'd never seen the knife as alive, but it carried so many souls inside of it. Maybe he should have.

Then, a thought occurred to Derek.

Niran nodded, reading his unspoken thoughts. "Yes. Enya gave me the knife. I don't think that was a coincidence. I think she knows more about it, about us, than she lets on. She knew that I could wield the knife, and I'm guessing that her son can't do anything with it. She's going to try and convince you to kill Shion, just like she did to me. If you recall, that's how I died."

"Yeah, yeah. You killed yourself so she couldn't use you."

"That's only part of it," Niran said. "I did it so she couldn't use me anymore. I did it because she was going to make me kill Shion. But more than that, I did it because time was running out. The man was going to become me. He had no attachment to Shion, and he had no qualms doing Enya's bidding. I couldn't let that happen." He took a deep breath. "I couldn't let her die. So, I died instead."

Derek had no words. It was clear that Niran had a part of the story that either none of the Iravata knew, or Shubishi was keeping a secret. If so, why was he keeping it a secret? How much more did he know?

He bit the inside of his lip before saying, "Okay, then, if you become me, or I become you, or whatever, what are you going to do? Fight Enya?"

"That's the plan." Niran clenched his fists. "You're strong, but you are nowhere near as powerful as I was when I was alive. If I can just get back the other part...."

"What other part?"

Niran waved him off. "Nothing. We should get moving. We need to find Blair and get out of here, right?"

Derek frowned, but didn't press. Niran would tell him in time if he wanted to. If not, there would be no getting anything out of him. Besides, they didn't have time to talk about this anymore. Blair had waited long enough, and Derek needed to get out of here before Niran grew too strong. Otherwise, things were going to go south real fast. Derek couldn't explain why, but he knew that he couldn't let Niran take over. He needed to fight just long enough to stop Enya. Then...well, he didn't want to think about that.

Gulping, Derek continued through the snow, brushing flakes off his shoulders and his chest as the wind picked up and the snow attacked his face.

Chapter Six

He was out of breath. Not enough to make this difficult, but enough that it felt like the beginning of a cold. At first, after escaping the hellscape of blizzard land, he thought that he *had* caught a cold. It wasn't like him to get sick, but this place had its own rules and he wasn't naive enough to think that they didn't apply to him.

However, when his nose didn't start to stuff, and his throat didn't grow sore, and his temperature didn't rise into a fever, he realized it wasn't a cold. He wasn't sick, and this had nothing to do with the blizzard world.

This place was draining him of his energy. It was sucking out his life and giving it to the ever stronger, ever more present, Niran.

Getting out of here was always at the forefront of his mind. At times, when he struggled to get through a particularly stubborn tear, it even overtook his mission. Why keep going if he was going to die? Why keep going if this was going to make him incapable of getting her out? Why not leave?

Every time his mind went down this rabbit hole, he shook his head and continued on, gritting his teeth and clenching his fists.

This was not the time to give up. No one said this would be easy. In fact, all the literature stated otherwise. He still had to do it. Even if it killed him, even if he couldn't be the one to put an end to Enya and all of her scheming, even if he couldn't get his revenge, he would save Blair. And maybe, just maybe, if he died another way, if he died not by the knife, and not because Niran took over, then the cycle would be broken.

As he plunged through another tear, coming to another version of England, though this one much earlier by the looks of it, he let his thoughts run wild. All the things he'd put out of his mind came forward as he contemplated the idea that he might, in fact, die here.

He'd never given much thought to how he'd die. Maybe once or twice, back in the days when Steven and Kathleen were trying to kill him. When the bookshelf had fallen. When the car had come out of nowhere. When the mountain lion had leapt through the air with a snarl revealing its teeth. He'd thought, in those moments, about his mortality, but he'd always fought against it. He hadn't wanted to die.

Well, he still didn't *want* to die. If he could, he would do everything in his power to stay alive. To find Blair, get her out of here, and make things right with Mia. To show her that she didn't have to waste away in China, hating her life. To give Cody hope that the magical world wasn't entirely a shit show, even if it seemed that way sometimes.

But this wasn't in his power. There were too many factors out of his control. Which meant he thought about it. Now, as his power drained and Niran became stronger, he thought about what it might be like to die. As far as he knew, every person in the reincarnation chain had killed themselves with the knife. No one had been taken over. What would happen to *him*? To his mind? To his soul? Okay, sure. He had Niran's soul technically, but he had to have his own too. He wasn't Niran. He was Derek. He always had been, but he might not always be.

It terrified him. There was no other word for it. If Derek could sense his own emotions like he could others, then he would certainly feel the sharp claws ripping at his skin. It would overwhelm him. Make him numb to anything else. And maybe he already was. His heart raced at the thought of never being able to talk to Mia again. Not being able to hold Blair. Laugh with Cody. Roll his eyes at his parents.

His parents.

When was the last time he'd spoken to them? When was the last time he'd *seen* them? Was the last time really going to be the last time?

If he failed here, it certainly would be. Would his death be his parents' worst nightmare? Would it be Mia's? Would they move on? Would they even notice?

He breathed out, finding the next tear. But before he could grab it, before he could tear it open, a firm hand caught his wrist.

"Stop it," Niran said.

Derek blinked, staring at the man. "Stop what?"

"Those thoughts." Niran's grip tightened on Derek's wrist, and Derek flinched before trying to pull away. Niran wouldn't let go. "They're not going to do you any good. Maybe I'm wrong. Maybe there's a way we can both end up happy. But if you give up now, if you let this place get to you, then I will always be right. Don't let me be right."

Words failed Derek. Niran had never encouraged him. Never made it seem like it was possible they could both win the fight.

He pulled his wrist from Niran's grasp and faced the tear. It glinted in the sunlight, like all the others, but when he looked closer, there was something else there. Something ethereal. Something unique. He hesitated, brow furrowing.

"You think you found it?" Niran asked.

Derek shook his head. No, this wasn't Blair. Blair was magical

56

in her own right, but there was something otherworldly about this.

"We going in?" Niran's voice was quiet. There was no sass. No petty amusement. A hint of concern flickered against Derek's skin.

He brushed it off, heart pounding. "It's the only tear near here. Got nowhere else to go."

"I guess."

Derek reached for the tear, pulling it open far enough that he could step into the blinding white light. He took a deep breath. What were they going to find here? What trouble was awaiting them on the other side?

Part of him expected something close to Dante's version of hell when he entered the white light. But the minute he did, the minute his limbs tried to separate from his body, uncomfortable but not painful, he realized he was wrong. And the minute the white light vanished, he was certain the world stopped.

They were in a mountain range. Stuck on a steep hill with peaks rising to the sky. The trees, lush and green, looked untouched by man. They too, reached toward the heavens, and he followed them up, staring at what should have been a bright blue sky. The sun shone, as it had for the past three or so Family Trees, but the area around it brought Derek a mass of confusion. Because instead of blue, he found himself staring up at a mix of purple and green swirling together with light maroon clouds floating lazily in the atmosphere like oddly-colored sheep grazing on grass.

Derek breathed in a sharp gasp. In all of his research, he'd never found anything that described a scene such as this. Yet, for some reason, it was familiar to him. Something he'd seen in his mind's eye. A memory flittered around, bugging him just enough that he wanted to grab it and watch. It evaded him for a moment, but when he managed to hold on, it took him back six years to that summer of stories. When he'd broken up with Blair and everything had fallen apart.

The Iravata had described the sky, but he'd never taken it seriously. They were remembering wrong. There was no scientific basis for a sky made of dancing purple and green. But why would there be? When their world had been filled with so much magic.

"Oh." Niran breathed the word so softly Derek thought he might have imagined it. But when the man stepped in front of Derek, staring up at the sky with wide eyes, shoulders relaxed for the first time, it was clear that the shock and awe tickling Derek's skin wasn't part of his imagination.

They stood under the same sky that the Iravata had once stood under. Or, at least, the version of it that existed in the Realm of Death.

Derek took a step. His foot sunk into soft earth, warmth climbing up his leg as energy returned to his limbs. He tore his gaze away from the sky to stare at the fertile soil. Even in death, this world had so much life.

"She told me so much about her home," Niran said in that same, soft voice. "She was born here. Lost so much, gained so much, experienced so much in her immortal time here. Even though she never said she missed it, I could tell she did. Everyone knew she did. She would get this faraway, gentle look when she talked about the city Death had confined her in. And when she looked at the sky— our sky—there was always pain."

Niran never spoke of his relationship with Shion. Derek had always sensed that it was a point of internal contention with his shadow. Whenever something slipped out, pain gripped his voice. Pain that Derek knew all too well, even without his empathy.

"She didn't grow up *here*," Derek said. "We're in the Realm of Death."

"I know." Niran closed his eyes and breathed in. "But the sky...I never thought I'd see her sky."

Derek dropped his gaze again, paying close attention to the grass snaking up his legs. It curled. He'd never seen curly grass before. "You really loved her, didn't you?"

Niran let out a stark laugh, and regret and pain scratched Derek's skin. "You know, it's been killing me to watch her through you. You don't *see* her. Her beauty. Her power. Her kindness and gentle soul. To you and your friends, she's a strange woman who doesn't understand your world. And maybe she is, but I knew her. Not the her that Death wanted her to be. I knew *Shion*. Not the queen. She was my everything. I would give the world to hold her. To kiss her. To tell her all the things I couldn't the night I sealed her away.

"I regretted it the moment I did, but I couldn't take it back. I knew that Enya had tricked me, but it took too long to figure out how deep that deception went. Now I know I should have trusted Shion, I shouldn't have ever lost my faith in her, but it was so bad. You don't understand, Derek, what it was like to live in that war. The mages blamed the Iravata for everything. They wanted Shion's head on a spit. Whatever they did to Adelia changed her. You should have seen her after. I never thought she'd speak again. I'd convinced myself that Enya had the answers, but when it came time to do it, I couldn't. I couldn't kill the woman I love."

A tear streaked down Niran's cheek, glinting in the sun. Derek stiffened, jaw clenching, hands curling into fists. With every passing second, Niran became less of a ghost and more human. At what point would Niran be alive and Derek the ghost?

"You love Blair the way I love Shion," Niran continued. He wiped away the tear and faced Derek. They mirrored each other. Two men with the same face. Both fighting to make right on their failures. "But you're stronger than I am. Even now, you fight me. Your determination to save Blair puts me to shame."

Derek breathed in. "Do you hate me?"

"Yes." Niran's soft smile was nothing like his normal smirk. "But more than you, I hate myself. The only way I can make things right

59

is to hurt someone. You don't deserve what's going to happen. Just like I didn't. Just like Shion and Blair didn't. Fate is cruel sometimes."

"Yeah. It is." Derek had no other words.

Niran nodded. "Maybe I don't hate you. Maybe I hate what you're keeping me from doing. But, there's always a possibility."

"Anything is possible when it comes to magic," Derek said.

Niran smirked with a slight laugh. "Esther believes that with every ounce of her soul."

"She does."

"Maybe we should too."

"Maybe."

They fell silent for a moment. A light breeze rustled their clothes, Derek's backpack weighing down on his shoulders. He gripped the straps, turning away from Niran.

"Do you hate me?" Niran asked.

For as long as Niran had been his very talkative mirror, the man had been cocky. Full of sarcasm. Bitterness. The world had broken him and he'd taken it out on Derek. Derek had ignored him, wanting to keep him far away from his life. Wanting to push his impending doom to the furthest reaches of his mind.

That wasn't the Niran who stood in front of him now.

"No."

That was all Derek said before he moved on. His footsteps filled his ears, squelching mud the only sound under the noon sky. Niran's footsteps soon followed.

What would happen to Niran if Derek managed to break the curse? Would he disappear into the ether? Would he come here and live out the rest of time as a dead soul in their shared Family Tree?

Was that fair?

They needed to find another way. But not now. Not when Blair needed help. Not when he'd made her wait for so long. Derek didn't know what was going to happen to him, nor to Niran, but what he did know is that Niran had made his bed three thousand years ago, and it wasn't Derek's job to make it right. He'd lost his chance to make things right with Shion. It was Derek's turn to make things right with Blair.

The moment Derek saw his first Vilaim, he tensed. The woman, hair blond and eyes gray, walked toward him with a stride that seemed akin to a stone skipping on water. She didn't move like the spirits had in the other Family Trees. Her jerky movements raised goosebumps on Derek's skin, and he searched for somewhere to hide. He found nothing. The mountains, filled with sparse trees, didn't give him much cover. All he could do was step aside and hope she didn't notice him, as spirits in other Family Trees had not.

When she didn't spare him a glance, the tension fled from his shoulders, though he wasn't entirely convinced she wasn't dangerous.

"Weird," Niran said. "She looks like Adelia."

Derek glanced at him, then back at the woman. He was right. There were differences, of course. Adelia had a slightly different face shape. Her eyes had a light in them, a fiery determination that the spirit lacked. But if Derek hadn't been looking closely, and if he hadn't known that Adelia couldn't die, he might have mistaken this woman for her.

"Must be from the Tep tribe." While Derek couldn't recall all the tribe names, since there had been so many and he'd heard the story so long ago, Tep and Seshen had stuck. Maybe it was because the Seshen were the first—and in his opinion the worst—while the Tep were instrumental in changing everything the day that woman fell into the arms of one of their own. Halise. Her death had changed the Vilaim's lives forever. If she hadn't died, if she hadn't run from her city and fallen in love with Amir, what would have happened to the Vilaim? Would they have killed each other, lost without the influence of their creator?

Niran stepped toward the woman who had passed them, movements still jerky. "I've never met a Vilaim. Not a normal one, anyway. It's always just been the Iravata and Enya. I hadn't...." He sighed.

"Hadn't what?"

"I hadn't realized they would look so similar."

Maybe they didn't. Maybe this woman was somehow related to Adelia. Her mother, possibly. But when others appeared, looking even more similar to each other than the woman did with Adelia, Derek couldn't voice his theory.

The newcomers jerked forward, as the other Tep woman had, and they didn't interact with one another. He was reminded, at first, of his first moments with the dead in his Family Tree, but as the jerking movements stopped and the dead Vilaim became more corporeal, their attitude didn't change. They didn't interact. They moved aimlessly. They didn't touch. Some passed through each other, but if they noticed, they didn't react. A few spoke to the air in a language Derek had never heard before. It sounded like none of the languages he knew from home. Or maybe it sounded like all of them at the same time.

"We should move," Derek said. "I don't think they're any danger to us."

"They don't seem to even know what's going on. It's almost like–" Niran shook his head. "You're right. Let's go."

What had he been about to say? Derek frowned but didn't question Niran. The two headed off, Derek still searching desperately for a new tear.

He didn't know how long they'd been walking for when he felt eyes on him. At first, he thought nothing of it. This place was

62

messing with his head, clearly. But the further they went into the mountains, the more silent dead they met, the stronger the feeling became.

Derek came to a halt and spun around, searching for those eyes.

"What are you doing?" Niran stopped as well, a few paces ahead of Derek. "Did you find a tear?"

"No." Derek wished. "I think someone's watching us. Me. I don't know if they can see you."

Niran groaned. "No one's watching you. This place is messing with your head."

Derek didn't believe him and kept searching. Searching and searching until he found someone who did not fit. It was not only her appearance—though her lighter blond hair and soil brown eyes were a dead giveaway—but her movements. Namely, her lack of movement. Others jerked past her, but she stood still, eyes alive with the light Derek had always admired in Adelia.

Was she alive? Were the Vilaim able to enter this place?

The woman tilted her head, holding out her hands. An apparently universal sign of peace.

"Don't," Niran snapped. "She's going to hurt you."

But the feeling in Derek's gut, the one that had kept him alive so far, said otherwise. If she'd wanted to hurt him, she would have already. Instead, he took a deep breath and stepped toward her. She did the same, and before long they stood a body length away from each other as the dead continued to move past them.

The woman examined him, emotions non-existent. She was dead.

"You're alive?" Her voice crackled, like she hadn't used it in years. The English caught Derek off guard, and he crossed his arms. How was she doing this? She cleared her throat and tried again. "You look like a Narumi, but you aren't. There's something different about you."

63

"I'm not a Vilaim," Derek said.

She furrowed her brow. "Vilaim? I'm not sure what you mean."

"Uh...." Derek waved his hands. "I come from a different place than you. It's hard to explain. You're a Vilaim, I'm a human."

Her scrutiny made him shiver, and behind him Niran called him an idiot. Derek ignored the priest. No reason to acknowledge him if this woman didn't know he was there.

"I see." She examined him again. "You have power. Your life force is very strong."

"Excuse me?"

Then, she held up a hand, placing the edge diagonally on her chest, and bowed at the waist. "It's a pleasure to meet you, human. My name is Halise. I suppose I am from the Nimbon tribe, though once the Tep adopted me I rejected my heritage. Not that you understand–"

"Wait, are you serious?" Derek asked.

She blinked. "I am quite serious, human."

"*You're* Halise?"

She was beautiful. The Iravata had never described her, as they'd never met her, but she had this ethereal beauty to her that only Flora could compete with. Her hair was thick and wavy, falling to her waist, while her eyes were soft and warm. It was no wonder Amir had fallen in love with her. It was no wonder they'd fought a war over her.

Her hesitation let him know that she didn't realize how famous she was. "You know me?"

"No. Not, uh, not really." He crossed his arms. How could he explain? "I've just heard stories about you."

"Stories?" She tilted her head, taking a step back. "What stories?"

How much could he tell her? "I know some Vilaim. Well, they're not really...they have...they're immortal. The Iravata. They told me your story. About Amir dying and you–" He hesitated. This wasn't the time to talk about that.

Halise seemed to understand what he was saying anyway. "They know my story. Why do they know my story?"

"You're kinda famous," Derek said. "You ended a war."

"I did no such thing."

"I don't think you *meant* to but—"

"You're getting off topic," Niran snapped. "Ask her where Blair is."

Derek grimaced. "Anyway. That's not important. Look, I'm here looking for a friend. Another human. She doesn't look like me, and she might bite your head off if you look at her wrong. But she's important to me, and I'm not leaving without her. Can you help?"

Halise thought for a moment before slowly shaking her head. "I'm afraid I have my own journey to complete. Even if I didn't, I wouldn't know how to help you. I've never met a human before. Only, what did you call us? Vilaim? I've only met other Vilaim, and none of them speak to me."

What a depressing life. Derek frowned. "Okay, well, thanks."

He turned to leave when she called out to him. "You need to be careful, human. Other living beings have foolishly attempted to save someone from Death, but he has no mercy for those who upset him. If you do not go insane, a lost dead might take your life force. Escape is impossible."

"That's the second time you've mentioned life force. What is it?"

Niran hissed something under his breath that Derek didn't catch. Was he annoyed? Did it matter?

Halise let out a heavy sigh. "There are many dead who did not want to die, human. Those who come here unwillingly will take any chance they have to become alive again. The living who come here have energy. A life force. At least, that's what I've always called it. They believe, incorrectly, that if they take yours, they can be alive once more."

Fear struck at Derek's heart. He took a step back. "Let me guess, you want my life force?"

Her smile shone bright. "No, human. I have no interest in living again. If my love is here, then I am here. I will find him, and we can finally be together again."

Her love? Amir? She was still looking for him? A shudder ran through Derek's limbs. She'd been searching for millennia and she still hadn't found him. He'd thought, maybe foolishly, that the two of them had been happy here all of this time.

Would he ever find Blair? Would he get stuck here for the next million years as he went slowly mad? Would he die here in his attempt to save her?

As Derek was about to assure Halise that she'd find Amir, her eyes widened and she spun around. A gust whistled through the trees, and the shuddering dead vanished into mist.

"You have to go," Halise said, words so fast Derek almost missed them.

"What?" Derek reached out to touch her shoulder, but she vanished before he could. He tripped, almost falling flat on his face. The wind picked up speed. Derek struggled to stay upright against the gusts. The minute he stood upright, a roar exploded through the forest.

"What the hell?" Niran asked.

What the hell indeed. Derek spun in a circle, fighting the wind which, annoyingly, didn't bother Niran. At least he wasn't completely a person yet. But that meant whatever was coming would be coming for Derek and Derek alone.

He considered running, only to find an invisible force nailing his feet to the ground. Fear? It had to be fear. Regardless, he couldn't move. He could only watch as a mass of pure darkness slinked out from the shadows of the trees. It was large. Large enough that if it lay on Derek he would suffocate to death. From the darkness, two long arms—legs?—crept out and landed on the ground, shadows spiking up like electrocuted fur, while glowing yellow eyes peered out from what would have been a face if it wasn't pure darkness.

It leaned the shape of its head back and howled again, revealing two rows of razor sharp teeth. The trees rattled. Leaves fell to the ground. Derek slammed his hands over his ears to protect them from the explosion.

Run.

It was the only word he could think. But he couldn't obey the command, feet still pinned, heart thumping in his chest.

Run, you idiot.

The creature hunched what had to be its shoulders, rearing back before it pounced.

All coherent thought vanished from his mind. His body reacted before he could tell it too. A hand lifted into the air. Energy pooled in his palm. The creature flew closer. Niran screamed something. Magic exploded from Derek's hand, a mass of raging light. The ball collided with the creature, sending it flying away with a yelp. It slid through the trees and vanished into the shadows.

Derek's mind caught up to his body, but he still couldn't move. The creature, picking itself up, growled and morphed from a black mass to a mountain lion. The same mountain lion Blair had saved him back before he understood anything. Back in the days when magic had turned from a fun quirk to a death sentence.

The mountain lion growled. The trees of the forest transformed from deciduous to pine. Blair screamed at him to move. To do *something.* Wasn't she supposed to save him? Wasn't she the one who had made all the bad things go away?

Blair wasn't there. He wasn't in the Colorado wilderness. He was in the Realm of Death. He told himself this over and over, but it didn't stick. The black creature remained a mountain lion.

Rage flooded his system. If he was going to do this alone, then it was going to be an explosion of magic. One that the creature never saw coming. It wanted him dead, but he needed to live. Which meant that it needed to *die*.

More energy welled in his palm and he focused it. No ball of light this time. No fire. He needed something stronger. More refined. An element that would destroy the creature at first hit. As the creature leapt toward him once more, he shot out his hand and a bolt of pure lightning crackled through the air. It collided with the creature, shooting right through where its heart would be if it had one.

The creature screamed. A scream that almost sounded human. And then it fell to the ground at Derek's feet in a cloud of black sand.

For a moment, the briefest moment, relief was the only emotion Derek could feel. But then came the nausea. Then came the jellied legs and the shaking arms. He collapsed to his knees, panting, stomach turning as it threatened to expel its contents. He knew there was no fire, but still, fire spread from his body to the trees, burning bright. Destroying everything in its path.

Steven's powers.

His breath shortened. He couldn't get enough oxygen. Placing a hand over his mouth, he tried to push down the memories of those days before his secret had come out. When tea and bookshelves were his enemy. When he was too sick to do anything but sleep. When the dreams started. When he'd pushed his sister away, thinking it was going to protect her from this world. He'd had no idea that other ideas had taken form in Kathleen's head. He'd had no idea that Lady Shion had been saving him, not trying to kill him. He'd had no idea that he would have to take a knife and stab Steven with it.

He could still feel it. The knife sliding into Steven's body. It was a physical memory he would never forget, but it was one he'd tried hard to ignore. It all came forward.

When the hand touched his back, he jerked away from it, scrambling to get away from his foe, only to turn and see himself.

He blinked. His mirror twisted and changed, turning back to Niran who held up his hands.

"Derek?" Niran asked.

No. He wasn't going to answer any questions. He didn't have *time* to answer questions. The fire in his vision vanished. The trees returned to normal. His breath came back in heaving gasps. He wasn't back then. He wasn't in Colorado. He was safe. Ish. He was safeish.

"Derek," Niran tried again, but Derek ignored him and pushed himself to his feet.

"Let's go," he muttered.

He didn't give Niran time to say anything before he rushed off, shoes pounding against the ground. He needed to get out of here. Away from the trees, from the mountains, from whatever that monster had been. No matter what happened, once he left this Family Tree, he was never going to return. The Iravata may have missed their sky, but he preferred blue.

Chapter Seven

There was no saying how long they'd been walking for. The mountains sloped down, and before long they were out of the woods and into an expanse of fields. Since the monster, they hadn't seen any Vilaim wandering around, and Derek wasn't sure if that was a good thing or not.

Niran hadn't said a word since they'd started moving, for which Derek was grateful. He didn't need the dead man questioning him, and he certainly didn't need a lecture about not letting his trauma get the better of him. He knew it already. He'd known it for years. He was stronger than his demons. It should be easy for him to fight them off.

Except it wasn't, and there was no saying when they'd hit again.

They came to an unnatural circle of rocks. At least, it didn't look natural. They formed a perfect circle around a flat center stone. If Derek had been his normal self, not the sweaty, emotionally drained mess standing in the center of the circle, he might have questioned what it was there for. As it was, his mind wasn't working the way it normally did. It was still stuck in the past. Every sound, every rustle of wind, startled him. He needed a moment.

Niran said nothing when he sat on the center stone. All he did was watch Derek shift his backpack to the front and zip it open, looking at the bottles of water and the crackers. No, he wasn't hungry. No, he wasn't thirsty. But part of him longed for the normality of eating and drinking, so he pulled out the bottle and cracked it open. The water was surprisingly cool against his lips, and he chugged what must have been half of the bottle in one go.

Gasping for air, he pulled it away and looked out over the field with the bottle between his hands. Even though he hadn't been thirsty, the water calmed him. It brought him clarity he hadn't had before.

There was no explanation for why he'd hallucinated the fire and the mountain lion. Trauma, probably, but it'd happened so suddenly and so out of his control. He needed to get it together. He needed to think about what had actually occurred, not what his brain wanted him to see.

A monster, a strange monster of pure black energy, had attacked him. But why? Had it wanted his life force? Where had it come from? Halise had recognized the change in the wind, so it must have been something she'd encountered before. But how? When? Why?

Too many questions. He took another gulp of water. Smaller this time.

Niran, who had been standing in his periphery with crossed arms, settled on the stone next to Derek. Without acknowledging him, Derek went back into the backpack and pulled out four crackers. Two for himself. Two for Niran. He held them out to the man, refusing to make eye contact.

Niran sighed. "I'm dead, Derek. I can't eat."

Right.

He seemed so real now.

Derek replaced two of the crackers in their sleeve and then

nibbled on the other two, relishing in the salt against his tongue and the crunch whenever he took a bite.

"You gonna talk about what happened back there?" Niran asked. Derek said nothing, but Niran wasn't taking his hint to drop it. "You panicked. Why? I've never seen you panic like that before."

"I thought you were always in my head," Derek said.

For a moment, Derek thought Niran wasn't going to reply. The man didn't say anything for a long while. Long enough for Derek to finish the two crackers and fish out a third after another gulp of water. When he did speak, his voice was very quiet.

"I don't hear all your thoughts anymore. Just bits here and there. The longer we're here, the more separate our minds become."

Well shit. Derek absolutely did not like the sound of that. "Oh."

"Yeah." Niran sounded almost sad.

Derek frowned. "What? You like being in my head all the time?"

Niran snorted and looked at the sky. "Frankly, yes."

"Oh great."

"It's not that I like spying on you, though it's quite fun to annoy you. It's more…." He sighed. "Never mind."

"Don't do that!" Derek twisted to look at Niran. "It's so annoying when people start to say something and then stop. Just tell me what you were going to say."

"You'll make fun of me."

"When have *I* ever made fun of *you*?"

Niran hesitated. "Okay. Fair. It's just that I spent so long alone. I had no one to talk to. No stimulation. I floated half in and half out of consciousness. Being with you gave me stimulation. It kept me from going insane as I watched you grow into a man, while I waited for my chance. I was *lonely*, Derek. You saved me from that."

Derek dropped his gaze. Three thousand years. Alone for three thousand years. He couldn't imagine it. It was a miracle that Niran wasn't batshit insane.

"So," Niran said, "are you going to tell me what happened, or do I need to keep guessing?"

Derek couldn't stop his scowl. Niran may not have been batshit, but he was still incredibly annoying at times. "Nothing happened. I'm fine."

"No you aren't."

"If I say I'm fine, it means I'm fine."

"Did you relive it?" Niran clenched his hands together, and Derek faltered.

"Relive what?" he asked in a quiet voice.

"I remember it, you know." Niran stood, still staring at the sky. "When you killed Steven. Everything before. I was aware even back then. I know how much it's tortured you all of these years. How you refuse to think about it. You didn't see me. You didn't know anything about me. But I knew you, and I felt everything you felt when you did what you had to in order to survive.

"So, I ask again. Did you relive it?"

Derek joined Niran in staring at the strange sky. All this time, he'd thought he'd been alone in his guilt and the pain that had come with killing his sister's first boyfriend. A boy. Steven had been Derek and Mia's age. He hadn't wanted to hurt Mia. He'd wanted to protect her, though he'd failed miserably. It wasn't fair that he'd died. It wasn't fair that Derek had killed him.

"Yes," Derek said. "And I don't know if I'll ever stop reliving it."

"I understand."

Derek didn't doubt he did.

Joining Niran on his feet, Derek zipped up the backpack and threw it back on. "Let's go."

Derek sped up the minute he felt a tear. It wasn't far off, but he didn't want to dawdle. He'd already spent too much time in this Family Tree. He was so focused on getting to the tear that he didn't notice that he and Niran weren't alone until Niran muttered a fervent, "Oh shit."

Considering Niran wasn't one for swearing, Derek came to a stop and looked around at the ghosts who had joined them.

For a second, he thought that he'd somehow transported through another tear without noticing. Family Trees were just that: a collection of family. But the dead sailing along next to him weren't the jerking Tep from up in the mountains. They didn't have the blond hair and the gray eyes. These ghosts were taller. Willowy, as though a single breeze could knock them over. The men and women both had long, brown hair, and their eyes, lifeless as they were, still seemed to glow the most beautiful shade of blue.

They did not belong to the Tep tribe.

No, these were Seshen.

They were everywhere, floating aimlessly. None of them spoke. Some of them held wild fear in their eyes. A few had mouths that opened and closed, miming speech with no sound. And with them, moving at a pace a snail might consider slow, a wall of mist.

Derek swallowed thickly.

These Vilaim had an ethereal quality about them. A species forever lost to time.

Shion used to look like them, Derek realized. Before the Iravata's betrayal, she'd had the brown hair and blue eyes. She'd been the last remaining Seshen, speaking for her people when she didn't want to. Death had been her goal. The end of the pain the Seshen had caused.

Death had taken that from her.

In the end, Death took everything from everyone.

He didn't flee the mist. The tear was through it, and he wasn't afraid. Even when the fog grew so dense he could barely see in front of him. It didn't matter that he couldn't see nor hear Niran. That the ghosts glowed in the cloud, little shimmers of floating light. He kept going. Because even though Death had taken so much from the world, both deserved and not, he was not going to let him take Blair. She deserved to live and be happy. Five years. Death had stolen five years from her.

That was going to be it.

Derek burst through the other side of the fog, stumbling. He looked around, searching for the tear, and found it right in front of him. A small glimmer of wrong in front of a palace which stood taller than any Derek had ever seen. He would have paid more attention to it, but something else caught his attention.

Or, more, someone else.

A woman with her back to him. Her brown hair was pinned upon her head, underneath a gold and silver crown, and her clothes spoke of riches Derek could only imagine. Her head was tilted back as she stared up at the palace.

"Who the hell is that?" Niran asked.

Derek wasn't sure, but they had to get past her to get to the tear. He took a deep breath and stepped toward her. She didn't flinch or turn. He kept going. Maybe she wouldn't notice him and he could escape from this strange Family Tree without any more trouble.

But when he got closer, he realized that not only was she staring at the palace, she was also whispering. Muttering the same phrase over and over. It wasn't loud enough to make out at first. Just similar sounds. Similar breath patterns. The exact same cadence. Then, as though someone had turned up the audio, Derek understood what she was saying.

"I tried to fix it."

He stopped next to her, unable to take his eyes off her pale face. Her hollow eyes.

"I tried to fix it."

This was the queen. Not Shion, but her predecessor. The last true queen of the Seshen. Shubishi had said she was going to make things right and fix the mistakes of her people. She'd died before she could.

"I tried to fix it."

He opened his mouth to say something to her, but no words came out. How could they, when he pitied her so?

The dead here didn't see each other. They wandered aimlessly, souls lacking conviction. And the queen of the Seshen stood before her home, haunted by her failures. She wasn't young. Beautiful, yes, but not young. She'd had time to go against her people's history, and she hadn't. Maybe she was waiting for the right time, but that time would never come. Had she hesitated? Had she questioned her resolve? Why, if she'd tried, if she'd wanted to, had she not fixed a broken system?

"I tried to fix it."

Derek shuddered and glanced behind him. Niran knew the history as well as Derek did. They locked eyes as pain washed over Niran's expression. If this queen had fixed everything, if her mother had fixed everything, her grandmother, her great-grandmother, Shion would never have suffered.

"Leave her," Niran said. "We can't fix her regrets."

Derek nodded. The tear—and possibly beyond it, Blair—waited for him. He couldn't help the unnamed queen. Her regrets, her mistakes, were her burden to bear. But his burden, his regrets, he could do something about.

Reaching for the tear, he spared one last glance at the muttering queen, and as he pulled it open and entered, the last words he heard were, "I tried to fix it."

Even though the tear brought him back to a Family Tree of humans, there was something so vastly different about this one that Derek almost threw up the minute he landed in the green rolling hills. Magic emanated from the air, suffocating him. He managed to stay on his feet, but he had to lean over, hands on his knees. Blair wasn't here. That much was clear. Her emotions were stronger, but still muted, and this didn't look like the Wyoming countryside. In fact, he had no idea where he might be.

He didn't care.

"We need to get out of here," Niran said. "There's something unnatural about it."

Derek wanted to say, "I know, but I can't sense a tear, give me a minute." What came out was garbled nonsense.

Niran sighed. "Oh come on. It's not good, but it's not that bad."

Derek took a deep breath, pushing himself upright so he could try again. "Speak…for…your…self…," he gasped out.

What was going on with him? Why did this place step on his chest and make it so impossible to breathe?

He took a step. Then another. There was no tear nearby, so they'd have to find one. Maybe, just maybe, if Derek kept going, he'd get used to the strange magic oppressing his nervous system. Niran followed, using one hand to support Derek's elbow. Derek didn't even have the energy or the focus to shove him off. Besides, even though he'd never admit it to Niran, he was grateful for the help.

Together, the two stumbled through the hills. If the Vilaim's Family Tree had given Derek life, this one took it away. Or maybe corrupted it. He couldn't quite tell. All he did know is that there was something eerily familiar about the magic in the air. It was almost as though he'd experienced it before. But where? When? Why?

Too many questions. He blinked in an attempt to clear his mind, even though it didn't work. They must have trudged on for at least ten minutes—though time meant nothing here—before a thought occurred to him. It broke through his jumbled mind and screamed at him in a crystal clear voice.

DANGER.

Danger? Derek paused. Niran tugged at his arm, but he wouldn't move. This place was dangerous. But why, and did it have to do with the magic?

That's about when he saw her. It should have been obvious, when he thought about it. The familiarity. The negativity.

She stood maybe twenty feet away, gaze locked onto Derek. Her bleach blond hair was let down, hanging the exact same way it had been the night she'd died, and even from this distance, her blue eyes haunted him. Or maybe that was from his memory. He couldn't tell.

"Oh fuck," Niran said.

Derek swallowed thickly. Kathleen tilted her head.

Mia had never told Derek what happened to Kathleen. She'd died, yes, but how? That was a mystery. Mia had tried to tell him once, but the words had caught in her throat and she'd never tried again. He'd never pushed.

"You're dead." She didn't ask. She told. Her voice was as chilling as Derek remembered, and he tried to get his legs to move. To flee. They refused to listen.

"Yup," he said instead. "Dead as a doornail. Just gonna leave now. Sorry to bother you."

Her eyes scanned him, and he tensed. It felt like every inch of his body had been put under an extra strong x-ray, a feeling he was not fond of.

Kathleen snorted. "I wondered when one of you idiots would

end up here. Always wished it would be Mia, to be honest. Annoying bitch."

Derek couldn't help but narrow his eyes.

"Don't let her antagonize you," Niran said.

"She was so whiny. 'Look at me, my life is terrible. I'm so scared. My brother won't tell me why he had sex with his girlfriend. Boo hoo.' Spare me. If I hadn't had orders to take her in, she would have ended up here, not me." Kathleen flipped her hair and in half a step stood directly in front of Derek. She reached out with a bony hand and touched his chin. Even though he was fully grown now, she still had at least an inch on him.

"Though," she continued, "you don't seem dead."

"Use magic." Niran tugged at his elbow. "She won't expect it."

Using magic was not a good idea. He was certain the only reason he hadn't collapsed the last time was because of the energy from the Vilaim Family Tree. If he tried anything here, he might actually die.

Kathleen's blue eyes narrowed. "You aren't dead."

"Derek, do *something*."

He couldn't. Even though he begged his body to move, to run, to flee, it stayed completely frozen. Even the words wouldn't come out.

"Well, isn't this interesting," Kathleen said. "I found a live one. Perfect. Now I'll get your energy and return to the life I should be living. Fitting. You kids took my life away, and now I'm going to take yours to get it back. Maybe I'll find Mia and make her regret ever catching Jae's eye."

Anger coursed through Derek like a fire in southern California. Mia hadn't done *anything*. She didn't want to be part of this world, and she'd fought hard to escape it because of Jae and his *obsession* with her. Punishing her, attacking her, doing anything to her, was not something he would ever allow.

The pure, unadulterated rage broke whatever spell this Family

Tree had cast upon Derek. His hand came up and energy swelled in his palm. Kathleen, too focused on taunting him, didn't look down or acknowledge his magic. The ball of pure magic shot from his hand and into her stomach. She flew back, fingers leaving his chin, and she let out a screech. Maybe from surprise. Maybe pain. Derek didn't know if the dead could feel pain.

"Finally." Niran grabbed at his arm again. "Thought you were going to die."

"I'm not going to die until I *kill her*," Derek spat. He stepped toward Kathleen, but Niran held him back.

"She's already dead. Leave her. Let's find the next tear before she–"

Too late. She hopped to her feet, face screwed up in the same anger Derek felt.

"Run," Niran snapped.

Derek finally did. The two bolted, Kathleen shouting after Derek. The names she called him bounced off the hills and echoed in his ears. She blamed them for her death, even though she'd been the one who attacked them. That wasn't going to change. She hated Mia. She would always hate Mia. Derek couldn't let that impact his actions. He had to keep running forward, even though all he wanted to do was turn and fight. Give Kathleen a piece of his mind.

But his mind lost all focus on Kathleen for a moment. A brief moment when he felt the strong, rushing wave of contentment against his skin. Blair's contentment. His heart dropped into his stomach. Had she given up? Was he too late?

Kathleen screamed something, bringing his attention back to the present. She was closer. So much closer. It really sucked that the dead were so fast.

And that's when he felt it. The tear. It was there. Right there. It had appeared out of nowhere, a gift from someone looking out for Derek apparently. He reached it and ripped it open. Kathleen couldn't follow him, right? She was dead. She couldn't move between family trees.

Right?

Wrong. The flash of light disappeared almost as quickly as it had consumed Derek. He didn't stumble, but kept running, bursting into a flatland of emptiness. He came to a stop away from the tear, thinking himself safe, only to find Kathleen lying on the ground next to the tear. She groaned, pushing herself up to her feet. Derek breathed in, taking a step back. He searched, quickly, for Niran, but the priest was nowhere to be found.

Odd.

But he didn't have time to think about that. Not with Kathleen rising to her feet. She observed the new scenery, and a vicious grin spread across her lips.

"Oh," she said. "This is good."

What had he done?

She stalked toward him, lip curling like a predator about to hunt its most prized prey. Derek knew there was no reasoning with her, so he didn't even try. He could use magic again, but he had no idea what would happen or if it would do anything to her. He was stuck. She was going to get his life force and then unleash hell on whatever Family Tree he'd dragged her into.

His heart raced.

When a hand made of pure blackness shot out through the tear.

It wrapped around Kathleen's waist and yanked her back. Her eyes seemed to bulge out of her skull. She screamed, but her scream vanished back through the tear and into her family tree. Derek wanted to cheer, thrilled that this dark creature had saved his life, but the creature didn't leave. It clawed its way out of the tear, howling toward the blue sky as it did so.

A thought occurred to Derek. The creature hadn't killed Kathleen. It'd merely put her back in her Family Tree. It didn't want to harm the dead. It wanted to make sure everything was in its place.

Derek's face went cold.

He didn't belong here.

The creature hunched, pure white teeth chattering between a snarl. This wasn't good. It was beyond not good. Derek didn't have the burst of magical energy anymore. He had no idea what this creature was, or what it would do to a living, breathing, person. AKA, Derek.

When it pounced, Derek reacted without thinking. Instinct took over, and he jumped out of the way just in time to avoid the claws. But he wasn't graceful. He fell to the ground, face smacking against the dirt. Still, he managed to scramble away, turning over. The creature snarled again, turning to face him. Derek could only look into its glowing yellow eyes. His chest heaved. His face hurt. His hands stung. He tried to climb to his feet, only to find fear locking them in place.

This was it.

He was out of options.

He needed a miracle.

God, he missed Blair.

Closing his eyes, he prepared for the worst.

The worst never came. Instead of his death, a screech rang through the air, blue light peeking in through his eyelids.

Blue light.

Magic.

Blue magic.

A gasp expanded his lungs and he snapped his eyes open in time to see the owner of the magic leap onto the creature's back. The creature howled and jerked, but she held on to its shadowy fur and spun a spear over her head. It came down, accompanied by another flash of blue light. The creature dissolved into ash, and the woman landed on the ground, tip of her spear touching the ground.

With his fear subsiding, her annoyance flickered against his skin. The familiar wash of warmth sped up his heart until he thought it was going to burst from his chest. She stood up straight, staring directly at him. She wore a tank top and a pair of cut off jean shorts. Clothes he'd never expected to see on her. She'd lost weight, the pudginess of youth turning into hard muscle, and her hair was short and unbraided.

She eyed him, then headed his way, footsteps cautious, emotions still screaming "annoyed".

He waited for her to say something. To greet him. To yell at him.

But Blair Arbour didn't say a word. Instead, she held up her spear and pointed it directly at Derek's throat, eyes narrowing as the annoyance against his skin turned to rage.

He'd always wanted friends. All of his existence, he'd desired someone at his side who lived as he did. Who connected to him in the way he so desired. He wanted to hold onto those who came into his life. He didn't want to take their souls. He'd never wanted to become the *Grim Reaper*.

But fate had other ideas in store for him. He couldn't have the only thing he'd ever wished for. Because he was a monster. He was a deity who had nothing more than a million lifetimes to live. He had the power over life, but he would trade it for one year, one decade, one century, with a friend.

All he wanted was a friend.

Yes, he'd had many friends over the years. But none were like her. He'd tried to recreate it. Their friendship. But there was nothing like her curiosity. Nothing like his smile when he was with her. How she made him laugh. He loved her, as much as he knew how to love.

And it is precisely because of that love that he continued on his trajectory. Seeking, searching, desiring to recreate the impossible. He hadn't been enough for her, and in the end she'd died, just like the others. She'd gone to the other side where he couldn't reach her.

This love drove him. It'd driven him to create the first immortal, and it drove him now. His love for her was never ending. And that was okay, he decided. It was enough. It was time.

It was time for the end to come.

Cody

Chapter Eight

Even though it had been six months, Cody couldn't get that moment out of his head. Mia wrapped in his arms. He knew he was being ridiculous, clinging to the memory of her soft, brown eyes that watched him as he whispered that he loved her. The feel of her smooth skin pressed against his. The joy overtaking his heart when he kissed her.

He had to cling to it, because the memory that came after destroyed him. He didn't want to remember waking up in an empty bed. No note, no hint of why she'd disappeared. He'd panicked, calling her phone. She hadn't answered, and he knew better than to leave a voicemail. He'd texted her. Texted Derek. Asked what the hell was going on. Derek had responded with three words.

Let her go.

At some point, she'd gotten on a plane. Her number was disconnected, and she'd blocked him on the chatting app she used in China. He'd even resorted to sending her an email.

It'd gone unanswered.

After a month, he'd given up.

After two, he'd turned to hating her. Cursing her name and wishing he'd never opened his mouth.

After three, missing her had become so unbearable that he'd begged Derek to give him updates. News. Confirmation that she was at least alive. Even though he'd been reluctant, Derek had eventually given in. Mia was in Beijing. She was living with their grandparents. She didn't want to talk to anyone. Derek only knew because he'd called his grandmother. Apparently, Mia hadn't spoken to him or their parents either.

Now, six months later, he longed to hear her voice. To see her smile and listen to her laugh. He got why she'd rejected him. He was so intrinsically linked to the magical world that if she spoke to him, she would never escape it. He was not only a mage, but also a Natara, and *also* the half-brother of the man who had kidnapped her and led to her best friend's death.

He halted. A warm, dry breeze rustled the leaves of the trees in the CSU Oval. All around him, other students chattered about classes and clubs and homework. He recognized a few of them as people in his dorm, but they didn't seek him out. Maybe they didn't notice he was there, walking to clear his head, or maybe they didn't want to talk to him. He didn't know, and he didn't care. If he was meant to make friends, he would eventually. No need to force it.

Besides, he wasn't sure he wanted friends. He'd tried the friend thing. One had left him without a word after a one night stand and confession of love. Another had holed himself up in an apartment, obsessed with finding the third. The third who was dead.

Cody closed his eyes, breathing in the fresh air of the afternoon. He didn't let himself think of Blair. They'd just started to become friends, having bonded over their road trip. Sure, it'd had ups and downs, but he'd enjoyed her company. He was only sort of certain she'd enjoyed his too.

Thinking of her hurt. Derek kept insisting she wasn't dead,

but Cody knew better. Her mist was gone. Derek was holding onto a phantom. Something to make him feel better for the way he'd treated Blair in her last few months of life.

He opened his eyes and stared up at the crystal blue sky. White clouds floated above him as gentle wisps. He'd been in school for a month now. Classes were easy, but he knew they would be. He hadn't used his magic since the night Mia had left, and he planned to keep it that way. He'd get through university. Move on with his life. Prove to the universe that he could be *normal.*

Even if the two mists hanging out in the center of The Oval reminded him it was going to be almost impossible to prove.

Dropping his gaze, he examined them. Every now and then he felt the Iravata's mists. Lady Shion often appeared in the corner of his eye. An invitation to talk. He ignored her every time. But Heba and Parker hadn't come to speak to him since before the mage clan attack. It was odd seeing them trying to blend in with the students around them. But while the other young adults had an ease to them, a normality, Parker and Heba remained tense. Their mouths moved. Were they arguing?

Cody sighed. He could ignore them, but they probably wouldn't get the hint. It was better to stamp this out. Besides, they'd been there when he'd needed them. The least he could do was see what they wanted.

He diverted his path and crossed the small road to the grass oval. The two of them stood under a tree and neither reacted to him.

"This is a bad idea," Parker was saying.

"Well, it's not like we have many other options."

"He's gonna—"

Cody cleared his throat. The two jumped and faced him. He came to a stop far enough away that they could barely hear each other, but close enough that others wouldn't notice anything weird.

Crossing his arms, Cody said, "Why are you here?"

A grin spread across Heba's face. "Told you he'd come over."

Parker mumbled something incomprehensible. He shoved his hand into his jeans' pocket and pulled out a crumpled five dollar bill. Heba flattened it before folding it in half and slipping it into her own pocket.

"That's not an answer," Cody said.

Heba stepped forward. Like always, she towered above both Parker and Cody, and Cody shrunk. He wasn't used to being around women who were taller than him. It got to him every time.

"We heard what happened in Willow Creek," she said. "We're so sorry."

Cody scowled. "That was months ago. Fire's out." It'd raged for two months. The most destructive fire in Colorado history. It'd left a scar on the mountains, having decimated everything in its path. It was a miracle that the firefighters had managed to put it out. Ash had fallen from the sky, creating unsafe air for a month after containment. People mourned the loss of the town. The loss of vegetation. The loss of life.

"Sorry," Parker cut in. "We've been kinda busy."

"Good for you. What do you want?" Cody knew they weren't there to give their condolences.

The two exchanged a look before Heba took another step toward him. "No need for attitude. We have a proposition for you."

Great. Just what he needed. "What proposition?"

Another glance passed between the two of them. Cody was about ready to throw up his hands and leave when Parker said, "We want you to help us find Natara kids who need help. You can see mists. That's how Jae always found us. We're trying to rebuild his mission to help Natara kids in shitty situations, but we're having trouble actually finding them. Some parents are terrible because they're just terrible, not because of magic. So, if you came with us and–"

"No." Cody didn't hesitate.

Parker sighed. "Told *you* he'd say no."

"Oh shut up." Heba clenched her fists. "You didn't even think about it, Cody. Just give it some thought. You still have our numbers, right? Call us when you've had time to–"

"I *have* thought about it." Cody took a deep breath. "Look, after Willow Creek burned, I thought about abandoning everything and helping kids like us. But shit happened and I just want to be normal. No mage or Natara bullshit. Just me going to college and getting a job. Hell, maybe I'll get married someday and have a big house with ten cats. I don't know. But if it has to do with your world, I want out. I can't be normal and also help you hunt down abused Natara kids."

Fire blazed in Heba's eyes. Clearly she didn't approve, but Cody was going to hold his ground on this. It wasn't fair of them to ask. Besides, what could he do besides seek out mists? He lived in a dorm. He had no job. He only had a place to live because of scholarships.

Parker grabbed Heba's arm, drawing her a step back. "Look, dude, I get it. It's a lot to ask. We won't bug you about it again. But please don't pull away from everything. Not us. We get you and there are things you can't run from forever. Keep in touch, at least? I'd hate to lose you as a friend."

Friend? Is that what Cody was to them?

He frowned, crossing his arms. Maybe they could be friends. At least acquaintances. People he could rely on. People who could rely on him. Not for magical stuff, but something else.

"Fine," he said. "I'll keep in touch. But don't expect more than a text or call now and then."

Parker smiled. "Fair enough."

Heba, on the other hand, snorted and muttered about annoying wastes of time. Parker shot her a look. She shrugged before slipping her hand in his. "Later."

"Yeah. Later." It took all Cody had not to stare at their hands. Longing pierced his heart as the two walked away from him. From The Oval. From the normal life he wanted to build here. That could have been him and Mia, if he hadn't messed it up. They could have been happy together. If only he'd told her sooner. Before the world had broken her.

He turned away from the couple and headed in the direction of his dorm. He shoved his hands deep into his pockets and tried to push any and all thoughts of Mia out of his mind as the sun beat down on his neck.

Five Years Later

Chapter Nine

Cody slipped out of the woman's room, closing the door quietly behind him. She wouldn't wake. Her mist, a dull pink, remained deeply under. His doing. Still, he figured it was better not to piss off her neighbors or draw any unnecessary attention to himself as he escaped from her apartment in the middle of the night. When she finally woke in the morning, this night would be nothing but a haze. He was some guy whose name and face were just out of reach. Not that he'd given a real name. Better safe than sorry. But he wasn't Eran. He couldn't erase memories. The smallest hint could bring back everything, and that could be a problem if they ran into each other again.

He hadn't done anything bad to her. After Derek had snapped at him to get out of the apartment, he'd found himself at a bar where she'd flirted. She'd been nice enough. Cute, with curly blond hair and wide blue eyes. She'd spoken with a bit of a lisp and mentioned that she was trying to get herself out there again. They'd talked into the night, both nursing their drinks as she talked about her past relationships. About the possibility of looking for something new.

Really, he should have bidden her goodnight before she'd kissed him and asked him if he wanted to have fun. But he'd been horny, she'd been willing, and he'd wanted something to take his mind off the insanity of his day.

Once outside of the apartment, Cody locked the door with magic. It was as easy as breathing. He was only certain it worked because he heard the click of the deadbolt.

The night air was warm. Downtown Denver smelled like metal and pollution, and even this late at night, car engines roared to life and tires squealed against pavement. Cody hurried down the street, eager to get home and get some sleep before work. He wasn't far from his apartment, so he didn't bother to check the light rail schedule. Besides, a walk would do him some good.

Honestly, if someone had told him that this would be his life at twenty-three, he would have laughed in their faces. For one thing, he lived in Denver. He'd lived his entire life before the fire in a small mountain town, venturing out of the town limits only in desperate times. Or when Mia had begged him to. For another thing, he didn't have any trouble charming and sleeping with random women. Five years ago, he'd been so convinced that he and Mia were meant to be that the idea of being with anyone else had disgusted him. Not to mention the fact that he hated strangers. And finally, he never thought that *he* would be the most well-adjusted of his friends.

Mia, depressed and living in China.

Derek, obsessive and self-destructive. Also possibly hallucinating, based on the way he watched empty air when he thought Cody wasn't looking.

Blair, dead.

How had he, out of all of them, slipped into a normal, functional, adulthood?

A police car rushed past him, sirens blaring, red and blue lights flashing, and he flinched. He shouldn't have. The police had no business with him, but the sound and the lights had caught him off guard. He paused, watching it disappear down the maze of streets.

It was strange that he was so okay with this life. But what other option did he have? Mia wouldn't talk to him. Derek wouldn't let go of Blair. And while Cody loved his parents, his mom was constantly in and out of the hospital, getting mentally and physically weaker, and his dad had enough trouble managing her without also dealing with Cody. He had no one. Even Parker and Heba didn't contact him as often anymore. They were busy with their mission, and he couldn't hold that against them.

Really, it didn't matter that he'd found the love of his life at ten. That she wanted nothing to do with him because of powers he'd never asked for. It absolutely, positively, didn't matter that most of his social life came from work, one night stands, or checking in on Derek.

And most of all, it didn't matter that he was one of the most powerful and dangerous beings in the world: a ticking time bomb, waiting to explode.

All that mattered was this moment. His need to get home and sleep so he wouldn't be a coffee addled zombie at work in the morning. So, he kept walking, keeping his head high and watching the glinting moon lighting up the night sky.

<<Come over. I need your help>>

Cody stared at the text with a raised brow. This couldn't be good. Derek didn't often *invite* him over. In fact, usually the man hated Cody's presence in his apartment and did everything in his power to kick him out as soon as possible. According to Derek, Cody was a distraction. Derek needed to focus. It'd gotten worse in the past year, as Derek insisted he'd almost found a way to save her.

Sighing, Cody locked his phone and turned his attention to the computer screen hanging over his work desk. He'd been gone for lunch for thirty minutes. Thirty freaking minutes. Why did he have so many unread emails? Were people really that incompetent without him?

He should have focused on those, but instead he kept thinking back to Derek's text. One-by-one, he either deleted or responded to emails. Most of them were quick to deal with. Others he would have to save for later. And between each one, he glanced down at his phone and pondered whether he'd calmed down enough to even consider going to see Derek.

Unfortunately, Cody felt responsible for his unhinged friend. Not because of years of friendship, but because Dr. Sòng had practically begged Cody to watch over her son. It'd happened after Cody had graduated from university and gotten this job. She must have found out through Cody's dad, or maybe Derek had mentioned it, but she'd shown up at his apartment two days after he'd moved in and offered to help him unpack.

She'd lost weight, no doubt worried about both of her children, but she'd still been strong. When she'd asked him to look out for Derek, to make sure he didn't destroy his life looking for Blair, Cody hadn't been able to say no. This was the woman who had always been so kind to him. Who had fed him. Offered to buy him clothes when his were torn. Who had sat with him while he'd studied, just to make sure he did his homework. She'd been a second mother to him, and he couldn't tell her how uncomfortable it was for him to go to Derek's apartment and make sure he was still breathing.

"I know this is hard for you too, but please don't abandon him. Not while he's still grieving."

The problem was, Cody didn't know how much longer Derek would grieve for. But he could do this for Dr. Sòng.

He sensed the mist approaching his desk before he heard the footsteps, and he sighed. Normally, he wouldn't think twice about someone passing his desk, but George wasn't going to just pass. He was going to stop and talk, just like he always did. The man had it in his head that he and Cody were friends.

"Hey, Cody," George's bright, yet deep voice said.

Cody glanced over his shoulder at the smiling man. Even though he and Cody were the same age, having graduated from CSU at the same time, George looked five years younger. He didn't sound like it, but he had a baby face devoid of any facial hair.

"Hey, George." Cody returned to his emails. "What's up?"

"Nothing much." The man leaned against Cody's cubicle wall. "Did you get that email from Harris?"

"Looking at it now." He clicked on the email from their supervisor and skimmed it. "Another temp is leaving?"

"Yeah. Annoying, isn't it? What's with the retention rates here? I think we're the only ones left from our orientation group."

Cody shrugged. "Guess it's the way of business."

"Think they're gonna do another round of hirings?"

"Probably." Cody's hand hovered over his phone. Derek was waiting for his reply, and knowing Derek, if Cody didn't reply soon, his phone would go off with an "urgent" call.

George fell silent but didn't move from his spot. Cody snatched his phone up from the desk and unlocked it, staring at Derek's unanswered demand. He had little patience for George's need for attention, especially when he had to deal with Derek's bullshit.

"You wanna get a beer after work?" George asked. "I hear there's happy hour at this bar downtown every Friday. Could be nice to relax, especially after this week."

This week hadn't been especially difficult for Cody. At least, not at work. But then again, he'd never had a difficult day at work. "Sorry, can't. I'm meeting with an old high school friend. He needs help with something."

He'd feel bad about using Derek as an excuse not to socialize, except it wasn't an excuse. He hoped, possibly like an idiot, that if he helped Derek with whatever this was, Derek would finally let go of the past and move on. Maybe he'd even go to college. Put that academic brain of his to work.

"Right. Well, maybe next Friday."

"Maybe." Cody ignored George, who took off toward his own desk. His fingers hovered over his keyboard as he tried to think of something to say to Derek. This was a bad idea. Derek had these weird ideas about this realm where the dead lived. He was *convinced* that Blair was there. That he could feel her emotions. After all these years, he refused to let it go.

Then again, who was Cody to talk? It's not like he'd gotten over Mia, and Mia had made it clear that she wanted nothing to do with him.

Sighing, he typed a message to Derek and hit send, before focusing on his emails again. Four more hours of work, and then he'd see what Derek needed from him. Even if this was a terrible idea.

Cody probably didn't need to knock, but he did anyway. Derek was, no doubt, on the other side of the door, lying in wait to ambush Cody with a too-fast, possibly manic, explanation. Still, he didn't want to be rude.

That is until Derek yanked the door open, grabbed Cody's arm, and dragged him into the apartment so roughly Cody almost tripped.

"Hey!" Cody ripped his arm from Derek's grasp and fell against the wall with a loud *thump*. "What the hell?"

"I figured it out." Derek reached for Cody's arm again, but like hell was Cody going to let Derek manhandle him. He yanked his arm back and glared. Derek, clearly not in the mood for pleasantries, rolled his eyes. "Come on. We don't have a lot of time."

That wasn't ominous at all. "Have a lot of time for what?"

"The ritual. Pay attention." Derek stepped carefully into the apartment, and Cody realized that it had transformed. It was still a disaster zone, but the middle of the living room was clear of books and furniture, replaced instead with…something. A summoning circle? Was Derek going to summon someone?

Cody's eyes flickered up in time to see Derek glare at the kitchen doorway, but there was no one there. Derek had officially cracked.

"I need your help," Derek said.

Cody tried to hold in his laugh. It came out somewhere between a bark and a scoff. "No. Screw that. I'm not helping you with anything. I'm done with magic. You know that."

"*You* can't be done with magic." Derek's words came out fast and clipped. "Just give me three days. After that, Blair will be safe and we never have to speak again."

Blair would be safe? What the hell was he planning? "I don't want to not speak. I just–"

"Just what?"

Derek shuffled through a pile of papers, and in seconds he was at Cody's side again, shoving said papers into Cody's hands. Cody struggled not to drop them.

"Never mind," Derek continued. "Come on. I need you to act as an anchor here. You have more magic than pretty much anyone, so it should be simple. All you have to do is stay put until I can get Blair out."

"Excuse me?" None of this made sense. If Cody was staying here, then where was Derek going? Was it worth questioning his sanity? Would it be a good idea to just go along with whatever delusion was going through Derek's head? "I can't do that. I have work. I have a life."

"You owe me this," Derek snapped.

"Owe you? You haven't done shit for me. I don't owe you anything." It was true. Even when Cody had struggled to adjust to life after the fire, Derek hadn't been there. Every time Cody's mom ended up in the hospital for something new, Derek was nowhere to be seen. After the first two times, Cody had stopped mentioning any of this to Derek, knowing full well he'd just be let down.

Derek crossed his arms. "I keep you updated on my sister."

Cody's face heated. Derek had never thrown that in his face before. He bowed his head. "I don't need you–"

"Save it." Derek's tone was derisive. "She doesn't want to talk to you, you want to know how she is. I'm doing you a favor, and now you owe me."

Cody scowled. "I don't owe you. I will not let you drag me back into the world of magic. It's done nothing but destroy my life."

"It's just for a few days!"

"No." He had to set boundaries. If Derek wouldn't respect them, then that was it. The end of their communications. Dr. Sòng would be disappointed. Or maybe she'd understand that Cody wanted *nothing* to do with this life.

"So, you're going to punish Blair because you're a coward?"

Cody hesitated, hand gripping the doorknob. When had he stormed toward the door?

Derek was wrong. He wasn't a coward. He just didn't believe Blair was alive. That she was in this Realm of Death place. Mia had seen her go up in flames five years ago. Cody had come to terms with it, it was time for Derek to as well.

Except a small voice in the back of Cody's mind asked him if he was certain that Derek was wrong. Maybe, just maybe, Derek hadn't cracked like a bad egg. Maybe he had found Blair and would bring her home. How could Cody stand in the way of that? If she was still alive, that would fix everything. Mia might come home.

He breathed in. "I don't want to be part of this world."

"I know." Derek stepped toward him with an extended hand. "I wouldn't be asking if I had any other choice."

Cody calculated the logistics. He had so much saved time off that his employer was actually hounding him to use it. It would be a little short notice, but whatever. He was a model employee. He could spend a weekend in Derek's apartment. If Derek was wrong, then no harm no foul. If Derek was right though, it would change everything. "All I have to do is stay here for a few days? Nothing else?"

"Nothing else." Derek always sounded serious, but this took on a new quality. One that Cody was certain meant that Derek believed his own words.

Still, he didn't know. It wasn't an easy decision. He glanced around the room. Derek had spent five years preparing for this. It was his chance to prove he was right, or fall flat on his face. Either way, maybe it was a good idea to give him this.

"Cody, I need an answer," Derek said. "Are you in or out?"

If Blair was alive, he couldn't let her suffer any more than she already had. He sighed. "Fine. But you owe me."

"If this works, you can have whatever you want."

Derek couldn't give Cody what he wanted. But that was fine. Despite his words, he wasn't doing this to be in anyone's debt.

"All right. Let's do this." Derek faced the circle.

Right this second? Cody raised a brow. "You might want to take a shower first." He skirted the edges of the circle to stand on the other side. It really was magnificent. Like something out of a movie exorcism. "Pretty sure you want Blair to want to go home with you. She might do it if you look like shit, but you have a better chance if you don't."

Derek glowered at him. "Fine. But after that, we're doing this. No running away. If you try, I will hunt you down."

Cody raised his hands in self-defense. "I won't run away."

"Good."

Derek said nothing else. He disappeared into his room, slamming the door. Cody flinched. That seemed unnecessary. Cody was giving him what he wanted. What had angered him?

As if it were second nature, Cody went about organizing and cleaning the apartment, careful not to mess with anything ritual related. Mostly, he dusted shelves and looked at titles. The sound of the shower pounded through the entire apartment, drowning out his thoughts. Which was for the best, because they wanted to go haywire.

Once he'd dusted all the shelves of a bookcase, he went to the notes Derek had shoved at him. They were mostly gibberish. A mix of unreadable English and Chinese characters. They meant nothing to him, though written at the top in big letters were three words:

The blood of the anchor.

Sighing, he put them down and grabbed a book off the shelf, letting it fall open to a random page. It was in English. A history of magic. Cody grimaced. This was all stuff he wanted to escape, not learn more about.

He hadn't realized how much time had passed until Derek spoke from the door to his room. "You ready to do this?"

Cody closed the book before replacing it on the shelf. "Frankly? No. But if this works, you're going to make a lot of people happy."

Mia would be happy. But he wasn't about to say that aloud. Besides, Derek probably knew who he meant.

"Then let's do it."

Derek walked to the table and picked up a knife that Cody hadn't thought much about. But now he stared at it. It looked like the Knife of Souls. A bad sign. How long had Derek had that knife? Why did he have that knife?

Derek walked to a bowl of water and unsheathed the knife. When he pricked his finger and held it over the bowl, Cody grimaced. This wasn't good. What the hell was Derek planning?

When Derek held the knife out to Cody, he figured he needed to do the same.

"Are you—"

"Just do it," Derek snapped.

It hurt. Pricking his finger. The blood welled before slipping into the bowl. The water hissed, as it had with Derek's blood, and Cody's eyes widened at the sight of gold and purple magic dancing together.

A pang shot through Cody's gut. He placed his non-bleeding hand on it.

I can do this, he told himself. *I can do this.*

A small breeze rustled the pages of the books around him, and in the center of the chalk circle, a human shaped oval swirled into life. Cody's jaw dropped. He didn't know what it looked like to Derek, but to Cody, it was a mass of colors fighting with one another for control. Maybe to flee whatever lay on the other side of the portal. They were souls. Souls of the dead.

Maybe Derek really was on to something.

"Whatever happens," Derek said, "don't leave this apartment."

Dread filled Cody's heart. "I won't."

Derek stepped toward the portal. He glanced to the side. At whoever he was seeing. Then he breathed in deep and entered the oval. It shuddered and then collapsed in upon itself. Wind kicked up all the loose papers in the room. They blew toward Cody, who lifted his arms to protect his face. There was a simple *pop*, and then an eerie calm settled over the room.

Slowly, and not sure that this was actually happening, he lowered his arms to stare at the place where Derek had disappeared. Only to find it wasn't empty.

Cody let out an involuntary yelp, jumping away from the circle. Because standing in the middle of it was a man. A man with sallow skin and sunken eyes. A man who looked more bone than flesh.

A man with no mist.

Cody stared at him, eyes wide. "Who the hell are you?"

The man tilted his head, and then smiled with perfect teeth.

"I am Death. I have a task for you."

Chapter Ten

Cody had thought that he wouldn't know what Death looked like to him until the day he died. By then, it would be too late to care, since Death would be ferrying him to the other side.

Ever since the Iravata's story, he'd tried to imagine what he would look like. The Iravata always referred to him with male pronouns, though they'd made it clear he could be any gender. Any race. Any species. However a person imagined them, that's how they appeared.

In all honesty, Cody had not expected him to look so human. Yes, there was something unnatural about him, but if Cody saw him on the side of the road, he'd think Death was a frail, middle-aged man. Maybe not middle-aged. Late twenties? Thirties? He blinked, taking a step back. The deity didn't seem to have an age.

Heart racing, Cody went over his options. He could attack. He could verbally spar with the ruler of all things dead. Question his presence in Derek's apartment.

None of those were good ideas, though.

He knew better than to trust Death. Death didn't need anything from a mortal.

Cody took a deep breath. Death waited for him patiently, hands clasped behind his back. They both knew that Death could wait all day for Cody to answer him.

He could wait forever.

"What task?"

Death observed him as if Cody were a contestant in a dog show. Cody shuddered. The lack of mist was not something he'd experienced before. Everyone had a mist. It was their soul. But while Death had no soul, he did have an energy about him. A presence, maybe, that kept Cody nailed to the spot. A presence that increased his heart rate, and brought a bead of sweat to his temple. He couldn't stop his breath from speeding up until he was about to hyperventilate.

He wanted to run.

To escape.

Especially when Death stepped from the center of the circle, careful not to step on any chalk lines. He dropped his hands to his sides as he moved.

Move, Cody told himself. *Don't let him touch me.*

"Possibly, 'task' is not the correct word." Death reached out with a bony hand to stroke Cody's cheek. Cody jerked back, maybe out of instinct, and Death's lips curled into a smile. "It is more of a demand, young one. You see, there are issues that you and your father have created. Issues that are getting in my way. It is time for a correction."

Death waved his hand and a piece of golden paper appeared in it. He held it out, dark eyes drawing Cody closer until he found himself taking the paper.

It was soft and worn. A tingle ran up his fingers and into his arm. He didn't need to ask to know that this wasn't normal paper. He'd accepted it. It was going to haunt him forever.

Cautiously, he looked down at three lines written in the most beautiful, clean handwriting he'd ever seen.

Fix Leo
Save your mother
Bring Mia home

His breath caught in his throat. Why did Death care about any of this? Why were any of these things getting in his way? And in his way of what?

He looked up at Death. "I don't know how to do any of this."

"You will discover the way," Death said.

"And if I say no?"

Death's gaze dropped to the chalk ritual. "You cannot say no. Your friends are in my care, and they will remain in my care until you complete the list. I may not be able to enter—what does Derek call it? The Realm of Death?—but I still command it. I decide who enters. I decide who leaves. If you ever want to see your friends again, you will do as I say."

Cody's eyes widened. "Excuse me?"

Death waved his hand at the chalk circle. "It has been many years since I took Blair there. It's hard to say what it has done to her. A living being has never spent so much time beyond the veil. Not that it matters if Derek fails in finding her. If he succeeds, however, the two of them will remain in my realm until you complete my tasks."

Death had taken Blair? She was alive? Derek wasn't crazy? Cody's head spun and he wanted to sink into the couch. His knees trembled. What in the world was going on here? "But why?"

Death turned his back to Cody. "Because it is time for this to end."

And then he was gone. One second Cody was staring at his back, and the next he was staring at the doorway to the kitchen. The oppressive energy vanished along with Death, and Cody sucked in a deep breath. His chest hurt. His legs turned to jelly and he collapsed to his knees, panting.

The piece of paper remained crumpled in his fist. What did he do next? Could he trust Death's words? The deity had his own agenda, that was for sure. What if Cody did as he asked and messed everything up for everyone? Or, what if he didn't, and Death was telling the truth? Blair had spent the past five years struggling to survive, and who knew what Derek had gotten himself into.

"Dammit!" Cody gripped his hand into fist and slammed it against the ground. Derek had told him not to leave the apartment. But what else could he do? He didn't know what the list meant, or how to complete it, but he couldn't give up. Even if this was dragging him back into the magical world. Even if he was certain that this was going to go poorly. He had no choice but to trust Death.

A bitter laugh escaped his lips. Trust Death. That was going to be a mistake.

Pushing himself to his feet, he un-crumpled the piece of paper and stared at it. Fix Leo. Save his mother. Bring Mia home. His eyes went to Mia's name, and a pang attacked his heart. Mia didn't want to see him. She didn't want to talk to him or ever step foot in America again. This wasn't her home.

He pulled his phone out of his pocket, staring at the lock screen. On it was a picture of the four of them. Back when they were teens. He'd never been able to let go of that brief time when things were okay. When Mia knew about magic and was recovering from Steven and Kathleen's mental torture. When he could be honest with her. When he didn't feel so alone.

At the moment, he felt so incredibly alone.

Unlocking his phone, he found Parker's contact and dialed it, hand shaking, still out of breath.

"Sup?" Parker asked.

"I need your help," Cody said. He'd never asked them for help before. He'd kept in touch, but he'd mostly stayed out of their business, and they'd stayed out of his.

Parker was silent for a moment. Then, "My help with what?"

Cody didn't know how to answer that exactly. He wasn't sure what help he needed from Parker, just that he couldn't go through this alone. He knew that it was a mistake, asking Parker and Heba for help. They'd want something from him in return.

But he didn't have anyone else.

Quickly, he explained the situation, Parker silent the entire time. Once he was done, Parker let out a heavy sigh.

"Derek is such a freaking idiot. But okay. We'll be there as soon as we can. Don't do anything stupid until we're there."

Cody rarely did anything stupid. But he said "Okay," anyway and hung up, staring at the room around him.

Blair was alive.

Derek was in the Realm of Death.

Death himself had come to Cody with instructions.

None of this was okay.

Cody left the minute Parker and Heba arrived. They'd exchanged few words. Asked to eat whatever was in Derek's fridge—though Cody had warned them that Derek's diet didn't involve meat—and wished him luck. As he took off, heading toward his car, he wondered if they thought he'd gone crazy. They knew about Death, but why in the world would a deity visit Cody and give him a list of tasks? Yes, he had the paper as proof, but he could have written that himself. Not that it was his handwriting. And where the hell would he have gotten gold paper?

He shook his head. It didn't matter. He had to get downtown. Slipping into his car, he glanced at the list again, a scowl forming on his face. He could have gone directly to the last one, but he had a feeling it was better to do them in order. Fix Leo. What did that mean? Was he supposed to give Leo his magic back? How the hell was he supposed to do that when he didn't know how he'd taken it to begin with?

The drive downtown took longer than normal. Derek didn't live super far, so it should have taken a few minutes. Instead, it took half an hour. Something about an accident on I-25. Eventually, he managed to exit and took the back roads to the abandoned street where the mage hospital sat with magic protecting its existence. He'd only been there once, but he knew how to find it. Nothing else exuded magic quite like an entire building of sick mages.

He parked and got out to walk the last half mile. No need for them to know what his car looked like, in case this went south. It would only take a second for them to know he was here. They had ways about them. Sure enough, the minute he stopped in front of the run down building, a rainbow of magic shimmering in the air, a woman in a white coat strode out of the broken doors.

"Cody Velt." Her voice was smooth and thick, like poisonous honey.

Swallowing, he held up his hands. Of course they knew who he was. Who in the mage world didn't at this point? "I'm here to see Leo Arbour."

The woman nodded. "Of course you are. But he's not taking visitors who aren't family."

"He might see me." He had last time. "Ask?"

Her smile unnerved him. "He knows you're here, Mr. Velt. He always knows when you're here or when you're close. It makes his condition worse. He won't see you."

"Can you tell him that I–"

"He's quite insistent." The doctor bowed her head. "I'm sorry. But you are not welcome in our hospital." She turned her back on him and walked quickly back into the abandoned building.

Cody's hands curled into fists. Leo had seen him last time, so what was different now? He'd asked if Cody had figured out a way to give him his magic back, so maybe that's what Cody was missing. An answer. He'd thought if he could see Leo, if he could experiment with his magic and Leo's empty mist, then maybe he'd have an answer.

Idiot. He was an idiot.

Groaning, he shook his head and turned to head back to his car. Or, maybe the mage library. Derek had mentioned it more times than Cody could count. Would it have answers for him? If it did, would he be able to find them? He was highly intelligent, but languages had never been his strong suit. That always had been—and he suspected always would be—Derek's specialty.

He cursed. He needed Derek's help. If only Derek wasn't the one he needed to save.

"Cody?"

His head jerked up, the familiar voice shocking him. Standing there, looking no older than she had five years ago, was Mrs. Arbour. Her hair, which she'd always had in two braids, was pinned up, and she wore flowing clothes, like the ones Enola had always worn. He'd heard from Derek that Mrs. Arbour had taken over as head of the clan, but part of him hadn't believed it. It must have been painful for her to be the voice her mother had been. The voice Blair was supposed to be.

Cody hadn't seen her for five years. Not since the day she'd wailed for her dead daughter, still grieving her mother, as Mia had choked out what happened. She was thinner than before. In her arms, a bouquet of flowers.

"What are you doing here?" she asked. Her blue mist fluctuated.

Hesitance.

"I–" Cody turned toward the building. "Leo. I'm here to see Leo."

She frowned. "Why?"

He didn't want to give her false hope. He couldn't tell her the truth. At least, not all of it. "I'm trying to figure out how to give him his magic back. Help him."

She gasped, and Cody flinched. He shouldn't have said anything. It was too late to take it back, though. She closed the gap between them and touched his arm. "You can do that?"

He swallowed, mind racing to find an answer for her. Like hell did he know if it was possible. Death had said he'd find a way. Maybe he would. No, not maybe. He *had* to. He couldn't let his mistakes take away another one of Mrs. Arbour's children. She'd grieved enough.

"I don't know," he admitted. "But I have to try. I think the answer might be at that library. Derek talked about it a lot. I'm headed there now."

Mrs. Arbour nodded. "Yes. I know of it. We got books from there for...well, for our children to help with their studies."

Blair. The two middle boys had gone to boarding school in France for a few years, while the youngest had been too young to formally study magic. Now, Cody had to guess they all got their education in Sangota. Why attend a boarding school in France when their teachers lived down the street?

An idea popped into Cody's head. He shouldn't do it, but he was desperate. The list burned in his pocket, begging him to finish it. "Can you help me?"

Mrs. Arbour glanced down at the flowers, and then up at the abandoned building. "I'm not sure. I've researched your power before, hoping that I might find something to save Leo, but your power has never been recorded in our lore. If there is something about it in the library, it might not be in a language I speak."

"Right." He ran a hand through his hair.

"But maybe ask someone who has your power?"

Cody grimaced. There were only two known people, besides Cody, who had power over souls, and neither of them were an option. Jae because screw him, and Shubishi because, well, same, but also because Cody didn't want to be indebted to the Iravata.

"That's not an option," Cody said.

"Are you sure? I'm sure he'd help–"

"Trust me." He'd only go to Shubishi if he had no other options. Getting involved with that man terrified Cody more than anyone else. Even Enya didn't scare him the way that Shubishi did.

"Okay." Her smile said it wasn't okay, but Cody didn't comment.

Instead, he looked at the flowers. "You're here to visit him, aren't you?"

She nodded.

"Ah." He backed away. "Sorry to bug you. I'll go find the library and come back if I find anything."

She bit her lip. Her gaze trailed up to the building again while Cody prepared to leave, but when she spoke, he froze. "You aren't bothering me. I'm not sure I can be of much help, but two sets of eyes will be better than one. Leo doesn't know I'm here yet. Delaying for an hour won't hurt him."

Seriously? She was going to help him? Derek was probably the best person for the job, but since he was trapped in the Realm of Death, Mrs. Arbour was the next best thing. She knew so much about magic. Her power was unmatched in the mage world. Even out of practice, away from Sangota, and the tired mother of five kids, she'd kicked so many mages asses. And that was five years ago. Her mist was brighter now. A sharper shade of blue.

It looked like Blair's.

"You don't have to," Cody said, but Mrs. Arbour was already walking down the street, gesturing for Cody to follow.

"If you can help my son, I'm going to help you." She smiled, eyes filled to the brim with absolute pain.

Cody hesitated. She'd lost so much. Was it fair of him not to give her hope? Or was hope the enemy? Because if he told her what Derek was doing, that Blair was alive, but the mission failed, what good would it have done? He couldn't give it to her until he was certain he wouldn't have to rip it away.

"Thank you," he said instead.

She bowed her head and the two headed toward the library. They had to find something there. If not, then Derek and Blair were absolutely screwed.

Chapter Eleven

Cody gripped his hair, head between his arms, as he scanned the book lying on the table. Across from him, Mrs. Arbour flipped through a different book, her eyes narrowed in concentration. Her mist distracted Cody, flickering and jerking. He tried to ignore it, but it was difficult when he was having enough trouble deciphering the words in front of him.

With the help of a cautious librarian, they'd find every book on magic manipulation she had to offer—and that were in English—but it wasn't enough. They'd gone through at least three books, finding nothing. If only he could *remember* the day in question. When he'd taken Leo's magic. That's where the answer lay. It had to be. But that day was so hazy for him, and Mrs. Arbour hadn't been there when it'd happened.

All Cody remembered was fear. Then pain. Then screaming. Then tears. His. Leo's. Mrs. Arbour's. Blair's.

Maybe he could contact Eran. Ask him to help. Not that Cody knew how to ask Eran for help, nor did he want anything to do with that particular Iravata. He seemed nice enough, but his constant manipulation of Cody's mother's memories had never sat right with Cody. Besides, there was no saying that Eran *would* help.

Cody gripped his hair tighter, sending annoyed pains through his roots into his scalp. There were too many variables in all of this. *If* Cody managed to give Leo his magic back, *if* Cody managed to save his mother, *if* he could convince Mia to come back, then *maybe* Derek and Blair would be free of the Realm of Death, and *maybe* things might go back to normal for all of them.

Then again, when were things ever normal for any of them?

Cody gave up on this book. It wasn't getting him anywhere. He released his hair and slammed the thick tome shut, slouching in his chair. "Any luck?"

Mrs. Arbour sighed. "No. I don't think we're going to find anything in these books. Your powers aren't from a mage clan. They're from your father."

"I know. I know. I *know*." Cody returned to his previous position, squeezing his eyes shut. He was going to have to do it. He was going to have to find Shubishi and ask him for help. "I don't know what else to do. I can't go to my father. He's an ass of epic proportions, and he'd hold it over my head until I died. Since, you know, he can't kick the bucket."

"You really shouldn't talk about him that way," Mrs. Arbour scolded. "Even if it is true."

Cody laughed bitterly. "I don't know what else we can do besides research."

Mrs. Arbour closed her book and leaned forward on her elbows. "Cody, dear, I have to ask: why now?"

Cody hesitated. "It's complicated."

"I'm sure it is." She reached out and untangled one of his hands from his hair. She held his hand, staring him directly in the eyes. "But it's been over fifteen years since you took his magic. You'd convinced yourself you couldn't give it back. What changed?"

"I...I...." He groaned. "It's *complicated.*"

Her eyes softened. "We have time."

But they didn't have time, and Cody couldn't tell her the truth. The list burned in his pocket again. He resisted reaching for it.

"It's just something I have to do." Cody released his hair and clenched the first Mrs. Arbour wasn't holding. "I've been running from my powers for too long. It's time to stop."

Mrs. Arbour watched him with her deep brown eyes. They reminded him so much of Blair that his stomach turned, threatening to expel what little breakfast he'd eaten that day. Two of her children's fates were in his hands. It was difficult to look her in the eye knowing that he might fail both of them.

"I know you're lying," Mrs. Arbour said, "but I can't figure out why."

Shit.

Cody looked away from her, toward the window leading out into Denver traffic. Unlike the hospital, the library didn't pretend to be anything but a library, but it had wards that would make non-mages walk the other way. See a creepy library in the middle of Denver? Why not go to the local one ten miles the other way? Even now, people glanced at it, frowned, and kept going. It was getting late in the evening. Cody was lucky it was summer. The sun wouldn't go down until at least nine, giving them another three hours of sunlight.

Mrs. Arbour pulled her hand away and opened her book again. "For the past five years, I've been trying to figure out what happened that night. I never blamed Mia for not explaining. She was inconsolable. She *insisted* that Blair was dead. Burned to ash. But there was something wrong about the way she died. One second she was there, and the next she wasn't.

"I know I'm supposed to feel this way. I'm her *mother*, and mothers don't give up. But I can't shake the feeling that we've been wrong all of these years. The elders don't understand why I refused

121

a funeral. They have given me grace and they don't question me to my face, but I know they whisper about it. They think I'm grieving and in denial. Maybe I am. But it doesn't matter, because all of these years, I've wondered if maybe Derek is right. Maybe Blair isn't dead. Maybe she is a hostage in this place he calls The Realm of Death."

Cody flinched, and Mrs. Arbour eyed him.

"The necklace never picked another wielder," she continued. "The elders say it's only a matter of time before we find the new seers. I'm starting to think that they're only half right. We will find *one* new seer. The other is still alive. My daughter is alive, isn't she?"

He didn't want to admit it. He didn't want to give her hope. He had to give her hope. So, he nodded.

"Cody." She gripped his hand again. "What's going on?"

Before he could stop himself, he spilled his guts. Everything Derek had been up to. The past twenty-four hours. Death's visit. The list. He pulled out the list and showed it to her, watching her eyes widen and her hand cover her open mouth. Tears appeared in her eyes.

"Why didn't you tell me?" she asked.

"Because I didn't want to give you hope, only to fail." Cody couldn't stop the words from tumbling out. He couldn't keep them in anymore. He needed to talk to someone, to an adult, to a mage who knew the magical world. "I can't imagine what all of this has been like for you. Watching Leo deteriorate, losing your mom, then your daughter. I don't want anyone else to get hurt because of my mistakes. And I'm still making mistakes. Look at me! I can't figure out how to complete the first item. How am I supposed to do the others? How am I supposed to save Blair and Derek when I can't even fix Leo?"

He blinked back his own tears. "I already have the burden of telling Dr. Sòng that her son is gone. She doesn't know where he is. He didn't say goodbye to her. I don't think he even thought of it.

It's going to break her heart if he never comes home. I couldn't do that to you too."

Mrs. Arbour wiped away her tears. They streamed down her face, staining her cheeks. "You kids. You think you have to handle all of this alone when you don't. I am here for you. I always have been, and I always will be. I appreciate that you want to protect me, but, Cody, it's *my* job to protect *you*. It's my job to protect my children, and you have always been one of them. Until Blair comes home, I am the leader of the Cokori clan. I will do whatever I can to help you complete your tasks."

Cody didn't know how to describe the overwhelming emotions raging to get out of his body. Mrs. Arbour always *had* been there for them, and they hadn't utilized her help. She'd always been an authority figure. Someone who might get them in trouble for their mistakes. But six years ago, she'd helped them find the knife. Five years ago, she'd fought against the mage clans to protect them.

Five years.

It'd been five years.

Without warning, Cody's emotions coalesced into one: anger. So much had happened since the night of the museum opening. Nothing good had come from it. Even though for five years he'd rejected magic, Derek had continued to research. Blair had fought to survive in a completely different realm. She might not even be sane anymore. And Cody's magic had continued to grow. It'd built up behind a dam of his building.

The dam sprung a leak.

Mrs. Arbour gasped.

Cody jerked his head up, blinking rapidly as he came back to the present. Mrs. Arbour wasn't crying anymore.

"What?" he asked.

"Your magic." She pointed at the air. Cody eyed it, spotting the signature purple hue.

"Sorry." Cody tried to call it back, but it was difficult. The dam didn't want to be fixed.

"Why is it purple?" she asked.

Cody eyed her. "It's always been purple." Or, it had been since the first time he'd seen his mist. "My soul is purple."

She looked him straight in the eye. "It wasn't purple when you were a child."

Cody couldn't believe his ears. "Excuse me?"

"I haven't seen you use your magic since you were a child, but back then it wasn't purple. It was red. It used to scare Blair because it was so different than the magic she was used to. Everyone in the Cokori clan has blue magic, but yours was red."

Red.

Blue.

Purple.

It all snapped into place. Not only the answer, but also the memory of that day. Leo had harassed him. He'd gotten on Cody's case for being from a non-magical home. He'd pushed Cody. Cody had snapped. And he'd felt the moment that he'd taken it. His magic had reached out and latched onto Leo's, yanking. Pulling. Shredding it from his soul.

He remembered the burning as Cody's soul mixed with Leo's magic. It'd been a fire deep in his heart. And Leo's soul had turned from brilliant blue to crystal clear. Empty.

Cody stood, knocking his chair back. The woman on the other side of the library shushed him, but he ignored her.

"I took his magic," Cody said quietly.

"Yes?" Mrs. Arbour stood as well.

"It became part of me," Cody continued. His words came out rushed and quiet. "My mist didn't used to be purple but if you mix blue and red—"

"Oh." Mrs. Arbour's face lit up for a moment, then drained of color. "You think you have his magic?"

"I don't think. I know." He looked at his hands. If his soul wasn't purple, if it had been mixed with Leo's magic all of these years, then this wasn't going to be easy. "And I know I can give it back."

Excitement flooded him. He'd always been more powerful than Derek and Blair. Was this the reason why? Was it because he had the magic of two people inside of him?

Could he be normal if he gave Leo back his magic?

"We gotta go," Cody said. "We're running out of time. Do you think you can make Leo talk to me?"

Mrs. Arbour frowned. "I've never been good at getting Leo to do anything." She grabbed the flowers from next to her. "But it's worth a try."

Cody nodded and took off, Mrs. Arbour right behind him. His heart raced. Maybe this wouldn't be a disaster. Maybe, just maybe, he could finish the list and save Blair and Derek. This didn't have to be a failure.

His mission was simple in theory: get in, give Leo his magic back, get out. In execution, though, it was much more difficult. It wasn't getting into the hospital. Since he was with Mrs. Arbour, no one came to stop him from entering the building, though the receptionist on the first floor asked what they were doing there. Mrs. Arbour stopped to talk to her.

Cody did not.

The hospital was as clinical and cold as he remembered. White walls. Tile floors. High ceilings with fluorescent lights. There weren't many people here today. Patients, yes, but not visitors, which was probably for the best. Cody didn't need an audience for what he was about to do.

He took the stairs to Leo's floor two at a time. By the time he got to the top, he was panting, and he hesitated with his hand on the doorknob. This would be so much easier if no one knew he was there. He had no doubts that the doctors would try and stop him, and he didn't have the time nor the patience to try and fight them off. Besides, he wasn't here to make enemies. He was here to fix one.

With a deep breath, he focused on his mist. Making it invisible. Something he hadn't done in five years. And five years ago, it'd been one of the most difficult things he'd ever done. Today, though, he barely had to think before the color drained from his mist and he disappeared from prying eyes.

The door opened. He jumped back and two doctors walked past, arguing about the correct dosage of some medicine Cody had never heard of. Perfect. He slipped through the door before it closed.

They'd moved Leo from the pediatric floor years ago, so the walls were empty of children's art and friendly paintings. It was as cold as the first floor. Two nurses stood behind a counter, gossiping, while three healthy mages sat in chairs, all ignoring each other. Cody walked across the floor. None of them could see him, but he didn't want to take any chances with his power giving out on him.

Leo's room was at the end of the hall where no one could see. With a deep breath, he opened the door and stepped inside.

He was in a bed this time. No wheelchair in sight. He wasn't mobile, his body wasting away with a million wires hooked up to him. His eyes were closed at first, but at the sound of his door locking, he looked over at the empty space in front of his door. There was no life left in his eyes. It occurred to Cody then that Mrs. Arbour hadn't just come to visit her son.

She'd come to say goodbye.

"Who's there?" Leo asked.

Cody released the color back into his soul, enjoying the way that

Leo's eyes widened.

"What, come to kill me?" Leo asked. "Can't you see that's going to happen soon anyway?"

Cody had no idea why Leo might think that. He didn't care. "I'm not here to kill you. I'm here to help."

Leo snorted, which turned into a coughing fit. "Help me? How can *you* help me?"

"You asked me, five years ago, to give you your magic back," Cody said. "Sorry it took so long."

It was clear Leo didn't believe him. "You can't. You said so yourself."

"I've been known to be wrong before." Back then, on the day it had happened, all Cody had been able to think is how much safer he would be if Leo didn't have his magic. He captured those thoughts, holding them close, and then banished them from his mind. Yes, at that moment, Cody had been safe. But at what cost?

Leo said nothing. His dead eyes examined Cody, and Cody shifted. Even half-dead, Leo still unnerved him. "What, do you not want your magic back?"

"I do." The words were quick and harsh. Spat out.

Cody walked over to the bed. There was a knock at the door, then someone, a nurse perhaps, tried the doorknob. A voice called out. Cody ignored it and held out his hand for Leo to take.

Leo stared at him, and Cody stared back. He wasn't afraid of this man anymore. How could he be afraid of him? How could he ever have been afraid of Leo? It was amazing how things had changed over the years. How Cody had gone from a panic driven shut in to sleeping with random women and working in an office filled with people. How he'd gone from a frightened child to someone with a fire inside of him.

He couldn't hesitate. Even if doing this, if completing this list, might change everything again, he had to do it. There was no going back. Bringing Mia to America wouldn't change the last five years. Seeing her again, seeing Blair again, letting Derek out of his obligation to save her, wouldn't bring back their high school dynamic. Maybe he didn't want to bring back their high school dynamic.

There was no going back.

There was only the future.

Leo lifted his fragile hand and flopped it into Cody's. His skin was thin. His hand small. His muscles non-existent. Cody had done this to him. Now he would fix it.

There was shouting. Someone banged at the door, but he didn't want that. He needed it to be quiet so he could focus. If this failed, Leo was going to die. He refused to let another Arbour die. The world around him fell silent. It was just him and Leo. Him, Leo, and their mists.

Leo's was empty. Cody's too full. For the first time in his life, he saw his mist trailing down his hand. It pulsated. It screamed for an escape. This wasn't like when he'd intertwined his mist with Mia's to save her life. This wasn't his magic, but his soul. His and Leo's, mixed together for fifteen years.

But the thing was, when he thought about it, this wasn't the first time he'd seen his soul. The first time had been that day fifteen years ago. It'd been traumatic for him. The flashing red hadn't been anger, it'd been his soul. He hadn't realized it at the time, but now he did. He knew. He understood.

He furrowed his brow and pushed every bit of his mist that felt *blue* out of his soul. It thrashed. It screamed. His ears filled with howls of pain and anguish. The mist pulsated stronger and stronger, until the blue lifted and the purple shifted to red. A beautiful, ruby red. The blue, meanwhile, slithered down Cody's arm, red repelling it, and latched onto Leo's empty soul with a vengeance.

Leo screamed.

Cody gripped his hand tighter, refusing to break the connection.

The blue mist wanted to go home. It did. But Cody's mist didn't want to let go. It'd gotten so used to the power of blue that it clung to its companion. Cody panted. He pushed. He didn't need Leo to be weak anymore. He didn't need the protection of the blue magic.

He deserved to be free of his past.

And Leo deserved to live.

A loud snap exploded through the room and Cody's breath vanished from his lungs. He collapsed to his knees, letting go of Leo's hand as the hospital room came back to him. The door behind him slammed open, voices shouting. Someone grabbed Cody's shoulders and pulled him away from the bed. He didn't fight them. He couldn't fight them. Even if he'd wanted to, his limbs wouldn't respond. His brain was a mess of fog, and he wanted nothing more than to crawl into bed and sleep for the rest of eternity.

"Leo!" a deep voice said. "What happened?"

Cody forced his head up. A security guard was holding him, but he didn't pull away. He understood how this looked, and he waited for Leo to clear up the situation. But all Leo did was stare at his hands.

And Cody stared at him. Because his mist was no longer empty. Instead, it was filled to the brim with a sky blue light.

Leo, with shaking arms, pushed himself into a sitting position. He still looked like he was on death's doorstep, but there was something different about him now. He had life in his eyes.

"Let him go," Leo croaked.

"I will not," the security guard said.

The doctor by Leo's bed nodded, though he had a strange look of confusion on his face. "Leo, this man assaulted you."

"No," Leo said. "He just saved my life."

Chapter Twelve

While doctor's fussed over Leo for the next hour, a nurse set Cody up with an IV and a cold compress for the headache that wouldn't leave him alone. They were transfusing him with something—he hadn't asked for details—and it was helping him feel better. Every now and then, a doctor came over to him and asked in a serious tone what he'd done to help Leo, but Cody never had an answer for them.

Mrs. Arbour was a mess. Not a bad mess. But a mess all the same. She kept blubbering out gratitude to Cody, asking Leo how he was feeling. Cody and Leo both responded the same way every time: Cody said it was no problem, and Leo said that he was feeling better and better by the second.

It would take time, the doctors said, for Leo to get his muscle mass back. He'd probably be in a wheelchair for quite some time. But he already had color back in his cheeks, and he was *finally* keeping down food and water. It was amazing, really, that Leo had lived as long as he had, considering his condition.

When the room finally emptied of hospital personnel and Leo

had fallen into a deep, restful sleep, his blue mist settled and content, Cody removed the cold compress from his forehead and glanced down at his hands. Once more, he couldn't see his mist. He'd only seen it for a moment, but he longed to look at it again. To see the ruby that marked his soul. At the moment, his magic was angry with him. Hiding in case he tried to give up some of it again. Or maybe it was just tired. He couldn't really tell. Either way, he had a feeling that it would build up again, growing to fill the now empty space that Leo's magic had once occupied. Before long, he would be as strong as he'd been before.

That both terrified and pleased him.

"Are you feeling better?"

Mrs. Arbour's voice drew his attention from his hands. She sat by Leo's bed, holding his still frail hand. Her eyes were red from all the tears, but her smile spoke of pure joy.

Cody shrugged. "Not every day you shove out half of the magic you've been holding onto for over a decade."

She nodded. "True. You worked a miracle today."

He hadn't, really. He'd done what he'd had to do to protect his friends. It'd been the right thing to do, but still. If it hadn't been for Death's tasks, he might never have tried. Leo might have died without the color in his soul. What would have happened to him then? Could a colorless soul enter the Realm of Death?

Cody reached into his pocket. The list warmed his icy fingers and he pulled it out with a thought that he should ask for a pen to cross off the first item. Make it official. But when he unfolded the paper, he realized that he didn't need to. Someone had already done it for him.

~~Fix Leo~~
Save your mother
Bring Mia home

"What the hell?" he asked, frowning. Mrs. Arbour tilted her head in question, but he shook his and shoved the note back in his pocket. Death had been here. Of course Death had been here. He was everywhere all the time. But when had he crossed off the first task? Had he, or was the paper magical? Did *it* know when Cody had succeeded?

He shuddered, and once more he asked himself why Death cared if Leo had his magic back. It had to do with all of this somehow. An issue Cody had caused. But if Death cared so much, why hadn't he just taken Leo's life? How had Leo lived so long on the brink of death?

Had Death not been able to reap his soul?

Panic flooded Cody. He stood, ignoring how his body swayed. Leo slept peacefully, chest rising and falling in a rhythmic pattern. His heart rate was good. Better than when Cody had entered the room. He was getting healthy. Would Death want to take his soul now? Was Leo going to die?

"Cody, what's wrong?" Mrs. Arbour asked.

"I'm worried about Leo." He didn't want to lie to her anymore.

She nodded. "I am too. It's strange that Death wanted you to fix him. But I'll keep an eye out for him. I think...I think if Death wanted his soul, he would have taken it already."

So, she'd had the same thoughts. At least Cody wasn't completely paranoid. "Are you sure?"

With a laugh, she shook her head. "Of course not. But he's in good hands here. They know what they're doing now that he's responding to treatments. He'll be okay. You should rest. The doctors said you can stay the night here. They're worried about you."

"Me? Why would they be worried about me?"

She smiled. "No offense, Cody, but you look like hell."

He did? Fishing out his phone, he turned on the front camera and looked at himself. Sure enough, his face was sheet white, dark circles under his eyes. Sleep was probably the right option, but he couldn't stop. Even for a moment. The longer he delayed, the more danger Derek and Blair were in. For all he knew, Derek had found Blair already and they were stuck wandering the Realm of Death.

"I can't stay," Cody admitted. He put his phone away and then stared at the IV in his arm. Who knew how long it would take to save his mother, whatever that meant? Time was running out. "Can you get a nurse in here to get this out of my arm?"

Mrs. Arbour hesitated with a frown. "Cody, that's not a good idea."

"I have to finish the list. If Derek finds Blair before I do, they won't be able to escape. Blair shouldn't be in there any longer."

"I appreciate you wanting to save my daughter, but you need to take care of yourself too."

"I'll take care of myself when the list is finished."

"Cody…."

He shook his head. This was his final answer. He needed to see his mom. Yes, he felt like shit, and he had no doubts Ava would freak when she saw him, but none of that mattered if he could save her like he'd saved Leo.

Mrs. Arbour nodded and then went to the door to call for a nurse. There was a moment of fussing and arguments.

The nurses didn't want to let him leave looking like he did, but he put on a smile and told them that he wanted to rest in his own bed. A damn lie, but they didn't know that, and Mrs. Arbour kept her mouth shut.

Once they'd freed him from the IV and given him some herbs that helped with magic recovery, they bustled out of the room again with an invitation to come back and see Leo whenever. To them, to Mrs. Arbour, he'd performed a miracle.

Maybe he had.

Cody faced Mrs. Arbour. "I'll let you know the minute they're back."

She smiled up at him, tears leaking from the corners of her eyes, and nodded.

With one last look at Leo, then at his monitors which held strong, he headed out of the room. To the elevator. Down to the first floor. Into the evening.

The sky had a tinge of pink to it. It was getting to be night. Would his mom even be awake? He figured it was worth trying.

The picture of his friends still mocked him, but he ignored it and unlocked the phone. He found his mother's contact. She was the most recent person to call him, so it didn't take long. Still, he hesitated. He never called her. It's not that they didn't talk, but she always called *him*. Somewhere in the past five years, he'd built that boundary with her. She decided when they talked. When she was okay enough to talk.

Today, he was breaking down that wall.

The phone rang twice before she picked up. "Cody?"

"Hey, Mom." Cody breathed in and looked up at the reddening sky. "I was just wondering if I could come over for a bit."

She was silent for a second. Then, with so much joy in her voice she said, "Of course. You can always come over."

Cody clung to that happiness. "I'll be there soon. Is Dad home?"

"No, he's away on business. I'd love some company. It's too late for dinner, but your room is ready if you want to stay the night."

Good. It might be better if Dylan wasn't there. "I don't know how long I can stay. But maybe. I'll see you soon, okay?"

"Okay. Love you."

He hesitated. "Love you too."

Then he hung up before she could say anything else. A light breeze rustled his clothes, pulling him toward his car.

Leo was okay, he told himself. Leo was okay. He'd fixed Leo, he would save his mom.

The moment Cody stepped inside the condo where his parents lived, Ava hugged him. She had to stand on her tiptoes to wrap her arms around his neck, and he couldn't help but wonder when she'd gotten so small. It wasn't like she'd ever been particularly tall. Maybe when he was a kid he'd thought of her as larger than life. But she hadn't seemed so tiny the last time he'd seen her. Had he grown? He must have been somewhere around six foot at this point, so maybe.

When she pulled away, she said, "It's been too long. Welcome home."

Home. This wasn't his home.

He forced a smile. Ava hadn't changed much. Or, maybe, she'd changed just enough that he didn't notice. She had more gray hairs. Was a tad thinner. Her smile wasn't as forced. But she still ushered him inside. The condo was filled with pictures of him as a kid. Pictures of family, of friends. Of a life he knew nothing about. His parents had flourished—mostly—in Denver. Especially Dylan, who found he enjoyed not living in poverty.

"How are you doing?" Ava asked in a cheery voice. She always had a cheery voice when they spoke. How much of that was her not trying to burden him with her issues? He was grateful that she wanted to protect him from the worst of it, yes, but he also wished she would see him as an adult. After all, he was an adult now. He could handle it. And it wasn't like she'd protected him when he was younger.

"I'm all right," he lied.

She frowned. "You look sick. Are you sick? Have you been eating well? Sleeping? Come on, let's get you something to eat."

"Mom, I'm not hungry," Cody said.

"Tea then. A nice hot cup of tea will bring some color to your cheeks."

He couldn't argue with her. He followed her to the kitchen—a room filled with warm brown furniture and cabinets, granite counters, and a windowsill of purple flowers. She gestured for him to sit, and he did, taking in the warmth of the room. He hadn't actually been here in a while. Sometimes he came home for the holidays. Dylan still liked to do Christmas, even though Cody had insisted he was too old for it.

"It brings Mom joy. We should do it," Dylan had said to him one time.

As she put on a kettle for tea, taking mugs out of the cabinets, the questioning began. "You're still working at the same company as before?"

"Yeah."

"How is it?"

It was a job. But that answer wouldn't be enough, so he babbled. "It's good. The people are nice. The work is easy but not too easy. I'm glad to be developing software for their project, though I'm not sure exactly how much my work actually means to them. Half the time someone finds a bug in my code."

Ava nodded along as she returned to the table with two steaming mugs of tea. "I still don't really understand what you do."

"That's okay, I don't either half the time."

She laughed and Cody smiled. It was good to hear her laugh. Overall she seemed okay. Better than right after the fire, at least. It was difficult to gauge her mood over the phone. Sometimes he could tell when she was slipping into depression, but other times it was nearly impossible to know if she was wearing a mask or not. In person it was much easier to tell, especially with her mist dancing like it used to when he was very young.

"How have you been?" Cody asked.

His mom sighed. "I've been okay. It's lonely with you and your father working all the time. Most of my friends have moved out of Colorado. I'm thinking of joining a hiking group. Maybe a sewing group. Something to meet new people."

He was glad to hear that she was looking forward to socializing and getting into new hobbies. But if she was doing okay, if her mist was happy, then why did he need to fix her? What exactly did he need to fix?

"You know, I've been having those dreams again."

She said it so plainly and absentmindedly that he almost missed her comment. She stared at her tea with a faraway look in her eyes.

It'd been a long time since she'd mentioned those dreams to Cody. Not since he'd learned that the Iravata were involved with her hospitalization. That Eran had been manipulating her memories.

Memories.

They weren't dreams at all, were they?

Excitement flooded Cody. Was this what he needed to fix? Did he need to ask her about her dreams and treat them like memories? It would fix her mood. It would give her a sense of peace to know that she wasn't crazy. That her dreams weren't just her imagination going wild.

He leaned forward. "Tell me about them."

Ava flushed. "They're silly dreams, Cody. I shouldn't have even brought them up. Let's talk about you. Tell me more about what's going on in your life."

Cody would not relent. "I'm serious. You've talked about them a lot, but you've never really gone into detail. I'm curious about them."

"But why?" She looked up at him, cheeks still a slight shade of pink. "They aren't important."

"Because–" The truth caught in his throat before he could get it out. He swallowed and tried again. "Because I want to know more about you. I've been a bad son, and I want to change that."

"Cody, sweetheart, no. You haven't been a bad son. I know that things aren't always the best between us, but you try. I'm the one to blame for our complicated relationship." She smiled down at her tea. "Me and my dreams."

It tore at Cody's heart to hear her say that. Because it was true. She'd always had her moments of good, but most of his childhood hadn't been and it *had* been her fault. But she was trying now. She'd been trying for years, and he'd been too scared of letting her in.

But he *wanted* to. Dammit, he wanted a mom like Dr. Sòng or Mrs. Arbour. One who would do anything to protect her children. He wanted that love. That unconditional, special love that he'd heard so much about on TV shows and read about in books. It was too late to have it in his childhood, but maybe he could have it now.

"You tried your best," he said weakly.

She shook her head. "I didn't. I'd like to try now, though."

"Me too." He gripped his hands. "Can you tell me about them? The dreams?"

"I've always said they're just dreams, but they don't feel like them." There was a quiver in her voice. "I see the same people, the same sights, the same buildings. Sometimes the dreams are different, but usually it's the same ones. And when I wake up, I feel like my mind is clear for a second. I know it's just the mental illness. I *know* that the medicine is supposed to help, but they keep breaking through. It's exhausting. It's freeing." She sighed. "I don't know how to explain it."

"What do you see in them?" He was on the right track. He had to be.

"A magical place," she said with a slight smile. "The sky is nothing like what we see here. It's a beautiful mix of green and purple, and there's magic everywhere." She laughed, shaking her head. "Magic. Such a strange notion. But it always feels so much closer to reality than people think."

Dylan had always known about Cody's magic. Not all of it, but some things. He'd mentioned them to Ava before, and she'd always brushed him off. But why? Why hadn't she taken it seriously? Why had Dylan noticed those things, but Cody's mother hadn't?

It all clicked into place. Answers he'd been seeking for so many years. She had never seen his magic because she *couldn't* see his magic. The Iravata wouldn't let her.

Maybe it wasn't his place to break the spell. Or maybe he was the only one who had a right to. How many times had Dylan told her about magic and she'd brushed him off? And more than that, why did the Iravata keep her from knowing?

"Mom, magic is real."

Her eyes widened and she reached out to grab his hand. She held it so tightly, her own shaking, that he flinched. "Are you seeing things too? Having dreams? It all started when I was about your age. I think. We can get you help. It'll be okay, Cody. Everything will be okay."

Therapy and medicine helped those who needed it. Cody and his mom were not in that category. Magic was real, magic ran his life, and magic had destroyed hers. But it didn't have to be terrible for her. If she remembered, maybe *he* could save her.

"I'm not imagining things." He withdrew his hand from hers. "I've never talked about it before because I didn't want to upset you or Dad. Turns out, Dad's known the whole time. But I have magic. There are skies like the one you describe."

"You're talking nonsense."

"I'm not." He was too weak to prove it to her. He was too scared that if he tried to use his magic, things would go awry. So, he focused on her memories.

"Think about your dreams," Cody said. "Think about what you see in them and how real they feel. That sky? I've seen it before."

"No," she said, tears springing to her eyes. "No. No. No. It's not real. The doctors, Dad, everyone tells me that it's not real. It can't be real. It's my stupid brain. It doesn't work right. It…."

But she hesitated before she could finish her sentence. Her eyes widened, tears drying up, and she looked at her hands. Cody tensed, waiting for her to say something. Was it working? Had he gotten through to her?

"Greece," she whispered.

"What?"

"Have I ever been to Greece before?"

Cody blinked. "I don't think so."

"But that's where those dreams take place. They're from a long time ago. Back before ancient Greece fell. Back when the gods ruled the world. That's when I met him."

Ancient Greece? That would make his mother over two thousand years old.

Cody's stomach turned. Shubishi. She'd met Shubishi. He had power over souls. Just like Cody. Just like Jae. But he'd been doing it for longer than Earth had existed. What could he do that Cody and Jae couldn't? How far did his powers range? What had he done to Ava?

"Are you talking about Shubishi?" Cody dared ask.

Her jaw slacked and she nodded.

Cody hesitated. There was a wild look in her eye. But he couldn't stop now. "What happened?"

"I was the daughter of a mage," she said. The tears returned, streaming down her face. "Father was a clan leader. He was powerful. *I* was powerful. But then I met Shubishi. I knew there was something wrong with him. He never aged. We met when I was seventeen and I fell in love with him. But he always told me it wasn't time. He kept insisting it wasn't time. Then my father found out about us and he banished me from the clan. Shubishi took me in and we lived together for years until I found out I was–" She gasped. "I was pregnant."

With Cody. She'd been pregnant with Cody.

"I don't know anything after that." She shook her head. "How did I end up here? In this time? Why didn't I die? What did he do to me?"

Her words grew frantic and she stood, pacing the room.

Cody wasn't sure if he was helping her or hurting her at this point. He considered calling for one of the Iravata. Eran, specifically, to help her calm down. To take away the memories of this conversation, but it was too late.

"Do you know him?" She rounded on Cody.

Cody nodded. "I don't know him well. I only know a few things about him. But I know he's my...father."

The tears came faster, accompanied by sobs. This couldn't be right, Cody told himself. This was hurting her so much.

He scrambled over to her, nearly knocking over a few chairs, and placed his hands on her shoulders. "Mom?"

She didn't bat away his hands, but she didn't seek comfort from him either. She placed her face in her hands and sobbed.

"I know about magic," she spluttered. "I know about your magic. I know so many things. But I can't do anything with them. Because there's this fog. Every time I get close to finding out answers, there's a fog and it's coming back now."

Her head jerked up, sobs halting.

At first Cody thought the fog had returned. That she was going to forget all about this. This conversation was going to disappear, just like every other time.

But then a look of calm washed over her face. There was no fog behind her eyes. Her mist was bright and alive in a way it hadn't been for Cody's entire life. A force pressed against Cody's chest. Not her hand, but her magic. He coughed, shocked, and fell back as she bolted from the room.

It took a second for him to recover. Ava had used magic? The fog wasn't back. It absolutely, positively, wasn't back.

Scrambling to his feet, Cody took off after her. She'd left the door open, and he grabbed his shoes, shoving them on before he ran. He hadn't fixed her. He'd broken her. He'd failed completely and he had no idea what was going to happen next.

As he ran, he tried his best to think of how to fix this for her. To make her stop remembering all these awful things. That was how he had to save her. To help her come to terms with all of this. He had to encourage the fog.

Still, it felt wrong. Because the fog kept her from being herself. She'd been dealing with it for all of her life in Colorado.

For all of his life.

She ran along the street, barefoot and quick. Groaning, he chased after her, hating himself for giving up on exercise. It wouldn't have killed him to go to the gym once a week. But the gym reminded him of Mia, and he'd decided he'd rather not. Now, as he panted, running after his very agile mother, he wished he hadn't stopped. He wished he hadn't let Mia control so much of his life.

They came to an overpass. One with a sidewalk but no gate. His mom clambered onto the edge and Cody realized what was going on. He halted, mostly out of instinct. If he got too close, she might jump.

He'd caused this.

He'd made her remember.

She faced him, back to the highway below her. There were no more tears, and for a second he thought that the fog might come back to her.

But she smiled. "I can't go back under the fog. I can't live this life anymore. It's not mine to live. I'm so sorry, Cody. I know you don't deserve this, but I can't do this anymore."

"Mom," Cody said. A few people had stopped on the street, watching the situation. "Mom, come on. You don't have to do this. It'll be okay. You don't have to go under the fog anymore."

She shook her head. "I remember now. All the times I went to the hospital, it's because the fog didn't come in time. Someone has been messing with my head for a very long time, and I won't let them do it anymore. I'm going to take control of my life the way that Shubishi and his friends haven't let me all these years."

"Please," Cody begged. He couldn't lose her. She was his mom. Despite all of the pain, all of the frustration and the bad moments, she was his mom. "Mom, *please.*"

"I'm so sorry, my little bird," she whispered.

And then she jumped.

"MOM!" Cody sprung forward, reaching to grab her arm. When he missed, he shot out his mist. But it didn't listen, sagging as the exhaustion came over him.

She fell.

Chapter Thirteen

Chest tight, Cody sank to his knees. He couldn't do it. He couldn't look at the highway where people were honking and shouting. Someone touched his shoulder, asking him what had happened.

He'd failed. That's what had happened. He'd failed his mother. He'd pushed when she'd begged him not to. If he hadn't done that, if he'd just ignored her dreams like she'd wanted, she would be alive still. She would be happy behind her fog, never knowing what really had happened to her.

What Shubishi had done to her.

He'd failed to save her. Reaching out, he searched for her mist. For any trace that she might be there, but there was nothing. The familial bond that tied him to her had snapped. He hadn't even realized it was there. He'd always taken it for granted. A string between mother and son.

"Young man." The voice was louder than the rest. It broke through his concentration not only because it was loud, but because it was familiar.

Cody looked up and found himself staring into a pair of green eyes. Eran.

He couldn't move. Eran lifted a finger to his lips, begging him not to scream. Cody obeyed, in part because he couldn't find his voice, and in part because he didn't want people to notice him. Already they seemed to be ignoring him, focused instead on Ava's lifeless body.

Eran gestured for him to come with. He was wearing a police uniform. Was he a cop now? Or was it all pretend? Either way, like hell was Cody going to go with him. He hadn't seen the Iravata in five years. *Five years.* They'd kept their distance, avoiding Cody, Derek, and hopefully Mia, and now they were here to do what? Fix the situation?

There was no fixing this.

He pushed himself to his feet, eyes burning.

"What happened?" Eran asked.

The people around them dispersed. One second Cody and Eran were surrounded, and the next, they were alone. No doubt an Iravata trick. Magic. They were using their magic.

The words tumbled out of his mouth, heat overtaking his face. "You assholes did this to her."

Eran must have guessed Cody's anger because he didn't flinch. "We were just trying to fix what Shubishi broke. We were trying to atone for his mistake."

"You failed," Cody spat. They weren't the only ones. He shoved his hand into his pocket to pull out the list and throw it over the ledge. Fury raged through him, making him almost blind to the rest of the world. But one thing did catch his eye. The list.

The changed list.

~~Fix Leo~~
~~Save your mother~~
Bring Mia home

Everything stopped. All the honking turned into white noise, screaming in the background, as Cody stared at the list. At that single line drawn through the second item. His stomach turned. His breath shortened.

He hadn't failed.

He'd succeeded.

He'd *saved his mother.*

Why? Why when he'd finally stopped running away did this happen? Why did Death want her soul? Death had told him to fix his and his father's mistakes, but why did that mean Cody had to lose his mother?

He didn't recognize the feeling in his gut. It burned through his stomach, spreading into his limbs. His face. His heart. Eran spoke to him, but the words floated away without meaning. Adelia appeared next to him, reaching out to touch his shoulder. To comfort him.

His body tensed, raring for a fight. Absolute unfiltered *rage* destroyed any exhaustion in his bones. It was indescribable how much pain he felt consuming his heart. All those years of his mother suffering, all those years of his suffering, led back to one person. No, not a person.

An Iravata.

The world snapped back to reality and he glared at Eran.

"Where is he?" Cody asked in a trembling voice.

It was clear Eran didn't want to tell him. "You're angry."

Of course he was angry. Shubishi had caused this. Shubishi was the reason that his mother was now lying dead on the street. Why he'd grown up in such a complicated and difficult way. It was all because of Shubishi and his *obsessions.*

He was the reason Death had created the immortals.

He was the reason Lady Shion had suffered as the immortal she never wanted to be.

He was the reason that the Iravata had come to Earth.

146

He was the reason that Cody's mother was dead.

Shubishi was the cause of all of Cody's pain.

"*Where is he?*"

Eran breathed out heavily. He glanced at Adelia, who nodded, and then said, "He's home."

Cody didn't need to be told twice. He charged away from Eran and Adelia, who both called after him. He mentally dared them to try and stop him, but neither of them moved from their spot.

He was still weak, but his anger fueled his magic. He closed his eyes and imagined himself at Shubishi's house. The crashing waves of the Gulf of Mexico. It was far away. Thousands of miles, but he'd traveled further and under more duress.

And then he was there, feet digging into the sand, cars and shouting replaced with ocean waves crashing against the shore.

He opened his eyes and looked up at the looming house above him. Shubishi stood with hands gripping the railing, and he stared down at Cody.

For a moment, they stayed like that. Father and son. Bastard and child. But when Shubishi turned, disappearing into his house, Cody's feet moved on their own. They took him away from the ocean and toward the man who had made his life a living hell.

When he entered, he made his way to Shubishi's study. The house was as haunting as he remembered. The hallways were long and thin, and he stopped for a moment outside of the bedroom where he'd watched over Mia while she'd slept. They'd been kids back then. Seventeen and traumatized. Terrified of the tale the Iravata had spun for them. A tale that supposedly had all the answers.

A tale that did not explain everything.

It had been, Cody realized, the beginning of the end. Telling the kids about their history was a big step for the Iravata. For Lady Shion. They'd laid as much on the table as they were willing to, and it'd caused so many issues. It'd led to Blair pissing off the clans. To

Mia trying to escape and be normal. To Derek becoming obsessed with Death. For the longest time, Cody had blamed Jae and Enya for it all, but it was more than them. It was also the story.

With a shake of his head, he pushed his way into the study where Shubishi kept all of his most treasured items. Shubishi stood with his back to Cody, holding open a book that he flicked through with ease.

There was a moment of silence before Shubishi faced Cody. "You've come."

Cody said nothing.

Shubishi sighed. "Eran warned me that you were angry. I take it Ava is dead?"

Still, Cody said nothing, but the rage in his heart grew. Shubishi didn't care. He didn't care about anyone.

"It's a shame," Shubishi said. "She was brilliant. It's why I took an interest in her in the first place. Willing to rebel. Willing to question her clan's choices. Willing to tell me when I'd gone too far."

He spoke with a light tone, almost like he'd actually loved her. But Cody knew better. Shubishi wasn't capable of love. He had been, and always would be, more interested in observing. Staying on the sidelines to watch and never interfere.

Cody saw that part of Shubishi in himself. And he hated it.

"She was a magnificent woman."

"Didn't stop you from destroying her," Cody snapped.

Shubishi frowned, tilting his head. "Destroying her?"

"How did you do it?" Cody asked, wracking his brain for an answer. "How did you get her here from Ancient Greece?"

Shubishi closed his book and placed it on the table. "Simple. I froze her soul."

Cody balked. "Excuse me?"

"I'd never done it before and I will never do it again. I knew it had to be done for the sake of the world, but I didn't intend to hurt her. I didn't know what the consequences would be."

Cody couldn't believe his ears. Shubishi had frozen her soul? It had to be done for the sake of the world? What did that even mean? How could tormenting his mother even be an option?

"You're an ass," Cody said. He didn't care that this man was immortal and had seen much more of the world than Cody ever would. Shubishi was, entirely, an asshole, and Cody wasn't going to take it anymore. He wasn't going to take the cryptic messages or the cocky attitude.

It was enough.

"I'm not an ass," Shubishi said with a shrug of his shoulders. "I merely know more than you do."

Cody's hands gripped into fists. "Yeah? Well, I know plenty. I know that you tormented my mother. I know that you caused her so much grief that she felt the only thing to do was take her life. I know that you're the reason all of this has happened, and I'm sick of you playing with our lives!"

"I'm not the one who handed you the list," Shubishi said.

Cody flinched. "I don't know what you're talking about."

"Of course you do." Shubishi stepped toward Cody. "You know very well what I'm talking about, and it would be easier for both of us if you stopped pretending like you are an excellent liar."

Okay, so he knew about the list. It wasn't like it interfered with his life at all. He would continue living, pretending like nothing was wrong, for as long as it took for him to get bored of humanity and leave Earth forever. There were other dimensions out there. Who was to say that there wasn't one that Death didn't rule over? One that Shubishi could visit and continue his studies?

"I'm merely following the plan, Cody," Shubishi continued when Cody didn't speak. "Everything I've done has been for the good of your people, and none of you seem to care."

"What you did was for the good of *my mother*?" Cody yelled.

4type

He grabbed a glass figure from the desk and chucked it at Shubishi. Shubishi's eyes widened as he ducked. The glass figure shattered against a bookshelf.

For a moment, there was silence as glass tinkled to the ground, but after a few moments, Shubishi glared at Cody.

"How *dare* you," he growled. "That was an antique."

"So what?" Cody took a step toward him. "You think that you can mess with people's lives and there won't be consequences? My mother is *dead* because of you. She would have been happy living with her family, dying at an old age with children and grandchildren if not for you. Now she's *dead*."

His magic mixed with his anger and the area around him exploded. Another crack in the dam. Shubishi flew back, slamming against the wall with a gasp.

Cody startled. Shouldn't he have no magic? He'd given so much of it away to Leo.

He didn't have time to think, though, because Shubishi pushed himself away from the wall and narrowed his eyes. Something tugged at Cody's clothes. No, not his clothes: his mist. A voice in Cody's head whispered for him to get on his knees and beg forgiveness.

Cody refused. He held his ground and fought Shubishi, face screwing up with concentration. With anger.

It took a moment for Shubishi to understand, and Cody realized Shubishi had never fought someone with the same power.

Shubishi's frustration grew. His brow furrowed, a look Cody had never seen on the normally calm and collected man, and then Cody felt the power tugging at his mist again.

This time, he fought back. He pushed against the pressure with so much force that it knocked Shubishi back. He grabbed onto his desk to steady himself, growling in an almost animalistic way. He didn't tug at Cody's soul again. Instead, he stood and held up a hand. Cody had never seen any of the Iravata use any magic besides their own gifts before. It was strange, seeing Shubishi's pure magic explode from his hand and fly toward Cody.

It was red.

Shubishi's magic was red.

Just like Cody's.

Fear controlled Cody's body. He held up a hand, trying to create a shield, but it didn't work. The magic flew directly into his hand. It didn't hurt. In fact, it was warm. Well, hot, maybe. But not painful. It disappeared into Cody's arm. Filtered into his body.

The dam shattered.

Cody flew back as his own magic burst from his hand. He landed on the ground, coughing oxygen back into his lungs. The house shuddered. Brick burst into dust, the sound deafening. And then it was silent. The only sound in the room was Cody and Shubishi's breathing. Panting.

Shaking, Cody pushed himself to his feet and watched Shubishi appear from behind his desk. The wall behind him had a gaping hole in it. In fact, most of the wall was gone, revealing a well-manicured lawn and a grove of orange trees. Shubishi's hair was disheveled, a look of pure malice on his face, but Cody didn't care. In fact, Cody was enjoying the look, possibly a little too much. For all the years he'd known Shubishi, every conversation he'd ever had with him, Shubishi had always been in control.

Cody had taken that from him.

"You are an insolent brat. You have no idea who you are messing with." Shubishi gripped his hand into a fist.

Cody narrowed his eyes. "And you have no idea what you've done. You are the reason for everything. All of our pain is because of you. Without you, none of this would have happened."

"Without me, you children would be in worse shape."

"Keep telling yourself that." Cody was in no mood to play games. "I want nothing to do with you or your lies."

"I am your father," Shubishi snarled.

"No, you're just some guy who fucked my mom." Cody turned his back on Shubishi. "I don't know why you think you're so important that you can do whatever you want, but I won't stand for it. I wash my hands of you."

The words had barely left his mouth before there was a piercing slash across his back. He gasped, eyes flying open, and he collapsed to the ground, shirt soaking with blood. Pain consumed him. He couldn't move. His ears rang, but through it all, he heard Shubishi walk toward him.

"I am only doing what my sister told me to do," Shubishi said in a low, dangerous voice. "I am following the path set by the woman that little girl used to be."

Little girl? Was he talking about Olivia?

"What she told me was so much worse. You children should be *grateful*."

Grateful? Cody didn't have the energy to respond. Instead he lay there, bleeding, while Shubishi walked away.

Cody wasn't sure how long he'd been lying there when he heard a scream. It might have been two seconds, it might have been two hours.

Hands touched his back. He was too tired, in too much pain, to wail. Warmth spread across the gash on his back. First warmth, then burning. His skin stitched itself back together and tears leaked from his eyes.

Then, it was all over.

"Cody?" a gentle voice asked.

He shuddered. Warm blood dripped down his sides. His shirt threatened to fall off when he pushed himself with shaking arms to his knees. Shubishi had tried to kill him. He would have succeeded if Flora hadn't been there. Had he known Flora was there?

He glanced over at her. She watched him with big, worried eyes.

Yes, he hated all of the Iravata. *All* of them. But it was difficult to be angry with Flora. All she wanted to do was help. All she'd ever done was what people asked of her. She was so kind and gentle, it was hard to believe she'd been the center of the controversy that had led to the Iravata getting kicked out of their home. Enya had a nasty streak, that was for sure.

"Are you okay?" Flora asked.

He damn well was not okay. But he nodded. "Is he gone?"

"Yes." She looked at her hands. "I don't know where. He can hide himself."

"I know."

"Are you sure you're okay?" Flora touched his shoulder, and he found he didn't want to shove it off.

"You healed me. I'm fine."

"I meant your mood. I can't heal anger."

Cody pushed himself to his feet. He was quite cooled, actually. Fueling his magic with anger had calmed him. Of course, Shubishi's attempt on his life hadn't helped. He knew then that he would never forgive Shubishi for what he'd done to Ava. Shubishi didn't deserve forgiveness.

But Cody did have questions.

Shubishi had mentioned a sister. A path that she'd laid out. And he'd mentioned Olivia. The girl who had collapsed into a coma when she'd seen Shubishi in the woods five years ago. As far as Cody knew, she was still in the same hospital, comatose.

"Flora," Cody said, "who is Shubishi's sister?"

Flora remained kneeling, but she looked up at Cody with wide eyes.

"I didn't know he had a sister."

Cody frowned. "He's never spoken of her?"

"No." She rubbed her hands together, expression soft. "Shubishi is a man of many mysteries. We've known each other for a very long time, but I still don't know about his life before he was immortal. As far as I know, his life was insignificant until he approached Death."

But he'd had a sister. And Olivia had recognized him. In the way that only a sibling would recognize another sibling. It was a familial familiarity that was difficult to deny. Derek was a reincarnation of a priest, so why couldn't Olivia be a reincarnation of Shubishi's sister?

Cody realized what he had to do.

First, he had to get a new shirt. Second, he needed to shower. But then he needed to seek out Olivia and ask her what she knew about Shubishi.

"Thank you," Cody said to Flora.

She nodded. "Please be careful. I don't know what Shubishi or Death are planning, but it can't be good. When the two of them scheme, it's never good."

Cody watched her for a moment, and then asked, "Why do you stick around him if he scares you so much?"

She jumped, eyes going wide. "He doesn't scare me."

"Are you sure?"

"I'm sure." Finally she got to her feet and walked over to a shattered window. "Shubishi doesn't scare me. It's horrible of me to say, but I pity him. He has so much potential to do good, but he's obsessed with things going exactly his way. He doesn't keep anyone around who doesn't interest him. Enya never interested him. Jae never interested him. He longs for something, though he's never told me what. Honestly, he's lonely."

Cody hesitated. She spoke of him like he had a human side to him. Cody still couldn't forgive him, but he wanted to know more about the man Shubishi pretended not to be. "So, he's like Death."

Flora let out a laugh like bells. "Yes. He's like Death."

A match made in heaven, Cody thought, though he wouldn't say that to Flora.

"I should go," Cody said. "Don't want to be here when he gets back."

"No, of course." She faced him and smiled. "Take care. And say hello to the others for me. I've missed all of you."

Had she really? And would he ever see the others again? "I will."

Flora vanished from his view, as did the broken study. In its place, Derek's apartment materialized, and he collapsed to his knees in the center of the chalk circle.

Chapter Fourteen

"Shit on a biscuit, Cody!" Heba screamed.

Disoriented and exhausted, Cody glanced at her. In all the chaos and drama, he'd forgotten that she and Parker were watching over Derek's apartment. Parker sat, back straight, on Derek's couch, while Heba stumbled over to him with wide eyes. He needed a moment to recuperate. Just a simple moment to catch his breath, change his clothes, and take a shower. He didn't have time for anything else. Olivia waited for him, though she'd be useless if she was still in a coma.

"What the hell happened to you?" Parker asked. He stood, and together with Heba they pulled Cody to the couch. His mind didn't work.

"I pissed off my father."

The two of them exchanged glances, but didn't press further.

"I can't sit," he said. "I'm covered in blood. Derek'll kill me if I get blood on his couch."

"You need to sit down." Heba tugged at his arm, but he pulled it away. "Cody."

"I'm going to take a shower." He didn't wait for their response before escaping to Derek's bathroom. He would have to borrow some of Derek's clothes, since he didn't have any here. It would be fine. Derek wouldn't miss a shirt.

Really, he shouldn't have been thinking about clothes. He should have been thinking about what Shubishi had said, but his mind was a jumble of confused thoughts and emotions. Anger, frustration, and curiosity were only overshadowed by the million questions.

When he got to the bathroom, he stopped and stared at himself in the mirror. There were splatters of blood on his face. He reached up to touch them, finding them mostly dry, and bile rose to the back of his throat. He swallowed it down and turned to look at his back. The shirt was destroyed—which was a shame because Cody had really liked this one—and covered in blood, but there was no evidence of a wound. Flora's gift was incredible. It was no wonder that Death had wanted her to be immortal, and that Shubishi had taken such an interest in her.

He recalled the pain. The pain of getting his back slashed open. A wave of dizziness came over him, vision blurring, ears ringing.

He wanted to forget he'd ever gone to see his mom.

But he couldn't.

The events of the day crashed over him. His energy, depleted, failed to keep him upright as he collapsed to the ground. The last thing he saw before slipping into unconsciousness was Ava standing over him, telling him that everything was going to be okay.

When Cody woke, he was in a soft bed. The room was dark enough that he could barely make out the outlines of furniture. At first, he wasn't sure where he was. He wasn't home, that was for sure. His blankets were heavier. Had he fallen asleep at some random woman's house? No, that wasn't right. He'd gotten a text from Derek. He was in Derek's bed.

Derek had gone into the Realm of Death.

He jerked up, head whipping around. His heart thumped in his chest, pounded in his ears, and made it difficult to breathe. Sure enough, he was in Derek's mess of a room, shirtless, but still caked in blood.

His hand snaked around to his back and he felt for a scar. The skin was warm to the touch, possibly a side effect of Flora's gift, but there was no scar. He lay back down, breathing out.

This wasn't good. None of this was good.

The list had marked off the second task, but why? If he'd really been able to save his mom, she would be here. Happy and healthy. Instead she was dead. Gone forever. Never able to come back.

Tears dripped down his face as he covered his eyes with his arm. He'd never thought he'd live in a world without his mom. She hadn't been the most amazing mom, but she'd tried. She'd wanted to be there for him. She'd wanted to make things better for him. She'd loved him, and he loved her.

She was gone.

He hiccupped as the events of the past twenty-four hours washed over him. He tried to keep quiet, so as not to let Heba and Parker hear him crying. They didn't need to know what he was going through. His emotions were his and his alone.

His grief was his and his alone.

Eventually, the tears stopped, his nose completely plugged up, eyes hurting, and he sat up again. With his eyes adjusted to the darkness, he could make out Heba sleeping curled up in Derek's desk chair. Cody didn't want to wake her, but he was desperate for a shower. Slipping out of bed, he sneaked out of the room. He found Parker in the living room, passed out on the couch.

This was fine, he told himself. Let them sleep.

He headed to the bathroom and turned on the water. Even though it might have woken the two of them up—since Derek's shower was not the most quiet thing in the world—neither of them came to check on him. Instead, he let the hot water wash away everything.

His tears. His blood. His grief.

He didn't have time to grieve. He didn't have time to process that Shubishi had nearly killed him; if it weren't for Flora, he would have. All he had time to do was shower, and then he needed to figure out what the hell was going on with Olivia.

Cody walked out of the shower, wearing nothing but a towel, and found Heba and Parker talking quietly in the living room. Not wanting to deal with them, he focused on turning his mist invisible and slipped into Derek's room to at least put on some pants. The last thing he needed was to embarrass Heba or piss off Parker. He had questions he refused to let them dodge.

"Cody?" It was Parker's voice at the door.

"I'll be there in a sec." Cody went to the closet and found some clothes that he had cleaned only a few days before. God, had it really only been a few days? Regardless, he pulled them on, squirming at how they didn't exactly fit him, and then braced himself for two interrogations: his and theirs.

When he opened the door, he found Parker standing there with crossed arms, Heba watching them both from the couch.

"Sup?" Cody asked.

Parker sighed. "You scared us half to death, man. What the hell happened?"

Cody shrugged. He didn't want to get into it. "It was just a stressful day. Nothing I can't handle. Got one more thing to do for Death and this can be done."

"I'm sorry, but you can just 'handle' all that blood?" Annoyance laced Parker's tone.

"Yes." Cody's wasn't going to budge on this. The last thing any of them needed was for him to break down. He'd just finished collecting himself. It wasn't the time for more tears. "I have questions for you two."

Parker and Heba exchanged one of their infamous glances. No doubt, they were debating whether or not Cody was sane and if they needed to ask *him* more questions.

"What about?" Heba eventually asked.

"Olivia."

Immediately, Parker and Heba's demeanors changed. Parker dropped his arms to his side, and Heba sat up straight, looking anywhere but Cody.

"What about her?" Parker asked.

"I think she's important," Cody admitted with a shrug.

Parker laughed. "What are you talking about? She disappeared six years ago. Haven't seen or heard from her since Heba lit up Jae's mansion."

"Which I will *not* apologize for," Heba said quickly.

Cody ignored her. "She's not missing, she's at a hospital in Denver. Fell into a coma before Willow Creek burned."

"Excuse me?" Heba asked in too loud a voice. Parker shushed her, and she glared at him. "What are you talking about? What the hell happened?"

Cody quickly explained to them what he knew about Olivia. Her omniscience, her visit to them in the woods six years ago, her meeting Shubishi, and her falling into the coma. It was a lot to get through and Cody tried to do it as quickly as possible. Heba kept trying to interrupt him, but he wouldn't let her, pushing on through her protests.

When he got to what Shubishi had said to him while he lay bleeding on the ground, Parker's eyes widened.

"Shit," he said. "That explains so much."

Cody latched onto that. "Explains what?"

"Look." Heba sighed. "We didn't know Olivia that well. She was always kind of mysterious and clung to Steven."

Steven. Cody hadn't heard that name in years. He hadn't thought about that name in years. But the memory of the boy who'd hurt Mia made him want to punch something. Possibly Steven.

"But she was weird," Parker continued. "She had this way about her. Like she always knew more than she was letting on. She told us she knew things, but never said what exactly that entailed. But it was like she belonged in a different era altogether."

"If she's Shubishi's sister's reincarnation," Heba said, "then that explains so much. But why didn't he tell you he had a sister?"

"Hell if I know," Cody muttered. "So, you can't tell me anything about Olivia? About what she might or might not know? Maybe a way to wake her from the coma?"

Both teens shook their heads.

"It's like Heba said. We barely knew her." Parker sighed and joined his girlfriend on the couch.

Cody shifted. This wasn't giving him the answer he'd hoped for. He had to talk to Olivia. She was the one with all the answers to everything.

"I'm going to visit her," Cody decided. "Maybe she'll wake up. If she does, she can tell me things that no one else can. Things about Death and his motivations."

Like why mom had to die.

Heba shrugged. "Maybe. I wouldn't bet on it though. Like I said, she was super mysterious. Sweet kid, but she gave me the creeps."

There was no denying that. Olivia had always felt off to Cody, even in the short time he'd known her. The whole omniscient thing was wrong. It wasn't possible to know everything at all times. There had to be some limitations. Some reason why.

Cody swayed, and Parker caught his arm.

"You should get some sleep," he said. "You had a day. Go in the morning. It's not like you can just burst in there in the middle of the night and demand to see a comatose sixteen-year-old."

Cody wanted to argue, but found he couldn't. Morning sounded good. Sleep sounded good. Besides, Parker was right. Even if Cody was welcome at the hospital whenever, they wouldn't take kindly to him disturbing the peace of midnight.

Sleep. He needed to sleep. "Go sleep in Derek's room. I'll take the couch."

The couple didn't argue with him. After a simple dance of goodnights, they disappeared into Derek's room and Cody collapsed on the couch. He needed sleep. He needed to rest, but he couldn't stop thinking of the last task he had to complete. One he didn't want to even consider doing.

But he had to, if he wanted to see Derek and Blair again. The thing was, he wasn't sure he wanted to see Mia after all of these years. He'd managed to put her in a tiny box and shove it in the back of his mind. She was a memory to him. A wonderful, painful, memory. If he saw her again, there was no saying what he'd do. Hug her? Kiss her? Yell at her for abandoning him? Did he have a right to do that? She'd slept with him and then shoved him out of her life. But he'd told her he'd loved her. He'd kissed her. He'd pushed her into it.

He didn't want to think about it. So he didn't. He closed his eyes and allowed himself to drift off into a dreamless, painless, sleep.

Chapter Fifteen

Cody stared up at the hospital, energy flowing through his veins. There was something off about it. A feeling that gave Cody a sense of dread.

He stepped inside, desperate for Olivia's knowledge. Her answers. As he walked to the pediatric ward, feeling out for Olivia's mist, he thought about making a visit to Death, but decided that wasn't going to do any good. Death had been MIA, and he wasn't going to show up now to answer Cody's questions. But Olivia would have them. Just Olivia.

So, he continued on, trudging over to the room he knew to be Olivia's. His feet were like lead, not wanting to move, and he had to force them to take each step. It was long. It was grueling. And when he finally came around the corner, he found a group of doctors and nurses outside of her open door.

"What's going on?" he asked.

A nurse, one he recognized from five years ago, looked at him with wide eyes.

"She's gone," the nurse said. "We don't know where or why, but she's just gone."

Of course. That was the bad feeling. That was why he couldn't track her mist. Nothing was going right, Cody decided. He'd gotten cocky after Leo.

He didn't say anything else. He turned around, knowing full well that he had to complete his tasks. Olivia didn't have answers for him, or if she did, she wasn't going to reveal the secrets of the universe to him today.

Besides, he had another task ahead of him. He needed to make sure Blair and Derek got home safe.

It was time. After five years, it was time to do the one thing he'd promised himself he would never do.

He was going to bring Mia home.

He knew it was coming to an end. The wheels were set in motion. The story was coming to a slow, bitter conclusion. He didn't know how it would end. He didn't know what was in store for him, or what he would have to sacrifice—what he would lose—to make sure that he saved those he had hurt.

But he was willing to do anything to make this right.

For thousands of years he had tried his best. For thousands of years he had done what he thought was right without listening to counsel. He did not take into consideration what anyone else thought or might think about his actions.

Because he was the only one who had to live with the consequences. While everyone else died, he lived, so why not be selfish? Why not do what made him happy?

After all, he deserved happiness too.

Blair

Chapter Sixteen

Blair was in a dream. She was in the middle of a field, staring up at the sky of Sangota. Every bone, every muscle in her body ached, which should have been her first clue that something was wrong. But in her dazed state, she continued to stare up at the beautiful sky. Clouds floated lazily—white against swirling purple and green.

The day preceding the dream hadn't been her favorite in the world. She'd gone back to Willow Creek to say goodbye to everyone. Honestly, she hadn't wanted to, but her mom had made her.

"It will be good for you to get closure," Esther had said with sad smile.

Blair hadn't had the energy to fight. Losing her grandmother had stolen any of her motivation to do much of anything except sit in her room and wait for the grief to pass. She'd expected saying goodbye to Cody would be nothing. Saying goodbye to Derek would break her heart. And saying goodbye to Mia?

Well, Mia had already said her goodbyes.

Still, she hadn't been able to resist seeking her out. It hadn't been difficult. Mia had left the gym, wearing her prom dress—had it really been prom?—to get air or something, so it only took a second to find her. Blair was going to find her, then find Derek, and then leave.

But it'd turned into a fight. Mia had accused her of so many things, and Blair hadn't held back all of the feelings she'd hid for all those years. Mia and Blair didn't often fight, but when they did, it was explosive.

Blair closed her eyes, chest tight at the memory. They'd both cried. Blair hadn't wanted to leave things on such a bad note. She was lucky that they hadn't. They hadn't. Right?

Eyes opening, Blair pushed herself into a sitting position. Her arms protested the movement, which she tried to ignore.

Was this a dream? It was a strange dream. For one thing, Blair was aware that it was a dream. For another, the hair on Blair's arms stood on end, pissed and annoyed at the heightened magic in the air. She swallowed thickly, trying to gain her bearings. The beautiful fields of Sangota stretched out before her with the city rising over the horizon. Behind her, a grove of trees she'd never seen before. Granted, she hadn't seen all of Sangota's lands, but the trees didn't fit. They were thick and wild, rising high into the air. They called to Blair.

This was a dream. It had to be a dream. But what had happened after her fight with Mia?

She placed her face in her hands. There were no memories of saying goodbye to Derek or Cody. She hadn't sought out Esther, who had gone to the house to collect things for the boys. The last thing she remembered was watching Mia's pained face.

It hit her like a hammer against her head. That wasn't the last thing she remembered. Enya had arrived. Blair's first instinct had been to protect Mia. Why else would Enya come but to get her son's angel? Except the immortal hadn't been there for Mia.

She remembered Mia screaming her name as crackling fire overtook her vision.

"Oh shit." Her voice wasn't her own. It was, but it was quiet. Half there, half not. She'd died. Enya had killed her. This wasn't Sangota, but a facsimile. She'd never thought much about what would happen after she died. Even when the Iravata told their story, she'd never pondered it. Why should she? She would see when she died.

Her breath caught in her throat. She had seen. All those visions of fire. They hadn't been about Jae killing her grandmother.

A tear streaked her cheek and she wiped it away. Could the dead cry? Could they breathe? No other explanation made sense. Her grandmother's sacrifice had been for nothing. Blair had failed to live on. And it wasn't *fair*! None of this was fair. Why had Enya killed her? Because of her gift? Had she been a threat? She'd had so much life left to live. So many things she'd wanted to do. How was it fair that she was—

-You are not dead.

A voice on the wind tickled her ear and destroyed any semblance of thought. She jerked her head up and searched for the source. She was alone.

-You are my prisoner.

She scoffed. "Excuse me?"

-Until my list is complete, until the gears are set in motion, you are my prisoner.

Blair focused on the voice. It was familiar in the way that all voices were when you weren't paying enough attention. Not enough to know who it was, but enough to wonder if you should. Who could it be? And why would they want to hold her prisoner? How could she not be dead?

-It was not your time to die. I took you from the flames. I healed your wounds and brought you to the place I cannot enter. You are within my realm, caught between life and death. And you shall remain that way until my list is complete.

171

"Who are you?" Blair asked. She pushed herself to her feet, hands curling into fists.

The voice laughed.

-I am Death, young one.

Her jaw dropped. Death? What the hell? How could they have taken her from fire? What did they mean that it wasn't Blair's time to die?

-I can do as I please. It shall be interesting to see how well you survive here. The living have entered before, but never with my permission.

Blair couldn't stop her scowl. They were getting on her nerves with that cocky attitude of theirs. She wasn't about to try and survive with the dead. Not without food or water. Not without clean clothes. Not without her friends. Death had brought her here, but they'd seemed to forget that Blair was a mage, and she'd dealt— albeit briefly—with other realms before.

She held up a hand and focused her energy into it. The last time she'd escaped from another realm, it'd taken a lot out of her, but she could still do it. Just focus on breaking through. Tearing a hole in time and space.

-Foolish girl.

Her body rebelled against her. The magic fizzled out, taking her energy with it, and she collapsed to her knees with a gasp.

-Magic is different here. There are ways to use it, yes. But you have not yet figured that out. Until you have, you will have to learn to survive without. Just as your friend has had to do all of these years. My advice? Fight, Blair. Fight and remember how to live.

What did that even mean?

Blair leaned her head back and shouted toward the sky, "Why are you doing this?"

There was a moment of contemplative silence. And then, the voice said:

-Because it's time for everything to end.

172

Blair meant to ask more questions. Really, she did. But a deep growl interrupted her. She spun around, heart racing. Standing not far away was a creature of pure blackness. Its eyes glowed red, and whisping claws dug into the ground.

Blair stumbled away from it. Panic rose in her throat. She had no magic. She couldn't fight. There were no weapons. No way to survive.

The creature padded toward her.

She fled.

Five Years Later

Chapter Seventeen

The hallucination of Blair's ex-boyfriend stared up at her with both wonder and fear. It held up its hands in a peaceful manner, still on its back, but she didn't buy the act. Her hallucinations were never peaceful, and the one time she'd fallen for the trap, it'd led to a close encounter with her end. It wasn't often she hallucinated. Just when she was particularly lonely, after a bad dream or maybe if she hadn't left her grove in a long time. Sometimes she wondered if Death was messing with her. Or maybe she'd gone mad. After being in Death's realm for so long—though she wasn't quite sure how long it'd been—that was bound to happen.

When she didn't strike, the hallucination lowered its hands. A mistake on its part. She jabbed the spear at its face. Better to get rid of it before it turned into one of those monsters.

The hallucination gasped and rolled out of the way. The tip of her spear dug into the ground as confusion overcame her. That wasn't normal.

Yanking the spear from the ground, she glared at the hallucination as it scrambled to its feet. They usually didn't avoid her attacks. Granted, they normally didn't get attacked by the monsters either. Not to mention that it looked different than the Derek she remembered. Whenever she hallucinated him—and he was a frequent visitor to her rotation—he was the exact same idiot from that day in the woods. Short hair, strong but still lanky with bits of baby-fat around his face, wearing jeans and a t-shirt.

The clothes were the same (except the t-shirt, which was a different color), but the rest of him didn't match her memory. His hair was longer and pulled back into a ponytail, while he'd filled out and lost whatever baby-fat he'd had left. He looked like a man, not a teenage boy.

Why was it different? Had Death found a new way to torture her? Their old hallucinations had stopped giving her hope, so they'd created different ones? Or maybe the dead had discovered a way to shape shift?

No, that wasn't right. They weren't the kind to be purposefully malicious. They were all stuck in a loop, living life like they had on Earth.

It didn't matter. A hallucination was a hallucination, and she wasn't in the mood to prolong a fight against her mind.

She lifted the spear, pointing it again at its throat. Was it taller too? That was annoying. Death had gotten really creative. Or maybe this is what Derek looked like back home. If she ever got out of here, she was going to have to tell him to ditch the ponytail.

When she took a step forward, ready to strike, it held up its hands again. Then, it spoke.

"Blair. It's okay."

Her eyes widened and she hesitated. It didn't sound like Derek did in her memory, though at this point she wasn't sure she remembered what anyone back home sounded like. And that was part of what caused her to pause. The hallucinations had never spoken before.

Face screwing up, she tensed. Maybe it wasn't Death. Maybe it was the monsters. They were known to try and draw her out of the grove. Had they perfected a hallucination she couldn't resist?

Its eyes widened and it muttered, "Oh shit," as she charged. But instead of letting her spear it through the chest, the hallucination twisted. A dodge. It grabbed the spear right above her hand and yanked.

She gasped. Her hallucinations couldn't touch things.

Maybe it wasn't a hallucination. Maybe it was actually Derek. Had he died?

Tears threatened to burn her eyes. He couldn't have died. The idiot was too stubborn to die. She yanked the spear back, but he kept his grip on it and jerked. She let go. They fell apart, him with the spear, her stumbling into a position she'd seen Mia take back when Mia spent her days practicing martial arts with her dad.

The hallucination—or maybe it was Derek—caught its footing. His footing. The footing. Whatever. Derek stared at the spear in his hands. She didn't wait for him to use it before she rushed him. He didn't fight her for the spear, eyes widening as she snatched it from his hands and jumped back far enough to swing.

Cut it in half. Cut the hallucination of Derek in half.

Her spear hit a solid rib cage.

Derek yelped. He reached for the spear, but she pulled it back as more confusion clouded her mind. She stared at her spear. Then at him. With a whip, she smacked it in the arm. Another solid hit. Another yelp. Another attempt to grab her spear. She twisted it and smacked him in the other arm.

"Stop that!" The hallucination—or maybe it really wasn't one—rubbed his arm.

The tears broke through. What was happening? How did she make it stop?

This is cruel, even for you. Blair wasn't sure Death got the message. They didn't respond, so it was hard to say.

Charging once more, she went for where a heart might be if Derek were actually there and alive. A kill shot. It wouldn't take long. Except that it turned. Her spear faltered in empty air. Derek then stepped into her space, grabbing. She tried to pull back.

His hands caught her wrists.

The warmth caught her off guard. The spear dropped from her hands. Sometimes, when she was lonely, she'd hold her own hand. Try and remember what someone else's skin felt like. There were no words to describe how amazing it felt.

Frozen, she didn't stop him from grabbing her other wrist. She didn't fight him when he pulled her close enough that she could smell his shampoo. Memories flooded her. The day before her grandmother had died, she and Derek had lain together and she'd smelled his shampoo. It was the same one.

Why was he here? What was this? What was going on? Was Death punishing her?

The ice in her joints melted and she regained composure. Her arms tensed and she struggled to pull away. He held onto her wrists, grip tightening. How was he stronger than her? After everything she'd gone through, he shouldn't be stronger than her.

"Blair, it's okay." Pain laced his tone. Desperation. "I'm not going to hurt you. It's me. It's Derek."

She couldn't take it anymore. "You're just a hallucination."

It hurt to speak. Yes, she ranted to herself, but the only conversations with someone not dead was, well…Death. And they weren't chatty. Nor did they require her to speak aloud.

It laughed out, "I'm really not."

Wow, so it was a jerk too. Laughing at her. She screwed up her face before stomping with as much force as possible on his foot. He groaned, but didn't let go of her wrists. Still, she tried to yank away. He didn't let go. There was a tangle of legs and confusion. Somehow, through it all, she tripped over his feet. Or maybe he tripped over hers. It didn't matter. They both fell. She landed on her back, free from his grasp, but he hovered over her, a hand on either side of her head.

Tears once more burned her eyes. "Just leave me alone."

Derek didn't laugh this time. He watched her with the gentle look he'd always reserved for her. One of understanding. One of adoration.

"I'm not a hallucination, Blair."

"Then how are you here?" Her voice cracked. This was cruel. Death had done some nasty things to her while she'd been here, but this was the worst of all. To bring her a fake Derek. One who could touch her. Who could speak to her. Assure her that he was real.

All this time she'd longed for him. She'd wanted a chance to apologize. To wrap her arms around his neck and never let him go.

She closed her eyes. This was it. The end for her. At least she'd go at the hands of the man she loved. Even if he wasn't real. Seeing him, getting to say goodbye, was good enough.

The strange Derek didn't suck out her life force. Instead, he shifted until he was no longer hovering over her. His presence moved, though didn't vanish, and her eyes snapped open. He was on his feet, holding out a hand for her to take. There was a small smile on his face.

"Trust me," it said.

It was probably a trick, but damn did she want to fall for it. She was tired. So freaking tired. No one was coming for her. The list was never going to be completed. Whatever that even meant.

She reached up and took his hand.

Derek hauled her to her feet. Their hands, hers still in his, remained between them. A barrier. His thumb stroked her skin and a shudder ran up her arm.

"You aren't hallucinating, though we'll get back to that in a bit. I'm actually here." Derek took her hand and placed it flat against his chest. She paused, waiting for the trick to fail. The monsters, the dead, they didn't have hearts.

Derek's raced.

She looked into his eyes. Those warm, green eyes.

"How?" she asked.

"I found a way into the Realm of Death." Derek reached out and brushed her cheek. "Took forever. Sorry about that. Turns out this isn't an easy thing to do. But I made it. And I've been through some weird shit to get here. But I did it. I found you."

"You're not dead?"

"Not dead."

"You're real?"

"I'm very real." He smiled.

Her own heart thumped in her chest. She pulled her hand away from Derek's. He let her go, concern crossing his expression. She reached up and pressed a hand against his cheek. His very warm, slightly prickly, cheek.

"What's wrong?" Derek asked.

Because it *was* Derek.

"It's been so long," she whispered, "since I was able to touch someone."

Derek's eyes widened before he wrapped his arms around her. She found herself enveloped in her first hug in who knows how long. He was warm. So warm. And soft. So soft. She gripped the back of his shirt, biting back a sob. If this was a trick, if this was a trap, then it was absolutely worth it. But it wasn't a trick or a trap. Derek had found her. All those times, lying in bed, wishing for a miracle, had come true.

"I'm here," he said.

Her breath shuddered and she pressed her face against his chest. He was here. Running a hand along her hair. Arm pinning her to his body. This was it. This was real. Whatever had happened in the real world, it'd finally come to help her.

It was time.

-It is time to go home.

Chapter Eighteen

Even though Death wouldn't let her die here, they weren't opposed to her feeling pain. The monsters often came back with a vengeance after she shattered them, meaning if they didn't get out of the open soon, then there was a chance they'd both get shredded.

Still, she didn't want to pull away from Derek's grip. He was real. So freaking real she could cry. And she was crying, unable to stop the tears from pouring down her face. She'd given up crying a while ago, as it did her no good here. Frustration, fear, regret, and sorrow all came with unhelpful tears that she'd locked away deep in her gut.

These were happy tears. Relieved tears. Excited tears.

She squeezed him tighter, eliciting a low rumble of a laugh. It vibrated against her ear. A feeling she'd never thought she'd feel again.

"You're real," she whispered.

"Yup."

"You're actually real."

"Last I checked anyway."

She gripped his shirt, no doubt leaving indents in the fabric, and squeezed her eyes shut. "Don't be snarky. You have no *idea* what this is like for me."

He relinquished his grip on her and pushed her away just enough to look into her eyes. His hand cupped her cheek. She couldn't stop herself from leaning into his warmth.

"No, I don't." His smile made her face flush with heat. She'd missed that smile. "I don't know what you're going through, but you don't know what *I'm* going through right now." He leaned in, pressing his forehead to hers. "I missed you."

Before she could tell him how much she'd missed him, the wind shifted and the hairs on the back of her neck stood up. She tensed.

"We have to go." Her words were quick; her actions were quicker. She grabbed Derek's hand and pulled him toward home, bending to pick up her spear without breaking stride. Through their connected hands, she felt Derek stumble, but then he caught himself and she picked up speed.

"Wait, where are we going?" Derek asked. "Why are we going?"

"A monster is coming," she said.

"A monster? You mean that creepy creature?"

"Creature, monster, it doesn't matter what we call them, they're dangerous."

Derek didn't say anything. Blair took this as a "I'm going to take you seriously" silence and so she pulled him along, half running to pick up speed. The trees in the distance marked their safety. There was no doubt the monster would be pissed that she'd shattered it, so when it roared behind them, she let go of Derek's hand and broke into a full run.

The hair on her arms stood. Her heart pounded. She should have moved much earlier, but what was done, was done. No point in dwelling on it.

The trees grew closer. A roar shook them. Blair narrowed her eyes. Derek's footsteps pounded on the grass next to her. A good sign. He hadn't neglected physical exercise.

The roar sounded again. Closer. Blair didn't dare look over her shoulder. They were almost there. Almost to the tree line. Any second and–

She crossed the border first. Derek flew past it half a second later, and she slowed to a stop. Daring to look, she found the monster prowling outside the boundary. A grin spread across her face, even as she panted so hard she tasted iron. Stupid things couldn't come into her Safety.

Flipping the creature off, she faced the shadows of the grove where she found Derek standing not far away, also panting.

"It's...not...coming...after...us?" he asked between breaths.

Blair breathed in deep, calming her heart rate. It wouldn't take long to return to normal. "No. Can't. It wants to though. We shouldn't stay still long. No saying if the rules will change now that you're here."

"Rules?"

She ignored his question, instead grabbing his hand to pull him further into the forest. The minute their fingers intertwined, a jolt of joy, and possibly a little desire, shot through her arm and into her heart. It thumped wildly. Was she ever going to get used to touching another human again?

They didn't run this time. They walked, very carefully, through the woods. Derek's head whipped around, taking in her Safety, which she found amusing. She'd had the same reaction to it the first time she'd decided to see what it was. There wasn't a grove of trees like this in Sangota. At first, she'd thought it was a horrid place and she would die if she entered. Turns out, it was the only place the dead couldn't stalk her. Whenever she went into the city—usually to steal something—she heard the dead whisper rumors about the grove. It was haunted, they always said.

186

Haunted by her, sure.

"Where are we?" Derek eventually asked.

"Home," she said.

He shot her a glance, frowning, though she couldn't figure out what it meant. Was that concern she'd detected in his tone?

"I'm safe here."

He gripped her hand, and not for the first time, she wished she could feel *his* emotions.

Leading him through the forest, she checked her wards to make sure they were still active. Her magic wasn't the best here, and it took a lot out of her when she used it, but she'd found simple wards were okay. They didn't take much to activate, and were often ritual-based anyway.

The stones guarding her cave were intact—if anyone had passed through without her approval, they would have fractured—and the dried flowers she'd stolen from the city were untouched. They would have flatted if anyone had tried to break in. She relaxed, passing through the boundary while still holding Derek's hand.

She never wanted let go of his hand.

The minute they crossed the boundary, a cave popped into view. It looked small on the outside, and maybe it actually was small, but it had suited her well. Sometimes, when the weather felt like it, it rained. Sometimes the winds were so bad she thought she might blow away. But her cave held sturdy, extending mostly underground. It was cool on days when the heat was unbearable, and warm when snow decided to dump everywhere.

Small and hidden, the entrance didn't stand out, but she didn't even have to think to know where it was. She slipped inside, following the natural incline to the bottom where it spread out into a room about the same size of the one she'd grown up in.

With regret, she let go of Derek's hand and strode over to her makeshift bed. It'd held sturdy every night, made of wood from one of the trees outside, stolen nails, and a stolen mattress. It wasn't the most comfortable thing, but it worked well enough to help her recover from magic use or injuries. Or boredom.

And when she faced Derek, sinking into the plump mattress, the rush of relief overcame her once more. He was here. How could he be here? He had so much explaining to do that she wanted to tap her foot, impatient. But he wasn't looking at her. Instead, he was focused on her little home, completely silent, eyes wide and confused.

She'd never pictured herself as a kleptomaniac, but now, paying attention to everything in her cave for the first time, she understood that she'd become one. The only things she hadn't stolen were the clothes she'd been wearing when she'd arrived, and her dead phone. Both sat out of view, since she didn't want to get rid of them, but also, screw looking at them every day.

Her phone had brought her comfort before it'd died. She'd spent as much time as she could scrolling through old photos on her phone to remind herself that she was loved. That people out there would be looking for her.

The day the battery ran out, she'd given up on the notion that anyone was coming.

All the other things in her room were scattered about, many stacked on the floor, some on small, natural ledges. Books, paintings, letters, weapons, even a broken BluRay player, because why not? Anything and everything to make her feel *alive*.

"It's not much," Blair said. "But it's home, I guess."

Derek frowned. He reached up and touched a painting she'd stolen from an elder's house. One of a wolf pack howling at the moon.

"I'm sorry," he said.

"For what?"

He breathed in. "For taking so long to find you."

It occurred to her then that she had no idea how much time had passed. Derek looked *very* different. Older by at least a few years. But how many years?

"How long has it been?" Blair dared ask. She wasn't sure she wanted to know, but if Derek was breaking her out of here, she'd find out sooner or later. Better now when she could process it without having to deal with the real world.

Derek kicked at the ground. Was he embarrassed? He had nothing to be embarrassed about. He was here now. That's what mattered. She'd survived—somehow—through all of this hell and he'd come for her.

"Just tell me," she said.

"Five years."

"Oh."

He faced her, tilting his head. "You aren't shocked."

She should have been. Really. Five years as a prisoner. Five years of missed memories and life changes. "Time passes weird here. Sometimes it feels like it's been two days. Other times it feels like it's been twenty years. Night and seasons aren't stable. It can be bright out and spring when I go to sleep, and dead of winter and night when I wake up. I know that a day hasn't passed." She gestured at him. "You don't look nineteen anymore."

"You don't either." He crossed his arms, and for some reason, his comment made her flush. She hadn't realized she'd aged. Yeah, her hair grew (though she kept cutting it short), and she knew she'd lost weight since her old clothes were too baggy on her, but she hadn't looked in a mirror since she'd gotten here. Those didn't exist in this place for some reason.

Breathing in, she decided that it was time to ask questions. All the questions she'd delayed when the wind had changed on the plains.

"How did you find me?"

Derek laughed, almost bitterly. "A lot of research. Took me a

189

bit to figure out *where* you were. Spent the last few years figuring out how to get in here. It wasn't easy, and I guess I owe Cody now."

"You owe Cody?"

"He's acting as an anchor on the other side." Derek grabbed the back of a wooden chair Blair had stolen and sat in it, stretching out his legs. "Really didn't want to. Both he and Mia like to pretend like magic doesn't exist. Especially Mia."

Blair grimaced. "Can't really blame her, can you?"

"Guess not." He shrugged. "Anyway, all these years, I've felt your emotions. Not well, but enough that I knew you were alive. Not that anyone believes me. Well, maybe your mom does. She never held a funeral as far as I know."

Blair's jaw dropped. "Wait, are you telling me the whole world thinks I'm *dead*?"

"According to the official report, you died in the fire."

"*The* fire?"

Derek hesitated, then nodded. "Yeah. Enya caused one of the most destructive and deadly fires in history. Worst in Colorado history. You can still see the black scar on the mountainside."

All to kill Blair. Which Enya had failed to do. Blair shuddered. Would the crazed god go after her again? "Okay, so I'm guessing Willow Creek is...?"

"Ash." Derek suddenly found his hands very interesting. "I haven't been back. I don't think anyone has."

"Oh." Derek had mentioned Cody, her mom, and Mia. But.... "Did your parents make it out okay? What about my family? Cody's parents?"

"Everyone's fine." Derek took a deep breath. "I mean, not *fine*, but they aren't dead. It's been a rough few years."

"You said my mom hasn't held a funeral for me?" Blair's heart thumped in her chest. Funerals in the Cokori clan were a big event. Her grandmother's had lasted days. It was important to usher the soul into the next life, and just as important to return the magic to the world. If her mom hadn't held one, she must have been holding onto hope that Blair would come back. It must have pissed off all the elders.

Derek shrugged. "As far as I know. She's the head of the Cokori clan. I talk to her sometimes, though I've mostly kept my distance. Figured my studies might upset her. But your brothers are doing okay last I asked. They miss you."

She missed them. Annoying as they were, they were her brothers. She would give anything to talk to them again and hear their sass. See the innocence in their eyes. "What about your parents?"

At this, Derek sighed and slumped in his seat. "They moved to D.C. Work there now, I guess. Mā comes to visit sometimes, though Bà keeps his distance. I'm a disappointment. He'd had such great academic hopes for me and Mia, and neither of us delivered. Mā fusses. She thinks I don't know she asked Cody to keep an eye on me."

"Cody?"

"Went to college. Works as a computer something." Derek waved his hand in the air. "He thinks he's doing the right thing, but anyone can tell he's miserable. Spends his time working or sleeping around."

Blair choked on air. Cody? Sleeping around? What the hell happened to cause that? She swallowed and tried to think of a delicate way to ask. When nothing came up, she instead asked about the last person she'd seen before the fire. Her best friend. The person Blair had the most regrets about. Their fight hadn't been good. Necessary, but interrupted. Blair hadn't had a chance to make things right.

"How's Mia?"

Derek's sigh echoed in the cave and he got this faraway look in his eyes. "Mia's coping the best she knows how."

191

Blair didn't like the sound of that. "What's that supposed to mean?"

Derek hesitated, which was never a good sign. How bad was it? How broken had Mia become? "I haven't talked to her in a few months. Got really focused, and we've been drifting apart for a while, I guess."

"What happened?"

"She moved to China after the fire. Lives with our aunt right now in a big city in Sichuan. Last time I checked in, she was working a menial job and had no friends. She doesn't talk to me or our parents very often. Usually when we call her. I know Bà gets updates from our aunt."

Blair's brow furrowed. "Doesn't she talk to Cody?"

"Not since they slept together."

"Excuse me?"

Derek rolled his eyes and groaned. "Idiots. It was right before she left for Beijing. No idea what happened, but it ended with her cutting all contact with him, and him pining after her for five freaking years." He grumbled something that sounded like a string of cuss words before again saying, "Idiots."

"Wow." Blair couldn't wrap her mind around all of this information.

"Sorry." Derek grimaced. "This all probably sounds super stupid to you. It's just drama. After living here—"

"It's refreshing." She leaned forward. "I've spent so long alone and fighting for my life. This, right here, is the first time in five years I've felt even remotely alive."

She looked at her hands, trying to remember the last time she *did* feel alive. It wasn't the night Death had taken her. It was before that. Before her grandmother's funeral. Before Jae had stolen the knife. Before the mages had swarmed Willow Creek like the insects they were. Hell, it was even before they'd gone to save Mia from

192

Jae's mansion. She'd been running on fumes for so long and hadn't even realized it.

"Blair?" Derek ventured.

She breathed in. "We've been through a lot."

"Yeah." He stood but didn't move toward her. The chair scratched against the cave floor: a piercing sound.

"I'm trying to remember the last time I felt alive," she said. "I'd thought, before coming here, that I was living the best I knew how. But maybe it wasn't enough. During all the *shit* we've been through, one thing after another, I'd lost bits and pieces of myself until finally I was a husk. And maybe I still am one."

Her gaze trained to the ceiling. "I've learned to survive here, but I don't want to survive anymore. I want to *live*."

Derek crossed the cave with slow steps. Blair watched him. How could she not. He was here. Alive and here. And even though he looked different, he was exactly the same man she'd fallen in love with when they were idiot teens. The man she'd hurt. The man who had spent five years researching and risking his life to find her.

When he reached her, she took his hand. It was warm. Everything about him was warm.

"Once we get back," Derek murmured, "you'll get to live for a long time."

He looked at her with such soft, gentle eyes. But there was a hint of sadness there. She didn't understand it.

She wanted it gone.

Tugging at his hand, she tilted her head back. "Who says I have to wait until then?"

At first, she didn't think he'd pick up what she was laying down. Some part of *her* didn't catch on. Namely her brain. But her body did. It tingled with anticipation when their eyes met and he smiled. No, smirked. The sorrow disappeared from his eyes, replaced instead of knowing amusement.

"Really?" he asked. "Now?"

She tugged his hand again and he leaned in. The hand not entwined in hers came up to cup her cheek. He was so close. He smelled like soap and shampoo. Maybe a little bit of *him*.

"Blair," Derek whispered.

"Yes?" she asked. What was going on with her? This was the first time she'd seen him in years! Or, at least it was the first time she'd seen the real him. And in person. He'd frequented his dreams. She'd fantasized about this moment. Him touching her. Holding her.

Kissing her.

Why wouldn't he just kiss her?

He leaned in closer, their noses brushing. Her eyes closed.

"Do you want me to help you feel *alive*?"

She answered him with a kiss.

As they lay together, clothes strewn across the floor, with Derek's fingers running up and down her arms, Blair relaxed. She'd found time to relax before, but this was different. There was something so special about being entangled with the man she'd loved since she was fifteen. He gave her peace. The sex, of course, had helped. Nothing like getting a release after five years of being alone. But it was more than sex. It was about his arms wrapped around her. Her head on his chest. Feeling his heart beat and his chest rise and fall.

She couldn't believe he was here.

"You were stupid to come after me." They were the first coherent words she'd spoken in a while.

Derek snorted. "Was I now?"

"Of course." She snuggled closer to him. "You could have died. Or worse."

"Yeah. Worth it."

"For sex?"

"Of course." His tone was teasing, and she laughed along with him. How much research had he done? How many bridges had he burned? Why, when another man might have given up, had he not?

She pushed herself away, just enough to look at his relaxed face. He smiled at her, and her heart jumped. He was here. And they were going to get out of here together. She just knew it.

Leaning forward, she kissed him gently. "Thank you."

There it was again. His sad eyes. What wasn't he telling her?

"Hey," he said.

Blair tensed. Was he about to reveal something?

"What?"

"When we get out of here, what are you going to do?"

What was with that question? She shrugged. "Probably go back to Sangota. Guess I'm the rightful leader of the clan. Mom can't run it if I'm alive. Necklace already moved on from her."

"Oh." Derek watched her, then reached out and brushed his fingers against her cheek. "Take me with you."

She raised a brow. "To Wyoming?"

"Yeah. Why not?" He pulled her against him again, silencing her million reasons why it was a bad idea. Her clan would disapprove. He wouldn't fit in. They might all hate him for the trouble he'd accidentally caused.

Or, maybe, they'd welcome him a hero. After all, he had found her.

"I don't ever want to be apart from you again," he whispered.

She closed her eyes. She didn't want that either. He was her everything. The main person who had gotten her through five years of hell.

If he wanted to come with her, then she was going to let him. She was going to welcome him with open arms and never let him go again.

Nothing, no one, was going to take her from him, nor him from her.

Chapter Nineteen

She wasn't sure how long she'd slept for, but when she woke, she was alone. Panic settled in and she jerked up. Had it all been a hallucination? Had Death really tricked her?

"You okay?"

At the sound of Derek's voice, she relaxed, pulling the blanket up to cover her bare chest. He stood half-turned to her, holding a notebook she'd written her thoughts in. It wasn't open, and she hoped he hadn't read it. That one in particular—the one with the purple cover—had a lot of her anger. At the world. At Mia. At her grandmother.

At Derek.

He was already dressed, watching her with a tilted head and a frown. Her heart thumped wildly in her chest, still recovering from the shock of waking alone. She could barely breathe, and Derek put the notebook down before he crossed the cave and sat on the bed.

"Blair." He reached out to take her hand.

"I thought I'd imagined it all." She slipped her fingers in his.

He leaned forward and kissed her forehead. "I'm sorry. I

didn't think about that. You were *out*, but I wasn't tired anymore. Thought I'd read when I found your stash of notebooks." Her heart fluttered. Embarrassment. Derek chuckled. "Don't worry, I didn't read anything. Just amazed at how many there are. Didn't realize you were one to journal."

"Had to find something to keep from losing my mind." Blair scooted toward him, pressed her head against his shoulder. His hand traced circles along her bare back. "Turns out the dead get whatever they want here. If I steal something, it shows up again in seconds. They never even notice that it's gone. Made for stealing little things super easy."

Derek hummed a response.

She didn't want this to change. Of course she wanted to escape this place and go home, but being here with Derek made it almost bearable. If they never escaped, it would be okay.

The minute she thought those words, her eyes flew open and she pulled away. That wasn't good. This was a temporary moment. Her happiness would eventually fade, but worse than that, Derek's happiness would fade. He didn't want to be here. *She* didn't want to be here.

They had to leave.

"I'm going to get dressed." She gripped his hand and forced a smile. Not that he would believe it. It was hard to believe fake happiness as an empath.

He didn't comment, though. Instead he stood and turned, giving her privacy despite the fact that they'd *just* had sex. Or maybe he didn't want to get turned on again. Not that she was totally opposed to the idea of that.

He chuckled and Blair shot him a glare. She'd forgotten what it was like to have not only someone there, but someone there who could read her emotions.

As quickly as she could, she got dressed and looked around

the room. Derek's backpack—which she assumed had survival supplies—rested on the floor next to the bed. He'd no doubt take that. It didn't look super full, so maybe she could take something with her.

Then a thought occurred to her: could she take anything with her? Even her clothes, she'd stolen from the city. But they were objects of this realm. Would it be possible for her to use any of these things when she got home?

In the end, she grabbed her old phone—which after five years probably had fifteen upgraded versions—and nothing else. There was no need to take her used notebooks. The books she'd read a million times. The paintings on the walls. They wouldn't do her any good, and it was time to move on.

She was moving on.

"You ready?" Derek asked once she'd slipped her phone in her pocket. She hadn't had it on her in so long that it felt strange against her leg.

Was she ready? Logically, she should have been, but the idea of leaving her Safety behind struck a nerve with her. She glanced around. It was all familiar. It'd been *home*. The only place in the entire realm where she'd felt safe. What if they didn't escape? What if the list Death kept mentioning wasn't complete yet?

With a deep breath, she decided that it didn't matter. They couldn't escape if they didn't try.

She reached out for Derek's hand. He took it without hesitation and she led him out of the cave. Through the woods. She refused to look back, just in case she changed her mind about leaving. It was difficult to explain to herself why regret overtook every other emotion at the thought of never coming back here. This was what she'd wanted. All of her time here had been about surviving just long enough to escape.

Well, she could escape.

So why did it feel so wrong?

They exited the grove and Blair chanced a look over her shoulder. They were only a few feet away when the trees shivered. She halted, eyes widening. Leaves drifted to the ground, falling one at a time, but as though someone had turned up the gravity. They thudded against dirt, and the branches shriveled up. Then, as if disappearing into mist, the grove vanished. A mirage that had lost its grip on reality.

That's when it hit her. Why she didn't want to leave.

She knew how this world worked. It'd taken time, but she'd figured it out. The dead were predictable. The monsters were easy to get rid of once she'd learned their patterns. This place was her hell, but she'd grown used to the sweltering heat. Things here didn't change. Sometimes they were unpredictable, but it was all static.

Home was not static. Everyone had transformed, and she wasn't sure she'd recognize them when she got back. Things were already changing when Death had taken her. She wasn't going back to familiarity, but surprise. Derek had tried to prepare her. He'd told her about his life. About Mia and Cody and Blair's family. But from the sounds of it, he'd become kind of a shut in. What didn't he know?

"Are you okay?" Derek asked.

She looked at him, heart racing. "Yes."

Derek frowned. Sometimes she really hated his innate ability. She wanted to *feel* things without her boyfriend immediately knowing. He didn't press, but she knew he wanted to. He always wanted to know what was going on in her head, but her head was private. At least, from Derek.

Death on the other hand seemed to have unlimited access.

"Well," Derek said, "I guess we should find a tear."

"Right."

Blair knew about the tears, though she hadn't really explored them. The monsters hated when something was *off* about the order of this realm. They tolerated her being here, in what Derek had called her Family Tree, but they did *not* enjoy her traveling to others.

"What's the plan?" Blair asked.

Derek, still holding onto her hand, led her in the direction of the city. She grimaced. It'd been a while since she'd been there. Considering the last time she'd gone, one of her dead relatives had tried to take her life force, she wasn't eager to go back. But if that's where Derek thought they needed to go, she wasn't going to question him. He'd seen more of this place than she had.

"I think we need to get back to my Family Tree," Derek said. "Let's at least head there and see. It's where I came in, so maybe it's where we can get out."

"Okay." She glanced over her shoulder again at the empty space where her Safety had been only seconds before. Her chest tightened, and she gripped Derek's hand tighter. It was okay, she told herself. It was all going to be okay.

As they drew closer to the city, and to the tear, Blair realized that there was something wrong with Derek. It was subtle at first. He'd glance behind him and then focus on finding the tear again. At first, she thought he was just being paranoid that a monster was stalking them, but when he rolled his eyes, she knew something else was going on. Every now and then he'd mutter under his breath, though when she confronted him about it, he'd brush her off.

"Just trying to focus," he'd say with his loving eyes and grin. "I think we're getting closer. Can't you feel it?"

No, she couldn't feel it, and after they'd been walking for a time, she wasn't certain Derek could either. Maybe that's what the muttering was about?

The outskirts of the city rose high above the horizon. Blair eyed it, then glanced at Derek again. He wasn't looking ahead. Still walking, but his head was twisted to the side and his brow was raised like he was listening to someone. Was he hallucinating too? He hadn't mentioned his brain going to war against him, but she also hadn't really told him about *her* hallucinations. He knew about them, but it was a topic he seemed eager to avoid.

"Are we almost there?" Blair asked.

Derek flinched, then smiled at her. "I think so. It's kinda hard to feel. They're usually around the dead though. Are there a lot of dead in the city?"

"Yeah." Blair had experienced her fair share of moments with the dead. Sometimes, when she was stealing something, they would notice her. Usually not the newer ones. Not the older ones either. The middle-aged dead who were starting to lose their natural life force, but hadn't quite lost their way yet. Especially if she used magic, they would take notice of her. Of *her* life force. And they'd try and take it.

Usually she avoided any situation that could lead to a chase. But sometimes, when she'd felt especially dead inside, she'd provoke them. Just to see. Just to run. Just to feel the adrenaline of fear. Of life. She never fought back, even in self-defense. She ran every time, and every time she managed to escape through the winding streets of Sangota. Fighting her ancestors felt wrong. Like a betrayal, and she'd already betrayed them enough.

"Shit." Derek's curse brought her out of her thoughts.

She frowned. "What's wrong?"

"Nothing." Derek let go of her hand to run both of his along his face.

Of course, it wasn't *nothing*. He was hiding something, and she was determined to figure out what it was. But before she could grab at his arm and demand he tell her his secret, a spark jolted her heart. She halted. Warmth bloomed through her body, pulsating with the beat of her heart.

She'd felt these tears before. Every now and then she'd run into one, but none of them had felt like this. Normally they exuded negative energy. They screamed at her to run in the opposite direction, so naturally she had to investigate. This one was almost inviting her in. It wanted her to step through.

Was this Death's doing?

"You okay?" Derek asked when he realized she'd stopped walking. He shoved his hands in his pockets, and for a second he looked like he had back in high school. The backpack, the jeans, the t-shirt, the concerned look of someone who knew all of her emotions. If it weren't for the ponytail and the fact that he was much taller, it would have been the same.

She swallowed. "The tear feels different."

"What do you mean?"

"Just...." She didn't know how to explain it, and she wasn't sure she should try. At least not right now. There was no need to go into everything she'd done to feel alive since coming here. Not until they were safe and she had time to process it all. "I don't know. It feels right to go through it."

Derek frowned, then his eyes flickered to his right. A scowl befell his face, and this was too much for Blair. He was definitely hiding something.

"Derek, what aren't you telling me?" she asked. "Are you hallucinating?" It'd taken her a while to have her first hallucination, but there was no saying how long Derek had been here. Was this place starting to affect him already?

Derek shook his head. "No. Not hallucinating. Look, I'll explain later. Let's get out of here. The longer we stay put, the more danger we're in, right?"

Yes, but she wasn't in the mood to wait. She'd pulled that herself on him many times. Delay the conversation until he forgot about his question.

Crossing her arms, she shook her head. "Tell me now."

"Uh, no." He started walking again, but Blair stormed forward and grabbed his arm to stop him. He groaned. "Blair, it's not important right now. I'm not hallucinating. It's complicated and we don't have time."

"We're not going anywhere until you tell me," she said. "I'm not letting you get out of this conversation. There's no monster. We're not near any dead. Take two minutes to explain."

"You are so freaking stubborn," he snapped.

"I do believe you knew this when you came to find me." She raised her brow and he rolled his eyes. "Besides, you're *just* as stubborn."

"Guess I am. So, are we just going to stand here in silence until something goes wrong?"

"Looks like it." Blair raised her chin. "Or, you could tell me what's going on and we can go on our merry way."

They stood in silence, stuck in a stupid game of chicken. What she didn't get was why he didn't tell her. If it was complicated, that was okay. She could handle complicated. But maybe it wasn't just complicated. Maybe it was difficult for him to talk about. But why? What could be so difficult to reveal? And if it was difficult for him to talk about it, was it because of the topic, or because of her?

Did he not trust her still? Was pushing him the right thing to do?

Blair breathed in deep and then tried with a softer tone. "It's okay to tell me. Whatever it is."

Derek opened his mouth, maybe to tell her the truth, or maybe to tell her to leave it alone, and she tensed for either one. Instead, his eyes widened and he grabbed her arm to yank her away as he shouted, "Watch out!"

A *thump* sounded behind her, accompanied by a frustrated howl. Unnatural wind buffeted her back and she stumbled, completely caught off guard.

The pit of her stomach turned to acid and she caught herself, spinning. The monster—who had *not* been there seconds ago— reared up on its hind legs and leapt.

She pushed Derek out of the way, sending both of them flying in opposite directions. The monster landed where they'd been. Dirt scraped up her bare arms, and she flinched. That was gonna hurt when the adrenaline passed. For now, she ignored it and scrambled to her feet. She didn't have her spear. Why hadn't she grabbed her spear?

The monster faced Derek, crouching to stalk him. Blair's heart nearly stopped. If she used magic, it would draw its attention away from Derek, but it also might call to the dead. They were so close to the city. Would the middle-aged dead notice her if she attacked the monster?

Did she have a choice?

Maybe two seconds passed as those thoughts raced through her mind, and she made a decision. It was either use her magic, or die.

She held out her hand and the warmth flowed through her arm. It tickled her fingertips before elongating into an energy rope. A whip. She had no idea how to use a whip, but it couldn't be hard, could it? All she had to do was get the monster's attention.

Flicking her wrist, she sent the whip flying. It collided with the monster's back. The monster howled again and spun. A top with four legs. Its glowing eyes flickered in and out, still adjusting to her magic, and she released the energy in the monster's direction. Blue light flew toward it, hitting it right in the chest.

Another howl.

It fell back, flickering in and out of existence.

Without much thought, she ran around to the other side of the monster to grab at Derek's hand. He'd managed to get to his feet. He was stunned. That much was clear. Had he hit his head?

"We gotta get out of here!" she shouted.

He shuddered and nodded before she took off, dragging him behind her.

The monster whimpered and whined. It would take a moment for it to gain its bearings again, but not enough of a moment.

She focused. Derek wasn't running at his normal speed, which concerned her, but she tried not to focus on it. Even when the monster's whimpers turned into a roar. Even when its feet pounded against the ground. They were getting closer. So much closer. It would only take a few seconds.

If she'd had her spear, she would have killed it already. But what was done, was done. Maybe she'd make another one so they'd be prepared if this happened again.

Then, without warning, Derek let go of her hand. She skidded to a stop, prepared to grab at him if he'd fallen, but he hadn't. Instead, he was facing the monster.

"What are you doing?" she shouted.

He didn't answer her. The monster grew closer and she made to grab for him but something held her in place. Not a feeling. Not fear or understanding. Not even magic.

A hand grabbed her wrist. But it wasn't Derek's hand.

She gasped and spun around, coming face to face with another Derek.

He smiled, and then flickered into non-existence.

Then the monster howled. A flush of energy washed over her, warming her to the depths of her soul. Gold light caught her attention. She faced Derek, eyes widening. The monster vanished into mist and Derek stood there, panting, holding out his hand.

The monster was gone. The tear was right there. Derek dropped his hand to his side and shook his head. Then he faced her with the same smile as the man who had grabbed her wrist. At least, on the surface it looked the same. On the surface, the two had been identical. But when she recalled the other man, she realized they did look different. Slightly. Like identical twins. Same face, different skin tones, different mannerisms.

"Well, that was exciting," Derek said. "Probably should be more careful in the future. Last thing we need is to use all of her energy fighting those creatures."

But Blair wasn't listening to him. Her mind had transported her back five years to the park in Willow Creek. They'd just gotten back from France. Derek was pissed for no good reason. If he'd bothered to talk to Blair or Cody, he would have known of their plans. But that's not why she remembered it. It wasn't his anger, but his admission.

"Derek," she said.

Concern crossed his face. "Are you okay? Are you hurt?"

No, she wasn't hurt, minus the scrapes on her arm. At least, not physically. But her heart, thumping against her ribcage, screamed in pain.

"Blair." Derek crossed the gap between them and took her hands. "What's wrong?"

His fingers felt different than the man's had. They were softer. The hands of an academic.

Niran's had been rough. The hands of a farmer's child.

"Derek," she tried again. "What aren't you telling me?"

Five years ago, standing in that park, he'd told them that Niran was going to take over his body. He hadn't known when, or how. Blair's stomach had turned then. Now it flipped like an Olympic gymnast. Because it was happening. Wasn't it?

Derek looked over her shoulder. At Niran. He was looking at Niran.

"Let's go through the tear," he said in the softest voice she'd ever heard from him. "I'll explain everything. I promise."

When he leaned down and kissed her, his hands shook. She closed her eyes and kissed him back, but only for a second before he pulled away and led her toward the tear. And as she walked, a shudder ran up her spine. She looked into air.

Niran flickered into existence, nodding at her, before the space became empty once more.

Chapter Twenty

The tear brought them to a mountain. It wasn't the Rockies, or maybe it was from hundreds of years ago. She didn't know, and she didn't care. The minute they were through it, she pulled away from Derek and wrapped her arms around herself.

Niran.

How long had he been seeing Niran?

"Blair," Derek said. He touched her shoulder, but she shrugged it off. He sighed. "You know, don't you?"

Her face burned, not from embarrassment, but from holding back tears. She'd just gotten him back, and now this? Had he known that coming here might mess with his life? He'd said it was worth it, but was it?

"I'm sorry." Derek placed his hands on her hips, resting his forehead against the back of her head. She placed a hand over her mouth as the tears escaped her eyes. "I didn't know how to tell you."

"How long have you been seeing him?" Blair asked through a strained voice.

Derek hesitated. Then sighed. "A few years."

Years!?

Blair squeezed her eyes shut. Maybe to keep the tears in. Maybe to force them out.

"How did you know I was seeing him?" Derek wrapped his arms around her waist. His voice trembled.

"He stopped me."

"What?"

She took a deep breath. "I was going to stop you from using magic. But he grabbed my wrist."

Derek cursed and pressed against her hips. Turning her. She let him, but refused to look him in the eye. "I knew that coming here might make him stronger, but no one's seen him before. I thought it would just be me until...."

He didn't have to say the words. She could remember the fear in his eyes when he'd admitted to them that he would one day become Niran. This terrified him as much as it did her. Probably more. He was the one who was going to disappear.

Her hands curled into fists, and she pounded one against his chest. "You shouldn't have come after me! You're an idiot!"

When his arms wrapped around her shoulders, she fought him. She didn't want a hug. She didn't want to be placated. But he refused to let her push away and crushed her against his body.

"You really think I was about to let you waste away in here?" Derek squeezed her tighter. She could barely breathe. "I told you before and I'll tell you again: this is worth it. Even if I become Niran, I'm still getting you the hell out of here. You deserve to live and be happy."

"So do you," she said, though her voice was muffled against his chest.

Derek didn't respond. At first, she thought he was thinking, but then it occurred to her that he might be listening. To Niran. And when he sighed and let her go, she knew that's what he'd been doing.

"What's he saying?" Blair asked.

Derek shrugged. "He's being a dick. Like he usually is. But he has a point."

"What point?"

There was another pause, then Derek kissed her. Gently. Like his lips weren't there at all. "I deserve to live, but he didn't deserve to die. He's hoping that I can stop being a stupid idiot and find a way to let us both exist."

Her eyes widened. "Is that possible?"

She finally caught his gaze. It was sad. Pained. He kissed her again. "I don't know."

Of course he didn't know. Who would know? Reincarnations weren't well documented in mage history. Derek was the most famous, but that's only because people had known Niran. The asshole had made an impact on the mage world—on the entire world, really. But if it was possible, then he needed to survive long enough to get out of here.

She grabbed his shirt. "I know that we're in a lot of danger, but I need you to promise me you won't use magic again."

"I can't promise that," he said immediately. "It'll be fine."

"It won't be fine!" She needed to get it through his head. "Don't you get it? Every time you use your magic, he gets stronger. He'll keep getting stronger until he sucks the life out of you. You'll stop existing! I can't…."

She couldn't lose him. She'd *just* gotten him back.

There was a look in his eye that she hadn't seen since before Mia had been kidnapped six years ago. It was a look she'd always wondered if she'd ever see again. It'd embarrassed her before. It was hard to understand why Derek had looked at her with such love. Why he'd loved her at all. But now, she never wanted him to lose that look. It was her look. And if he lost himself to Niran, she'd never see it again.

"It's okay," Derek said. "I know what I'm doing. You won't lose me." He pressed his forehead to hers.

She closed her eyes. He didn't know what he was doing. He was a complete idiot. But telling him that wouldn't change his mind. Instead, she whispered, "Please?"

He tensed, then let out a sigh. "Okay. I'll do my best not to use magic. But I won't promise. I'd rather save you, even if it means I cease to exist."

No. That's not what she wanted. But she knew it was the best she was going to get out of him.

Pulling away, she turned. They couldn't stay here much longer. The monsters took time to find her whenever she decided to travel, but they always did in the end.

"Let's find a way out of here," Blair said. "We need to find your Family Tree, right?"

She could feel Derek's eyes on her, and it brought her such pain. Knowing that he was going to disappear soon changed everything. She'd thought that no one could take him from her, but she was wrong. They needed to keep moving because if they didn't, she'd say "screw it" and just hold him. She wanted this time with him. Alone. Once they were back in the living realm, there would be other people. There was a war waiting for them. Blair wouldn't be able to just *be* with Derek.

The only thing she wanted was to be with him.

"Yeah." Derek didn't touch her again, but he stood next to her and stared up at the sky. "I'm hoping I'm right. I don't know where we need to go if I'm wrong."

She hoped, curling her hand into a first, that he wasn't wrong. Finding his Family Tree wouldn't be easy, but it was a goal. They didn't have the time to change the goal. Not when Niran appeared out of the corner of her eye. She didn't look at him. He disappeared, and she stepped forward.

They passed through the next few tears without speaking. Some of them were close together. In some Family Trees, they only spent a few minutes searching. In others, it took an hour or more. At least, that's what it felt like. Derek did all of the looking. He could always feel them before she could, which was annoying because it meant that he was the one who used his magic to lead them through to the next Family Tree.

Blair didn't enjoy the fact that they weren't speaking. There was so much she wanted to know about the world she was about to re-enter. But what could she do? Every conversation she thought of failed to leave her lips. The words caught in her throat, more tears threatening to fall.

Any conversation could be their last. She couldn't tell if Derek felt the same way—it would explain why he was silent too—and she longed to ask him. At the same time, if she asked him, that would acknowledge the not so silent elephant in the room, and that was the last thing she wanted to do.

Still, she hated the silence. She needed to break it. To hear his voice for as long as she could.

"Derek?"

They walked together, hands intertwined, through a field of empty grass. Somehow, they hadn't run into any dead, and she was grateful for that. The last thing they needed was another fight.

He squeezed her hand. "What's up?"

With his words, she realized he was out of breath.

She frowned, but didn't comment. "Tell me more about the living realm. I want to know what I'm coming back to."

"I already told you most of what I know," Derek said.

"You know nothing about the state of the world?" She nudged his arm. "Come on. What shitty politics are going on? Tell me the stupid reality TV drama."

He shrugged. "I don't know. I don't read the news or watch television."

"Not even a little?"

"Don't even own a TV."

That was impressive. Derek had never been one for television shows or movies, but he'd always played video games. They'd had many nights during that summer they were dating and Mia was in Asia when they would hang out in his room while he played video games. She would look up guides and try and convince him to do the wrong thing. Sometimes the right thing, just to keep him on his toes. It'd always made him laugh.

"What do you do for fun, then?" Did he even have fun?

A laugh echoed through the fields. He looked at the sky, shaking his head. "Haven't had time for fun, unless you count learning languages. Already took too long to find you."

"So, all you did was research?"

"I worked out too."

"For fun?"

"To make sure I was strong enough to survive here."

She frowned, not liking the sound of his life. "So, you basically became a shut-in?"

"I suppose."

"That's not healthy."

"Probably not." He shrugged again. "Cody comes to check on me now and then. And my parents. I used to go see Mia, but she usually ushered me away after less than an hour of talking. Besides, I wasn't exactly *alone*."

Right. Blair looked ahead of them where sometimes Niran flickered in and out of existence. He never looked back. Never

214

spoke—at least not that Blair knew. Maybe he was a chatterbox and Derek had gotten good at ignoring him. Either way, he walked ahead of them, hands behind his back. Each time he appeared, he stayed a little longer.

"How often does he talk to you?" Blair asked.

"He only shuts up when I'm asleep."

Blair frowned. And then mortification hit her. "Wait, does that mean he was there when we—"

"No!" Derek stopped, facing her. "Of course not. He disappeared when I got to your Family Tree and didn't show up again until the grove disappeared. No idea where he went, but he wasn't around."

A look crossed his face and he glared ahead of them.

"What?" Blair looked for Niran. He wasn't there. "What's he saying?"

"He's being an *ass*," Derek muttered.

This was not ideal. Derek was losing himself. How could he be so used to Niran's presence? Why wasn't he fighting it more? Entertaining the man who wanted to take over his body?

Blair, needing to change the subject, asked without warning, "How are the Iravata?"

Derek frowned at her, then his expression softened and he continued walking. "No idea. They haven't talked to me at all. Cody's mentioned Shion a few times. I think Lior might watch over Mia, but mostly they've kept their distance. Even Jae and Enya have been quiet. It's like they're waiting for something, but I can't figure out what. I get that they're immortal, but we aren't."

Blair halted.

"You okay?" Derek asked.

No. She wasn't okay. They were waiting for something. They'd been quiet for years. Since her supposed death. There was no way Enya and Jae had just *stopped* their crusade against the Iravata. Not when things were finally moving. And it occurred to Blair, in that moment, that Enya was waiting for something to happen.

For Derek to become Niran.

"Twenty-three," she said.

Derek raised his brow. "Uh, yeah? What about it?"

"What if Enya is waiting for this year?" Her breath caught, heart racing.

It took a moment for Derek to catch up with her thought process, but then his eyes widened. "Oh shit. She's going to try and manipulate Niran again?"

"After everything she's done to you, there's no way she'd trust you to kill Shion."

"And only we can," Derek said. "Me and Niran. We're the wielders of the knife."

"Even though Jae has it?"

"If he could use it, why hasn't he already?"

Well, he'd already killed two people with it. But Derek had a point. And why had Enya come to finish off Blair? There were too many questions and not enough answers. Blair squeezed Derek's hand, and he placed his palm against her cheek, lifting her head.

"It'll be okay," Derek said. "We'll figure this out. But we can't do that here. Let's keep going."

They fell silent again, moving at a slower pace than before. Blair could have gone faster, but Derek seemed to struggle. She didn't comment, though she knew he was getting tired. If she lectured him again about using his magic—and the tears were definitely taking magic from him—she had a feeling it would lead into a fight. He was being stubborn, and at some point, one of them had to concede or they weren't going to get anywhere. She didn't want to fight with him. Especially not if these were their last moments together.

After they'd been walking for some time, and the tear's energy pricked at Blair's heart, Derek spoke again.

"Hey, did you ever wonder why we all met?"

Blair wasn't sure what he meant by that. "What are you talking about?"

Derek shrugged. "Just seems weird. Been thinking about it for a while, but how did we all end up in Willow Creek? You, me, and Cody. We all seem to be part of this huge puzzle, but it can't be a coincidence that we all ended up becoming friends."

"People with magic are drawn toward each other."

"Yeah, but in Willow Creek?"

Blair sighed. "Sometimes shit just happens."

"I don't think it did this time." The tear appeared in the distance. They kept walking, but Derek didn't stop talking. "Look, I get that coincidences are a thing, but what are the chances that your parents moved to the one place where Shubishi's son was living? And then out of all the places in the world, why did *my* parents move us there? They didn't even stay there half the time. Since moving to D.C., their careers have exploded. I get that my mom wanted to move back to America to be near my grandparents and my aunt. But they live in Los Angeles. We could have moved to Denver where their job was, but we *didn't*."

He took a deep breath. "I don't think it was an accident that we all ended up there. Someone planned it. Someone's been manipulating our lives for *years*, and I don't think it's going to stop anytime soon."

"Who do you think is doing it?" Blair asked. It made too much sense to argue against. Willow Creek had been her home, but her dad wasn't from there. Her parents had met at college in Wyoming. The fact that her dad had gotten a job in Willow Creek had never bothered her or Esther before, but maybe it should have.

Derek didn't respond. They reached the tear and he held out a hand to open it. But his hand trembled. It hadn't trembled at the last tear.

Question forgotten, Blair reached out and snatched Derek's

217

hand from mid-air. The tear remained untouched.

"What are you doing?" Derek asked.

She didn't want to fight. She didn't want to fight. She *didn't want to fight.*

"Let me do it," she said.

Derek immediately shook his head. "We're almost there. I can sense my Family Tree. It's calling to me. I think if you start opening the tears, it'll mess with everything."

"Or it won't," she said. "And you won't lose even more of your energy."

He smiled. "It's just a little exhaustion. I've dealt with worse."

But he shouldn't have to. Did he not get it? "Derek, please—"

He kissed her to shut her up. She didn't fight him, but she didn't kiss him back either. He was being stubborn still.

When he pulled away, she glared. "A few more?"

"Just a few more."

"What if when we get to your family tree, it's the wrong place?"

Derek paused, then let out a heavy sigh. "If we need to keep traveling, I'll let you take over. Okay?"

She hoped that they wouldn't have to leave his family tree. It was the only place they could go, right? It's where Derek had entered, and it was where they needed to leave from.

Behind Derek, Niran came into view again. He caught her eye and mouthed something, but she couldn't understand it. She'd never been great at lip reading, and it was possible Niran wasn't speaking English. The dead in Sangota didn't. Why would he? English didn't even exist as a language when Niran was growing up. He never would have learned it when he was alive.

White light encased her vision, blocking her view of Niran, and the tear sucked them through. Derek breathed heavily next to her, not quite panting, but clearly struggling to breathe normally. He kept going the minute the white light vanished and a new landscape of flower fields extended out before them. Pretty, but she didn't care. All she could do was look at Derek, memorizing every contour of his face.

She slipped her arm in his and held it against his body. He paused, but she kept walking, tugging him along so they could find the next tear. He could ask about her emotions later. Maybe when she understood them herself. The anxiety overwhelmed her, and all she knew was that she wanted to hold on as tightly to Derek as she could. Because this might be her last chance to.

Chapter Twenty-One

The river rushed along muddy banks. The water wasn't clear. Blair couldn't imagine jumping in and taking a nice bath, though she felt like she could use one after all the walking. In her Safety, there'd been a stream that was cool when it was hot outside, and steaming when it was cold. She'd loved that stream, and had sometimes soaked in the perfect water for hours when she was bored. Once or twice, she'd fallen asleep.

The Mekong River was nothing like her stream.

And yet, it was magnificent. Trickling along, wider than any river Blair had seen in her life. She could see why Derek loved this place. Why, even though he'd always called Willow Creek "home," his heart had belonged to these banks. It was a part of him, just as much as Sangota was a part of her.

Blair breathed in the smell of fish and muddy water, closing her eyes. Derek stood next to her, refusing to let go of her hand. She wished she could see this place in the living realm.

When all of this was over—when she'd found a way to save Derek from Niran's invasion—she would take a trip with Derek.

They'd visit all the places Derek had told her about when they'd lay together in his empty house in Willow Creek. She'd let him show her around Beijing, and then they'd take a trip to Thailand. He'd show her Bangkok and all of the temples, and they'd travel around the countryside, where she'd try and fail to speak Thai. He'd haggle with artisans, surprising them with his natural fluency despite his clearly non-Thai companion.

It would be an amazing trip. One that neither of them would forget. And maybe then she would understand him better. He'd spent the first ten years of his life growing up outside the United States, and though he'd assimilated well, it had impacted him. No, he hadn't grown up in Thailand, but to see the East, to experience cultures so unlike her own—or maybe similar in ways she couldn't imagine—with him was all she could think about.

"We found it." Derek's words were the first they'd spoken in a while.

Blair glanced up at him. He'd lost some of the color in his cheeks.

"You sure it's yours and not someone else who has family ties to Thailand?" Blair asked.

Derek's smile crinkled the corner of his eyes. "I know it's mine. It feels like home."

Well, she couldn't argue with that. But still, she questioned how he knew. It was no different than when she'd find her Family Tree again after trying to travel. Often, a monster put her back, but sometimes she found her way back and it was obvious when she did. There was something unsettling about the other Family Trees. They didn't want her there. Even this one, as beautiful as it was, clawed at her skin, begging her to leave. It wasn't her home.

Then again, where was home? Enola had always insisted it was Sangota, but Blair hadn't grown up there. Those few weeks in the summer when she went to Sangota to train, to spend time with family, she'd always felt like an outsider. Like a person with a foot in two different worlds. And whenever she returned to Willow Creek, it was *wrong*. Just for a little while before she adjusted again, but still. Wrong. Completely wrong.

Now, there was no Willow Creek. Her family had moved to Sangota. But Sangota wasn't home to her. She'd left her home—her Safety—to escape this place.

But was that even home?

Where did she belong?

Where did Derek belong?

And could they belong there together?

"Did you know I'm related to Niran?" Derek asked.

Blair jerked, startled by both the sound of his voice, and his revelation.

"You're what?" she asked.

"When I first got here, I ran into his sister." He let go of her hand and then looked at his. "We have the same family tree. I think, somehow, I'm related to him through her."

That would make sense. "Might explain why you ended up as his reincarnation."

"That's what I was thinking." He breathed in deep and closed his hands into fists. "She attacked me. At first she thought I was Niran, then she thought I was an imposter, and she went all crazy. Grew wings and fangs. I don't know what I did to her, but she turned into dust and this glowing orb floated toward the sky."

She'd never seen something like that happening before. "It sounds almost like you killed her."

"Is that possible?" Derek asked.

"No idea."

He hummed his response before turning away from the river. Blair joined him, and together the two stared out at the jungle of Derek's Family Tree.

Part of her wanted to go and search through it. He'd seen her Family Tree—though they'd managed to avoid any dead—so why couldn't she see his? But when she reached out to take his hand, to lead him through the jungle, he pulled away.

"Derek?" she asked.

"It should be here," he said. He shoved his hands in his pockets and searched around. "I came in here. I should be able to leave through here. Unless Cody broke his promise and left the apartment like an idiot."

"He wouldn't do that." Right? "He's a mess, and sort of weird, but he wouldn't abandon you when you asked him not to."

Derek hesitated. "Then why can't we find the door?"

Blair crossed her arms, watching Derek's back. His shoulders were hunched over, which was a bad sign. Was he getting weaker? He had to be getting weaker. But she couldn't do anything about it.

"What exactly did you need Cody to stay in your apartment for?" Blair asked.

"He's the anchor," Derek explained. "I used a couple drops of his blood, his magic, to open the portal. He doesn't actually have to stay the whole time, but he needs to be near the ritual for me to get out. I think."

"You think?"

"This hasn't exactly been done before." Derek faced her. "People have gone in, but no one's come out before. I went in blind, so to speak."

"Because you're an idiot."

"We've covered that." Derek rubbed his eyes with the heel of his hand. There were dark circles under them that hadn't been there before. Had she just missed them? Or was this Family Tree in particular draining him faster than the others?

Niran appeared next to Derek. For the first time since Blair had started seeing him, he didn't look at Blair. Instead he examined

Derek. His mouth moved. Speaking. He was saying something to Derek. Derek waved him off and the man vanished again.

"What if we don't need to be here?" Blair asked.

Derek looked at her. His hand shook. She wanted to grab it, but refrained.

"What are you saying?" Derek asked.

She took a deep breath. "Cody is your anchor, right? What if we need to go to *his* Family Tree?"

Her revelation must have hit Derek like a brick, because he smacked himself in the forehead. "Holy crap! You're right! We're in the wrong place." Excitement sprung to his face, then vanished in the same second.

"What's wrong?" Blair asked.

He shook his head. "How are we going to find Cody's family tree?"

"The tears." Obviously.

But Derek kept shaking his head. "Niran and I have a theory that we can only go to the Family Trees of people we know who have died. Or people we know who had relations with one of the dead. Personal relations. If we need to go to Cody's Family Tree, and the Family Trees are matrilineal…."

"Oh." Blair did not like the sound of this. "Cody's mom doesn't know anyone in her family."

"Shit!" Derek kicked the ground.

Blair reached for him, placing a hand on his shoulder. "It's okay. We're going to be okay. Maybe we're wrong."

Derek groaned. "I don't think we are. We're stuck here."

They couldn't be stuck here. Blair refused to accept that. She reached up and grabbed his face. "Derek, listen to me. We can't lose hope. We *will* get out of here. Let's think. There has to be another option."

He reached up and grabbed her hand, never breaking eye contact with her. She could tell his mind was working overtime. Going over his research in his head, no doubt.

Then, without warning, he pulled away from her. Anxiety tinged her stomach.

"What are you doing?" she asked.

He watched her, and a look crossed his face that she didn't like. He was planning something, and he knew she wasn't going to approve of it.

"Don't you dare," she said. "You promised!"

Derek took a few more steps back. "Actually, I didn't."

Then, before she could stop him, he focused his golden magic into his palm. Was he doing what she thought? Was he going to try and open the door himself? From the wrong Family Tree?

"Derek, stop!"

Her scream went unanswered as a burst of golden light overtook her vision. She covered her eyes. The magic shoved her away from Derek, maybe because of his own doing, maybe because it was such an explosion of power. Either way, she couldn't stop him.

Warmth enveloped her, and for a second she thought he might have done it. But when the warmth disappeared and the light faded, she found him gripping his hand and falling to his knees. There was no door. No portal. The magic hadn't done anything.

She didn't know whether she was angry or terrified. Probably a mix of both. Either way, she ran, skidding to a halt in front of him. She crouched, and he fell onto his ass, panting. Full on panting.

"Stupid!" she shrieked.

Derek nodded. "Yeah. Stupid. But I had to try."

"No you didn't!" She could slap him! "You think I haven't tried that? Death won't let us leave until they're satisfied. They aren't satisfied right now because we're in the wrong Family Tree. I don't know how we're going to find Cody's, but we *have* to. You exhausting yourself even more—"

She faltered. Niran stood behind Derek, looking at his hands. They were firm. He didn't flicker. He just stood there, waiting.

No!

She focused on Derek again. "I don't care about your pride or your stubbornness anymore. You are *not to use magic.* I won't let you. You try again, and I will knock you unconscious. Don't think I can't, because I absolutely can."

Derek's chuckle enraged her. But before she could tear him a new one, he reached out and pulled her against him. One hand held her head. The other wrapped around her waist. Her face pressed against his shoulder. Her cheeks burned.

"Don't try and placate me," she said, though she didn't fight him. "I'm mad at you. This isn't the time for this. We need to move."

Derek hugged her tighter. "I'm not sure how much time I have left. I'd like to spend it holding you, if that's okay."

Her heart threatened to stop. Was he giving up? Was this it? They'd *just* gotten back together. After everything they'd been through—after all the pain and the frustration—he needed to stop being an idiot. Could he do that? Could he, for two seconds, not be a complete and total idiot?

How could she help him? If the tears would stop for two seconds, maybe she could focus on a way to make this better. To help him the way he was helping her. He'd given up college, fought with his parents, learned who knows how many languages, and put his life on hold for five years to find her. What could she do to help him?

It occurred to her then what she could do. She pressed her hands against his chest and pushed him away. He fought it, but only for a second before her strength was too much for him.

Looking him directly in the eye, she said, "Let me give you energy."

Derek's jaw dropped, eyes widening. "What?"

It was probably going to go poorly, but she had to try. "I've done it before."

"No." Derek shook his head. He grabbed her hands and held them against his chest. "I won't let you hurt yourself for me."

She wasn't taking no for an answer. "You don't get it, do you? I just got *you* back. I've been alone in this damn place for five years. The rest of the world thinks I'm dead. They've given up on me. You are the only person who didn't. Through all the hallucinations, and the times I thought I was going to die—from the moment I woke up—the only person who helped me hold on was you. The hallucinations of you always hurt the hardest because you were the person I wanted to see most. You. No one else." She placed her hands on his cheeks. "*I can't lose you.*"

Derek closed his eyes. "Blair–"

"You can't be okay with becoming Niran," Blair said. "You can't accept this. You have to fight it. Let me help. I can't give you much energy, and who knows what it'll do to me, but I have to try. I wouldn't be able to go back if I didn't try."

Derek smiled at her, reaching up to brush a lock of loose hair out of her face. His fingers left a trail of electricity along her skin.

"Please." She didn't care that she was begging. If there was any good reason to beg, it was for her love to *live*.

Derek tilted her chin up. In a low whisper, he breathed, "You've changed."

She said nothing.

"I've always liked you. You were my first crush. We must have been eleven when I decided that I wanted you to be my girlfriend. Not that you ever cared about that. You were always hard headed and didn't give a shit what anyone thought of you. It got you in trouble, but it made me feel like it was okay to make mistakes. Before you, I thought I had to be perfect. You saved me from myself. You let me *be*. You even seemed to like me for who I was. Even when I was stupid.

"That part of you is still there." He leaned in and kissed her cheek. "But you never would have said any of that to me when we were teens." He kissed her other cheek. "Honestly? I think I love this you even more, if that's possible."

"Derek…."

He shook his head. Behind him, Niran spoke, but Derek ignored him. "Remember the first time I kissed you?"

It wasn't a memory she'd ever forget.

"Do you know why I did it?" Derek asked.

"Because you were horny?"

Derek snorted, then shook his head. "No. Well, yes, but no." He trailed his fingers along the side of her face. "You were so pretty. Maybe I was fifteen and stupid, and maybe I was just listening to my hormones, but when you looked at me with such intense, furious eyes, I saw passion that I'd never had for anything. You were *so* mad about getting a B on that paper. This was before you knew about my empathy. Before you tried to hide your emotions from me. My skin was on *fire*, and it'd lit a different flame within me."

He laughed. "Probably should have asked first. Might have stopped you from slapping me. I couldn't stop myself."

"I slapped you because I was shocked," Blair admitted. "I wasn't mad about the kiss."

"I know." He shook his head. "Still hurt like a bitch."

She couldn't stop her snort. Tears poured down her face and she didn't even try to stop them. She leaned in and kissed him lightly. Then whispered against his lips, "Don't let this be our last kiss."

"I don't want it to be."

"Let me give you energy."

He closed his eyes. "Okay."

This time, when their lips connected, it wasn't just love she pushed onto him. She pushed her own waning energy into his body.

It fought her. It didn't want to leave her body, especially not when Derek's remaining energy latched on and yanked. She had to be careful or he would accidentally take all of her.

It was okay. She would be careful. She'd been trained to do this.

"This could save your life one day. Or it could save the life of someone you love."

How much had Enola known? Had she *seen* Blair saving Derek? Is that why she'd taught this to Blair at such a young age?

When she pulled away, her limbs turned to lead. They dropped to her sides, and her chest heaved as she tried to catch her breath. She could still stand, she decided. It would take a minute, but she would recover. And when she looked up at Derek, she knew she'd made the right choice. The dark circles had lightened, and color returned to his cheeks. His eyes, now alive with the spark of life, locked onto hers, and he smiled.

Then, without warning, he pushed himself to his feet and pulled her to hers. She couldn't fight him, and even if she could, she wouldn't. It was just so nice to see him energetic again. Especially when he pulled her against him and locked their lips together in a furious kiss. Her eyes closed while he kissed her with a passion he normally only summoned during the throes of intimacy, and she all but melted in his arms.

They were both out of breath when he pulled away.

"I never should have broken up with you." Tears glistened in his eyes. She reached up to wipe them away.

"No, you should have," she said. "I hurt you. I betrayed your trust and I'm not even sure I deserve it again."

"You do." He kissed her. "I forgave you a long time ago. It was a terrible situation and you did the right thing. I would have made the mission fail. I was being petty. I was angry at the world because I was so useless. And because of it, I missed out on a year of being with you."

She kissed him so he'd shut up.

It didn't matter to her. Yes, they'd lost time, but they'd get it back. They were going to get out of this place and Derek was going to fight against Niran. Once they were back home, she would do everything in her power as the rightful leader of the Cokori clan to help him. They would fight her on it. She didn't care. She would do whatever it took to make sure that Derek was safe.

Because she loved him more than she'd ever loved anything in the world. Five years in the Realm of Death hadn't changed that, even if it had changed her.

Chapter Twenty-Two

At first, Derek was back to normal, but Blair's energy didn't give him long. She watched out for the signs. Derek's hands trembling. His breathing growing labored. His slowing pace.

Niran appearing more often.

Blair's energy levels came back, but the stronger she grew, the weaker Derek became, and before long she wrapped his arm around her shoulder and let him lean on her. They'd passed through multiple tears as they searched for Cody's Family Tree, but it seemed like they were going in circles. They didn't speak, as Blair wanted Derek to conserve his energy, but Blair didn't need to confer with him to recognize the landscapes they traversed across.

A scream built in her throat, never releasing. It grew and grew until it was all she could think about.

And when Niran flickered into existence and didn't leave, she almost let it out.

Niran didn't have a look of glee on his face, at least. It was more pity. He didn't speak, and Derek didn't acknowledge him. But now and then, when Derek stumbled, Niran and Blair made eye contact.

They'd stare at each other, Blair silently daring him to do something, until he'd look away and continue on ahead of them.

If Derek was aware of these exchanges, he didn't say anything. Blair preferred to keep it that way.

As they reached the newest tear, Blair hesitated. There were no others around—at least not that she could feel, and Derek wasn't much help—so it was this one or risk running into more dead. The problem was she recognized this one. It tugged at her, welcoming her with warm arms. She knew where it would lead.

They'd gone backwards.

Niran waited next to the tear for her to pass him. To bring the three of them back to *her* Family Tree. He tilted his head as if asking why she wasn't barreling ahead. Not that she *could* barrel ahead with Derek about to collapse. She almost put him down and waited, but when the wind changed, bristling at her skin, she knew they had to move.

Hoisting Derek up again, she trudged forward toward the tear. She refused to look at Niran when she passed him, though out of the corner of her eye she saw him nod.

This was the easiest tear to go through. Usually they pulled at her limbs in an almost agonizing way, but this time it was as simple as walking through a very bright door. It led them to the outskirts of the city, the sky a beautiful purple and green.

They were safe here, at least for a little bit. Derek didn't speak, but he let go of her shoulder and stumbled a few steps before collapsing to his knees. She rushed toward him and helped him onto his back. His eyes were closed, chest heaving. Sleep. He needed to sleep.

She lay next to him, on her side, pulling her knees to her chest. They would rest for a moment. Sleep had always helped her feel better when she'd overdone it with magic. It would be the same for Derek. It *had* to be the same for Derek.

Her eyes slipped closed. Maybe she'd doze off too.

In her dream, someone wrapped their arms around her. She recognized the scent. Jasmine with a hint of vanilla. When she was a kid, she'd loved the smell. Whenever they passed by the perfume section in the Cherry Creek Mall—not that they went that often— she'd seek out jasmine and vanilla because it reminded her of Sangota. It reminded her of sitting in her grandmother's lap as the older woman told her stories in their language while her bumbling grandfather brought her homemade cookies. Even now, she could picture herself there, safe in Enola's arms during those years before her first vision.

She pictured herself there. The unassuming house filled with magic and wonder and happiness. She'd never understood why her mom had left Sangota. How could she leave somewhere so wonderful? How could she fight with people who loved them so much?

"Blair." She could almost hear her grandmother's voice in her ear. "Blair, sweetheart, you have to wake up."

Why? Why wake up? Sleep was so nice. It let her exist in happy memories.

"I need to talk to you and I don't have much time."

The urgency was so real. Maybe it wasn't a dream? Maybe her grandmother was there. But in all of her time in the Realm of Death, she hadn't seen her. And even if she had, would Enola be able to touch her? To speak to her rationally?

Blair forced her eyes open. The lids fought against her. They wanted to stay closed, stay leaded and heavy. She had to do this. She had to see if her grandmother was actually there.

The body holding her wasn't warm. It wasn't cold either. More like it didn't have a temperature at all. It didn't exist in this time or space. Blair pulled away and stared at a woman who looked incredibly like Enola Demini.

"Grandma?"

Enola smiled. "It's been a while. Sorry I haven't come to visit sooner. Turns out the knife is a stronger force than even I could have imagined."

What was she talking about? Blair straightened. "You died."

The words weren't her own. Or maybe they were. She couldn't tell. Her mind was hazy and the world spun.

Enola bowed her head before reaching out to place her hands on Blair's shoulders. "I did. I'm so sorry you had to experience that. I was hoping that my visions were wrong. But if there's one thing seers know for sure, it's how they're going to die."

Blair's heart leapt into her throat. "Grandma, I'm so sorry. I should have listened to you. Rejecting you was the worst thing I could have done. I was just angry and hurt and—"

Enola shushed her. "It's okay, I know. The fault lies with me. I told myself I was trying to protect you, but really I was being selfish. I didn't want the world to find out I was a seer. There was no saying what the other clans would have done if they'd learned that a seer once more ruled the Cokori Clan. There's no saying what they will try to do to *you* when you return. They've already tried to take you once, and if you think for a second that was about Amahle and her artifact, then you are mistaken. They were looking for an excuse to weaken us." She let out a bitter laugh. "The Mauvais Clan especially has always been jealous of our power."

Blair's head spun. "Why would they be jealous of our power?"

"It's a long story, my dear. One that goes back ages and transcends mage politics. But I'm not here to talk of the issues you will face when you claim your place as the next clan leader. I don't have enough time. I'm here to warn you about the Knife of Souls."

Blair longed for more time. But this might have been an exhaustion fueled hallucination. It felt real, but so had some of her others. She desperately wanted this to be real.

"The Knife of Souls is not like the other artifacts," Enola continued. "The others were created to protect the clans from the world. To give insight and enhance our powers. But the Sixiang Clan's powers come from emotion, not from the soul. Their artifact was destroyed a very long time ago and the Knife of Souls was put in its place."

"What?" Blair had never heard any of this before.

Enola held up her hand to keep Blair from speaking more. "It's a long story, one that the immortal Enya has much importance in. She is responsible for the knife's existence. She and Shubishi made a mistake many years ago."

Shubishi? What did that–

"You and your friends need to destroy the knife." Enola grabbed Blair's shoulders, squeezing them tightly. "Once it's destroyed, all those trapped souls will escape and Enya will lose the power to win this war. She cannot win. She cannot trap the souls of the Iravata. If she does, then her plans will come to fruition, and our world will burn."

"What are you talking about?" Blair asked. Her tone rose in pitch, frantic. "How do we destroy it?"

Enola's body shimmered and began to turn translucent. "I don't know, but you will figure it out. There's a reason you four ended up friends. It was no coincidence."

"But–"

"I have to go. Get out of here. Derek was foolish to come in, being what he is."

"Grandma!"

She pressed her forehead to Blair's. "Just remember that I love you. I love your mother. I love your brothers. You are my family, and I'm so sorry I stopped acting like a grandmother. You needed my warmth, and I took that from you. Your mother will do better for you."

"Don't go," Blair pleaded. She grabbed for Enola's arm, but her hand fell through the ghost.

Enola smiled. "Good luck, Blair. Learn from my mistakes. You will be a better seer—a better leader—than I ever was. You will lead our clan into greatness. I love you."

Then, she was gone.

Blair breathed in a shuddering breath. All the things she'd wanted to say to Enola rushed forward, the dam breaking, but it was too late. It was always too late. She didn't have time for anything anymore. Not even to grieve. To process. Because her grandmother had given her a job. Get out of here. Find the knife.

Destroy it.

They needed to get *out* of here.

She pushed herself to her feet, body trembling. Niran stood next to her, arms crossed. She didn't care. He could stare at her all he wanted. She had work to do.

Even though she couldn't make a door out of the Realm of Death, maybe she could open a tear. Magic was dangerous here, and she wasn't exactly flush with it. Still, she was powerful. She was one of the most powerful mages in the world. Her powers to *see* things couldn't exist in someone who wasn't powerful. So what if she was almost tapped out? It was still enough.

A surge of energy rushed through her. Mind over matter, she told herself. She'd survived for five years, alone, in the Realm of Death.

She could get them to where they needed to be.

The fabric of time and space warped. It twisted around her and the still sleeping Derek, fighting against her power. She pushed harder, brow furrowing. Small jolts of lightning crackled around her. The realm groaned. It jerked. It *screamed*.

Then it split open, encasing her, Derek, and the grinning Niran, in all consuming light.

She found herself in a grove of olive trees. The warm air settled on her skin with enough water in it to make her lungs fight her. Growing up in Wyoming and Colorado had made her weak against humidity. Or maybe that was just her body complaining that she'd used too much magic.

Either way, she let herself collapse to her knees, though this time she didn't stay there. She crawled over to Derek and lifted his head into her lap. He was pale again. His chest rose and fell, but in shallow breaths. This wasn't good. He wasn't getting better. He was getting much, much worse.

Niran appeared at Derek's feet. Blair glared up at him, though he looked at her with nothing but pity in his eyes.

"Go away!" she snapped.

This time, when Niran spoke, she heard him. "I can't do that."

Her heart stopped. It was happening. Niran was finally stronger than Derek. Strong enough to talk. To take over Derek's body.

"Trust me, Blair, I don't want to do this. I've been fighting against it as much as he has. But our souls are one. We are forever tied together, stuck in a never ending loop. If I don't become him, he and I will both die and the cycle will restart once more. You don't want that, do you?"

"What I want is for you to fuck off," Blair snarled.

A smile lifted Niran's lips. "I'm glad you love him. He deserved to be loved like this. He was a good guy, even if he made so many mistakes. But I guess mistakes are what make us human."

"Stop talking about him like he's gone!" Blair gripped Derek's shoulders. She had to hold onto him. To remind him to keep fighting, even if he was asleep. Even if this coma wasn't going to end anytime soon. She believed that he would be okay. "Go away. Leave us alone. You had your chance at life and you squandered it. That's not Derek's fault."

Niran shook his head. "That's not how this works. It's time. I tried to think of another way, but there isn't one. That's not Derek's fault, but it's not mine either. He made his bed when he came into the Realm of Death, and now it's time for him to sleep in it."

Blair, filled to the brim with unrelenting hatred and rage, sliced her hand through the air. A blade of pure blue magic flew toward Niran, but he dodged it.

"The only way to stop this is to kill him. Are you willing to do that, Blair? Are you willing to kill the one you love?"

"No," she snapped. "I'm not you."

Niran flinched, frown turning into a glare.

She didn't let him speak. "You don't scare me. You might scare the Iravata, and you might scare Derek, but I'm not afraid of you. You wanna try and take Derek? You're going to have to go through me first."

"Nothing scares you, Blair. It's what makes you foolish. And it's part of why he loves you so much."

But so much scared her. She was terrified of losing the people she loved. Of losing herself to grief and darkness. She was absolutely *terrified* that her powers would take over her life and she'd hurt everyone in the process. That there was no happy ending for her.

She was scared.

But she would keep going, because that's how life worked. If she let the fear take over, then that meant she'd lost.

Blair refused to lose.

"Screw you."

Niran chuckled. "You're so different than Shion. Guess that shows the difference between me and Derek. We both fell for strength, but Shion's is quiet while yours is explosive. I don't understand why, but maybe it's not for me to question it. It was his life."

"It's still his life, and I'm the best thing to ever happen to it." Blair tensed, preparing for a fight. "You're not going to touch him as long as I'm alive."

"That can be arranged."

The world shifted. He held up his hand, clear magic swirling around his body. Blair knew her words were just that. Words. She couldn't fight him. Still, she would die to protect Derek.

Niran opened his mouth, maybe to say something, when his eyes widened, and he vanished.

Blair gasped. Standing in his place, at Derek's feet, staring down at the two teens, was a woman Blair didn't recognize. She was dead, that was for sure, but she didn't look like the other dead Blair had run into. She wasn't aimless. She wasn't crazed in the eyes. She just stood there.

Blair clung to Derek tighter. "Who are you?"

The woman glanced around. She looked almost familiar. Like Blair had seen someone who looked like her before. The blond hair. Eyes brown like freshly turned soil on a fertile farm.

"The boy knew my name," she said softly. "He's the first human I've run into. I found him fascinating, so I followed. He was like me. Searching for the one he loves."

Blair narrowed her eyes. "Answer my question!"

The woman nodded. "Of course. My apologies." She bowed at the waist. "My name is Halise."

Halise? "Wait, *that* Halise?"

Halise frowned. "I'm not sure what you mean by *that* Halise, but the boy–"

"Derek."

"Derek, said something similar. It would seem I've made my impact upon history."

She certainly had. Blair weighed the situation. This could be some kind of trap. Halise didn't appear to have lost her mind, and she wasn't attacking. But that could change in an instant.

"What do you want from us?" Blair asked. "What are you doing here? You're super old. Why haven't you lost your mind yet?"

Halise's smile was sad. "I told you. I was searching for my love."

"Amir?"

She laughed. "So, you know his name too." She wrapped herself in her arms, eyes closing. "Oh, Amir. My love. I miss him so much. He understood me in a way that no one else could. He forgave me for my faults, even when I didn't think it was possible. It feels as though no time has passed since he left me for this realm. Even less time since I'd followed. But it has been a very long time. I can't imagine what our world looks like now."

Blair didn't have an answer for her. Instead, she asked more questions. "Okay, so now what do you want? Why did you...do whatever it is you did to Niran."

Halise sighed. "I sent the man who looks like Derek away. I've watched Derek fight for you, and you fight for him. You two love each other. Maybe I'm no one important to the world now, but the importance of a person depends on each situation. In this situation, I am important because I can help."

"Help?" Blair tensed. "Why would you help? What do you want in return? I'll...." She glanced down at Derek's peaceful face. "I'll do whatever you want if you help us get out of here alive."

"You really love him."

"Yes."

Halise looked toward the sky. "I knew what love was once. I'd grown up in misery and someone gave me salvation. I'd had everything I'd ever wanted only to lose it without warning. I still don't know how or why Amir died. But what I do know is that even if his family hadn't blamed me for it, I would have forever blamed myself. The day they told me he was dead, I lost a part of myself that I knew I couldn't get back. I was devastated. In shock. Terrified that I'd brought this upon him and his family.

"I'd gone from almost becoming his, to losing him. After I took my life, I searched. And searched. But I cannot find him. We didn't have enough time together. Maybe it's selfish of me to defy fate, but I feel it is my right to do so. I don't want you to fall to my fate."

Blair didn't understand. "What are you talking about?"

"The love you have for each other is magical," she said. "All I want, in return for my help, is for you two to *live*. Love each other for as long as you are able, and when you come back here, when it's your time to join the rest of the dead, I want you to be able to do so with no regrets."

Halise crouched and reached forward to brush her fingers against Derek's cheek.

He shuddered, but didn't wake.

"You know," Halise said, "I always wondered what came after this. Sometimes, when I'm least expecting it, familiar faces disappear. Maybe that's what happened to Amir too. Maybe he moved on. Maybe he finally was able to let go."

Halise pressed her palm flat against Derek's cheek. "Maybe it's time for me to let go too."

"What are you doing?"

"Giving Derek the rest of my life," Halise said. "We all have it. The dead. Our life force doesn't disappear when we die. It lies dormant, sustaining us until we either move on, or fade away. If I give mine to him, it should keep him alive until you can escape."

Blair struggled to comprehend. Halise was giving up her chance to find Amir. She was going to kill herself again. Move on to whatever the next part of the cycle was.

The selfish part of Blair wanted to scream at her to do it already, but Blair couldn't do that. It wasn't fair. Halise didn't deserve any of what had happened to her.

But, then again, this was her choice. She knew the consequences. Who was Blair to tell her not to?

"Are you sure?" Blair asked.

Halise smiled. "Yes, I'm sure."

A brilliant pink light lit up the world around them. It focused on Halise's hand, swirling until it was a ball that transferred from Halise's skin to Derek's. The light flew along his body, jerking his limbs. He gasped, eyes flying open and he jolted up from Blair's lap. She barely moved in time for him to miss her chin.

His head spun. Searching. Looking.

But Halise was gone. She'd vanished, just like she'd said she would.

Derek twisted to face Blair. The dark circles under his eyes were gone, and his skin almost seemed to glow. He was flush with energy, and Niran was nowhere to be seen.

"What happened?" Derek asked. "Where are we? Where's Niran? What's going on?"

Words failed her. It'd all happened so suddenly. From her grandmother to Halise. She'd almost lost Derek. Only luck had saved them both.

A sob bubbled out from her lips. She bent over, arms wrapped around her stomach. She was exhausted. Her mind was filled with so much emotion that she couldn't hold it back. Even though she hated crying, and even though that's all she'd been doing for what felt like hours, she let it all out.

Derek didn't say another word. He scooted next to her, and pulled her against him, brushing a hand against her hair. He whispered something to her, but she couldn't make it out. Her sobs were too loud.

It was too much.

All of this had been too much.

It took time for her to stop sobbing. Derek held her the entire time, never speaking, never shushing her. He petted her hair, rocking just slightly in a motion that reminded her of her mom. Of her grandmother. Comforting. Gentle. Patient.

Eventually, the sobs turned into hiccups. Then into deep breaths. Then into silence. No more tears fell, though she wasn't certain they wouldn't start up again. Her eyes burned. She didn't want to leave the nest Derek had created with his arms. It was warm. It was safe.

They had to keep going.

She pulled away, refusing to look him in the eye. Her body was empty. Everything felt numb.

"Blair," Derek whispered. When she didn't look up at him, he pressed a finger under her chin and lifted it so she was looking in his eyes. "Are you okay?"

No, but she would be. "A lot happened."

"How long was I asleep?"

She breathed in a shuddering breath. "I don't know. Time here—"

"—Passes weird." Derek smiled. "Right."

God, she loved that smile. She told him everything. How her grandmother had visited her, Enola's warning, Niran almost winning, and Halise. Derek listened to her the entire time without a word. And when she finished, he slipped off his backpack and opened it, pulling out a bottle of water.

Blair stared at it, shocked. She hadn't thought to ask what was in the backpack. They didn't get hungry or thirsty here. In fact, she hadn't had anything to eat or drink in five years. Still, she took the half empty bottle and took a sip.

She'd forgotten what water tasted like.

She'd forgotten how refreshing it was. How it could replenish more than just the water in one's body, but also the life into a person's soul. She closed her eyes, letting the water rush down her throat. It filled her with energy. It took away the numbness and brought tingles back to her fingers.

When she finished, Derek stood and held out a hand for her. She took it, letting him haul her to her feet. Once the bottle was back in the backpack, Derek faced her with his smile.

"We're okay," he said. He brushed a lock of hair behind her ear. "We're going to find our way out of here, and everything will be good."

Blair didn't know what the side effects of Halise's gift would be, but she was glad that he was smiling. So glad, in fact, that she pulled his face down and kissed him like there was no tomorrow.

Because for him, there might not be.

He broke the kiss after a few seconds. "You all right?"

"Just happy," she said. "Just so happy."

And so sad.

"Hm…." Derek kissed her forehead. "Come on. Let's go find that door."

They were in the right Family Tree. She didn't know how she knew, and it made no sense, but something about it screamed "Cody". It had his energy. But more than that, it had his mother's energy. This was it. They were going to find the door, and then Blair would pour her heart and soul into figuring out how to save Derek, just like he had for her. Because she refused to lose him. Absolutely refused to.

Blair knew the minute they came across her. It didn't take long.

They'd been walking—searching—for maybe a few minutes when she appeared in the distance. Her energy, a deep maroon, trickled down from the sky and she stared up at the floating clouds.

Her hair, a deep shade of auburn just like Cody's, hung to her waist. Blair had only ever seen her with short hair. Granted, it'd been *years* since she'd seen the woman standing in front of her. Cody's mom, Ava Velt, didn't show her face very often. She was a mystery to the people of Willow Creek, which hadn't helped Cody's reputation. She'd arrived in Willow Creek one day, married the first man she'd met, and birthed his child months later. Or, so the town thought.

Some of Blair's earliest memories were playing with Cody at the park with Mrs. Velt watching them. Her own mom had always tried to make a connection with Mrs. Velt, but the woman had politely declined any sort of friendship. Then, after the accident with Leo, she'd just vanished from public view. If Blair could go back, if she could see the situation with Cody and Leo from the view of an adult, she would have done it all so differently. She would have been there for Cody. Gotten to know his family. Understood what he was going through at home.

Maybe she could have seen this coming.

"Oh," she whispered.

Derek looked at her. "What? Who is that?"

She was new. So new. Her soul wasn't even entirely in the Realm of Death yet. What in the world was going on outside?

"That's Cody's mom."

The woman's head dipped down and she turned to face Blair and Derek. In all of Blair's memories, she'd had a pinched face. A woman with many secrets she didn't know herself. But this Ava looked different. She had a smile on her face, and her eyes were warm.

She was free.

"You two are friends with my son," Mrs. Velt said. She stepped toward them, almost gliding. Blair should have feared her, but she didn't.

"Mrs. Velt, what's going on?" Blair asked.

She shook her head. "I know that's how you knew me, Blair, but that isn't my name. It became my name. It's how my son and my husband will remember me, but please, call me Calliope."

Calliope? Like the Greek muse?

"I remember who I am," she said, staring at her hands. "They tried to take it from me. Cody's father tried to take it all from me. But I remembered. I took it back. Death whispered in my ear. She came to me and told me it was time for all of us to move on. I was living on borrowed time. A borrowed life."

Blair looked at Derek, who shrugged. She swallowed. "Um…do you know where you are?"

Calliope nodded. "Of course, dear. I'm dead."

She said it with such acceptance that Blair's heart tore in two. Did Cody know?

"I didn't want to leave Cody or Dylan," she said. "I love them with all my heart. But it was time. I never should have lived to see the things I've seen. I don't regret my beautiful boy. He is the reason I needed to keep going. And now he's grown. He still has a lot to learn, and he will stumble many times. But he'll continue to rise to his feet and move on. He won't understand. Not now. Maybe not ever. This needed to happen, even if it will cause him pain."

She bowed her head, smile sad, but still present, on her face. "When you see Cody, please tell him I'm okay. He doesn't need to worry about me. I'm happy now." She sucked in a breath. Maybe a habit from life? "Please, Blair, tell him that I'm sorry. And that I love him."

"What—"

"It's time for you to go," Calliope interrupted. "You've survived here, but the living realm is far more dangerous. It'll be okay, though.

As long as the four of you have each other, it'll all be okay."

Blair opened her mouth to ask questions. A lot of questions. Maybe to yell at the woman a little bit for her appearance. She said she'd taken herself back, but did that mean she'd done this to herself? Why did she have to apologize to Cody? What was going on?

But before she could get the words out, a pressure sucked at her back. Energy burst from nowhere, nearly knocking her off her feet. She and Derek spun around and found themselves face to face with a wooden door. Intricate carvings adorned the sides, and a golden doorknob waited for them to take hold and yank it open.

On the other side, she felt life.

"Holy shit," Derek said. "We found it."

No, they hadn't found it. Calliope—Ava Velt—had given it to them.

Blair turned to thank her, to tell her she'd pass on the message, but the woman was gone. Had she let go too? Had she moved on?

Whatever had happened to Calliope, it was out of Blair's hands. She couldn't control this. There were so many things she couldn't control. But she could get out of here.

She faced the door again. She'd been waiting for this moment for so long it was hard to believe it was happening. But there it was. The door to home. Away from this hellhole. So what if it was more dangerous? It was her dangerous.

"You ready?" Derek asked.

Blair took a moment to breathe. It was over. Her prison sentence was done. A smile spread across her lips. So much had happened. So much was yet to happen. But it was okay. It was all going to be okay.

"Like you wouldn't believe." And then she reached forward, grabbed the doorknob, and opened the door.

One day, when he traversed his domains, he realized that he was the cause of all the issues. He did not know what made him understand. Was it because everyone always left him? Because he was always so alone? And was it that loneliness that had caused him to create so many problems for the universe?

He was not sure. Maybe one day it had just popped into his head. A new, important piece of information he had been craving for so many millennia.

However, he was sure of one thing. He was sure that no matter what he did for the rest of his existence, he needed to fix everything he had broken. He had created the Vilaim. He had set their positions in life. He had caused so many years of pain and suffering. Over all the years of his existence, he had done nothing but make mistakes.

It was time to fix them.

It was time to make sure that everyone he had hurt ended up happy.

Mia

Chapter Twenty-Three

Really, Mia did understand why her grandparents paced outside her door. They didn't need to explain their concerns. The last thing she needed was for them to come into her room and coax her out from under her blankets to talk to her *again* about getting help. Her grandparents. The people who didn't believe in therapy. They thought she needed someone to talk to. Herbal medicines to help with sadness. They thought what she was doing was unhealthy. Everyone thought what she was doing was unhealthy.

Maybe they were right. No, she was certain they were right. She curled into a tighter ball, squeezing her burning eyes shut. No more tears fell. How could they? She'd cried them all.

Not for the first time, she pictured herself back at prom. She was still with Chad in the dance and had decided against getting air. There was no need to go into the woods. No meeting with Blair. No explosive screaming match between two best friends trying to figure out if they could continue to *be* friends. Enya hadn't appeared. There was no fire. Mia's arms hadn't been burned so badly that it'd taken Flora an hour to heal them.

She could still feel her nerves crying out in agony.

It was all a nightmare, she told herself. Ignore the pain. Her brain was mad at her. She wasn't in her grandparents' house, curled under blankets on the bed she used to share with Derek when they were so small they *could* share a twin bed. Blair was alive and well, living in Sangota. Mia hadn't cut contact with Derek. With Cody.

She hiccupped. What she'd done to Cody was unforgivable. Because it wasn't a nightmare. No matter how much she wished for it to be one, she *was* in her grandparents' house. Blair *wasn't* alive and well. She *hadn't* spoken to Derek since she'd left him standing alone in the airport. She *had* slept with Cody and then left when he was asleep.

What a horrible person she was. A disastrous, miserable, pathetic excuse for a person.

Running away to China.

Hiding out in her room.

She hadn't been out of bed in a week. She couldn't remember the last thing she'd eaten. Every meal, her grandmother or her aunt would come in and bring her soothing food. Congee. Soup. Hard boiled eggs and mantou.

She'd tried to eat. She really did. But every time she went to take a bite, her throat closed up and she could barely breathe.

After two days, she'd given up and only drank the jasmine tea that came with each meal. Her grandmother had insisted it would make her feel better, but so far, it hadn't worked. How could it? It was *tea*. Derek might have sung its praises their entire life, but it couldn't bring back Blair. It couldn't fix the mistakes Mia had made. Maybe what she needed was someone to talk to, but who?

Derek was in denial about Blair.

Cody was not an option.

Her parents still didn't understand the magical world, though they did try.

And the rest of her family didn't know anything about it.

She was alone, and it was her fault.

More tears spilled from her eyes. So much for the theory that she'd run out. They dripped down her chin like raindrops on a cloudy day. Was she ever going to stop crying? Would those clouds ever part?

Did she care?

She felt nothing inside. Even the grief was muted in shades of gray. But it wasn't the same as what Steven and Kathleen had done to her. No one was manipulating her. The minute Blair had died, something in her soul had snapped, and she wasn't sure how to knit it back up.

Placing a clammy hand over her mouth, she tried to stifle the sobs. The last thing she wanted was for her grandmother to hear, come in, and try to comfort her. As much as she loved her grandmother, the woman didn't know *anything*. It wasn't her fault. And it was better that way. Safer.

She debated contacting Cody. He'd texted and called. Sent her message after message asking what he'd done wrong. What could she tell him? He'd told her he loved her and then kissed her. It was supposed to be *that* moment for him. But it wasn't for her. She'd felt nothing for him, and she didn't know if it was because she didn't love him, or if she was too dead inside *to* love him.

The door to her room opened. She swallowed down more tears but didn't sit up.

"Meilian?" Her grandmother's voice was soft. "Can we talk?"

Mia shifted to look at the old woman. She was getting shorter. Age did that to a person. But she was still the kind, warm, gentle grandmother that Mia had always loved to come see. Her white hair was pulled into a bun at the base of her neck, and she had a pair of thick, square glasses.

"Yeye and I are worried about you," she said. She settled on the floor next to Mia's bed. "You aren't eating. I know that grief can be consuming. I've felt my share of it. But you need to eat."

"I'm trying," Mia said, voice hoarse.

"I know." Her grandmother reached out and brushed Mia's hair out of her face. "Your gugu and I have been talking, and we think that maybe Beijing isn't the right place for you. I know you don't want to go back to America, and who can blame you, but maybe somewhere new will be a good change of pace for you."

Mia curled her knees up to her chest. "Where?"

"Lilan has a nice, two bedroom apartment in Chengdu. It's near the city center in a kind neighborhood. There are many young people there, and you can finish high school. I've also heard good things about the universities. It might give you purpose. Purpose helped me move on."

Mia didn't want to move on. Not yet. Not when it was still so fresh. But what else could she do? Blair wasn't coming back. Eventually, no matter what happened, she would have to let go of this pain and continue on.

The only question was, when and how?

"Maybe moving will be good," Mia said. She had no idea if they were right, but it was worth a shot. Beijing—while it was the place she'd grown up—held too many strange memories. Fights, complications, late night texting sessions with Blair.

Chengdu held none of those things.

Her grandmother smiled. "We'll prepare the paperwork. Yeye is going to come in with tea and soup in a minute. Try to drink both. It'll be good for you."

The old woman pushed herself to her feet, muttering about old bones, and then shouted through the door that they had work to do.

Mia watched her grandmother go.

She'd never imagined herself living anywhere in China besides Beijing, but maybe it would help. Maybe it would force her to move on. To meet new people and live a new life. She'd heard a lot about Chengdu. A vibrant city with many old temples and a thick dialect.

It would be good for her. She told herself it would be good for her. Because any other outcome wasn't an option.

Five Years Later

Chapter Twenty-Four

Mia sat at the cash register, legs crossed, with her chin in her hand. She glared out at her enemy, and the enemy mocked her in return. She considered flipping it off, just because it would make her feel better, but the last thing she needed was her manager catching her being a bitch. It wasn't that her manager really understood the significance behind a good middle finger, but he knew enough to know that it was inappropriate to flip off a convenience store.

She hated her job. Really, she did. The customers were rude. Her co-workers didn't get her and mostly stayed out of her way. The place was always a mess, no matter how many times she straightened up, and every shift she worked ripped out a little more of her soul. She didn't belong here. She was twenty-three, spoke two and a half languages, and had grown up with high-achieving parents who had met each other doing their PhD work. They'd raised her for the academic world. She was supposed to be in grad school about now. Instead, she was letting bitterness destroy her, one shift at a time.

Today was a particularly bad day at the store. It always was during the slow hours. Some days, she never stopped ringing people up, and then others she saw maybe two customers in five hours. There was no real pattern, so it wasn't like Mia could request the busy hours. Not that she wanted it to be busy either. In fact, she didn't want to be here at all. But it was a job, and the deal with Aunt Lilan was that she have a job or go to school.

She was *not* going back to school. The only reason she'd agreed to finish high school was because Derek had shown up one day and threatened to drag her back to America if she didn't. Even more than school, she refused to go back to that hellhole.

"Meilian?"

Mia sighed and then glanced at her coworker, trying to imagine that the poor girl hadn't called out Mia's name with a shaky voice. There was no reason to be afraid of Mia. She hadn't done anything worth being scared of. Still, the woman—whose name Mia couldn't recall—stood at the counter with a pricing gun in her hands, too-big uniform hanging off her.

"What?" Mia asked.

"Could you help me with pricing?"

Mia raised her brow. " Seriously? You know that last time I helped you, I got in trouble. Not going to do that again."

"Oh." The woman shifted. She was probably in her late teens. Not much younger than Mia, but they felt like worlds apart. The woman spoke in the Beijing dialect, probably because Mia did, but it was clear that she wasn't the most comfortable in it.

Mia refused to learn the Sichuan dialect. Probably wasn't the smartest decision, but what did she care? She could get around just fine, and it wasn't like she planned to live here forever. The minute she saved up enough money, she was moving back to Beijing. Her grandparents insisted they wanted her back, but they wouldn't help her move until she'd moved on from Blair's death.

Mia wasn't sure she'd ever move on from Blair's death, if she was being honest. It was too painful to think about. To talk about.

To let go of the fact that Mia had caused it. So, she was on her own. Moving in China was no small business. She had to get the right paperwork. Find another job. Get an apartment. But all of those things required money, and she wasn't exactly flush with cash.

"Well," the girl said, "I guess I'll get back to it. Let me know if you need help." She glanced around the empty store.

"Okay," Mia muttered and faced the front door. It mocked her, letting in the humid heat that wouldn't have existed in Colorado. She wanted to close it, but her manager insisted they keep it open so customers felt like they could come and go as they pleased.

It was stupid.

All of this was so stupid.

Still, she focused on the front door, ignoring the girl who moped around the store. Every now and then, Mia heard the *click* of the pricing gun, but she never took her eyes off the front door. It wouldn't have been difficult to talk to the girl, but Mia wasn't in the mood to chat. In fact, she was never in the mood to chat. All she wanted was to get through the day. Then the next. Then the next. Build up enough money to get the hell out of here and never look back. Because that was all she could do to keep going.

Mia hated the way she felt after getting off work. It didn't matter how much deodorant she put on, the humidity made her sweat, the air was sticky, and she couldn't stand it anymore. When she got home, she kicked off her shoes and turned on the heater. Why Aunt Lilan insisted on keeping it off when they weren't home, Mia would never understand. It made the apartment freezing, even though it was already March.

Aunt Lilan wouldn't be home for a while, so Mia went to her

room, stripped herself of her disgusting work uniform, grabbed a towel and scurried to the bathroom. A shower. A nice, hot shower to wash off the day was what she needed. Her feet hurt. Her head ached, and she pulled her hair out of the ponytail she'd shoved it into this morning.

As the water heated up, she ran her hands through her hair, letting it fall around her face. It was getting to be about time for a trim and style. Maybe she could ask Aunt Lilan for some money to go to a nice place. Maybe she'd play with hair dye. Some of the girls in Chengdu lightened their hair from black to almost brown. Mia had always been curious, though she had a feeling her grandparents would throw a fit.

Still, it was an idea. A change.

Once the water was warm enough, she stepped into the shower and slid to the ground, back against the tile. Water sprayed on her face and she closed her eyes. There was no doubt that Aunt Lilan would yell at her for running up the water bill again. Sometimes, Mia wondered if Aunt Lilan picked fights to see Mia react and make sure she wasn't dead inside.

Joke was on her. Mia was dead inside.

The water cleansed her of her day, and she did what she always did when she had a moment to sit and think: she pictured herself back in Willow Creek.

It was impossible, and she knew that. The town had burned and no one had rebuilt. According to Derek, people thought it was haunted. A rumor spread by the Iravata, no doubt. Still, she imagined herself in her parents' house, hanging out with her two best friends and her twin. Blair was making stupid jokes about a movie that Cody had picked, and Cody was doing his best not to snap at her, while Mia told both of them to behave and Derek laughed his ass off.

Was it wrong of her to long for that? For the days before she knew about magic? She'd harbored a grudge against the three of them for years because of their secret keeping—especially Derek—but they were right in the end. It was a dangerous world, and she had no business being part of it. If Steven had never come into her life, if he hadn't shown her the magical fireflies, would she even be in China right now?

Of course she would be. She opened her eyes and stared up at the shower head. She'd never really belonged in America. This was her home.

Even if it didn't really feel like it anymore.

Besides, it wasn't because of Steven that she was here. It was because of Steven's boss. The man who had taken everything from her in his attempt to protect her.

She hadn't heard from Jae in a long time. About two weeks after moving to Chengdu, he'd tried to talk to her. Aunt Lilan had sent her on a walk to get some sunshine—not that the sun shone very often in Chengdu—and there he was. Waiting for her with an apology. She'd turned and walked the other way with a desperate call out to the Iravata to save her.

"I'm so sorry," he'd said. *"I didn't know she would do that. I didn't want to hurt Blair."*

Mia hadn't said a word, and he'd vanished. The Iravata had never appeared.

The apartment door opened and Mia sighed. So much for getting a good shower in. She stood and washed everything. Her hair took the longest, as it always did, but once that was done, she soaped up and rinsed as quickly as she could. Then, she turned off the water, dried enough to slip on her pajamas, and then did her best to slip out of the bathroom without her aunt noticing her.

Her aunt noticed her.

"Meilian," her aunt said the moment Mia stepped out of the steaming bathroom.

Mia flinched, putting her best smile. "Hi. Sorry. I'm really tired.

Don't think I'll want dinner tonight. Just going to bed."

She couldn't move until Aunt Lilan dismissed her. Well, she could, but not if she wanted to avoid a fight.

Aunt Lilan eyed Mia for a moment. She looked much the same, as if the years hadn't affected her at all. Maybe they'd hardened her expression, but that was it. Her hair was still lush and black, her skin smooth and painted with light makeup, and she still wore the same business skirt and jacket that she'd bought five years ago.

"Are you sure you don't want dinner?" Aunt Lilan asked. "I bought enough for a feast tonight. I was just about to start on the jiaozi if you want to help."

Mia really didn't want to sit and make jiaozi. Jiaozi was code for, "let's talk about life" in her family. It was a social thing. Even if the result was delicious, she absolutely couldn't do it. Not tonight. Maybe not ever.

"I'm really tired. Work was exhausting."

It wasn't, but her aunt didn't know that.

Aunt Lilan nodded. "Right. Well, actually, I wanted to talk to you about that."

Oh crap.

"Talk about what?"

"I know you're saving up money to move back to Beijing, which I think is a fantastic idea. You never really adjusted to life here. But if you had a better job, you would be able to do that faster, and it would help you get a well-paying job near Yeye and Nainai. Plus, it might help you make some friends."

Mia didn't want friends. "I'm fine where I am."

"Okay. Well, I scheduled an interview for you tomorrow at my hotel."

Mia blinked. "What?"

"I know it's more engaging than your current job, but I think you'll like it. It's better pay and better hours. And the people will be better educated. You might find someone you get along with."

Mia couldn't stop staring at her aunt. It wasn't like Aunt Lilan to get involved in her life. Her grandparents, sure. They fussed over the state of Mia's everything. They'd even tried to set her up with a couple of guys, though that'd never gone well. The men had been nice enough, but she didn't want to date. She didn't want to get married. And she *really* didn't want a job at her aunt's hotel.

"You didn't have to do that," Mia stuttered out. "I'm fine where I am."

"You're not, and the fact that you can't see that worries me."

Was she serious? "There's nothing to be worried about. I'm okay."

"You've been saying that for five years, and for five years, I haven't believed you." Aunt Lilan sighed. "Come on. Just go to the interview. If you don't like the culture, you don't need to take the job. But give yourself a little credit. I think you'll be happier if you're in a better place socially and financially."

Mia wanted nothing more than to say "hell no," but she couldn't. Aunt Lilan had housed and fed her for five years. She'd dealt with Mia's depression, her anger, and her disinterest in the world. The fact that Aunt Lilan had stuck her neck out to get Mia an interview showed just how serious she was about this. If Mia didn't do well, it could make Aunt Lilan's working relationships very difficult.

Groaning, Mia said, "Fine, I'll go to the interview."

Aunt Lilan's face brightened. "Great! And how about making jiaozi tonight?"

"I'm tired," Mia repeated.

"All right, all right." Aunt Lilan grabbed her purse and headed over to her room, slippers slapping against the hardwood floor. "But make sure to be up bright and early tomorrow. You don't want to miss your interview. It's at nine, so you'll have to leave here around eight."

"Okay."

Mia retreated to her room. She closed her door and leaned against it with a heavy sigh. This was the last thing she wanted. Her aunt was trying to push her toward a normal life. But normal was long gone for her. She couldn't go back to the way things were before she found out about magic. She couldn't look Cody in the eye. She could barely speak to Derek. Whenever he showed up, she pushed him out the door as fast as possible so she wouldn't have to look at him.

Because looking at him reminded her of Blair.

With a sigh, she walked over to her bed and collapsed on it. Her phone buzzed on the mattress next to her. A call from her mom. She reached over, silenced it, and then curled into a ball.

This wasn't how life was supposed to go. She wasn't supposed to be twenty-three, without a college degree, living in her aunt's apartment in Chengdu. She'd had plans for life. To go out and explore. To get a PhD like her parents. She was supposed to make a name for herself, find a good husband, have children, and be happy.

Maybe this was a good thing. It was the fresh start that Chengdu was supposed to be. Sure, it'd taken five years for it to start, but better late than never, right? Maybe she could take a job that didn't make her feel like crap about herself, and maybe she could meet people who had nothing to do with the magical world. Maybe, just maybe, her life could turn around.

It was possible that she could become close to someone again. She knew she had it in her, even if she couldn't quite find that part of her. Maybe this time, it wouldn't end with heartbreak. No breakups, no mistakes, and no death. This wouldn't end like high school had: her with no one to talk to.

As she drifted off to sleep, forgetting all about her blankets, her mind reminded her that it was never going to happen. No matter what she did, she was cursed. People came into her life and they left broken or dead. People were better off avoiding her. She was better off alone. She was going to live the rest of her life never getting close to another person ever again.

Chapter Twenty-Five

Mia had planned out her entire morning. Aunt Lilan had woken her at six to say goodbye and remind her about the interview. At seven, she'd pulled herself out of bed to fix her messy hair and find nice enough clothes for an interview. She didn't have many business clothes, but she had one set. A black pencil skirt, a white button up shirt, and a black jacket with no buttons. She'd gotten it with her mom in the Before Times. Even though she'd lost some weight, the outfit still mostly fit, though she'd had to pin the skirt.

With that done, and a little makeup to hide the dark circles under her eyes, it was almost eight. It wouldn't take more than thirty minutes to get to the hotel as long as she caught the right bus. But that was the problem. Catching a bus in Chengdu was a whole disaster half the time, and only partially a disaster the other half. She was sure they tried to keep it organized, but traffic was traffic, and she had no way to predict if the bus would be late.

While getting ready, she'd left her phone in her room, and when she returned to retrieve it, she found two missed calls and three texts. All from her mother. The texts asked her to call and that she needed to pay more attention to her phone, and *I know you aren't at work, you don't work today.*

Groaning, she returned the missed calls. She had a few minutes. "There you are."

"Hi, I don't have a lot of time," Mia said.

"You don't work today." Her mother sounded irritated. Had Mia done something besides ignore her calls?

"No, but Aunt Lilan set up an interview for me. I need to leave." Like now. She glanced at the clock on her bedside table. She didn't want to be on the phone outside, as speaking in English always made her feel uncomfortable, and Intira had been spending less and less time speaking to Mia in Chinese.

Intira sighed. "Right, she mentioned something about that. Well, I want to talk to you for a minute."

"Can I call later?" Mia asked, desperate to not piss off her aunt.

"Yes, but first let me ask how you're doing. Are you eating?"

Mia rolled her eyes. "Yes, I'm eating." Probably not enough for Intira's liking, but it was better than a few years ago. She'd even gained back some of the weight she'd lost. "I'm fine. It's all fine."

"Have you spoken to Démíng recently?"

She had not, in fact, spoken to her brother recently. He'd texted, but she hadn't engaged. "Māmi, you know that we don't talk much anymore."

"I know, and that worries me." Something clacked on the other end. Intira's nails against her desk? "He's been more distant than usual. You should talk to him."

"I don't have time to talk to him right now."

"Not right now, but after the interview. According to Cody, he stays up late most nights researching anyway."

Mia bit her lip. Intira knew that Mia and Cody hadn't spoken in five years, and Mia hated when she brought up his name. He was part of Derek's life. He didn't need to be part of Mia's. "Maybe.

271

Look, I have to go."

Intira let out a heavy sigh. "Please call me tonight. I want a better update about your life."

"You know everything about my life."

"Then tell me how the interview goes."

"I will. I gotta go." She hung up before her mom could say anything else. No doubt she'd get an angry text later, but the English was making her head spin and she *really* needed to hurry. Intira would understand. Or she wouldn't, and Mia would get a lecture later.

Now frustrated and running late, Mia bolted from her room, almost missing her purse. She half put on her shoes before she was out the door to the elevator. The bus stop wasn't far from their apartment, but she needed to be on the other side of the road, and stoplights weren't known to be on her side.

The elevator took forever to arrive, then stopped at three floors on the way down as more people got on. She ignored them, tapping her fingers on her arm. She was polite and didn't push out of the elevator, but the minute she was out of it she picked up her pace and hurried out of the apartment complex and into the bright city morning.

Cars rushed past on the First Ring Road, and one of those cars wasn't a car, but a bus. The bus she was supposed to catch. She groaned. There was no way she would make it to the other side of the road before it took off. Immediately she took out her phone and texted Aunt Lilan that she'd be late. There was nothing else she could do.

When she finally got to the bus stop, the little electronic sign that gave estimated arrival times said the next bus was in thirty minutes. Which meant more like forty. Which meant she was going to be late.

Sure enough, the bus was late. She checked her phone every two seconds, heart racing. And when it arrived, she squeezed on and found her favorite corner empty. She settled in it and prepared to spend the next twenty minutes struggling through traffic. Aunt Lilan texted her back with a disappointed lecture about time management.

Mia ignored it.

Instead she let her mind wander. It'd been a long time since she'd heard Cody's name. Derek didn't mention him—at least not by name—and Intira usually didn't slip like that. Her mom must have been really worried about Derek. She considered sending him a text, since a call would be overheard, but the thought of checking in on him and his "research" gave her such anxiety that she had difficulty breathing.

He wouldn't let it go.

He wouldn't let Blair go.

What would it take to get him to move on? Mia didn't know the answer, and it wasn't her place to force him to let go when he wasn't ready. One day, he'd look back at this and regret it. Five years. He'd wasted five years searching for these lingering emotions he insisted were Blair's.

The gentle voice of a woman announced Mia's stop, bringing her out of her thoughts. Had twenty minutes passed that quickly?

Her mind went back to the situation at hand. She checked the time and found that the bus had arrived early. It must have done some amazing maneuvering to shave off five minutes. She pushed herself to the bus doors and hopped off the minute they opened at her stop. Her mind was only on crossing the street. Getting to the hotel in time to not make a bad impression at a possible new job.

She could have sworn the light was green. She could have sworn other people were crossing the street. Maybe it was stress, or maybe it was anxiety. Either way, she stepped into the moped lane. There was a series of honks and a moped shuddered to a stop right before it hit her. Another one sped in front of her, and she halted.

Heart pounding, she glanced at the moped that had stopped. It had almost hit her. What the hell? Why had it been moving?

"Hey!" Mia shouted. Heat filled her face and she kicked the tire. "Watch where you're going!"

The moped's owner, a woman wearing black jeans and a leather jacket, head covered by a helmet, didn't move.

Mia frowned. It was probably anger at her mom for the conversation earlier, and at herself for being stupid and not paying attention, but it took over her. She kicked the tire again. "People are walking!"

The woman tilted her head and in the same motion reached up with gloved hands. In a swift movement, she lifted the helmet off her head and Mia froze.

See, the thing was, Mia hadn't been expecting the woman staring back at her. Usually it was grouchy middle-aged women who almost hit pedestrians. Okay, that wasn't true. But still, that's who Mia had thought she was yelling at. Not the beautiful young woman who now watched her with curious, deep brown eyes.

The woman must have been around Mia's age. Maybe a few years older. Her hair—bleached—hung just beneath her ears and her skin was smooth and free of makeup. Her eyebrows were perfect, and her long lashes fluttered when she blinked. Around them, mopeds continued to fly by, some honking at them to move.

For some reason, the woman's eyes examined Mia from her toes to her head, and then she smiled. "It would seem at least one person is walking."

Her voice had an almost husky quality to it. Not like she was a smoker, but it wasn't perfectly clean either. Her words came out with the Sichuan accent, though she spoke with Beijing slang.

"I–" Mia bowed her head. Her face heated. Why was this woman so damn beautiful? And why did Mia notice?

"You're what?" the woman asked. "Sorry?"

Her tone held nothing but amusement, yet Mia couldn't keep the embarrassment from taking over. She couldn't speak. She knew better than to walk out into traffic. This could have gone so much worse!

The woman chuckled and Mia glanced up at her. She was still watching Mia. "You might want to be more careful in the future. Not everyone takes kindly to a stranger kicking their tires."

Mia's face burned. "Right. Well, I gotta go."

"Are you in a hurry?"

"I am."

"Maybe wait for the light to change." The woman held out a hand. It wasn't like she wanted Mia to shake it. It wasn't often Mia ran into people who wanted to shake hands here. It was more like she wanted something. "I'm Xue. You?"

"Meilian," Mia said without thinking.

"Hm…." The woman flicked her gloved fingers. "Okay, Miss Meilian. Give me your phone."

Mia blinked. "Why?"

"Because I'm going to put my number in it."

Mia's mind went blank. This woman—Xue—wanted to put her number in Mia's phone? Mia held out her cellphone and Xue took it, fingers brushing against Mia's. She shuddered while the stranger typed for a second. When she finished, she handed the phone back to Mia and lifted her helmet above her head.

"There. Go ahead and let me know when you get your voice back. I'm eager to hear your apology." She winked at Mia, replaced her helmet, and then sped off.

Mia stared after her, clenching her phone to her chest. Then someone honked at her and she jumped out of the way of another rush of mopeds. Her heart pounded. Her heart hadn't pounded like this in so long, Mia had forgotten what it was like to feel her pulse in her ears. She'd forgotten what it was like to blush.

Cheeks red, she waited for the light to turn green before she dashed across the intersection, still clutching her phone to her chest.

She needed to get her mind on the interview that she was officially late for. But she was still going to go. She was still going to make it. She was going to do her best.

Even if all she could think about was Xue and her winking smirk.

"You speak English?"

Mia shifted in her seat. The AC unit blasted her with cold air, chilling her nervous sweat. As if she wasn't uncomfortable enough under the unamused gaze of the interviewer. When he wasn't glancing at the resume Aunt Lilan had put together for her behind her back, he scrutinized her.

"Yes." Mia barely got the word out. "I lived in America for eight years when I was a child."

The hiring manager looked at her with narrowed eyes. "You would feel comfortable speaking English to international clients?"

"Yes."

He nodded, but there was no relief in his expression. Mia wrung her hands together under the table. Anyone could tell this wasn't going well. Hell, Mia was pretty sure even Aunt Lilan knew it wasn't going well, and she wasn't even in the room. From the moment Mia had arrived, exactly three minutes late, Aunt Lilan had shoved her to the back room for the interview. Mia hadn't even had time to take in the fancy hotel, nor explain about almost landing in the hospital.

The hiring manager had waved Aunt Lilan off and then set his steel-cutting glare on Mia. He was a stodgy old man with barely any hair and a suit that looked like it was worth more than Mia's rent. It was obvious he didn't want to be here, and she wondered how obvious it was to him that she *also* didn't want to be here.

"You currently work at a convenience store?"

"Yes."

"Did you not go to university?"

"No." She'd known this question would come up, and she had a whole speech prepared for it. One about how she was overcoming challenges in her personal life and had taken time off, but she wanted to go back to school and get a degree. The last bit was a lie, but it would sound better than the one word answer she gave. But when she tried to force the speech out, nothing happened. She stayed there, quiet, mind wandering to her conversation with Intira, and the fact that Xue had put her number in Mia's phone.

The hiring manager stood. "I think that will do. Thank you for coming in." He held out his hand. For a second, Mia imagined herself back in the street, Xue's long slender fingers asking for her phone. But he didn't want to contact her again. This was for a handshake. Mia reached out, trying not to wince—and failing miserably—at the dead-fish handshake.

"Thank you for taking the time to meet me." Mia released his hand, bowed, and then headed out of the room to escape the chill of the AC unit, and of the hiring manager's glare. If she hadn't been wearing a suit jacket, she would have been freezing. Who the hell turned on their AC unit in March? It was too early for that.

Aunt Lilan waited for her outside the room, arms crossed. There was so much worry in her eyes that Mia *really* didn't want to tell her how much of a disaster it'd been. If she hadn't been late, if she hadn't had that weird interaction on the street, then it might have gone much better. But she had been late, and Xue had given Mia her number, and so Mia had been flustered.

It wasn't so much that she'd almost gotten run over. That happened more times than she liked to admit in the gigantic city. It was that something about Xue had gotten to her. It'd made her feel something. At first, anger. Then embarrassment. Mia hadn't felt embarrassed about anything in years. She'd honestly thought she'd lost the ability to a long time ago. After all, you couldn't feel embarrassed when you were dead inside.

But Xue had been so beautiful. So amused. So confident. If she'd yelled at Mia, then maybe it wouldn't have ended up this way. Instead, she'd been calm and *entertained* at Mia kicking her tire. Who the hell was entertained when their vehicle was getting assaulted? Granted, Mia couldn't do much damage to a tire, but still.

"How did it go?" Aunt Lilan's question dragged Mia out of her thoughts.

She shrugged. "I doubt I got the job."

There was a flash of fury in Aunt Lilan's expression. Then it vanished and she crossed her arms. "Go home. We'll talk tonight."

Talk? Or fight? Mia absolutely didn't want to go sit at home and wait for her aunt to yell at her for messing up an interview. She could hear the guilt trip already. It must have taken a lot of pulled strings to get Mia an interview in the first place, especially considering she had no experience and no education in the hospitality field. This could come back and bite Aunt Lilan in the ass.

But that wasn't Mia's problem. She hadn't asked for the interview. She hadn't *wanted* the interview.

"I'll see you later." Mia didn't wave. She took off, head bowed. The magnificent hotel was a cage around her, and she needed to get out. She clenched the strap of her purse as she burst out into the city. Her chest tightened. The cage seemed to grow tighter around her. Maybe it hadn't been the hotel. Maybe it was the city itself.

Maybe it was just life.

She caught the first bus home and settled into a rare open seat. Her head rested against the window and she observed the city around her. There was a haze of gray over everything, making her wonder if it was pollution, the weather, or just her. Just once, she wanted to see the sun. It did shine sometimes, but rarely did she see the blue sky. Rarely did she get a moment of reprieve from the depression. Her mom was worried about Derek, as a mother should, but was she also worried about Mia still? Did she care that Mia was stuck? Stuck in a job she hated? Stuck in a city she had no connection to? And, the worst of it all, stuck in her memories of all her trauma and pain with no way out of them?

Or was Mia fading into the background? Was Intira, was Aunt Lilan, was Derek, giving up on her five years after she'd given up on herself?

And if they were, did Mia even care?

Mia didn't bother waiting up for Aunt Lilan. Exhaustion overcame her and she crawled into bed, still wearing her interview outfit. She didn't remember falling asleep, nor did she remember her dreams, but she did remember when a sharp rap at her door woke her up.

Her eyes flew open, heart pounding. A quick glance at her phone let her know she'd slept all day. It'd been a long time since she'd slept all day.

Groaning, Mia pushed herself out of bed and stumbled over to the door. She knew who was behind it. Only one person rapped on her door with their knuckles like that. And sure enough, Aunt Lilan stood there, waiting for her with crossed arms and a frown.

For a second, Mia saw her as Blair. That happened sometimes, whenever she saw someone who crossed their arms. Blair had always done it when she was uncomfortable. It was a defense mechanism. It protected her from criticism and judgment. It gave her control over her body when she felt like she had none. Or, at least that's what Derek had always said about it.

Aunt Lilan, however, didn't cross her arms due to insecurity and discomfort. She crossed her arms because she was pissed. "You messed up."

Mia rubbed her eyes. She was too out of it to fight. "I'm sorry. I tried, but—"

"But you're sabotaging your life?"

"What?" Mia covered her yawn with the back of her hand. "What are you talking about? I had a weird morning and it threw me off. I'm not sabotaging—"

"I don't want to hear your excuses. You always have a million reasons why you can't do anything to better your life. You can't go to school because you don't have money. You need to work. You'll go when you move back to Beijing. You can't get a better job because you don't have the right education. It's a vicious cycle, and I know exactly what the real reason is."

Mia scowled. "And what's the real reason?"

"You haven't forgiven yourself for what happened to your friend."

Mia's eyes widened. She hadn't told anyone she blamed herself for Blair's death. Not even Derek. How had Aunt Lilan figured it out? "I don't want to talk about Blair."

"You never do, but maybe we should."

Groaning, Mia pushed past her aunt and slid open the kitchen door. The kitchen was small. Smaller than it had any right to be. But it seemed to work well enough. No oven, but a small toaster oven that worked when Mia wanted to bake something. A pressure cooker sat on a waist-high cabinet, though it went unused most of the time. The fridge was the largest appliance in the room, save for the stove top, and it was filled with the food Aunt Lilan had cooked last night. Mia's stomach grumbled. She hadn't eaten anything all day.

Instead of food, though, she went for a bottle of water on the counter.

"I'm serious." Aunt Lilan followed her, standing in the doorway. "Your depression is getting out of hand. You need to talk to someone. If not me, then someone else. You're too young and too smart to throw your life away working at a convenience store."

Mia snapped. "It's honest work and it pays. Why do you care so much?"

"Because you're clearly unhappy."

"I am not! I haven't even cried in years."

"Yes, because that's healthy."

"You sound like a therapist." Mia once more pushed past her aunt, this time going to the living room to sit and drink her water. Her throat was parched. When was the last time she'd felt hungry and thirsty like this?

Aunt Lilan wasn't fazed. "Maybe I do. Maybe that's what you need if it'll get you to try."

"I am trying. I went to the interview, didn't I?"

Aunt Lilan let out a stark laugh. "You didn't try. You were rude and distracted the entire time."

Mia gasped. "I was not rude! Is he telling you I was rude?"

"You were late."

"Half of China is late to everything." Mia was not going to let a few minutes of tardiness ruin her life.

"I don't care what half of China does, I care what *you* do. If you keep going down this route, you're going to end up miserable. Is that what you want? To be lonely? To never get married? To never have kids? To punish yourself for something that isn't your fault?"

"You're single with no children. Guess that means there's something wrong with you too."

Aunt Lilan's eyes narrowed. "I don't *want* to get married. I chose this life because it suits me. I have something worth waking up for every day. What about you, Meilian? What do you have to wake up to every day? Because it sure isn't your job. It's not your friends. It's not even your family. So what is it? Why do you keep getting up every morning if you hate your life?"

Mia had enough. She slammed the bottle on the coffee table and stormed over to the front door.

"Where are you going?" Aunt Lilan asked.

"Out." Mia slipped on her shoes, grabbed her purse with her keys, and left the apartment, slamming the door behind her. As she waited for the elevator, she expected Aunt Lilan to come after her with another lecture, but the woman never showed. Instead, Mia stood there alone as tears pricked her eyes.

Her aunt was right. What did she get up in the morning for?

She yanked her phone out of her purse. Intira had told her to call Derek, and she did consider it. She went to his profile. But it was early in Denver, and there was no saying whether he was awake. Not to mention the fact that it'd been a while since they'd spoken on the phone. Texts only. What would he think if she called him crying, reaching out for the first time in five years?

But who else could she reach out to? Cody was *not* an option. Her parents would tell her that Aunt Lilan was right. She had no one else. There weren't many contacts in her phone, and most of them were family or work. Family, work, or Xue.

Mia saw the character for "snow" alone among her contacts. It was a strange name. Probably a weird nickname. Most Chinese people Mia ran into—and that included everyone in her family— had two characters for their names. Why did Xue only have one?

Again, did it matter?

Mia's finger hovered over the name. She could call this stranger. A woman close to Mia's age who deserved an apology. But what if Xue didn't actually want her to call? Why would she? Mia was a stranger. A violent stranger. And what if it was a fake number? But why would Xue have asked for Mia's phone only to give her a fake number?

She pressed Xue's name.

The woman answered after one ring. "Hello?"

Mia breathed in deep. "You told me to call when I could apologize."

There was a moment of silence before the woman chuckled. "I did say that, didn't I? All right. I'm ready."

The only problem was Mia didn't want to apologize over the phone. It was too impersonal. "How about I treat you to dinner tonight? Tell me where to meet you. That'll be my apology."

Xue laughed again, and tingles ran up Mia's spine. "Deal, Miss Melian. I know a great place."

Mia glanced up at the apartment building. She found her aunt's familiar curtains and glared at them. "How do I find this great place?"

Chapter Twenty-Six

Mia didn't like the way the waitress watched her. She tried not to look, but since she was still waiting for Xue, settled on a little plastic chair at a short table out in front of the restaurant, it was difficult not to glance in her direction now and then. Mia shifted, smoothing her skirt. Really, she should have changed, but there was no way she was going back into the apartment. Aunt Lilan was no doubt still fuming, and Mia wasn't too pleased with her either. It was a good idea to get some space.

The sun set in the distance, a deep orange glow behind thick gray clouds, and above Mia, fairy lights flickered on. Whether they were for ambiance or actual light, Mia didn't know, but she found them pretty.

She glanced at the waitress again. The woman hadn't taken her eyes off Mia since Mia had sat down. She hadn't come over to take Mia's order, but she also refused to move from her spot. Mia was tempted to ask her for a menu. Maybe prove that she wasn't loitering. Before she could raise her hand and beckon the glaring waitress her way, a familiar voice called out to her.

"You actually came."

Xue walked toward her. Every step was graceful and calculated. Her hips swayed and she had this smile on her face that Mia couldn't place. Like earlier in the day, she wore a pair of black pants and a leather jacket. She was taller than Mia would have guessed. Tall and thin enough to be a model. And when she brushed her hair away from her face, Mia noticed her left ear was pierced multiple times.

Mia swallowed thickly. "I told you I'd treat you to dinner."

Xue's grin widened. She sat across from Mia, never taking her eyes off her. Mia didn't know if she should look at her hands, or keep eye contact with Xue. On the one hand, she could feel the blush rise to her cheeks. On the other, the strange woman had such gorgeous eyes. It was difficult to look away from them.

The waitress rushed over the minute Xue sat and asked to take their order. Well, more like Xue's order. She barely acknowledged Mia. Xue broke eye contact with Mia and ordered two of the same dish and some tea. Then she was back to focusing on Mia.

"What did you do to the waitress?" she asked in an amused tone. "She cannot stand you."

Mia flushed and looked down. "I don't know. I haven't said anything to her."

Xue hummed and then placed her chin in her hand, elbow on her knee. When had she crossed her legs? "Well, it might be because you're dressed like you're about to take her boss' job."

"What?" Mia grabbed the lapel of her suit coat and looked at it. It wasn't that fancy, was it? "No, I don't...I just...I–"

"Don't worry. I think it's cute."

"Um, thanks. I got it a long time ago."

Xue tilted her head to the side, eyes glued to Mia. Mia shifted, throat suddenly very dry. Where was that tea?

Chuckling, Xue readjusted so her other leg was crossed. This time, when she leaned forward again, both her arms rested on her raised knee. "Well?"

"Well what?"

"Where's my apology?" There was no indication in Xue's tone that she *needed* an apology. In fact, there was no indication that she even *wanted* an apology. She was amused again, though there was far more laughter in her tone than earlier. Did she think that Mia had called her here for another reason?

Mia crossed her arms. "I'm buying you dinner. What more do you want?"

"The words."

"Why?"

"Because I like hearing you speak."

Mia snorted. What kind of answer was that? "Whatever you say."

"I'm not the one who has something to say." Xue straightened her back, still grinning.

What in the world had Mia gotten herself into? And why, despite how strange and uncertain she felt, did she enjoy it so much?

It'd been a long time since Mia had spoken to someone outside of work or family. She used to be good at this, right? Talking to people. Making friends. She'd had friends in America, even if most of them ended on the periphery. At one point in her life, she'd been popular. Capable. In control.

Or had that just been the illusion of high school?

Xue wasn't like anyone she'd talked to before. The woman had an air of confidence that Mia never could have matched. It was almost cocky. Not in the way that Blair had always presented herself. Blair's had been an act. This wasn't an act. Xue knew who she was, and she wasn't afraid of that person, whoever she was. Every action was intentional. She didn't give a shit what anyone said or did to her. Why should she? She was a queen.

At least, that's the impression Mia got from her. Maybe it was all an act. Or maybe it was because Xue looked at Mia with a hunger in her eyes. Maybe Xue was confident about one thing, and that was talking to Mia.

Mia coughed and looked at the table.

"Speechless again?" Xue asked.

"No."

"It's just an apology. Can't be that hard."

It wasn't, but Mia didn't want to apologize. She was buying a stranger dinner. Wasn't that enough? Xue seemed so determined to hear the words. Was it ego? Did she want to prove her dominance over Mia? And why didn't Mia want to just say the words and get it over with? Why did her resolve to *not* apologize grow ever stronger? It would take two seconds to ease the tension.

Maybe Mia didn't want to ease the tension.

When Mia glared, Xue let out a mystical laugh. Mia's heart fluttered and she opened her mouth to speak—though hell if she knew what she was going to say—when the waitress appeared with a pot of tea. Silence fell over the table, the only sound coming from the waitress practically slamming the cups on the table.

Once she was gone, Xue reached for the teapot, but Mia beat her to it. It was her treat. She should at least act like a somewhat gracious host. The other woman chuckled and withdrew her hands, replacing them on her knee. Mia breathed in deep and made to pour. Freshly boiled green water fell from the spout and steam assaulted Mia's hand.

"Crap!" She put the pot down, examining her scalded hand. It stung for the briefest moment.

"You okay?" Xue asked.

"Fine. Steam's hot."

Mia made to withdraw her hand and rub the condensation on her clothes, maybe scratch the skin so it wouldn't sting anymore, but before she could, Xue's hand darted out and grabbed her wrist.

Mia's eyes widened, and she tried to pull away. Xue was stronger, pulling Mia's palm out. The woman twisted Mia's hand and her fingers brushed against Mia's singed skin. They were soft. Xue's fingers. Gentle. Soft and slender and perfectly manicured.

"Steam is, in fact, hot," Xue murmured. "Surprised you got caught by it. Do I make you nervous?"

Mia was certain, in that moment, that her face was burning hotter than the steam. She yanked her hand back, holding it against her chest. "You do *not* make me nervous."

She always had been terrible at lying.

Xue chuckled. "If you say so. Do you need ice? Not sure the waitress will give you any, but I can always ask."

"I'm *fine.*"

"Are you sure?" Xue tried to raise her hand. Before Mia knew what she was doing, she reached over and grabbed Xue's arm, yanking it back down.

"I said I'm fine."

Amusement glittered in Xue's eyes. "Oh my. Someone has a temper."

Mia withdrew, realizing what she'd just done. "I do not!"

"My poor tire disagrees."

Derek had always told Mia she had anger issues. It hadn't been as prevalent when they were younger because Derek had secretly kept her calm with his empathy, but once he'd stopped, it had felt like a burning flame in her chest. Untamable. Uncontrollable. But could anyone blame her? She had a lot to be angry about. But did Xue deserve to have it taken out on her? All she'd done was not hit Mia with her moped.

"Look, I'm just having a bad day." When wasn't she having a bad day, though?

"Clearly." Xue finished pouring the tea and then held up her cup for a second. "Delicious," she said before taking a sip.

Mia frowned. What the hell was that? She reached out for her own cup. The steaming tea had heated it up enough that it stung against her hands, but she held it anyway. It was too hot to drink, so she waited for the wind to cool it down.

"So, if I'm not getting an apology, why did you call me out here?" Xue asked.

"I am apologizing. With food. Why won't you just drop it?"

"I might."

"Might?"

Xue leaned forward. "Tell me something interesting about you. Keep me distracted. I'll stop asking if I forget."

What was with this woman? "I'm not interesting."

"You absolutely are." Xue smiled and Mia's heart raced. "You're not from around here. That alone makes you *interesting*."

Mia glanced down at the tea, then back at Xue. It was difficult to keep eye contact. Xue never wavered, and Mia wasn't used to that. Yet, at the same time, Mia didn't want to look away. "Being from Beijing doesn't make me interesting. There are a lot of people from other parts of China in Chengdu."

Xue sipped her tea again. "And if you'd come here from another part of China, I wouldn't care."

Mia blinked. "Excuse me?"

"Oh, you speak the Beijing dialect perfectly. Almost flawlessly. But it's an almost. You have a foreign accent, though it's so slight I can't place where from. You spent time outside of the country, didn't you?"

How the hell…? Mia didn't have a foreign accent. Mandarin was her first language. It was all she spoke now. She sounded like anyone else on the streets of Beijing. Something else must have tipped Xue off to Mia's time abroad. Did Mia act like a foreigner? That was the last thing she wanted. To stand out. To be someone that people noticed. Being noticed was what had caused so many of her problems.

At that moment, the waitress walked up to them with food. Two plates of fried tomato and egg over rice. Mia hadn't had this dish in a very long time. Aunt Lilan wasn't a fan of tomatoes, and she cooked most of the meals. Mia's stomach grumbled as the savory, yet slightly sweet, scent of the dish tickled her nose.

She picked up her spoon, but Xue didn't move. Instead, the woman watched her like a tiger waiting to pounce on its next meal.

"Will you stop staring at me?" Mia asked.

"Why should I?"

"Because it's weird."

"But you're so pretty."

Mia's eyes narrowed. She did *not* appreciate being mocked. She dug her spoon into the rice. It was delicious. Sweet from the tomato, savory from the egg, textured from the rice, and with a hint of spice in the sauce. Must have been a restaurant recipe. She went for another bite but Xue reached out and ran her fingers up the back of Mia's hand. Then up her arm.

"I'm being serious, you know."

Mia dropped her spoon. It clattered against the plate, but neither she nor Xue looked at it. A million arguments came to the tip of her tongue, and then faltered. Deep down, she desperately wanted to believe Xue was messing with her. But the serious look in Xue's eyes—the deep, almost lustful look—took Mia's breath away. No one had ever looked at her like that. Especially not another woman. Especially not here in China.

She replayed the last five minutes. The staring. The comment about her clothes. The touching.

Was Xue…flirting with her?

Xue broke the eye contact, and Mia breathed. Her companion retreated, taking a bite herself, and Mia's hand dropped to her lap.

"Where did you live abroad?" Xue asked as if she hadn't just stolen the breath from Mia's lungs. "You never did say."

"America." Mia said the word quietly, afraid that Xue was going to judge her for it.

Xue's eyes widened. "America? You speak English?"

Mia nodded.

"Say something." Excitement brightened up Xue's tone. She ignored her food, focused entirely on Mia again.

Frowning, Mia took another bite of food and thought. She could say something. Like, the actual word, "something," just to mess with Xue. Or she could continue the conversation in English. Xue probably knew enough English to pick out a word or two. They did learn it in school here. But the idea of speaking English to a stranger made Mia's throat close up.

She swallowed. "I'm not going to speak English on command."

"Why not?"

"Because I'm not a monkey in a cage."

Xue's smile only grew. "No, you certainly aren't."

It was strange. All this time, Mia had rejected any social interaction. But here she was, verbally sparring with a woman who looked at Mia with hunger in her eyes. She should have hated it. The attention. She hadn't asked for it, and normally she would have paid for the food and left. Or maybe just apologized.

Yet, she didn't want it to stop. She found it exhausting, but exhilarating. She found it freeing.

When Mia didn't speak, Xue returned to her food. "Tell me more about yourself."

"There's nothing to tell," Mia said. A lie. But a practiced lie. Even if she wanted to open up about her life, she couldn't tell Xue. As far as she knew—and hoped—Xue wasn't part of the magical world. Mia couldn't tell her without breaking the laws and getting her brother in trouble. Not to mention that she didn't want to break Xue. Not in the way Mia had been broken.

"Nothing?" Xue tilted her head. "Are you sure? Not every day I get yelled at by a pedestrian for *not* hitting her."

Mia raised her brow and continued eating. Maybe if she didn't respond, Xue would change the subject. After a moment, she did.

"Fine, fine. We don't have to talk about you."

"I prefer it that way."

Xue smirked and Mia scowled.

"Why do you keep smirking at me?"

"Because you're cute."

"Yeah? Well, you're not."

"Don't know what you're talking about. I'm absolutely adorable."

She was adorable. Beautiful, really. Not that Mia would admit that to Xue. It would give her the wrong idea. Xue was flirting with her, but Mia had no interest. She was too broken to date, and she wasn't even interested in women. Except, when she thought of an excuse to leave, none came. Her heart raced. It took a moment, but she realized that she didn't mind the flirting. In fact, she kind of liked it.

"Tell me about yourself," she found herself saying. What was she doing? Why did she prolong this? She'd never see Xue again after today. Why did she want to know about her?

Xue laughed. "Well that's not fair! You won't tell me about you, but you demand to know about me?"

"I told you I lived in America."

She rolled her eyes. "Okay, fine. You told me where you lived. So I'll tell you where I lived." She gestured around her.

"Just Chengdu?" Mia asked.

"Just Chengdu."

"But you're speaking the Beijing dialect."

"Because you are."

"Oh. Right."

"But I can switch."

Mia didn't understand the next words coming out of Xue's mouth. They were familiar. She'd heard them before on the streets. Or, at least the accent. But it was a jumble of confusion, and Mia stared at her with a dropped jaw.

Xue cackled. "What? Can't understand me?"

Bewildered, Mia said, "I know some of the Sichuan dialect, but not *that*. What did you say?"

Mia didn't like Xue's grin. Or maybe she did. A little too much.

"Learn the dialect and I'll tell you."

"What? That's not fair."

"I never said it was."

Mia grumbled. She'd avoided the Sichuan dialect for a reason. She didn't want to assimilate here. This wasn't her home. She had no friends here. At least, she hadn't. Did Xue want to be friends? Did she want to see Mia again? Or was this the same situation as Steven? Or Chad? Or Cody? What did the flirting mean?

She couldn't stop her face from heating up.

"I–" Mia didn't know how to express what she wanted to say. She had no idea how to tell Xue she wasn't interested in women. She had no idea how to explain that she didn't want to date. That friends might be on the table, but nothing more.

In part, she didn't know how to express herself because she'd never had to before. In part, she didn't want to upset Xue, especially if Mia was wrong about Xue's intentions. But mostly, she didn't have the right words because deep down she didn't know how true any of it was.

To Xue's credit, she acted like Mia hadn't spoken one word and then went silent. "Okay, so I told you so something about me. Your turn."

They were back on this? "I told you. I'm not interesting. I'm just a normal angry person trying to live her life."

"Why so angry?"

"Because life sucks."

"It can, especially when you're all alone."

Mia's eyes widened. How had Xue known she was all alone? She opened her mouth to ask, but Xue changed the subject before she could speak.

"We don't have to talk about you, but I am curious what your views on the geo-political situation in America are. It's getting messy over there, but I only hear the news here. It'd be cool to hear your opinion."

All words caught in Mia's throat. That wasn't random at all. She coughed, then spoke. Then Xue countered. And back and forth they went, debating politics. Then literature. Then math. Then school. And it kept going, the verbal sparring as they ate their dinner.

And it was fun? Mia didn't know how to explain the exhilaration growing in her chest. When the conversation lagged, she came up with a new topic. Xue didn't seem to mind. In fact, she got more into it than Mia did sometimes.

Through it all, Mia learned three things about Xue:

She was intelligent.

She was confident.

And when she was animated about a topic, she was so amazingly, incredibly, beautiful.

They finished dinner, but the conversation hadn't ended. Or maybe it had and Mia just didn't want to go home. Xue entranced her. She had these views on the world that Mia had never considered. Even though they didn't talk about themselves, Mia had learned so much about her. She talked with her hands. She was mostly passionate about politics—international and domestic—but she also loved discussing culture. Mia knew about the ethnic minorities in China, but she hadn't really *known* about their impact on culture, politics, and even spirituality.

Xue did know. Xue loved talking about it. Mia loved listening to her explain the intricacies of minority representation in media and the political sphere.

The restaurant had filled with other patrons, and the waitress kept passing their table. A clear sign that she wanted their table for one of the waiting customers.

Reluctantly, Mia flagged her down—not that she was far—and paid. When Xue stood, Mia did as well, clutching her purse until her knuckles went white. It was still early in the evening. The idea of going home made her feel sick. Not only would she have to face Aunt Lilan, but she also wasn't ready to say goodnight to Xue.

"Do you want to walk a bit?" Mia asked.

Xue nodded. "I know a good walking path near here."

They took off together, walking side-by-side, hands occasionally grazing. Every time they did, Mia closed her eyes. It must have been from years of no physical contact, but she craved more. Her body was thirsty for touch, and she was perfectly okay getting it from Xue.

"You walk often?" Xue asked.

"Not anymore. Walked a lot back in America. But I lived in a small town so everything was close."

Xue blew out air. "Wow. I always imagine that everyone in America drives."

"A lot of people do." Mia shrugged. "Depends on where you live. I never actually learned to drive. I was supposed to, but then life happened. I don't think my brother knows how either, though he doesn't have an excuse like I do."

"You have a brother?"

"Oh. Yeah. Deming. My twin."

Xue threw her head back. "A twin! That's amazing. Don't meet many twins. What's it like?"

"Having a twin?"

"Having a twin, having a sibling, either."

"You're an only child?"

Xue gave her a look. "My parents could have had a second kid, try for a boy and all that, but it wasn't financially feasible. So, they got stuck with me."

"Stuck with?"

She laughed, but it wasn't the one she used when Mia did something amusing. It was sad. Regretful. "Turns out I'm a disappointment."

"Oh." Mia looked ahead. "That's okay. I am too."

"How could you be a disappointment?"

Mia shrugged. "My parents are *very* educated. They expected the same of me, but I'm not like that."

"No?"

"Nope. Never went to university. Work at a dead end job in a convenience store."

"But you're dressed like an office worker."

Mia laughed, bitterly. She'd forgotten all about her disastrous morning. "My aunt got me a job interview at her hotel. Completely messed it up."

Xue was silent for a moment, and Mia couldn't help but look up at her. She had a pensive look on her face. Then, she looked down. "That's where you were going this morning. Guess I should be the one apologizing."

"What for?"

"Flustering you."

"You didn't–"

There was that normal laugh. "If you say so, Miss Meilian. Still, I'm sorry that your interview went poorly."

"Oh. Thanks." Mia didn't know what else to say. She cleared her throat. "So, uh. Did you go to university?"

"Not yet." Xue reached her arms toward the sky. "Hard to do with no parental support. I'll go someday, but right now I'm content to just work and have a good time. School will always be there. Youth won't be."

"That's one way to look at it." Mia didn't agree, but she didn't want to debate. Xue would want a debate. "Where do you want to go?"

Xue grinned. "America."

"Seriously?"

"Seriously. Think about it. I could study my home from another country's point of view. Wouldn't that be fascinating?"

Mia grimaced. "It might not be as fascinating as you think. Americans have *ideas* about China."

"And Chinese people have *ideas* about Americans. Doesn't mean it's not worth looking at." She had a point, but she wasn't done. "Look, I'm not the most academically driven person in the world, but I think it'd be fun to see another part of the world. I've barely traveled. No time, no money. I haven't even left Chengdu on my own. My friends and I want to travel around China, but more than that, I want to see the world."

"The world is pretty great sometimes," Mia agreed.

Xue's eyes lightened. "You've traveled?"

"Some." More than she was willing to tell Xue. How did she explain midnight jaunts to France and Australia using magic? "My mom's family immigrated from Thailand in the early seventies when my mom was really young. Like two or three. So we've been back a couple times. I was born in Beijing. Lived there until I was ten when we moved to Colorado. Been to a few states—" she would *not* mention anything about Wyoming, "—and the summer before my last year of high school, I traveled around East and Southeast Asia with my aunt."

Xue stared at her with amazement, then threw her head back with a laugh.

Mia flushed. "What's so funny?"

"Nothing," Xue said. "Just knew you were interesting."

Her flush grew hotter. "I am not."

"Whatever you say." Xue caught her arm, pulling her off the path to a brick wall. Mia followed. Mia was pretty sure she'd follow Xue anywhere. Which was a disturbing thought that she pushed out of her mind. Especially when Xue sat down and patted the space next to her.

Mia hesitated. "Why are we sitting?"

"Because I want to see pictures, obviously." Xue patted the brick again, and Mia bit back a smile. Xue was acting like a puppy. It was adorable.

So, she sat. She pulled out her phone. The most recent photo was from years ago. Back when things were actually happy. They went through photos of her and Aunt Lilan traveling around Asia. Then further back to Mia and Derek in Beijing with their grandparents.

"You and your brother look *nothing* alike," Xue said. "You sure you're twins?"

"My mom insists."

Xue snorted out a laugh and then continued to scroll through the photos. They went back to pictures of Willow Creek. Of the forest surrounding the town. Of Denver. Of Derek and Cody. Of Mia and Blair.

"Who are they?" Xue asked when they got to a selfie of the four of them. Mia had taken it. It was amazing how much she'd changed. Her cheeks back then had been fuller. Her hair shorter and styled in such a different way. She'd worn an entirely different style of clothes, and she looked happy. She had been happy. Happy and young.

Xue pointed at Cody and Blair.

It'd been a very long time since Mia had seen pictures of her two best friends. She closed her eyes for a moment. "The boy is Cody. He was my first friend in America. We…we don't talk anymore."

"The girl?"

"Blair." Mia said her name in a whisper. "She was my best friend."

"Was?"

"She died."

"Oh." Xue lost all joviality. She touched Mia's arm, and Mia realized her hands were shaking. "I'm so sorry. I shouldn't have asked."

"It's okay." A small smile spread across Mia's lips. It'd been so long since she'd talked about Blair. So long since she'd let herself think about Blair. Everyone pushed her to talk. To let it all out and move on. She hadn't wanted to until this moment. Until this moment, she hadn't felt like she could talk to anyone about Blair.

"She was kind of a bitch," Mia said with a laugh. When Xue's eyes widened, Mia laughed harder. "She and I did not see eye to eye about so many things. Usually we were good. We'd talk it out, or she'd snap something at me about how she was feeling, and we had this understanding that we didn't fight. But the night she died we *did* fight. It was–" She blinked back tears. She didn't want to cry in front of Xue. "Anyway, she was a bitch, but she was also amazing. She was strong willed. Protective. Kind. She'd do anything to help the people she loved. She didn't always know how to show it, but she tried her best. I miss her so much."

Xue reached out and brushed a tear from Mia's cheek. "I get it now."

"Get what?"

"Why you're so angry. It must have been terrible to lose her."

"It was. Harder for Deming, I think. They had an on again off again relationship. He loved her, and I don't think he'll ever recover."

"Do you two talk much?"

"Not really. It's hard to talk to him when he reminds me of the past." In more ways than Mia was willing to admit to Xue. "My mom actually called this morning to talk about him. That's why I was late to the interview. Not because of you. Not that you helped." She grinned at Xue who chuckled. "She's worried about both of us, but I think she's more worried about him. He hasn't moved on yet."

"Have you?"

No. She hadn't. Mia breathed in and stared up at the sky. The clouds had parted, revealing an orange and pink sunset. "I will someday." Then she breathed out a sigh and jumped off the brick wall. "I should probably get home. It's getting late and I need to apologize to my aunt."

"So, your aunt gets an apology and I don't?" Xue's teasing tone was back.

Mia rolled her eyes. "I bought you dinner."

"If you think that's an apology then you are mistaken." Xue joined her, standing. "But you did pay. Which means I'm in your debt. How about I take *you* out to dinner tomorrow?"

Somehow, Mia didn't ask her if this was a date. Instead she swallowed down a blush and said, "I work tomorrow."

Xue nodded. "Okay. How about Saturday?"

"I also work Saturday."

"Do you ever *not* work?"

Mia took a step forward, shrugging. "Yes. Text me at the right time and figure out when. Sound good?"

Xue's grin released butterflies in Mia's stomach. "Sounds perfect, Miss Meilian."

Mia didn't wave goodbye. She didn't say anything either. The last thing she wanted was for this to be any sort of final. Instead, she walked away, phone in one hand, purse in the other. And on her lips, as her heart fluttered, she couldn't help but smile.

Aunt Lilan sat at the kitchen table. Mia slipped off her shoes and joined her. The moment she sat, Aunt Lilan stood and went into the kitchen, returning with two cups of water. Mia took hers without a word, and Aunt Lilan rejoined her at the table. If there had been a cricket in the apartment, its echo would have been deafening.

Mia didn't want to look at her aunt, but she had to. As much as Mia didn't want to admit it, Aunt Lilan had been right. It had been time to talk about Blair.

"Where were you?" Aunt Lilan asked after a minute.

Mia's fingers tapped on her glass. "I went out to dinner with a friend."

Is that what Xue was to her? A friend? It would be nice to have a friend, but there was an electricity there that Mia had never experienced before. With anyone. Something special. Something unique. Xue had come into her life and ripped all of her insecurities out of her. They'd known each other for one day. Not even a full day. But Mia could talk to Xue. Maybe it was the way Xue looked at her. Or maybe Mia was just that desperate. At the end of the day, did it matter?

"A friend?"

Mia nodded. "I met her today. That's why I was late. She almost hit me with a moped."

"Oh." Aunt Lilan was silent for a moment. "What's her name?"

"Xue."

"Strange name."

Mia shrugged. "I bought her dinner. We walked and talked for a bit. And...I'm sorry."

The surprise in Aunt Lilan's expression shocked Mia. Was it so weird that she was apologizing?

Aunt Lilan looked down at her glass. "Well, it's okay. I know you were angry. I shouldn't have pushed you to talk about...." She sighed. "It's okay. I'm glad you came home. I was worried."

"Of course I came home," Mia said, somewhat bewildered. "I'll always come home."

A sad smile crossed Aunt Lilan's face. "I hope you know that you can."

"I know." She took a sip of water. "But thanks."

Aunt Lilan stood, water unfinished. "I think I'm going to turn in early. Make sure to turn out all the lights before you go to sleep. You work tomorrow?"

Mia nodded.

"Guess I won't see you before I work. Have a good day. Let's make jiaozi tomorrow."

Jiaozi. A time to talk. Mia smiled. "Okay. Let's make jiaozi."

Even though Aunt Lilan had gone to bed, Mia stayed put at the table. She pulled out her phone and found a text from Xue.

<<Looking forward to treating you to dinner, Miss Meilian.>>

Now alone, she let her face burn with a smile. She didn't understand what was going on with her. Why the idea of getting dinner with Xue again pleased her so. But it did, and she wasn't going to fight it. She closed her eyes, holding her phone to her chest, and imagined a world where she could have friends. Where she could have a social life.

Where maybe—just maybe—she didn't have to be so miserable.

Chapter Twenty-Seven

Whenever Mia ordered coffee, Xue insisted that was the American in her. Mia always argued that plenty of people in China drank coffee, but Xue would still tease her every time. It got to the point, whenever they met up at their favorite cafe, that Mia would order a different type of coffee or latte. Just to mess with Xue.

Xue always found it delightful.

"I just don't understand," Xue said one day. It was just the two of them. It wasn't always. Sometimes, Xue's friends—and Mia guessed they were her friends now too—joined them. Today, though, Haoran had work, while Yutong and Yize were off in another part of the city with some of their friends from university.

Mia raised her coffee to her lips. The smell of slightly burned beans tickled her nose. "What's there to understand? Coffee is delicious."

"It's not, though." Xue lifted her own cup, one filled with jasmine tea. "It smells awful and tastes worse. Tea, on the other hand, is amazing."

"Tea is boring." Not to mention the fact that tea reminded Mia of Derek. "Besides, it doesn't have enough caffeine."

Xue waved a hand. "That's what sleep is for. Caffeine. Stupid thing."

Mia sipped her coffee. A nice, long, slurping sip. Xue grimaced and Mia almost snorted with laughter. "Oh come on," she said after swallowing, "you're telling the insomniac to just sleep?"

"All that caffeine you're drinking can*not* help your insomnia."

"Nothing helps with my insomnia. Might as well stay awake during the day."

Xue frowned at her, then sighed. "Fine. I guess. I like you better awake anyway."

"How would you know? Maybe I'm a joy to sleep next to." Mia froze when the words left her mouth, but Xue went on about the horrors of caffeine addiction as if she hadn't heard.

It wasn't that Mia had been thinking of Xue in that way. Okay, maybe she had a little bit. But not much. After that first meal, Xue hadn't flirted as much. It was as though she'd decided that Mia wasn't worth flirting with anymore, and that stung. Not that Mia understood why it stung. Xue was a woman! Mia had never had any attraction to women. Granted, Mia had never had any attraction to *anyone*, but that was beside the point.

The thoughts popped up sometimes. Not often. Just some nights when Mia couldn't fall asleep. When Xue had been texting her, complaining about her day, or asking Mia about hers. Whenever Xue sent her a picture, usually of Xue's face looking unamused, Mia occasionally imagined that that face was right next to her. That Mia could reach out and stroke her cheek and bring a smile to it.

"When did you start drinking coffee?" Xue asked. A direct question.

Mia blinked, forcing herself out of her thoughts. Away from the idea of Xue lying in bed next to her. "Oh. Uh. High school."

Xue's excitement rose. "Great. Tell me about American high schools."

Mia rolled her eyes. Xue's love of America was strange. "High school is high school. Too much homework. Too much drama."

"What kind of drama?"

"I don't know." Mia had been a source of gossip a couple of times, but she couldn't talk about that. Not that she wanted to. "People dating. Classes being rough. Family stuff. It was a small town. Everyone knew everyone."

"I bet moving there was hard."

Mia let out a stark laugh. "You can say that."

"Didn't have a good time?"

"Not at first. But the other kids eventually warmed up to me. Deming adjusted real fast. Had good friends on his first day. I, on the other hand, got to experience the joy of American bullying."

Xue winced. "That sucks. This Cody kid. Did he stand up for you? You said he was your first friend."

"No." Mia didn't want to talk about Cody. "We just hid together under the slide."

Xue must have sensed that it was a topic Mia wanted to avoid, because she changed the subject. "You mentioned dating. You ever date anyone?"

Okay, so the subject change wasn't the best one ever. Mia grimaced and sipped her coffee. What could she say? She'd had one boyfriend. Steven was unmentionable, and she'd slept with Cody once. Then broke his heart. "I dated a boy. He broke up with me after the fire. He and his mom moved back east to be with her family, and I came here."

Xue knew there had been a fire, but Mia hadn't told her how it had started. Apparently, news of the fire had made it all the way to China, so she'd heard about it on TV. It'd taken a moment for Xue to realize that Mia had experienced the fire first hand. They didn't talk about it.

"You had a boyfriend," Xue said. She stared down at her cup, then shook her head. "Of course you had a boyfriend. You're beautiful. Who wouldn't want to date you?"

Her sadness confused Mia. "Not many people. I was never super popular."

"Oh, I don't believe that." Xue placed her cheek in her hand. "I bet you have people knocking down your door every day."

There was one person Mia wanted to knock down her door. "You'd be surprised."

"You interested in dating?"

"Not sure. Depends on if I meet the right person."

"Describe your right person."

Xue's gaze intensified, and Mia's stomach clenched. "Not sure. I guess I'll know when I meet them."

"Me too." Xue's hand dropped from her face and landed on the table very close to Mia. It was difficult to explain the physical reaction Mia had to that action. To the way she said those words. It took all Mia had not to slip her hand in Xue's. Not to start describing the woman in front of her.

It wasn't right.

Mia had only dated boys. She'd only kissed boys. So why was it, when Xue smiled at her, a glint of mischievousness in her eyes, that Mia wanted to change that?

Mia wrung her hands together. "Maybe we shouldn't do this."

Xue glanced over her shoulder, basketball under her arm, and smirked. "Scared?"

"Of course I'm scared! We're breaking and entering."

The campus around them, leaves green and fluttering in the wind, was filled with people walking to and from classes. No one looked at them. They fit right in with the other group of people playing basketball in the court next to the one Yutong was currently slipping into.

"We aren't breaking and entering." Yize patted Mia on the shoulder with a laugh. He was the broadest of them all. He'd played basketball in college and this crazy scheme had been his idea.

"We aren't students," Mia said.

"No one knows that but us." He winked at her and then joined Yutong in the court.

Haoran, standing next to Mia, rolled her eyes. "Meilian is right to be nervous. She's a good girl. Doesn't break the rules."

Xue laughed. "Nah. Meilian has a bad streak. I just know it."

Mia did not, in fact, have a bad streak. Every time she went against the rules for anything, bad shit happened. Date the new boy and keep his magical secrets? Have a crazed woman stalk and try to kidnap her. Fight to break out of a captor's house? Best friend lights the house on fire and she gets thrown off a roof. Use magic to take artifacts from other magical clans? Piss off those clans and cause three deaths.

For the past five years, she hadn't broken any laws. Haoran had meant the comment as a teasing insult, but Mia heard nothing but truth in her words.

She shifted, crossing her arms. No one would notice them, and Yize had been dying to play basketball for a month now. It wouldn't be the end of the world. Right? She was in workout clothes, just like Haoran and Xue. A pair of leggings and a tight tank top. Other women—students—worse similar clothes. They did fit in. It wasn't like they'd broken into an elementary school to do this. They fit in.

"You coming?" Xue asked. She held out her hand, and Mia examined her. She looked damn good in her outfit. Normally, she wore clothes that didn't show off her body like this, and Mia hadn't realized just how toned she was.

Mia took her hand. Her very soft, very warm, hand.

Xue led her into the court where Haoran, Yutong, and Yize were arguing about teams.

"Girls against boys isn't fair," Haoran said. "You two boys play basketball, and none of us do."

"Didn't say it was fair." Yutong held out his hands toward Xue, who passed him the ball. He caught it easily and began to dribble. "Besides, three against two isn't fair either."

"How about Yize and me against you, Xue, and Meilian?"

"Why does Yutong get Xue?" Yize said.

"You think I'm not an asset?" Haoran asked.

"Not really."

Haoran's glare intensified and the boys laughed. Xue, still holding Mia's hand, squeezed it for a second before letting to and giving the final team list.

"Yize, you and I will go up against Yutong, Haoran, and Meilian. Then we'll switch around once we figure out the balance." She snatched the ball from Yutong and held it over her head. "Sound good?"

"Sounds great to me." Yize bounded away from the huddle toward the middle of the court.

It occurred to Mia about then that none of them knew her history with basketball. It'd never come up with Xue, and the others didn't ask her much about her time in America. They wanted to know more about the now. Not the then. She thought about telling them, but there was no saying she would remember how to play. It'd been years, and she wasn't exactly fit anymore.

She breathed out, then joined her team on the opposite side of the court.

"No tip off," Yutong said. "Just some good old fun."

"Let's destroy them." Haoran clapped her hands together.

Mia said nothing.

They broke and the game began.

At first, Mia held back. Every time someone passed her the ball, she took it but immediately returned it, mind back seven years when the world was so different. Senior year, she didn't remember basketball. But junior year? That had been all she'd thought about before the final game. When everything had been gray. When Steven and Kathleen had taken over her mind and Derek, Blair, and Cody had been keeping secrets from her.

How had seven years passed since then?

How could life have changed so much?

Before she knew it, she had the ball again, but her teammates were either covered, or out of range. Xue stood in front of her, grinning. Panting. She was having so much fun, and Mia hated that she wasn't. Why shouldn't she have fun? Why should she relive the past? So what if her last time playing basketball had been a total disaster? This wasn't then. It was now. Xue stood in front of her, waiting for her to move.

She dribbled the ball. It touched her fingers, then bounced against the ground and back up. The exhilaration of the game took over her mind. Xue stuck out her tongue.

"Just try and get past me," Xue said.

A taunt. Xue thought, for sure, that Mia had never played this game a day in her life.

Oh how wrong she was.

It all came back to her. Her muscles remembered. She stepped forward. She had complete control of the ball. And then she dodged around Xue and dashed down the court. Yutong cheered while Yize cursed. Haoran laughed. Mia knew where each one was. She was aware of Yize catching up to her. Of Xue catching up to the moment and whooping before running after her too.

She got to the three point line. She hadn't made a three pointer in years. No doubt she wasn't strong enough to do it. But she had the form, and Yize was going to catch her any second. She came to a stop and jumped, sending the ball soaring through the air.

It swished through the net. Didn't even rebound.

"What was that?" Yize groaned. Mia turned and found him on his knees.

Yutong and Haoran ran over to Mia, asking the same question, while Xue had this look of excitement in her eyes. She grinned at Mia before she patted Yize on the head.

"Didn't I tell you?" Mia asked, panting. "I played basketball in high school."

"That information was left out of the orientation packet." Yize lay on the ground.

Yutong patted Mia on the back before he went to chastise his friend for being overdramatic. Haoran said something about a great shot, but when Xue joined them, she said she was going to get the ball.

Xue's eyes were wild. Happy. "That was amazing. I didn't realize you could move like that."

"Well, I haven't played in a long time," Mia admitted. "Didn't realize I still *could* move like that."

Xue laughed and wrapped an arm around Mia's shoulders. The touch chilled Mia's skin, then it burned. "You are a surprise, Miss Meilian. What other secrets are you hiding?"

Too many. Mia knew that it was too many. But that was okay, she decided. Because they were in the past. She had no secrets about the now. Well, no dangerous secrets. No one would get hurt if she never said how happy she was when Xue touched her. How when she was alone in the shower, she imagined Xue in there with her. Hair damp. Skin dripping with steaming water. Lips pressed to Mia's collarbone.

Mia flushed. Those were alone thoughts. She was not alone.

"We going to keep playing?" she asked. "Might want to switch up teams."

"I want Meilian!" Xue shouted.

"No, I do," Yize said.

"Obviously the worst person should get her, and that would be me," Haoran said.

Mia laughed and took the ball from Haoran. She'd let them figure it out. Because to her, the choice was obvious. But if she voiced the obvious choice, then everyone would know her secret. And this secret was best left unsaid. Even if Xue was grinning at her like she already knew.

Even though Aunt Lilan hadn't bugged her to find a job since the disastrous interview at the hotel—and that had been three months ago at this point—Mia found she needed something more engaging. Which is why, even though it was hot in Xue's apartment, and Mia's phone was on the verge of dying, she sat in the ratty armchair Xue's roommate had bought two years ago and searched for a new job.

"Maybe narrow it down. What jobs are you willing to work?" Xue lounged on the couch next to her, wearing a pair of loose shorts and a billowing shirt. In one hand, she held an electric hand-held fan—which she pointed at her face—and in the other, her phone.

Mia did her best not to look. Not only because she had to focus, but also because she had a very clear shot of Xue's cleavage and she'd always been taught it was rude to stare.

"Anything," Mia said.

"Fast food?"

"Anything but that."

Xue's laugh filled the apartment. She sat up, dropping her phone in her lap and then brushed her hand against Mia's bare arm to ask for Mia's phone. All thoughts disappeared from Mia's mind and she held out her phone. Shivers went up her arm and to the base of her neck. Xue did that sometimes. When she wanted something from Mia. She didn't ask with words, but instead brushed against her.

"Let's see," Xue said. "Oh, these are no good. You need an in somewhere."

Mia couldn't speak. It was often that Mia couldn't speak around Xue. She'd hoped that it would get better as she got to know Xue more and grew more comfortable in her presence, but it'd only gotten worse. Everything had gotten worse. Mia no longer had her little fantasies when she was alone. Sometimes, they happened when she was sitting next to Xue. Sometimes—often, actually—they invaded her dreams. She longed to talk to someone about them. Not Xue. She didn't want to scare Xue away. But *someone* who wouldn't judge her.

She wanted to talk to Blair.

"I know! How about I get you a job where I work?" Xue grinned at her.

"I'm not answering phones in a call center." Mia didn't want to deal with angry customers anymore.

"Not that job. My other job." Xue had never mentioned another job before.

Mia frowned. "What other job?"

"I teach kids how to dance twice a week," Xue said.

Mia blinked. "You dance?"

"Haven't I told you that before?"

"No?"

"Oh, well, payback for not telling me about your short career in basketball." Xue stuck out her tongue.

Mia bit the inside of her lip. "Right. Well, I want to see you dance."

"No, it's embarrassing."

Xue? Embarrassed about something? Mia leaned across the armchair, getting as close to Xue as possible with a grin on her face. "Come on, Xue. Dance for me."

Shock crossed Xue's expression. Then the shock turned to amusement. Then darkened to something Mia couldn't place. It wasn't bad. But it was different. "I'll dance for you if you speak English for me."

And they were back on that. Mia sighed. "You know I only speak English with my mom. It's hard for me to switch back and forth now."

"Then no dancing for you."

"Not even a little bit?"

"Nope."

But Mia *really* wanted to see it. Xue wanted to hear her speak English? Xue didn't understand any of it. She'd said English had been her worst subject in school. Terrible teachers. No good motivation. Maybe it would be okay.

Mia took a deep breath, and then in English said, "I'd love to see you dance. I think you'll be beautiful."

Xue dropped Mia's phone next to hers, eyes wide. Mia's face burned so much she thought her skin was going to catch fire. It'd been the first time she'd spoken English to Xue.

"There." Mia switched back to Chinese. "I spoke English. Now dance."

Xue picked up her phone, gaze flickering down. Mia couldn't stop looking at her. The way her lashes batted. The way her slim fingers typed something into her phone. How elegant she looked, leaned over with a slight smile on her face.

Mia didn't know what to do with herself. These feelings were getting out of control. Where was Derek when she needed him? She hadn't heard from him or seen him in months. He'd basically vanished right when she needed him to explain her emotions. She'd never felt this for *anyone*. Steven and Chad had been beautiful in their own way, but they were nothing compared to Xue.

And when Xue's phone pumped out music, and Mia realized she was going to dance, glee spread through Mia.

Xue stood. She didn't move like other people. There was purpose behind every movement. She floated across the room, and Mia shifted to the couch for a better view.

"All right, Miss Meilian," Xue said, bowing at the waist. "As you have commanded. I shall dance for you."

And dance she did. Her movements were like water. So smooth, so controlled. She had excellent command of her body, moving it in ways Mia hadn't realized were possible. Mia couldn't tell if this was pre-choreographed or spontaneous. It felt like both and neither at the same time. A human becoming one with the song.

It was beautiful, but not as beautiful as the look on Xue's face. It was the look she got whenever she watched Mia. Soft, yet excited. Deliriously pleased with every aspect of life. She commanded the floor. Mia didn't notice anything else. Not her phone ringing. Not the music changing. Not her heart racing in her ears.

And when Xue finally stopped, she held out a hand for Mia to take and Mia couldn't stop herself from doing so. She didn't stop Xue from pulling her off the couch. From wrapping an arm around Mia's waist. From spinning her around. Xue was the lead, and Mia her princess. Mia could barely breathe. She locked eyes with Xue and only looked away when Xue twirled her out, then back in.

They were so close. The music changed again, but they didn't move away from each other.

For a moment, Mia wondered what it'd be like to kiss her.

Xue leaned in closer, capturing Mia's soul with her gaze.

"Next time, I'll teach you the tango," she whispered.

Mia shuddered. Xue let her go and went back to the couch,

leaving Mia standing there with a butterfly filled stomach, a red face, and a thudding heart.

Mia wasn't sure which felt better running through her hair: the brush or the fingers. Xue perched behind her on the couch's back, long legs on either side of Mia. Mia, meanwhile, sat with a perfectly straight back, hands in her lap as she tried not to move her head too much.

"Are you sure you want to do this?" Mia asked. It'd all started as a joke. With Mia complaining about how long her hair had gotten and Xue telling her that she was lucky to have long hair. They'd gone back and forth for a moment, Mia making them lunch, while Xue tried to convince her that long hair was better than short, and the only reason she didn't have it was because bleaching long hair was too expensive.

Before she knew it, Mia had agreed to let Xue play with her hair. A nothing decision in the moment. Mia was used to sitting still while Intira put her hair into intricate styles. But she soon realized there was a stark difference between Intira and Xue running their fingers through her hair. With her mom, it was annoying. With Xue, it was intoxicating.

"You have such amazing hair," Xue said, ignoring Mia's question not for the first time. "Have you ever dyed it?"

"No, but I've thought about it."

Xue hummed. "I like your hair the way it is. It's a pretty color. My natural color is so *dull*. No life. No spark. You have a little bit of light brown in yours. Did you know that?"

"Well, yeah. It's my hair."

Xue flicked the back of Mia's head lightly, and Mia jerked forward with a noise of complaint. But before she could say something about Xue's actions, the woman reached forward and pulled Mia's hair away from her face, fingers tickling Mia's cheeks.

She had to repress the shudder desperate to run through her body.

"If you did color it, I think you should go reddish-brown. Not a lot of red. Just enough to give it shine. Bring out the natural warmth of your skin tone."

Mia rolled her eyes. "Maybe I should just bleach it like you do."

Xue's stark laugh let her know that was a bad idea. "Bleach your hair? You'll just damage it. Your hair is so healthy. It'd be a shame to take away all this natural color. Especially since it's so long. It'd take you forever to grow it out."

"I could cut it."

The brush felt good against her scalp. Mia closed her eyes, relishing in the physical attention. Xue's perfume soothed her, almost lulling her to sleep.

"I can't imagine you with short hair."

"I did it once before. Before I moved to China."

"Did you like it?"

"Not really."

"Then I say keep it long."

Mia smiled. "Okay."

Xue put the brush down and divided Mia's hair into sections. Every now and then, she stopped to look at the video she'd found. Some beautiful, but intricate, braided style she wanted to try.

"Have you ever done something like this before?" Mia asked.

"Nope. Never really had a chance to play with someone's hair. Most of the people in my life with long hair either don't want it touched, don't want me to touch it, or I've been too intimidated to ask. But I've always wanted to. What about you?"

"Never had the urge, honestly." But that could have come from

Blair always having short hair, and having Derek as a twin. "If I'd had a sister, maybe. But until recently, Derek kept his hair in typical boy cuts."

"Does he not now?"

"Last time I saw him, it was pretty long." He'd gone on a rant when she'd asked him about it. Something about not having the time to get his hair cut. He had too much to do. Then he'd asked her if there was a mage library in Chengdu. As if she would know that.

"When was that?" Xue asked.

Mia shrugged. "It's been a while. He used to come visit once in a while, but that's stopped." Either he was too stuck searching for Blair and didn't have time, or he'd given up on Mia. Maybe he'd gotten the hint that she needed to move on, and if he wouldn't, he couldn't be part of her life.

"You should call him." Xue continued to braid, every now and then pinning a braid up with bobby pins. The last time Mia had put her hair up like this, it'd been the night of the museum opening almost seven years ago. Such a long time ago. What had she done with the past seven years? Where had the time gone?

"If I call him, he's just going to pull me back there," Mia said.

"Back where?"

Mia couldn't hold back her flinch. She'd meant in the world of magic, but Xue couldn't know about that. What came out next was an incomprehensible ramble about grief and depression and how she finally felt she was getting out of it. It was hard to say it made sense.

Xue placed a hand on Mia's shoulder, stopping her mid-sentence.

"I don't have siblings, but I know that if I did have one, I wouldn't give up on him. You've been struggling, but so has he, and he needs you. If you can help lead him out of this, maybe you should."

Mia's hand twitched, wanting to go for Xue's. But Xue pulled it away and continued braiding Mia's hair before she could. And Mia said nothing. Maybe Xue was right. Maybe Derek needed someone to help him get out of his obsession. The only problem was, there was more to the story than Xue knew. She didn't know about Derek's magic or his empathy. He wouldn't give up on finding Blair until he stopped feeling her emotions, and there was no saying when that would be. Their phantom existence was driving him to the brink of insanity, and Mia wasn't sure it was possible to bring him back. She wasn't sure he wanted her to bring him back.

Her brain refused to stay in the moment. Xue's fingers felt so good. She wanted to fall asleep. To rest her head against Xue's leg and use her as a pillow. Before she could build up the courage, Xue stopped braiding. No more hair rested on Mia's neck, and her head felt heavy when she moved it.

"All done!" Xue announced. She grabbed the mirror from next to Mia. Mia held her breath. Did Xue have any idea what she did to Mia? How being this close made Mia feel?

When Xue held up the mirror, the first thing Mia noticed was Xue in the reflection. Sitting behind Mia with a wide grin and that look in her eyes. The second thing she noticed was herself. She looked better. There weren't any dark circles under her eyes, and her cheeks were full. Flushed. She wasn't wearing any makeup today, but her skin was smooth and clear, and when she made eye contact with herself, she realized she was happy.

"Looking gorgeous, if I do say so myself," Xue said. She touched Mia's shoulder again.

This time, Mia didn't hesitate. She grabbed Xue's hand and gripped it.

"You okay?" Xue asked.

Mia twisted. She readjusted until she half faced Xue, still holding onto her hand. They made eye contact, and Xue's expression softened.

"Meilian," Xue whispered.

Her heart thudded. Stomach curled. Was it possible to tell Xue that she felt something? That all of this, whatever this was, held so much meaning to her? That whenever she was with Xue, all she could think about was kissing her?

She hesitated too long. A key entered the lock of the front door and Mia spun away, letting go of Xue just in time for the door to open and Aunt Lilan to enter.

Mia stood, smoothing out her pants. She rarely had Xue over, and usually had her leave before Aunt Lilan got home. The two hadn't met yet.

"Meilian?" Aunt Lilan peeked into the living room. "Oh, who's this?"

"Ah, this is Xue," Mia said.

Xue slipped off the couch and walked over to Aunt Lilan. "My name is Xue Huang. I'm a friend of Meilian's. Sorry to intrude."

Mia had to wonder what Aunt Lilan thought of the scene before her. Hair ties all over the couch. Mia standing awkwardly in front of the couch with her hair in a braided crown. Xue fidgeting.

"It's nice to meet you," Aunt Lilan said. She bowed her head at Xue. "I've heard a lot about you. Welcome to my home. I hope Meilian offered you something to drink."

"She made lunch," Xue said.

"Did she?"

Mia looked at the ground. She hadn't cooked much since coming to China.

"Yeah. It was delicious. Did you teach her?" Xue spoke smoothly, but there was something off about her voice. It was a little pitchier than normal. Was she nervous?

Aunt Lilan laughed. "Oh no. I mean, I know how to cook, but my brother, Meilian's father, was always the chef. He taught her and her brother."

"He taught her well."

"I'll let him know." Aunt Lilan placed her purse on the kitchen table. "Let me cut some fruit for you two. Meilian, can I speak to you for a moment?"

And there it was. Aunt Lilan was going to give her a lecture. Yell at her without raising her voice. Mia hadn't asked to bring Xue over, and there was no way Aunt Lilan approved of her. There was a reason Mia hadn't let them meet before now.

"Okay." Mia walked past Xue, shrugging at her. Xue nodded and then went back to the couch. Mia didn't dare look at her. Once she was in the kitchen, door closed behind her, she tensed and waited for the lecture.

But Aunt Lilan didn't lecture. Instead she smiled and grabbed some oranges from the fridge. "So, that's Xue. I was wondering if you were ever going to let me meet her. She seems very nice."

Mia, flustered, got out, "She is."

"Did she braid your hair?"

"Yes."

"It's beautiful. Can I sit and talk with you? Or do you want some privacy? I'd like to get to know her."

Mia wasn't sure what to say. "You can sit with us."

"Good." Aunt Lilan grabbed a knife and sliced the orange. "I'll be out in a few minutes. Go ahead and help Xue clean up the living room. It looks like a beauty salon exploded all over it."

"Okay." Mia turned to leave the kitchen, then she paused. "You think she's nice?"

"Well, I could do without the blond hair," Aunt Lilan said, thoughtful. "But I've never been one to judge based on appearance. She hasn't gotten you in trouble, and you've been happier these past few months. I doubt someone terrible would bring you such joy."

Mia smiled. "Yeah. You're right."

"She's very pretty," Aunt Lilan said.

Somewhere, Mia might have been aware of the hinting, but she didn't pay attention to it. Instead, she said, voice soft, "She's beautiful."

Chapter Twenty-Eight

Summer was upon them in full blast. Even though evening reigned, the warm air was almost suffocating. Mia, hair pulled into a high ponytail, clothes fit for a fabulous night out, couldn't help but laugh as Xue and her friends led Mia to a bar they liked to frequent. They'd invited her before, but she'd always been too scared. The last time she'd gotten drunk was the first time Cody had kissed her. She barely remembered the night at this point, but she remembered feeling so uncertain. So afraid of so many things.

She was tired of being afraid.

The bar was near the center of the city. High end restaurants surrounded it, making it stand out with its wooden siding and rickety staircase. Being on the second floor, hidden in the back, Mia had a feeling that this place was going to be a good time. A hole in the wall, almost literally. Even the inside was grungy, with spray painted walls and wooden tables with patrons' names carved into them.

Mia felt like she was in another world. A side of Chengdu she hadn't let herself see. It'd been five months since she'd first met Xue. Five months of new sights and experiences. But there'd always been a barrier between her and Xue. One that she'd kept up to protect herself. To protect Xue.

Tonight, she was smashing a hole in that barrier. The sledge hammer was poised and ready. While there would still be a lot of the wall, there was going to be a small part that she could crawl through. She was ready for it. And having a couple drinks would help immensely.

Xue placed a hand on Mia's lower back and leaned in to whisper, "Do you want me to get you a drink?"

"Surprise me," Mia said, smiling up at her.

Xue sucked in a sharp breath, then grinned, shaking her head. "Okay, but don't blame me if you get drunk." She took off toward the bar while Mia settled onto the bench. Yutong and Haoran sat across from her in chairs, while Yize pulled up another chair to sit at the head. Like always, whenever they got dinner or met up at a cafe, the three of them made sure that Mia and Xue sat next to each other. While she was certain they were doing it so Mia felt more comfortable, she didn't feel embarrassed or annoyed by it. In fact, she liked that she always got to sit next to Xue.

"Pretty sure Xue's bringing shots," Haoran said. She pulled out her phone, turned on the front facing camera, and checked her makeup. "If you want something else, you'll have to get it yourself or ask."

"I've never done shots before," Mia admitted. "I'm curious."

Yutong gasped. "How have you never done shots?"

"I don't really drink."

"We can change that." It wasn't Yutong who spoke, but Xue. She appeared with a tray of shots, a salt shaker, and some limes.

"Tequila?" Yize said. "You're gonna make her sick."

"Only if she drinks too much." Xue winked at Mia and then slid in next to her. Their thighs brushed and Mia's heart flipped.

Everyone grabbed a shot, and Xue showed Mia how to use the

salt and lime. It took a second, and almost spilling her shot, but she got it down, face screwing up even as the tart lime washed the bitter tequila taste out of her mouth. She shook her head and her face heated.

Xue laughed, having already done her shot, and wrapped an arm around Mia's shoulders. "Can't believe you've never done that before. Better get used to it. I have more coming."

Mia sighed. "I'd like to *not* drink my liver into exhaustion."

"Aw, just one more." Xue leaned in and whispered, "I promise it'll be fun."

"One will turn into five if you aren't careful," Haoran said. She stood. "I'm going to get an *actual* drink. Yize, Yutong, look out for Meilian, won't you? Xue is a *terrible* influence."

Before long, the table was filled with drinks. Xue convinced Mia to do another shot before Yize returned with a beer for her. Mia's head was light. Her limbs floated on air, and she sipped her beer with a smile, listening to her friends talk about their lives.

Yutong's parents were pressuring him to go to law school, which he absolutely didn't want. Yize's long distance girlfriend was bugging him to try and move to Xi'an. Haoran's older sister was getting married and was being a complete pain about it, fighting with their mom about how traditional it should be. Mia didn't participate. She should have, but how could she? The last time she'd spoken to her mom, Intira had just said that Mia seemed happier and to keep her updated. Liang hadn't said much on the call, but he'd seemed content that Mia wasn't a complete train wreck, at least. She had nothing to complain about there. And Derek...she still hadn't heard from him. Still hadn't sent him a text. Still couldn't bring herself to go back into that world.

After maybe an hour, something touched Mia's hand under the table. She jumped, shocked at the contact, then glanced down. Xue's fingers nudged hers, and when Mia didn't pull away, they slipped between them. Mia glanced up at Xue, but the woman didn't look at her. Instead, she chimed in about how work was kicking her ass and she couldn't wait to have enough saved up to go to school.

Mia found herself completely lost in the feel of Xue's thumb rubbing against her skin. If they were alone, Mia would have lifted Xue's hand and kissed it. If they were alone, Mia would have caught Xue's attention and kissed *her*. If they were alone, Mia might have let the alcohol win the fight in her brain and begged Xue to take off her clothes.

It was so odd, these feelings. These thoughts. She'd never had them before. Not with Steven. Definitely not with Chad. Yes, she'd slept with Steven, but what had that even been? Was it because he'd shown interest in her? Was it because she'd felt like that's what girls did with boys? Was it because she wasn't in her right mind?

Was she in her right mind now? The alcohol in her system said no, but her brain still demanded she ask Xue to accompany her to a dark, quiet corner where Mia could pin her to the wall and kiss her until the two of them could barely breathe.

Mia removed her hand from Xue's grip, but didn't pull away. Instead, she placed her palm firmly on Xue's thigh. At first, Xue stiffened, and Mia considered removing it. But when Xue shifted a centimeter closer to Mia, a small smile flickering onto her face, Mia decided against it.

The night came to an end in a blink of an eye. Haoran yawned, and Yize mentioned that he had work in the morning. Mia wanted to protest. She didn't want to get in a cab and say goodnight to Xue. Being away from Xue hurt.

"I'll walk Meilian home," Xue said. "I don't trust her to find the right apartment."

Mia pouted. "I'm not drunk."

"That's what all drunk people say." Yutong laughed and the others joined in.

Together, the group exited the bar. Haoran caught a cab with Yutong, and Yize insisted he could walk. The three disappeared into the night, leaving just Mia and Xue. Xue grinned at Mia. "Taxi, or on foot?"

"I feel like a walk."

"*Can* you walk? Or are you going to stumble home?"

With a roll of her eyes, Mia headed off toward home. Xue, laughing, caught up to her and together they walked in silence for about an hour. Mia resisted grabbing Xue's hand. Even though it was the middle of the night, there was no saying who was out and about. The last thing Mia wanted was to get in trouble. For people to *know* about the secrets thoughts in her head. The secret thoughts she'd let out just a little bit tonight.

When they finally got to Mia's apartment building, Mia stopped. They were out of the way of people. Not quite in the complex, but not in view of the street either. Xue faced her. Mia grinned and stepped closer. Xue reached out, tucking a strand of Mia's hair behind her ear.

"Why are you so adorable?" Xue asked.

All logical thought must have flown out the window, because Mia pressed against Xue, taking her hands. "I'm not the adorable one here."

A look crossed Xue's expression. She gripped Mia's hands and then looked at the glass door that blocked them from going inside. "You should go home. Sleep. It's late, and you're drunk."

Mia looked up at her through her eyelashes. What the hell was she doing? "You could always come up with me."

Xue chuckled. "Oh, Miss Meilian, you know I can't. Your aunt wouldn't approve, and I don't think it would be wise. I *really* shouldn't take advantage of you."

"You wouldn't be. I'd be thrilled to have you with me tonight."

Xue sucked in a breath and looked away. Her grip tightened

on Mia's hands. "You have no idea how tempting that is. But you'll wake up and regret all of this in the morning. I shouldn't add to your regrets."

"So, you don't want to kiss me?"

The forwardness caught them both off guard. Xue let go of Mia's hands and took a step back. Mia, realizing what she'd just said, lifted her hands to her mouth. How could she have asked that? What happened to just making a small hole? What happened to keeping all this a secret?

"I'm so sorry," Mia spluttered out. "I shouldn't have–"

Xue shushed her and grabbed her hands. She pulled them to her soft lips, leaving a gentle kiss. "It's okay. Just surprised me. Don't apologize. You're right. I do want to kiss you. You have no idea how badly I want to kiss you. How badly I've wanted to kiss you since the first moment I met you. When you stared at me, flustered, but furious. Every second around you has been torture. I want to kiss you. I do. But you seem confused. Drunk you might be ready, but until sober you is, I will continue to settle for torture."

Xue kissed the back of her hands once more. "Go inside. Get some sleep. We'll talk in the morning, okay?"

Mia could only nod, face burning.

Xue nudged her toward the building. Mia stumbled, watching her. She didn't want to go in until she saw Xue safely in a taxi, but she knew Xue wouldn't leave until Mia was inside. She smiled at her friend and then walked away, hands wringing together.

The entire elevator ride up, Mia banged her head against the wall. She was stupid. Stupid. Stupid. *Stupid.* How could she have blurted that out? How could she have shattered the barrier? Stupid!

At least she'd have all night to process it. She tried to be as quiet as possible when she entered the apartment so as not to wake her aunt, only to find Aunt Lilan was awake, sitting in the living room with a book and a single lamp on.

Mia had to collect herself. If she came in red, then Aunt Lilan might ask her what happened. She had to forget about the conversation. Forget about the hand kissing. Forget about it all. Just for a moment.

"You're up late," Mia said.

"I was waiting for you." Aunt Lilan closed her book and stood. "Do you want some water?"

Mia nodded.

There were already two glasses on the table, so Mia joined her aunt on the couch and grabbed one. The minute the water touched her tongue, she realized how thirsty she was, and she drank more than she should have in one go.

"I'm not used to you coming home drunk," Aunt Lilan said. "Is this going to be a regular thing?"

"No. Friends just wanted to relax after a stressful day. We had a lot of fun."

"With Xue?"

"And a few others."

"Hm." Aunt Lilan crossed her arms, watching Mia very closely. Mia squirmed under the scrutiny, not sure what Aunt Lilan was thinking. "Are you and Xue...more than friends?"

Mia's stomach dropped so far she was pretty sure she'd have to fish it off the floor. "What? No!"

"But you want to be."

They could *not* be having this conversation. "No. Of course not! That would be—"

"It's okay if you do." Aunt Lilan stood. "I know it won't be easy to be together, but Chengdu is pretty progressive about gay people and—"

"We're just friends." Mia couldn't tell if her flustered behavior was from the alcohol or the line of inquiry. "She doesn't want more. I don't want more. Friends. We're friends."

"Sure you are."

Mia squirmed under the scrutiny. If her face got any redder, she was certain it would turn into a beet. "I'm going to bed."

"Don't forget to drink your water." There was a teasing tone to her words and Mia all but ran into her room. A mistake, because it made her head spin, but she needed to get away from her aunt as quickly as possible.

Once she was behind closed doors, she let the events of the night wash over her. Being so close to Xue. Holding hands. Touching her thigh. Inviting her up.

And for a minute—or maybe more—Mia imagined that Xue had come up. That she wasn't alone in her room. She imagined Xue pinning her to the door, trailing feathered kisses down her neck. Pulling at Mia's shirt to reveal more skin. And as Mia took off her clothes, as her shirt fell, she pictured that it wasn't her hands stripping her, but Xue's. That Xue held her hips and kissed her, just as Mia wanted.

How had this happened? How had a singular person consumed so much of Mia's thoughts? It'd been five months. Only five months. And yet she couldn't imagine Xue ever leaving her life. Her intelligence. Her wit. Her cocky dominance. Her kindness. Her respect.

Her beauty.

Mia wanted all of it. In bed. With her. Right now.

Maybe she was confused. Maybe it was just the alcohol talking. Mia didn't know any of that. What she did know, and what she held onto with all of her might, was that Xue had taken her heart, and Mia didn't want it back.

Xue was late.

Xue was often late, but this time, Mia sat with trembling hands wrapped around a cup of coffee and stared at the door, waiting for her to show up. People stood in line at the counter, eyeing her table. Eyeing all the tables with only one person sitting at them. It was a busy day, and Mia had gotten lucky to sit at all. The warmth of the coffee shop walls was offset by the blasting air conditioning. Goosebumps rose on Mia's skin. She would have brushed them away, but she was afraid if she let go of her coffee her hands would shake so bad they might fall off.

There had been plenty of times in her life that Mia had made a fool of herself, but this had to be the worst. Every second of her conversation with Xue assaulted her. Sucker punches slamming into her face at high speeds. It was a disaster. Her entire life was a disaster and she didn't know what to do about it.

Her first friend in five years. Xue was the first person she'd trusted since Blair's death, and what did Mia do? Fall in love with her?

Okay, maybe it wasn't love. That was a little extreme. But there was definitely attraction there. Very intense attraction. Attraction that took over Mia's life and turned her into a bumbling idiot. She wasn't convinced it had been the alcohol. It had, maybe, pushed her to be more open about her feelings—and it had definitely forced her to shatter the barrier she'd put up to protect them both—but in the light of the morning, when she'd woken up alone, all she'd felt was incredible sadness that Xue wasn't there with her.

Now, Xue was late for their normal Wednesday afternoon meetup, and Mia wondered if it was because of what she'd said the night before.

She was going to give it another five minutes. If Xue didn't show up, then Mia was going to take off and hide in her room for a week to try and get over the embarrassment. She was a menace. She couldn't be let out in public, much less around Xue.

After three minutes passed with Mia sitting there with shaking hands and a turning stomach, the door opened. Xue walked in, head held high, and a smile on her face.

The world stopped existing. Mia's entire focus honed in on Xue. Her bright eyes. Her perfect hair. Her smooth skin. The skip in her step. When Xue spotted Mia, her smile grew and she rushed over to Mia's table.

Mia tensed. What was with the excitement?

"Take the weekend off," Xue said, speaking almost too fast to understand.

"Excuse me?" Mia asked.

Xue slid into the chair across from Mia and leaned over the table. "Take the weekend off. We're going on a trip."

A trip? The two of them? "What are you talking about?"

"Haoran texted me this morning asking if I'd be up for a trip out of Chengdu. Get away from the city for a bit. She wants to go to Mt. Emei. It's not the most fantastic destination in the world, but I think it would be fun!"

Mia had heard of Mt. Emei. Something about a temple and monkeys. While she really didn't have an interest in seeing more monkeys, the way Xue's eyes lit up as she rambled on about plans—taking Yutong's car and spending two nights at a hotel up there—incited excitement in Mia. They'd talked a lot about travel, but timing and finances had never been right.

"We'll pick you up tomorrow," Xue said.

"Sounds good." Mia loved that Xue assumed she'd be eager to join them. There was no question. Just a demand. No, not a demand. An expectation. Mia was part of Xue's life. Of course Mia would go with.

"All right. I'm going to get tea. Call your work and then I'll go over the full itinerary with you when I get back." Xue hopped up from her seat and darted to the counter.

All the while, Mia watched her go with an uncontainable smile. It was the first time in so long that she felt like she was part of something bigger than herself. Not huge. This wasn't the war with the Iravata, or the magical world. But it wasn't her alone. These past five months, she'd felt welcome in Xue's circle, but never as part of the core group.

In that moment, watching Xue wait to order her tea, Mia *was* part of the core. She wasn't an outsider that they put up with because they found her amusing. She was one with the group. Somehow, after years of pain and suffering, Mia was finding a place to be. To exist without hatred for herself. They were all on equal footing. No one had magic. There were no huge secrets. Nothing life changing. Nothing life *threatening*.

She'd finally gotten to the place in her life where maybe, just maybe, she could move on.

Chapter Twenty-Nine

Crisp.

Mia hadn't tasted crisp air in so long that it caught her off guard when they got out of Yutong's car. Xue called out to her to grab her bag, but Mia couldn't move. She stared up at the trees, expanding her lungs with the deepest breath she'd taken in years.

The foliage was different, and yet she was back in Colorado, hiking with Blair, Cody, and Derek. They were laughing, mostly at Derek for his lack of fitness. Mia had been strong back then. She'd held her head high and faced every challenge with confidence, whether it be an opponent in basketball, bullies, or a difficult test.

When had that changed? When had she become a coward, running from everything? Was it when she'd almost lost herself to Steven and Kathleen? Was it after Jae had taken her? Was it earlier than either of those things? Was it the night in the museum when *The Queen* broke and Derek fell ill?

Or, maybe all of her strength had been a face she'd put on to deal with the struggles in her life. From her parents almost divorcing to Blair's death. Had she ever been strong, or had she just wished she was?

"You okay?" Xue stood next to her. Mia looked up at the only person who had managed to break through. It'd been such luck that Mia had run into her that day. That the two had connected so deeply and so suddenly. That Mia had been at the right place at the right time to meet someone as amazing as Xue.

Mia nodded. "Just reminded of where I grew up."

Green surrounded them. Green and brown. Trees rose high up into the air, vines crawling up their trunks, while the sky hung above them, cloudless and crystal blue. Even the hotel was brown. Wooden walls. From where they stood, Mia noticed an outdoor fire pit, which she hoped they could commandeer for the night. It was like being at a summer camp, except they were adults and camp counselors weren't there to harass them to do arts and crafts. Not that Mia had ever attended summer camp, but she'd heard about them from kids at school.

"Wait, you grew up in a forest?" Haoran asked. She handed over Mia's bag, and Mia took it with a nod.

"Forests and mountains. Colorado is famous for both."

"Colorado?" Haoran asked. "Where's that?"

"America," Mia said.

"Well, duh. But *where* in America?"

"Oh." Mia fluttered her hands to try and explain. "I dunno. Center? It's a big rectangle near no oceans. Just a lot of mountains and rivers."

Yutong wrapped his arm around Mia's shoulder, hanging off her. "Sounds nice. You must have hiked a lot as a kid."

Mia laughed and shrugged her shoulders to get him off. "Almost every day. There was a hiking path in the mountains, so I'd run that every morning in the summer." Or, she had before the magic.

The others laughed, but Xue remained silent, watching Mia with her eyes flickering to Yutong every few seconds. Mia tilted her head to ask what was wrong, but Xue didn't give any signal back. Instead, she grabbed her bag and headed into the hotel after their friends.

That wasn't concerning at all. Mia followed, running to catch up. Unfortunately, Xue made it to reception before Mia could catch her and pull her aside, and from there the whirlwind started. Rooms were divided up. Haoran had demanded her own room during planning, leaving Yutong and Yize in one and Xue and Mia in the third. Even though Mia had prepared herself for this mentally, when they actually entered the room, just her and Xue, her heart thudded so loudly she was certain Xue could hear it.

Xue claimed the bed closest to the door, still quiet, so Mia decided she was going to ask what was wrong as soon as she put her stuff down. But she didn't get a chance. The moment her bag was on her bed, Xue grabbed her wrist and yanked her toward the door.

And like that, the funk was gone. "Let's go! We have so much to see!"

Mia barely had time to process what was going on before Xue had her out the door, closing it not super gently.

"Xue," Mia called out, wanting to tell her to wait a minute, but Xue waited for nothing.

They made it to the stairs of the temple and Xue led Mia toward a building where the gondola rose from.

"I'm so not climbing," Xue said. "Come on, let's ride up. The others will meet us there."

When had they decided that?

"Wait," Mia said, head spinning. "What if the others–"

"They want to take the stairs. I want to save hiking for tomorrow with the monkeys. Let's go, let's go!"

Mia really couldn't fight her. She wanted to, if only to figure out what the hell was going on. Even as Xue pushed herself toward the ticket line and bought two tickets for them, Mia was in too much shock to understand what was going through her head. Then, without a word, Xue gestured for Mia to follow her.

It wasn't super busy, so the two of them managed to get in a gondola by themselves. Mia sat on the far seat. Xue climbed in after her. And then they were off. Just the two of them in an enclosed space, with Xue staring out the window and not at Mia.

Finally, a moment alone. Where Xue couldn't escape from Mia's inquiry. "Are you okay?"

Xue stiffened, and then smiled. "Of course I'm okay. Why wouldn't I be okay?"

"I don't know. But you seem tense."

"Not tense."

Xue didn't lie to Mia. Normally, Xue was an open book. She talked about the things going on in her life with such candor that it made Mia jealous. Because Mia couldn't be candid about her life. There were so many things that she couldn't bring Xue into for Xue's safety. It wouldn't be fair of Mia to break Xue's perception of reality the way that Steven had broken hers.

Mia looked down at her lap. She didn't get why Xue was lying to her. Had Mia done something?

"Okay, now you look sad." Xue shifted, rocking the gondola, and sat next to Mia. "What's wrong?"

She didn't want to lie to Xue anymore.

Instead, she shook her head and glanced out the window. At the forests. Marveling at their beauty. Caught between the present and the past.

An arm snaked around her waist, and she jumped.

"You don't have to talk about it, if you don't want," Xue said. "Whatever is going through your head right now. But I'm here. Whenever. Always. I'm here for you."

Xue held Mia's gaze with such intensity that Mia couldn't stop the blush rising to her cheeks. Without thinking, she reached up and placed a hand on Xue's face.

"Are you okay?" she asked again, this time in a softer voice.

Xue closed her eyes and leaned into Mia's touch. "I'm okay. Just...dealing with a lot of weird emotions right now. It's hard to explain, so I'd better not try."

What did that mean? Mia tried to ask her, but Xue pulled away and moved back to the other side of the gondola, and the chatting began. It wasn't anything important. Mia wasn't certain she'd even remember the conversation later. What she would remember was Xue. The curve of her face. Her long lashes. The way her hair had grown—though she'd talked about getting it cut soon—and how her dark roots were showing. Mia would remember the way her thin, yet firm, frame was turned away as if she was embarrassed about *something*. She wouldn't look Mia in the eye.

Even though Mia couldn't take her eyes off her.

Eventually, the gondola slowed and the doors opened. Mia followed Xue out and the brisk air hit Mia like a brick. She breathed it in and more memories rushed her. Hiking in the woods with Blair and Cody. Learning to use a compass for the first time. Reading the signs of the forests. How to use the sun to find her way home. She remembered learning about animals. Plants. She recalled, all too well, the struggles of adjusting to her new life.

Before long, Xue wasn't in her mind. At least, not in the forefront. Before long, Mia was transported back to her teenage years that she'd tried to forget. Moments with Blair that she'd pushed to the side. Thoughts she'd tried to pretend weren't there for five long years. Guilt. Frustration. Anger. They all flooded her as she continued to walk with Xue. Xue talked the whole time, but Mia remained quiet. And in that moment, she *felt* all the things she hadn't been letting herself feel.

They arrived at the top long before Xue's friends, so the two of them climbed the last stairs and entered the temple at the top of the mountain. The temple was filled with people, but it was quiet.

All the voices were hushed. It was beautiful. Peaceful. Xue pulled at Mia's arm toward a shop to buy some incense. At some point, she'd gone quiet. When had that happened? How far had Mia retreated into herself?

"Here," Xue said after buying a pack of incense, "light this."

Mia took it, letting her fingers brush against Xue's hand. This was wrong. So wrong. There was so much she'd been running from. Even being friends with Xue had been her running. Not because Xue was bad for her, but because Mia couldn't tell her anything. Wouldn't tell her anything.

Still, Mia let her fingers brush against Xue's hand and smiled at the beautiful woman standing before her. Xue's eyes widened, but she said nothing while Mia went to the altar to light her incense and stick it in the sand. Smoke trickled from the tip, rising high into the air where it mixed with the smoke of other people's prayers.

She stared at it, taking a deep breath.

Xue appeared next to her. Mia didn't look at her, but she could feel Xue's eyes on her. Questioning. It seemed that both of them were going to act out of character today. Xue nudged her arm. "I heard there's a place to make wishes here. You want to?"

"I'm okay," Mia said. "But you should make a wish."

They wandered through the temple, and Mia took note of all the little elephant statues. The muted colors. The trees in full bloom. The little stream that ran under bridges. The main part of the temple. But Xue led her away from all of that to a little hut. She bought a wooden slab and grabbed a pen before she crouched and wrote something in the messy scrawl she called her handwriting.

Part of the reason Mia had said no was because she wasn't amazing at handwriting in Chinese, but she also had nothing to wish for. Blair couldn't come back. She wasn't sure if she wanted to face Cody ever again. She talked to Derek and her parents. And now she had friends. Everything else seemed superficial. Wishing for a better job, for more free time, for her own apartment, were all such small things compared to being with the people in her life.

Mia waited in silence until Xue stood and grinned at Mia.

"What did you wish for?" Mia asked.

"It's a secret."

"You don't keep secrets."

"I keep this one." Xue poked her cheek before heading over to the wall to tie her wooden slab to it. Mia placed a hand on her cheek, a small smile making it to her face. Xue was something else. Really, something else.

After a while, Xue's friends found them, sweaty and out of breath. Mia tried her best to smile, but more memories bombarded her. Memories of her and her friends. Of all the things she had lost. It was impossible to let go. She replayed the fight with Blair over and over in her head.

And as they explored the temple, Mia felt herself drifting further and further away, caught in the memories, stuck in the past, unable to escape.

They didn't do much else in the mountain on the first day. They retreated back to the hotel, all of them exhausted. This time, all of them took the stairs, and Xue kept looking back at Mia with a worried expression on her face. Mia tried to reassure her without words, but it was obvious she was failing.

They got dinner. Everyone chatted and laughed, talking about something stupid Yutong had done in the temple. But Mia wasn't paying attention. She couldn't bring herself back from the past. Maybe she should have made a wish. Maybe she should have wished to live in the now for the rest of her life. To never have to go back to the parts of her life she wanted more than anything to forget.

Once night fell, they gathered around the fire, chatting and laughing. No one questioned Mia's quiet. They all noticed, and sometimes they'd try and rope her into the conversation. She was good for a few lines before she went quiet again. It must have been obvious that Mia needed a minute to not be a person, because, while they didn't make her feel excluded, they also just let her exist in her memories.

Exist in a different time. A different place. A different mountain.

Until the fire died down and they all retreated to their rooms. Mia went to her bed and wasn't aware that Xue hadn't done the same until she turned back around. Xue stood with her back against the door, eyeing Mia closely.

"What's going on? Do you need to talk?"

Mia did need to talk. But she couldn't. She couldn't bring Xue into this. Not while they were friends. "I'm okay. Just been thinking a lot today. This place reminds me of Willow Creek. Which reminds me of Blair."

Sorrow crossed Xue's expression. She pushed away from the door, and before Mia knew what was going on, Xue had her in a tight hug. Mia's eyes widened as Xue's arms tensed around her.

"I'm sorry," she said. "I can't imagine how hard all of this has been for you."

Mia blinked back tears. She couldn't cry in front of Xue. Not about Blair, or Cody, or Derek, or the life she used to live.

When Xue pulled away, she held Mia at arm's length and smiled. Mia smiled back, though there was no heart in it. All of her thoughts circled around her pain and trauma, and she couldn't help but think: how could I have let myself become happy?

Xue didn't say another word. She collected her clothes and jumped into the bathroom to shower. And once Mia was alone, she changed into her pajamas, crawled into bed, and listened to the water splash against the ground. Maybe it would help her sleep.

Sleep wouldn't come.

When Xue got out of the shower, Mia didn't say a word. Xue paused at the edge of her bed for a long moment, but said nothing as well. The lights went out.

Still, sleep wouldn't come.

Instead, the tears did. She'd been holding them in all day, trying not to let the memories get the best of her, but they had. They plagued her mind, making it impossible for her to sleep. Impossible for her to do anything but hold a hand over her mouth so she wouldn't sob and wake Xue.

It was a lot, being here. It was a lot letting herself remember everything about Blair and their friendship. All the good things. All the bad things. All the fun times and all of the hurt that the two had caused each other. It tore at her heart, making the tears fall faster. She'd cried over Blair so much in the first year that the idea of crying more made her want to scream. But maybe she needed to cry. Maybe she wasn't done grieving her best friend.

There was rustling from the other bed, and Mia froze. Had she woken Xue?

When there was pressure on the edge of the bed, Mia turned to apologize for crying and waking her up. But Xue merely lifted the covers and said, "Move over."

Mia, startled, did. Xue climbed into bed with her.

"What are you doing?" Mia asked in a hoarse voice.

Xue didn't answer with words. Instead she slipped one arm under Mia's neck and wrapped the other around her body, pulling the two together so Mia was nestled against her.

"It's okay," Xue said, stroking Mia's back. "You can cry."

In her shock, the tears had stopped, but with Xue's assurance, they started up again with a vengeance. Mia's hand gripped Xue's shirt and she pressed her face against her neck, letting the tears flow without abandon. It was comforting and gentle. Xue stroked her back, whispering to her that it was okay, and that she would be okay.

Mia continued to cry until the tears dried up on their own, but she didn't let go of Xue, and Xue kept a hold on her. She was so soft. Her arms lithe and strong.

Xue reminded Mia of Blair, in a way. Always acting confident. Always with a soft side that she rarely showed. Maybe that's why Mia had clung to her so strongly. Maybe it wasn't a romantic attraction. Maybe it wasn't sexual.

Except, when Xue pulled away and wiped a tear off Mia's face, the electricity between them was undeniable.

"You should have told me you needed to cry," Xue muttered, finger stroking Mia's cheek. "I would have held you much sooner."

"I didn't want to be a burden," Mia whispered back.

Xue leaned in and pressed a kiss to Mia's forehead. Mia closed her eyes, relishing at the feel of her lips. They were soft and gentle. Just like Xue.

"You are never a burden, Miss Meilian."

Mia closed her eyes and pressed against Xue. Xue's arms tightened around Mia's body. She didn't push anything. She didn't kiss Mia, or shush her. It wasn't like that night with Cody. There was nothing secret about this moment. It was just the two of them, cuddled together in Mia's bed. And before long, the memories disappeared, replaced instead with moments of dozing.

And then, eventually, the darkness of sleep.

Mia woke to someone shaking her. She shifted, pulling the blankets tighter around her. Her eyelids, heavy with exhaustion, refused to open. The shaking got harder. It couldn't be Intira. She didn't shake Mia to wake her up. Derek did sometimes, but he was more the kind to wait for her. Maybe it was Blair?

No, it couldn't be Blair. Blair was dead.

Mia forced her eyes open. The room was mostly dark, but a lamp across the room lit it just enough that Mia could make out more than shapes. A figure crouched by the bed, arm the source of all the shaking.

"Wha?" Mia blinked a few times, and Xue came into view. She was dressed, hair pulled back into the world's smallest ponytail, and she had a gleam in her eyes.

Mia had been having a dream. One of the past. Of her hanging out with Blair when the two of them didn't have a care in the world. Tenth grade. Winter break. Snow piled up in the backyard. A fire roaring in the fireplace. Cups of hot chocolate in their hands with blankets wrapped around their shoulders.

"You know, I think you're the best friend I'm ever going to have," Blair had said.

Mia had giggled. *"Same."*

"Even though you're Miss Popular now?"

"I'm not popular." Mia had rolled her eyes. *"They're nice to me, but it's like they aren't real. When we get out of here, I'll lose contact with all of them. But not you."*

"Really?" There'd been hope in Blair's voice. *"Not me?"*

"Not you." She'd thought for a moment. *"Or Cody."*

Blair had scowled. *"All right, fine. Guess I can't compete with that. Let's try and go to the same college. It'll be cool to escape all of this."*

"Seriously." Mia hadn't understood the duality of that statement. *"Thank you."*

"For what?"

"Being my best friend."

"Hey, come with me." It wasn't Blair's voice, but Xue's. Xue. Xue Huang. She came into focus again, grinning.

Mia groaned. "Later. I'm tired."

"It won't be cool later."

What wouldn't be cool after another hour of sleep? Her eyes must have closed again, because Xue shook her once more and they shot open.

"Get dressed."

Before Mia could process what was going on, she had clothes shoved in her face. She sat up, holding the bundle of fabric.

"What's going on?"

"Get dressed!" Xue grabbed Mia's arm and pulled her out of bed.

Grumbling, Mia did as she was told. Xue all but pushed her to the bathroom and then shut the door to give her some privacy. To let her wake up and dress. Mia would have taken her sweet time, but she'd caught Xue's urgency and got ready as quickly as she could. Her hair was a mess. Her eyes a little swollen. She splashed her face with water and then ran her wet fingers through her hair to try and tame it. To make herself look presentable.

Then she was out of the bathroom. The moment Xue saw her, she hopped up from her bed and rushed over to Mia. She grabbed Mia's hand and led her to the door.

"Where are we going?" Mia asked, much more awake now.

"Mt. Emei has an amazing sunrise."

Sunrise? The sun hadn't risen yet? Mia groaned, but didn't complain. Even when Xue told her it was a thirty minute hike. Even when she was out of breath. She tried to take her mind off her protesting legs, but all she could think about was the stairs in front of her. And then, of her past. She used to be so active. She'd taken care of her body, making sure to eat healthily and to run every morning. Sports had kept her sane. Even before Willow Creek. When her parents were fighting all the time. When her grandfather favored Derek. When the girls at school poked fun of her. When the teachers ignored her.

She hadn't realized how much she'd given up on herself until this moment. It wasn't just all the things that brought her joy. She had given up on *herself*. Why should she be happy when Blair was dead? Why should she eat well when she'd hurt Cody? Why should she even exist if all she did was cause pain?

How long had she had those thoughts? Why hadn't she recognized it for what it was? Why had she pretended that all of these years weren't her punishing herself for things out of her control?

It wasn't her fault. Blair's death. She hadn't done anything except exist and fight for herself. For her happiness.

And it was okay.

It was okay to be happy.

When they got to the top of the mountain, Mia realized they weren't the only ones up there. She tensed, not wanting to be around other people, but Xue took her hand and led her to a secluded place. A little cliff that overlooked the mountain. The expanse of trees. The moon hung above them, but on the other side of the horizon, pink and orange light reached for the sky.

"I've always wanted to come here," Xue said. "Ever since I first learned about it in school. Some kid did a presentation on it, and I knew that it was my destiny to visit someday. This was before my parents' disappointment started, so I begged them to take me. But money was tight and things were rough for my dad's business. They didn't have time. I tried to understand, but it's hard to do that when you're a kid, you know?"

Mia nodded. She did know.

Xue looked at her knees. "Did you know that today's my birthday?"

No, she had not known that. "Why didn't you tell me?"

"Didn't want to make this trip about me." Xue breathed in.

"Guess I am now. But I wasn't going to tell you. Not this year, anyway. My birthday is always rough."

"Oh."

"I should have seen it coming. When my parents kicked me out. Just hadn't expected it to happen on my eighteenth birthday." She let out a stark laugh and Mia didn't know what to say. "Things had been tense. They wanted me to get married soon. Go to school, find a man, and settle down. They were traditional that way. When they introduced me to a matchmaker, I knew it was time to tell them that I'd never seen boys that way. But girls?"

Xue threw her head back and breathed in. "They didn't take it well. They thought they could fix me. That I'd grow out of it. Well, it's eight years later and I'm no different. At least, not in that way."

The sun came up over the horizon and its light caught Xue's face. Mia marveled at the way Xue's skin glowed. How her hair looked like a flutter of feathers. She was beautiful. The most beautiful person Mia had ever seen in her entire life.

"But they still won't talk to me," Xue said. "I don't think they ever will again."

How could anyone not want to talk to Xue? Mia reached out and took her hand. "Fuck them."

Xue looked down, eyes soft.

"It's their loss." Mia gripped Xue's hand tighter. "They don't get to know what an amazing person you are. They don't get to be part of your life, and that sucks for them. If they can't love you for who you are, then they don't even deserve to call themselves your parents. Who cares that you like women? Who *cares*."

Mia cared. Because, as it turned out, Mia liked women too. In fact, she liked one woman very much.

There was a new expression on Xue's face. It wasn't one Mia could place, but one that she wanted to stare at for the rest of her life.

"Do you know why I call myself 'snow'?" Xue asked.

Mia shook her head.

"It's not the name my parents gave me. I abandoned that name a long time ago. It's a name I decided fit me. Snow is cold. Snow covers everything alive. But it is the bringer of life as well. I wanted to give myself a fresh start. Once I got back on my feet and learned how to live. I've never seen it in person, but to me, there is nothing quite like fresh snow.

"I know it was strange of me to give you my number. When I did it, I wondered if I'd done the right thing. But you looked like you needed to live. And I thought to myself, 'who better to help than someone who has lost herself before? Who better than snow.' Maybe it was pretentious of me, but I felt called to you. Not just because you're the most beautiful person I've ever laid eyes on, but because through that beauty is sadness. I wanted to see you smile."

Xue pulled her hand away from Mia's and cupped her cheek. "I didn't realize how important you would become to me. I didn't realize how much I would love hearing about your life and seeing your smile. How much I'd want to protect you from all the pains in the world. How much I want to be there for you."

Her fingers trailed to Mia's chin and lifted it just slightly. Mia's eyes fluttered closed. Xue leaned in.

"You are beautiful, Miss Meilian," Xue whispered. "Please, be okay with me."

When their lips touched, Mia lost herself. She had no idea that this was what it was supposed to feel like when someone kissed her. It wasn't supposed to be terrifying. It wasn't supposed to be confusing. When Xue kissed her, she felt like she was floating on the clouds in the sky, hovering between the sun and the moon. She felt like she'd been stuck in another dimension for her entire life and had finally found her way home. Electricity shot down to the tips of her fingers, to the tips of her toes.

It must have lasted for only a moment, but it was the most exhilarating moment of Mia's life.

When Xue pulled away, Mia's eyes fluttered open and she couldn't look away from Xue's loving gaze. She wanted to be with Xue. She was one hundred percent on board with Xue. Every inch of Xue was perfect, as far as Mia was concerned. A woman who was worth living for.

But the perfect moment shattered. Because the sun rose higher into the sky and the moon slowly vanished with the light. Because before her lay the mountains and the forests and millions of memories over thousands of days. Because while she was okay with Xue, Xue couldn't be okay with Mia until she knew. Until the lies stopped. Until the secrets came out.

"I have something to tell you," Mia said.

Xue started and pulled back. "Oh. You...you don't like me."

How the hell...? Mia shook her head. "No! No, I do. I like you. It's something else."

Xue's brow furrowed. "What is it?"

"You have to promise not to tell anyone. Not our friends. Not my aunt. Not anyone."

"Okay." Xue didn't hesitate. Guilt wracked Mia. She might not be okay. All of this might fall apart.

She had to do it. Mia sucked in a breath, and then she told Xue everything.

Chapter Thirty

Xue was quiet while Mia spoke. She was quiet when Mia finished. She was quiet as the sun rose higher into the sky. As the voices of other people indicated the end of nature's show. Mia sat with her hands in her lap, staring at them. She hadn't been able to look at Xue the entire time, too afraid of the changes in her expression as Mia revealed her truths. This was the last thing Mia wanted to do, but if Xue was going to kiss her, then she deserved to know. She deserved to know everything because no matter how much Mia wanted to escape from the world of magic, she was intrinsically linked to it.

Derek linked her to it.

Five minutes passed. Mia squirmed. Why wasn't Xue saying anything? Was she angry?

"I know it's a lot," Mia said. "It's okay if you don't believe me. It sounds crazy. Hearing myself talk, it sounds crazy. But I promise–"

Xue held up a hand. "I believe you. There's no reason why you'd lie about any of this. I'm sorry. I'm trying to process."

Mia nodded. "It took me a long time too."

Xue breathed out, staring out at the dawn. "It's hard to believe, but at the same time, it makes so much sense. I always knew you were hiding something from me. I thought it might be family drama. Like maybe you didn't get along with your parents or your brother. I knew there had to be a reason why you always looked so sad. So broken. But I never imagined this." She placed her face in her hands. "My head hurts."

Mia reached out to rub Xue's back, but hesitated, then pulled her hand back to her lap. What if Xue didn't want Mia to touch her? What if she didn't want to kiss Mia again? What if she found Mia to be ugly? How could she still find Mia beautiful after learning all these horrible things?

It hurt, knowing that it was a possibility, but Mia couldn't keep her in the dark any longer. And if Xue did hate Mia now, then Mia would respect that. Even if it would destroy her.

"I'm sorry." Mia blinked back tears. "I shouldn't have told you."

"I'm glad you did." Xue faced her, took her hand, and gripped it so tight Mia flinched. "It's a lot to take in. And I'll admit that I'm a little scared of the future now. There's magic. Actual magic. And immortals. And reincarnations. I thought those were all legends. Stories."

"I wish they were."

"Me too." Xue breathed in, then out. "But they aren't. They're your life, and I'm glad you told me. I want to know you, Meilian. Everything about you. It just hurts."

"That I didn't tell you before?"

"That you've been through so much pain." She pulled Mia's hand toward her and placed it on her thumping heart. "I hate that you're looking at me right now like I'm going to disown you."

"I'm sorry."

"You don't need to apologize. But I'm not my parents. I'm not going to cast you aside because of something you can't control."

A tear dripped down Mia's cheek. Xue reached up and brushed

it away.

"You're beautiful, Miss Meilian. Nothing you say will ever change that."

Mia wasn't even aware that she was going to kiss Xue until it was happening. She threw her arms around Xue's neck and held her close, desperate for the intimacy that she'd denied herself for so long.

Xue was the one who was beautiful. Xue deserved the entire world.

When Xue pulled away, breathless, she smiled at Mia, then clambered to her feet. Holding out a hand for Mia to take, she said, "There's still time before the others wake."

She didn't need to say anything else. Mia hopped to her feet and the two hurried down the mountain. They snuck past the other rooms to their own, and the minute Mia closed the door, Xue had her pinned to it. Fire exploded through Mia's body. A tingle in her gut—one she'd only felt when close to Xue—encouraged her to kiss Xue with the utmost passion.

Somehow, through all the kissing and the laughing, Mia found herself on Xue's bed with Xue hovering over her and kissing down her neck. Mia couldn't think of anything but Xue's lips. Her body. Her hot breath on chilled skin. But through all the fire, and through the lust that consumed her, Mia realized there was one emotion settling deep in her heart: peace. Pure, sweet, welcome peace.

Friday passed. Haoran asked if they were a couple now, and Xue stuck her tongue out at her friend. Yize laughed. Yutong told them to be careful or the monkeys would steal their love for each other. Mia had flipped him off for that, eliciting more laughter from everyone.

And at night, they didn't even pretend like they weren't going to end up in the same bed. Mia thought of nothing but Xue kissing her. Of nestling so close to her girlfriend that it was like they'd become one.

The night ended too soon. Then another full day of walking around, though there wasn't much they hadn't seen. They got food, and as evening came, they headed back to the city. As the mountains faded away, Mia allowed herself to breathe. To process. To let go of her grief. She knew it would be back, and probably at the most inopportune time, but for now, she was ready to leave it behind her in the mountains.

Her phone, having lost service in the mountains, exploded with texts and missed calls. She'd told her parents and her aunt where she was going, but they kept bugging her to send them pictures. Mia wondered what pictures she *could* send them. There were a lot of her and Xue from the second and third day, but none of the temple. She'd have to bug Haoran for some later.

One text, however, wasn't asking her for pictures. It wasn't Intira telling her to watch out for monkeys. It wasn't from Aunt Lilan asking her what time she would be home. It was from Derek.

They were well into the city and the car had fallen silent. Yize was asleep, Haoran reading a book, and Xue had her eyes closed, gripping Mia's hand.

She didn't want to look at the text from Derek. She wanted to continue on in her bubble. Her happy weekend bubble. But part of moving on was forgiving him and allowing him back in her life.

She opened the text.

<<I know I haven't been the best brother to you. I kept secrets, I pulled you into this life, and I do nothing but bring you pain, even after all these years. But I wanted you to know that I could not have asked for a better sister. You took care of me when you shouldn't

have had to, and I know that you're stronger than I ever was. I love you. Just remember that.>>

What was with that message? Mia tried to think of a reply, but nothing came to her. It was early in the morning in Colorado. She could call him. But she didn't want to speak English in front of her friends, her Thai was awful, and she didn't want them to know what her conversation entailed. Instead, she closed the message.

She'd call him when she got home.

When Yutong pulled up to Mia's apartment complex, she prepared to get out alone, only to find Xue coming after her.

"Aren't you two sick of each other yet?" Yutong asked.

"Nope." Xue grinned at him. "Deal with it and hold onto my luggage. I'll get it later."

Mia giggled and the two headed out of the car. They fished Mia's luggage out of the car and then waved goodbye to the other three. Yize was still asleep, but Haoran waved with jubilance. Mia couldn't help but laugh. They were good people.

The night air was cool. A nice reprieve from Yutong's air conditonless car. Mia stretched her arms over her head and let out a heavy sigh.

"I'm exhausted," she said.

"Same."

"Why did you get out, then?" Mia asked.

Xue shrugged. "Wanted to say goodnight to you."

"You could have done that in the car."

Xue stepped forward and placed a hand on Mia's waist. This late at night there were no stragglers in the area. It was just them. "Not in the way I want."

Mia tilted her head back and Xue kissed her so lightly. "You absolutely could have done that in the car."

"You know," Xue said, "I could always come up for a bit."

Mia's eyes widened, glee overcoming her. "You would?"

"Might need to. I'm struggling to let you go."

Another laugh and Mia leaned up to kiss her girlfriend. This time, when she pulled away, she wrapped her arms around Xue's neck and hugged her tight. It would be hard to explain this to Aunt Lilan. Or maybe not that hard. But annoying. Confusing. She was expecting an, "I knew it" from her aunt, and she didn't want to deal with it.

Of course, there were worse things to have to deal with.

But then her entire body went cold. Her eyes widened. Because someone stood not far away from them. Immediately she pushed herself off Xue. She couldn't make out the figure, but he had his hands shoved into deep pockets. Was he going to yell at them? To harass them?

He stepped into the light.

Mia gasped. "Cody?"

Xue frowned. "What?"

"That's Cody!" The words came out in English. How could they not? It was Cody! He looked different. She almost didn't recognize him. He styled his hair differently, and he'd grown. His clothes were a little small for him, but they didn't *not* fit, and the scowl on his face looked right at home.

Still, it was him. The boy who had sat with her under the slides. Her best friend.

"Cody!" She couldn't explain the glee she felt at seeing him. She'd imagined this moment more than she liked to admit, and every time she'd felt nothing but guilt, regret, and anger. But now there was none of that. Just excitement that he was there.

She pushed past Xue. Cody halted, then his eyes widened as she closed the gap between them and hugged him.

"What are you doing here?" Mia asked. The English felt foreign on her tongue. She was also very aware of her accent. She didn't care.

"It's a long story." Cody's voice was cold, and Mia retreated. Was he still angry with her for what happened five years ago? If so, why was he here? Or maybe it was something else.

He saw me and Xue kissing.

Her face heated. Oh god.

He jerked his head toward Xue. "I can't explain with her here."

Magic. It had to do with magic. "It's okay. She doesn't speak English. Besides, she knows."

"She knows?"

Mia frowned at Cody's sharp voice. "Yes. What are you doing here? I haven't seen you in five years."

"And whose fault is that?" He hesitated, then sighed. "No. It's… whatever. That's not what I'm here for. It's about Derek."

His text message. "What did he do?"

"Something stupid." Cody ran a hand through his hair, letting out a heavy sigh. "He went after Blair in the Realm of Death."

Of course he did. He couldn't let go. "Is he going to try and bring her back to life? Is that possible?"

"No. But she's not dead."

"I saw her—"

"You saw Death take her." Cody reached into his pocket and pulled out a piece of golden paper. In beautiful handwriting were three lines, two of which were crossed off.

~~Fix Leo~~

~~Save your mother~~

Bring Mia home

"What is this?" Mia asked.

"A gift from Death." Cody's bitterness surprised her. He didn't used to be bitter.

"What are you talking about?"

"Death came to visit me after Derek left. Been working my ass off to get this list complete, and you're on it. I'm supposed to bring you home."

But she *was* home. "I don't understand."

"If you don't come back to America with me…," he said, eyeing Xue. Mia glanced behind her. Xue hadn't moved, but she'd crossed her arms and glared at Cody. "If you don't come back with me, Derek and Blair are going to be stuck in the Realm of Death for the rest of their lives. And I'm guessing those lives won't last much longer. You can come back here as soon as they're safe."

Blair was alive. Cody was telling her this. Not Derek. Cody believed it. Cody had never believed it before. After all of these years, after all of that healing, letting go, Blair wasn't *dead*.

Mia's chest tightened. She placed a hand on it, trying to breathe down a panic attack. "I'll be right back," she said. It probably wasn't smart to go back to America. There was no saying what danger lay ahead. But she couldn't abandon her brother. And if there really was a chance that Blair was alive, then she had to do everything she could to help.

When she reached Xue, Xue placed a hand on her cheek. "What's going on? That's the boy…your friend."

"Yeah. It's hard to explain. But apparently my brother is in trouble."

She stared down at the list which shook in her fist.

"I have to go back to America for a little bit," Mia said. "But I'll be back. Can you take my stuff to your apartment? I'll text my aunt and tell her I'm busy for a few more days. It'll be okay. It'll be okay." She wasn't sure who she was trying to convince. She looked up at Xue, eyes wide. "Will you wait for me?"

She'd never wanted someone to wait for her before.

Xue glanced over Mia's shoulder, and then lifted her chin to press a gentle kiss to her lips. "I'll wait forever if I have to."

Mia didn't want to leave. She wanted to grab Xue's shoulders and kiss her until she was weak in the knees. She wanted to drag her inside and make sure she didn't wait any longer than necessary. But she had to go. She had to go to America and save her idiot brother's life.

And Blair's.

"I love you," Xue whispered in English.

Mia's eyes widened, but then she smiled and kissed Xue back. "I love you too."

"Come back soon."

"I will."

They kissed once more before Mia pulled away. Her smile faded the minute she faced Cody. He looked like he was about to murder someone. It'd been five years. She would have thought he'd get over her by now, but apparently she'd misjudged, and that hurt. She didn't want him to think of her in that way. She never had, and would continue to never want to.

But it wasn't her emotions. It wasn't her heart. She knew now how consuming love could be. She just hoped that Cody could find someone who made him feel the way that Xue made her feel.

"Well?" she said. "Are we going or what?"

Cody nodded and held out a hand. She took it, and the last thing she saw before whiteness encased them both was Xue's wide eyes staring at her.

The chess board was set. The players in their places. Everything was going according to his plan. It would not be long now before his pieces clashed and the scheme went off. But it had to go off without a hitch. It had to go according to plan. If it did not, then there would be complications he could not foresee. If he was not careful, and if his players surprised him, then there would be issues with how he planned to end it all.

And he did plan to end it all.

The End

Chapter Thirty-One

The minute the white light receded, Derek collapsed to his knees. He never thought he'd be so happy to see a hardwood floor—especially not one covered in a chalk ritualistic circle—but he almost kissed it. Maybe he would have if Blair hadn't collapsed next to him, panting. The portal back to the living realm kicked up a storm of wind, knocking books all over the place. Papers flew into Derek's face and he swatted them away until the wind died down and the papers fell to the ground.

A mess. His apartment was a mess. But it was his apartment. And all around him, clawing at his senses, were his neighbors' emotions. Contentment from upstairs. Annoyance from downstairs. And was that lust he felt from the neighbor he shared a wall with? What the hell was that guy up to?

Derek shook his head. It didn't matter. He wasn't important. What was important was that they'd made it back. Somehow, through all of the struggles and warding off Derek's demise, they'd found the door. Or, Cody's mom had given it to them? Derek still wasn't sure what had happened in those last moments. One second he was falling asleep, and the next Blair was sobbing in his arms, and Niran was missing.

He still couldn't see Niran.

Next to him, Blair sat back, gaze darting around the room. Derek wanted to tackle her. Kiss her. Shout with excitement that they were *back*. He'd done it. He'd brought Blair back from the Realm of Death. No one had done that before. Everyone had told him it wasn't possible. That she was dead. That he'd never see again.

Screw them.

But he held back. Not because he wasn't excited, but because she wasn't. Instead, her caution rubbed his skin raw. Confusion came next, stabbing at his already fragile body. Then it was happiness. Then grief. Then caution again. The emotions cycled so fast that Derek's head spun.

He reached out and touched her shoulder. She jumped, facing him with wide eyes.

"You okay?" he asked.

For a second, she said nothing, and then, "Am I really here?"

"Yeah," he said, unable to contain his smile. "You're really here."

Tears welled up in Blair's eyes. These weren't the same as before. There was no sorrow in her emotions. Instead, pure, absolutely glee rained down on him. His breath caught in his throat just in time for her to tackle him, pressing her lips to his.

"Oh my god," she said. He was flat on his back, her hovering over him, but he didn't care. In fact, he quite liked it. "I'm back. I'm back. I'm *back*!"

He chuckled. "You are."

"I'm back." She touched his face and then kissed him again.

Derek was certain that he could kiss her forever, when the door to the kitchen slammed open and he couldn't help but groan. Cody had the worst timing.

Except, when glared at the man who had held down the fort, he realized that it wasn't actually Cody standing in the doorway. In all the excitement, Derek had failed to notice that two of the emotions around him belonged to people he didn't know. Two people who now stood in his living room, the young man holding out one of Derek's kitchen knives. The young woman stood behind him, but she looked even more fierce than he did.

Derek sat up. "Who the hell are you?"

Blair gasped. "Oh my god."

The young woman glanced at Blair, and all hostility died from her eyes. "Blair?"

"Heba? Parker?"

Derek's head spun. "What's going on here? Where's Cody?"

The woman, Heba, stepped forward. She pushed the knife down, giving Parker a look. "You must be Derek."

"Answer my questions," Derek snapped. He pushed himself to his feet. Blair might have known them, but Derek certainly didn't, and there was no way he was about to let two strangers ruin all of his hard work.

Parker let the knife drop to his side with a roll of his eyes. "Cody wasn't exaggerating."

"Seriously." Heba sighed. "Okay, fine. We're Cody's friends. After you went into the Realm of Death, or whatever, Death showed up and gave Cody a list to complete. We don't know much about it, but he asked us to stay here and make sure things went okay. He was here maybe an hour ago, but he went to get Mia. Something about needing her back in America."

Cody had friends? Derek crossed his arms, and Blair stood, placing a hand on his shoulder.

"Derek, it's okay. We've told you about them. They're the ones who helped us get Mia away from Jae."

When he thought about it, the names were familiar. Heba and Parker. Two Natara. That would explain why they were friends with

Cody, though that still seemed odd to Derek. Why hadn't Cody told Derek about them? Why had he left? What was this list? And how the hell was he going to convince Mia to come back to America?

He relaxed, though not entirely. "What is this list?"

"I literally just said I don't know much about it," Heba said.

Derek raised his brow, but next to him, Blair gasped.

"Is that what they were talking about?" she asked in a low voice.

Derek faced her. "What are you talking about?"

She bit her lip. "When I first got to the Realm of Death, Death spoke to me. They said something about a list. How I couldn't come home until it was complete." She focused on the two strangers. "You two know *nothing* about what was on the list? At all?"

Heba shook her head, but it was Parker who spoke this time. "Cody didn't show it to us. He called us here yesterday, told us to stay put, disappeared for a few hours, came back covered in blood—"

"I'm sorry, *what?*" Derek's jaw dropped.

Parker shrugged. "Wouldn't talk to us about what happened. He's okay, I think. Physically, at least. He passed out and then this morning went to go find Olivia and bring Mia back."

"Who's Olivia?" Derek asked.

"An omniscient girl in a coma," Blair said. "Why is he going to find her?"

It would seem Derek had missed a lot. And if Blair knew this, then it must have happened during their last year of high school. Not for the first time, he cursed himself for being so stubborn back then.

"He says she knows something." Heba sighed. "Look, we really don't know. He's not the most talkative person most of the time, but he was especially quiet last night."

That's about when the timeline occurred to Derek. Last night? It was morning, based on the way the light shone through the window. He'd been gone for less than twenty-four hours.

A wave of exhaustion almost floored him. He stumbled back, sinking onto his couch with his head in his hands. The world spun. It wasn't the same tired that had plagued him in the Realm of Death. It was more the kind that happened after a dangerous situation. When the adrenaline ran out and the body realized it was no longer about to die.

"Derek!" Blair sat next to him. "Are you okay?"

"Fine," Derek said. He looked up at Heba and Parker. "Has it really been less than a day since I left?"

They both shrugged, and Heba said, "Maybe. Cody didn't really say when you left. Just that we had to stay here."

How could they have made it back without Cody here? Had Derek's research been wrong? Or maybe he had misinterpreted it? Cody had taken a huge risk, leaving. But it'd all worked out, so Derek didn't plan on yelling at him. At least, not at first. Besides, if he'd been covered in blood, then something must have happened. Derek had no idea what Cody had been through the past sixteen hours.

"Well, thanks for staying," Derek said. "You can go now."

Parker laughed. "Yeah, no. We're staying until Cody gets back."

"I'll tell him you did your job," Derek snapped. "Leave."

"We don't take orders from you." Heba's emotions flared: defiance and annoyance. Derek groaned and placed his head back in his hands. It would take a minute to get used to emotions again.

"What's his problem?" Parker asked.

"He's an empath," Blair said. Derek had never appreciated Blair more than in that moment. She got him. He didn't even need to explain. "He's probably overwhelmed."

Exhausted, overwhelmed, a million other things. And when he looked up, he realized that there weren't four people in the room. There were five.

While Niran wasn't as stable as he'd been before going into the Realm of Death, he stood in the corner of the room with so much rage and disgust in his eyes that Derek couldn't help but grimace. The reprieve hadn't lasted long.

"Fine," Derek said. "Stay. But once Cody is back, I'm going to need you to leave. This place isn't big enough for everyone."

He resisted glaring at Niran when he said this. Heba and Parker nodded. Derek, meanwhile, grabbed Blair's hand and led her out of the living room and to his bedroom. They needed some privacy. Maybe some sleep. And he had a feeling that Blair would want to call her mom.

His phone had died, so he grabbed his charger and plugged it in, waiting while Blair closed the door behind them. Niran had followed them, as he always did, and Derek continued to ignore him. He'd have to tell Blair eventually, but she was already looking at him with such concern that he didn't want to add to it.

The moment his phone registered life, it blew up with texts and missed calls. All from his parents. None from Mia. The text he'd sent her still lingered on his mind, and he felt a little stupid for sending it now. But even though he'd known that he was going to save Blair, he hadn't been completely convinced he would survive it.

"Derek," Blair began.

Derek held up his phone. "Want to call your mom, or should I?"

Blair hesitated, and for a moment she seemed so much younger and less hardened than she actually was. "My mom?"

"Yeah. I can call if you want." Derek went into his contacts and found Mrs. Arbour's number.

Blair settled on the bed next to her. "Can you call? I...I don't think I'll be able to say anything."

Derek smiled at her. Her emotions were so young. So excited. So happy. He leaned over and kissed her lightly. "I'm sure she'll be here as soon as possible. Then you won't need to say anything."

He dialed Mrs. Arbour's number and as it rang, he glanced at Niran. The man stood in the corner, gaining stability, with his arms crossed. But the minute Mrs. Arbour picked up, saying Derek's name, he focused on the now. The future was coming for him quickly, but now they were back. They could find a way to save Derek, and maybe Niran too.

Blair felt her mother's magic the minute she arrived. Her head perked up and she rushed out of Derek's room. He called after her, but she ignored him. Heba and Parker sat up straight when she rushed past them. She ignored them as well. The front door was too far away. She stormed through the ritualistic circle Derek had drawn on his floor. Stumbled over books and crushed papers. Her heart threatened to explode out of her chest.

She didn't care about any of it.

Esther got one knock in before Blair yanked open the door, panting. Esther stood there, eyes red, hair graying and pinned back in the same style that Enola had always worn. She'd changed just enough that Blair noticed, but not enough to be someone else. Not enough to not be her mom.

Before she knew it, Blair was wrapped in Esther's arms, crying yet again. Had she used to cry this much? When was the last time she'd let herself *feel* like this? Did it matter?

Blair's legs gave out and she sunk to the ground, her mom's arms still holding her like she was a child. The woman stroked Blair's hair, and she whispered words to her in the language of Sangota. Words that Blair had been longing to hear for five years.

"You're home. You're home. I can't believe you're home. I've missed you so much. I've missed you."

All Blair could do was cling to her.

She'd missed Derek, yes. The idea of seeing him again got her through all of the pain and frustration. But this was her *mom*. She had to be strong for Derek. She didn't have to be strong for Esther. It was okay to let it all out. To forget that she was twenty-three. To pretend like with just a few words and a wave of her hand, her mom could take away all of her problems.

Being out of the Realm of Death was a lot. The softness of Derek's bed, Heba and Parker's magic. The fact that if she went outside, she could interact with the people walking down the streets because they weren't *dead*. When Esther kissed the top of her head, none of it mattered. She was home. She was safe. Everything would be okay.

"I knew something was going on." Esther said. Blair pulled away and her mom smiled at her, tears of her own in her eyes. "The necklace never chose a new wielder. And Cody visited Leo in the hospital. He explained what Derek was going to do. That you were alive. And I *knew* it. I couldn't feel your magic, but I *knew* you were still here. That I would see you again."

"I'm glad you had that hope," Blair said in a hoarse voice. "Because I was about to give up when Derek showed up."

Esther squeezed her eyes shut, gripping Blair's shoulders. "He never gave up on you. I never gave up on you. I'm glad you didn't give up on yourself as well."

Blair nodded and then hugged her mom again. They didn't have a lot of time before Cody would be back. It depended on if Mia came willingly, and how he was traveling. Still, she didn't want to let go of Esther.

"We should go inside," Esther said softly. "You and Derek have so much to tell me, and I'm curious who your friends are."

Blair had forgotten all about Heba and Parker. And kind of Derek. But her mom was right. She pulled away again and pushed herself to her feet before she helped Esther off the ground. They were the same height. They'd been the same height before Blair was taken, but it felt different now. The dynamic had shifted.

The two headed into the apartment where Derek waited for them. Blair closed the door as her mom went up to Derek and reached up, placing her hands on his cheeks.

"Thank you," she said.

Blair had seen Derek embarrassed before, but not like this. He looked anywhere but Esther and mumbled something inaudible. It was so unlike him that Blair couldn't help but let out a stark laugh, which earned her a glare from Derek. But she didn't care, because it didn't mean anything. He'd done the impossible, and he deserved all of Esther's thanks.

"And who are you?" Esther focused her attention on Heba and Parker.

"They're Cody's friends, apparently," Derek said.

Blair wasn't sure how she felt about Cody being friends with Heba and Parker. Yes, the two of them had helped them at Jae's mansion, but what did it mean that he kept in touch with them? That he'd asked them, of all people, to watch over Derek's apartment? Did he know how dangerous it was? Did he even question, for a second, *their* motives?

"It's nice to meet you." Heba's voice was quiet. Did she know who Esther was? The power Blair's mom held, magically and politically? She must have figured out something, because her normal sass had vanished.

Esther bowed her head. "You as well. I apologize for my bluntness, and my lack of hospitality. A lot has happened since Derek entered the Realm of Death, and I don't have a lot of time to greet you properly. But friends of Cody are friends of mine. Thank you for looking out for him."

Parker's jaw dropped, and Blair didn't blame him. She was shocked too. Esther and Cody had a relationship akin to foster mother and son, but there was something else there. Almost a hint of adoration.

"Mom? What happened?" Blair asked.

Esther hesitated for a moment, then she settled into the nearest chair. "Cody saved Leo."

"What?"

"Death gave him a list of things to complete. One of them was saving Leo. I'm still not sure what happened, and honestly Cody's power over souls terrifies me, but he did it. Leo has his magic back. He's already healing. It'll take time for him to be back to normal, but it should only take a year. Maybe less, depending on how much his magic fixes."

Blair sunk onto the couch, next to Parker. Derek stayed standing. Neither of them spoke. After all these years, Leo was okay? He was going to be okay? Blair definitely had questions for Cody the next time she saw him. Assuming he was willing to answer them.

"I was so caught up with Leo that I didn't realize the other clans had been trying to contact me," Esther continued. "That's where I was when Derek called: at a conference with the other major clan leaders. Everything is falling apart. The minute Derek entered Death's realm, issues appeared. Magic has grown weaker. Smaller clans have, almost like a coordinated attack, rebelled against the major clans. The Sixiang clan in particular is blaming the Iravata. They want action, but our treaties keep us from helping each other. We aren't allowed to band together against the smaller clans, even if it keeps peace. We don't know what's going on."

Blair groaned. "You have got to be kidding me. When is this going to end?"

"I wish I knew." Esther looked at Heba and Parker. "You two aren't mages, right? You're Natara?"

They both stiffened, but nodded.

"Do you know anything? Anything at all that could explain what's going on?"

"No." Heba's voice was quiet. "Jae didn't exactly explain anything to us when we lived with him. Now that we're on the out, he's gone radio silent. Haven't heard from him since Cody and Blair rescued Mia."

"I understand. Be on your guard, just in case. We don't need any more loss of life." Esther focused on Blair again. "What about in Death's realm? Did you discover anything there?"

"No," Blair said, brow furrowing. Except she had, hadn't she? In the mess of everything, when Derek was asleep. When she'd given up on ever escaping. As Niran grew stronger. Her eyes widened. "Oh shit! Grandma!"

"What about Grandma?"

"I saw her." How could she have forgotten that? Even if for a second? "We talked. About a lot, but also not. She didn't stay for very long. She said that the knife isn't a real artifact. Enya planted it a long time ago, after the original one got destroyed. The original one had to do with emotions." Blair glanced at Derek. He got his powers from his clan. Even if no one in his immediate family could use magic like he could, the blood still ran through his veins. "She said that her soul, and a lot of other souls, are trapped in the knife and we have to destroy it before Enya can use it against Shion."

How were they supposed to do that? The knife wasn't a real artifact, but it was still *incredibly* powerful. Probably more so than the others. And even if they did have a way to destroy it, how were they supposed to find it? Jae was in possession of the knife. Getting that back from him was going to prove difficult.

Blair groaned. "I don't know what to do."

Esther must have stood at some point, because she placed her hands on Blair's shoulders, sending a wave of calmness through her. They were heavy. Safe. Her mom was safe.

"It's okay. You don't have to know right this second. Maybe Cody knows something. Or Mia. Talk to them when they get back.

I want to stay, but I have to get back to my meeting with the clan leaders. They weren't happy that I had to leave. But it shouldn't last forever, and if you need me, I'm a phone call away either with them, or at the hospital with Leo."

She looked at Derek. "I know you kids like to do things by yourselves. And maybe I shouldn't get involved. But if you need me for anything, don't even hesitate. I'm here. I can help."

Derek nodded. "I'll call you if we need help."

"Thank you." Esther cupped Blair's cheek. "I'm glad you're home. Life hasn't been the same without you."

Home. Blair closed her eyes and let the word wash over her. She was here. In the living realm. In an apartment she didn't know, but still. It was home. All around her was home.

"I love you," Esther said.

"Love you too, Mom." Blair stood and hugged her mom one last time before Esther bade them goodbye and disappeared from the apartment, right in front of Blair's eyes. For a moment, Blair stared at the spot her mom had been seconds ago, and a part of her heart hurt. She hadn't wanted Esther to leave, but what else could she do? Esther had a lot to deal with, and Blair couldn't demand she stay. Besides, they'd have time later to talk and catch up. Blair had so much to tell her mom, and she wanted to know everything that had happened in the living realm over the past five years. Even the stupid things.

Her thoughts, however, were interrupted when her stomach rumbled.

Eyes widening, she placed a hand on it, and Heba and Parker snickered. She shot them a glare.

"I haven't eaten in five years," she said. "Excuse me if I'm hungry."

"Sorry," Heba said.

"Yeah, just a weird break in tension." Parker stretched his arms

374

over his head. "Why don't we eat? That's what Heba and I were doing when you showed up. Well, we were looking for food. Derek has shit all in his apartment."

Derek rolled his eyes. "Sorry, I didn't exactly expect two strangers to be staying over."

"So hostile," Heba said.

"I don't know you."

"Let's not fight." Blair gripped Derek's hand, smiling at him. He smiled back and her stomach lurched. Then growled again. "Why don't we order food? You can do that, right?"

Derek nodded. "What do you want?"

Blair thought for a moment. Her first meal in five years. What did she want? A smile spread across her face. "You know, I could use a really good burger."

She could have sworn Derek wanted to groan. He refrained, though, and instead went to grab his phone, grumbling about animal murder. She smiled after him. It'd been years since she'd heard him rant about meat. It was nice to know he hadn't given up that part of him. That even though he'd been through hell—and a lot of research if his apartment had anything to say about it—he was still Derek. He was still Derek, Blair was still Blair, and once they figured out how to end the shit Death had started, then they would have the rest of their lives to be themselves together.

Chapter Thirty-Two

When Mia opened her eyes, they were standing in the middle of an apartment parking lot. The morning sun shone down on her, brighter than she'd seen in years. She squinted, holding up a hand to protect her eyes. In the distance, the mountains exploded out of the ground and reached toward the blue sky. Even through the sky scrapers, she could see the mountains. Not only the beauty, but also the scar that Enya's fire had left. A black stretch across multiple peaks.

She dropped her hand at the same time Cody let go, and he and walked toward a three story apartment building.

Mia figured she should chase after him, but she didn't know if she wanted to. Follow him, yes, but even though she was excited to see him, even though *she* was ready, it was clear he wasn't. Was the only reason he'd come to get her because of Death's list? Would they ever have seen each other again if Derek hadn't gone into this Realm of Death place?

She took a deep breath and headed after him. "Cody, are you okay?"

He didn't respond. Didn't even slow down. They were almost to the apartment building when she caught up to him and grabbed his wrist. He halted, but didn't face her.

"What is your problem?" Mia asked, almost too afraid of the answer to press more. "Are you still angry about what happened five years ago?"

"You mean when you slept with me and then disappeared?" Cody asked.

Mia flinched and let go of his arm. "Well, yes."

He breathed in, then let out a heavy sigh. "No, actually. I'm not angry anymore. Maybe I never was. Hurt, but I get why you left. I shouldn't have tried to get you to stay."

That was unexpected. Mia had expected him to yell at her. To tell her all the reasons why he hated her. Or, maybe that's what she'd hoped he'd do. Anything to give her a reaction. But that wasn't Cody. Even after all these years, he was the same scared boy who couldn't express his feelings. He was hiding something from her. Something he was afraid to ask. "You can talk to me. I know that it's been a long time, but I'm still me."

Cody groaned. "It's just…how long have you been gay?"

Seriously? That's what he was concerned about? She had to admit that it must have been a shock to see her kissing a woman, but how could he be that surprised? Had his love for her really blinded him that much to the fact that she'd *never* found boys attractive? That her first boyfriend had been on a mission to seduce and kidnap her? That her second had been Chad Rogers? A boy she'd felt nothing for? If she were to ever fall in love with a man, it would have been Cody. Her best friend. The boy who had sat with her under the slide. The only one who had understood her pain and had been there for her through all of school.

If life hadn't fallen apart in eleventh grade, she might have figured it out sooner, but she was one hundred percent gay, and the fact that Cody found it shocking was almost an insult. Like he didn't see her for her, but for a woman that he desperately wanted to be someone else. Someone who loved him the way he loved her.

"I don't know," Mia said. "Maybe forever. I wasn't exactly in the right place in life for romance. But when Xue came into my life, everything changed. She makes my world come alive, and I'm not going to apologize for falling in love with her."

Finally, Cody faced her. They made eye contact and her defiance grew. She didn't owe him an explanation. He'd told her he loved her and she'd felt pressured to feel the same. But she didn't. She never would. Someday, Cody would find someone who loved him the way he deserved, but Mia would never be that woman. He needed to accept that.

"Your mist is brighter than I've ever seen it," Cody said. "I guess that's all I can ask for you. I want you to be happy and loved. If *she* gives you that, then who am I to complain?"

Mia blinked, surprised. "Oh. Thank you."

Maybe he had changed. Maybe he had gotten over her. Except, when he reached out and brushed her hair behind her ear, she knew he didn't completely mean those words. He was trying to save face. To look better in her eyes. And there was only one reason why he would want to do that.

But, did it matter?

"We should go inside," Mia said. "Wait for Derek and Blair there."

Cody withdrew his hand. "Actually, it would seem they're waiting for us."

Even though Mia had desperately wanted to believe Cody when he said that Blair was alive, part of her still hadn't. It seemed too perfect. Too unreal. Like a dream so far from a nightmare that nightmares were scared of it.

"What apartment?" Mia asked. Her voice hadn't shaken like this in so long she barely recognized it. She needed to see Blair with her own eyes. Otherwise, she'd always believe it was a trick. A trap. A lie. A dream.

Cody gestured at the building. "Two-oh-four."

Mia didn't even thank him. How could she, when she could barely breathe? Instead, she took off, bolting the way she used to back when she was athletic. It must have been adrenaline carrying her, because she barely noticed her exhausted legs complaining, nor the iron in her lungs. She was out of shape. She didn't care.

When she came to apartment 204, she tried to knock, but the door flung open before she could. In that moment, Mia decided that if this *was* a dream, then it was a cruel one. Because in front of her, hand gripping the edge of the door, hair shorter than Mia had ever seen it, figure slim and toned, stood Blair Arbour.

It was difficult to see through the tears brimming in her eyes. Mia didn't wipe them away. "You're alive?"

"It would seem I am." Blair smiled at her. It was different in a way that Mia couldn't place. Maybe a little less cocky. A little less insecure. More naturally confident.

Mia's legs shook. "I saw you burn. I was there. I tried to save you. You were gone." Her arms screamed in pain at the memory. She would never forget what it was like to reach into Enya's fire.

"I know." Blair leaned against the door. "I remember the fire. And you screaming. It haunted me. Thanks for that."

Mia blubbered out a laugh. "I had nightmares for years. I couldn't sleep. I couldn't eat. All I could think was that I should never have yelled at you."

Before she knew it, Blair had her in a bear hug. Mia blinked away tears and caught sight of Derek. He looked like he'd seen the depths of hell, but he was alive. He was alive and he'd done the impossible. She hugged Blair back.

"It's okay," Blair said. "I shouldn't have yelled at you either."

Mia choked back a sob. She hadn't let herself hope that this would happen. That she would ever get closure with Blair. She'd thought, for years, that their last conversation would be one of anger. That she'd have to live with that guilt for the rest of her life.

She wouldn't have to. Because Blair wasn't dead. And they were going to be okay.

Someone cleared their throat. Mia wanted to ignore it, to just hug Blair for a moment longer and let five years of emotion run dry, but the same someone spoke, and he didn't sound pleased.

"I hate to interrupt the reunion," Cody said, voice cold, "but a lot has happened and we don't have time for tears."

Derek sighed. "Seriously?"

Blair released Mia and rolled her eyes. "Wow. Nice to see you too, Cody. Glad you're still a dick."

Cody ignored her. He pushed past Mia, hands shoved deep in his pockets. For the first time, Mia noticed that there were two other people in the room. Two people she'd never thought she'd see again: Heba and Parker. Heba waved at her, then focused her attention on Cody. He said something quietly to them while Derek shot Cody a weird look, and then the two disappeared without saying anything.

"Are you wearing my clothes?" Derek asked Cody.

"Mine were a mess," was all Cody said in response.

Blair nudged Mia. "What did you do to him?"

Nothing. But she didn't want to have that conversation with Blair. Not yet. Not until she'd spoken to Derek. But as she walked into the apartment, glancing at Blair every few seconds to make sure she didn't disappear, Mia realized it'd been months since they'd spoken. He knew nothing about Xue. He knew nothing about the strides Mia had made to heal.

When she looked between the three people she'd once been closer to than anyone else in the world, she realized she didn't know them anymore. And they didn't know her. It'd been five long, excruciating years. They'd all gone down different paths, whether on purpose or against their will. It was normal for friends to drift apart after high school, but this was different. They hadn't drifted apart; the whims of immortal beings had torn them limb from limb.

Now, as Mia sat on the couch and watched her brother's gaunt face, her best friend's twitching hand, and her first friend's cold gaze, she realized there was a tension that maybe time couldn't fix. Tension Mia never thought would happen.

So much had changed, and she knew so much more was about to change.

Cody couldn't get the image of Mia kissing that woman out of his mind. At first, he'd thought he'd seen wrong. After all, it had been dark. But before long it became obvious that Mia and that woman were together. He'd never seen Mia's mist so bright. He'd never seen her laugh and smile the way she did with that woman. He'd hoped for it, with himself, but it'd always seemed just out of reach.

She was small now, sitting on Derek's couch while she glanced between her brother, Blair, and Cody. She wouldn't make eye contact with Cody. While he didn't blame her, it hurt. Because despite all of these years, despite trying to move on after she'd hurt him, he couldn't do it. Even knowing that she would never be his, he still wanted *her*. He still loved her.

"Okay, what now?" Blair asked.

Blair. Cody didn't know how to react to seeing Blair. She stood with crossed arms across the room from him, but her eyes darted. Her blue mist fluctuated like she was prepared to fight for her life, and maybe she was. Five years in the Realm of Death had changed her. Not just her physique—she honestly looked more like Mia than

Mia did—but also her expression. Defiance didn't rule her. True confidence had replaced it, but also concern.

It was obvious who she was concerned about. Derek looked worse than when he'd gone into the Realm of Death. He was also on edge, shifting from foot to foot, golden mist pale and slow. He was tired. Physically and in his soul.

Cody pulled the list out of his pocket. All three items were crossed off. He'd done it. He'd completed Death's list. Not that he knew what it all meant.

His gaze lingered on the second item. Saving his mother. He wanted to throw up just thinking about it.

"What's that?"

Cody jumped. He hadn't realized that all eyes were on him, and Derek's voice brought him out of his thoughts of his dead mother.

"Nothing," Cody said with a shrug. "Just a list Death gave me."

"Oh, my mom mentioned that." Blair crossed the room, holding out her hand. Cody hesitated. If they saw it, they would ask questions. But Mrs. Arbour had told them about it, so what was the harm? If he was lucky, they wouldn't say anything about the contents. Blair would already know about Leo, and no one needed to know about his mom.

He handed it over, but luck wasn't on his side.

"Save your mother," Blair breathed.

Derek stiffened, then sat down in the nearest chair. For the first time, Cody noticed take-out boxes with a half-eaten cheeseburger. Where the hell had they gotten cheeseburgers this early in the day? And why did he care? No doubt, he wanted to take his mind off Ava, but Blair's voice wouldn't let him.

"We saw her."

Cody flinched. "What?"

Blair handed the list back to him and then joined Mia on the couch. "She's the reason we're here. We couldn't find a way out until she showed us the door."

Cody bowed his head. All he wanted to do was disappear into the shadows and pretend like none of the past twenty-four hours had happened. "I don't want to talk about it."

"She had a message for you," Derek said. It wasn't often that Derek was gentle with his words. Especially recently. But these words were gentle. He waited for a moment, maybe to let Cody reject the message. Cody didn't want that, and Derek continued, "I mean, I never knew her, but she seemed happy. She said she was, and that you don't need to worry about her."

Blair cut in. "She also wanted you to know that she was sorry. That she loves you and she didn't want to leave you, even though she was ready."

Cody closed his eyes. She was sorry? For abandoning him? For causing him so much pain? They could have figured it out. He could have helped her come to terms with everything. He could have *actually* saved her. But it was too late. She was gone, and unlike Blair, there was no bringing her back.

"Like I said," Cody muttered, "I don't want to talk about it."

When he opened his eyes again, he found everyone watching him. The only one not staring at him with pity was Mia. She looked more confused than anything. He didn't blame her. She'd been out of this world for so long that all of this must have been a lot for her.

It took all he had not to comfort her.

Instead, he focused on Derek and Blair. "Did you learn anything in the Realm of Death about our next move?"

Derek and Blair exchanged a glance before Blair said, "Apparently we have to destroy the knife."

"We don't know how we're going to do that, though," Derek added. "I was asleep when Blair's grandmother told her about it."

"Enola?" Cody shuddered. He was not a fan of that woman, though he'd never speak ill of her to Blair. "Start at the beginning.

Tell us what happened."

Derek gestured to Blair. "You wanna start?"

"Start where?"

"At the beginning," Cody said. "When you first arrived until you left. Anything could be important."

Blair shrugged. "All right. So, turns out the Realm of Death is fucking weird."

And then she launched into her tale. It was obvious she wasn't saying everything, not because she was trying to hide anything, but because it was five years of her life. After a while—though it was hard to say how long—Derek chimed in with his side of the story.

There was so much.

Family Trees. Monsters. The Vilaim. Kathleen. Freaking Kathleen. And then more. How could all of that have happened in sixteen hours?

And when they finished, Cody found he couldn't stop watching Mia. In fact, he'd watched her through most of the explanation, wanting to keep an eye on her. She'd been so quiet. Watching, but not speaking. He couldn't imagine what was going through her head. She'd done it. She'd escaped. Successfully separated her life from magic. She'd even found herself a beautiful girlfriend to love. All of this must have been so much for her.

"So," Cody said when the silence came to be too much, "we have no idea what Death is planning, but it has to do with all four of us being together."

"Sounds like it," Derek said.

Blair grimaced. "I hate the idea of playing their game, but we don't exactly have a choice, do we?"

"No." Cody sighed. "Look, I get all of us want out of this, but until the knife is destroyed and Enya gets what's coming to her, we're stuck in this stupid game. Might as well play for a bit. See what he wants and if it aligns with what we want."

"What do we want?" Derek asked.

"To destroy the knife." Blair stood. "So, let's do it. How do we find the knife?"

Cody was very aware that all eyes went to her. Including his. She stared at them for a second before letting out a massive groan.

"Crap, I'm the seer."

"You forgot?" Cody asked, incredulous.

She glared at him. "I haven't had a vision for five years, Cody. Excuse me if it wasn't my first thought."

Blair, apparently, hadn't changed that much. "Fine. Well, have a vision."

"Yes, because I can just have one on demand."

"You can't if you don't try."

"What is your problem?" Blair snapped. "You've been hostile since you got back."

Cody hesitated. He didn't want to tell them about what he'd been through. He could blame it all on Mia and her girlfriend, but if Derek and Blair didn't know about that, it wasn't his place to out her, and it wasn't really about Mia. It was everything. He was tired. And frustrated. And pissed.

He wanted to go home. But where was home? Where did he belong?

"Can you just try?" Cody asked. "It can't hurt."

"Says the guy who's never had a vision," Blair muttered. But she closed her eyes and focused. Her mist thickened, filling with her magic. A stillness settled over the room. Cody didn't dare glance around. He didn't dare look at anyone but Blair, almost as if his looking away would break the spell.

She'd grown stronger. He had no doubts that she could do this. Force a vision.

And that's when it happened. Blair collapsed. Derek jerked forward to catch her and she shuddered. Her mist went wild, reaching out into the ether in search of a vision. Still on the couch, Mia paled and shrunk back. While Cody was used to seeing Blair's visions, Mia wasn't.

After at least a minute, Blair's body settled and she breathed out. Her eyes fluttered open as she pushed herself into a sitting position. Derek's arms remained around her, even as she waved him off and placed her head in a hand.

"Ow." Blair groaned.

"You okay?" Derek asked.

"No." Blair's voice shook. "That was not fun."

They didn't have time for this. "Did you see anything?"

Blair, once again, glared at Cody. "Thanks for your concern. But yes. I saw a lot."

"Anything specific?"

"Cody, maybe give her a second to process," Derek said.

Cody scowled. They didn't have *time*.

Blair waved Derek off again. "Snippets. I saw fire, which is *always* a great sign. I saw the knife. I saw Jae writing furiously. I saw the capitol building in Denver. I saw Olivia at a park near it—"

Cody started. "Olivia?"

"Uh, yeah?"

"We have to find her." They couldn't waste any more time. Olivia would know they were coming. He was lucky he'd grabbed his car from his parents' condo before going to look for Olivia earlier this morning. They'd have to drive there, as walking would take too long. She knew things. Of course she knew how all of this was going to go. If they could catch her, maybe they could get her to explain everything to them.

Derek helped Blair to her feet. "Cody, can you like, slow down for a second?"

"I'll explain in the car," he said. "Let's *go*."

He didn't wait for any of them to catch up to him before he

was out the door, shoes half on. The sooner they found Olivia, the sooner they'd find the knife and then he could go back to the life he'd built here. Pretend that the past twenty-four hours hadn't happened.

They just needed to end this stupid war.

Chapter Thirty-Three

B lair had never once thought that she'd miss the Realm of Death. That place had been dangerous and violent. She'd lived every second afraid that she'd make a mistake. There was only one place she'd been safe, and even then she'd taken strong precautions.

Yet, as they drove through Denver traffic, Cody behind the wheel, Blair next to him, and the twins speaking to each other in low voices—in Chinese too—in the back seat, Blair found herself completely overwhelmed. For one thing, Cody's car. It was a nice car. A sleek, four door sedan with a computer on the dashboard. Shouldn't have been anything too crazy, even if the technology did confuse her, and yet the idea that Cody wasn't driving a beat up truck disturbed her. The fact that he wasn't having a panic attack driving in Denver confused her. And the sheer fact that they were in the middle of a city with people everywhere who *didn't* want her life force, made her uncomfortable.

She'd gotten used to her hell. It made sense. It had rules.

The living realm had no rules.

She glanced at Cody. He hadn't actually done much explaining about why he was so pressed to find Olivia. Hell, she wasn't even sure they would find Olivia at the park. Blair wasn't great at knowing when her visions took place. But he was determined to try, saying something about her knowing more than they thought.

What had he gone through to complete that list? Fixing Leo was obvious, but saving his mother? She was dead. How had that happened? And why had Heba and Parker said he'd been covered in blood? Why wouldn't he tell them what he'd been through? What secrets was he keeping? And was it right for Blair to pester him until he told them?

Back in Derek's apartment, being in this realm had seemed manageable. Now? With Mia looking like someone had slapped her, Cody with his hands tight around a steering wheel, and Derek acting like Niran was back, Blair wasn't certain she wanted to be here.

Stop being stupid. You'll get used to it again.

That was true enough. She just had to push through. Get used to the unpredictability. To the changes. It was a lot, but she could do it. She'd adjusted to the Realm of Death, and she could adjust to the living world.

Except, when the world began to spin, her breath catching like she was about to have another vision, she wasn't so certain. She hadn't missed this part.

She closed her eyes and let the image of fire flicker against her eyelids. Not a good sign. She wanted out, so she opened her eyes only to find the world around her erupted with flames. Cars. People. Buildings. No one screamed. No one acted like they were burning alive. Cody continued to drive with his brow furrowed. But also on fire.

Blair swallowed thickly and blinked. The world returned to normal, but she trembled. The last time her visions had included fire…well, she didn't want to think about it.

A hand touched her shoulder. "Did you have another vision?"

Derek asked.

"Something like that," Blair said. "I don't know what it means. I'll keep you updated."

Even Cody glanced at her, concerned. She recalled, not too fondly, their trip to Wyoming, and the way he'd witnessed her intense string of visions.

"I'm okay," she said.

Cody shrugged. The twins had gone back to speaking to each other in Chinese. They hadn't seen each other in a long time. They probably had a lot to catch up on. Though Blair wondered if Derek was going to be completely honest with her about Niran.

When they finally arrived at the park, Blair pointed to a tree. The tree she'd seen Olivia sitting under. Poor Olivia. No longer a child, but instead a fully grown teenager, she'd lost so many years of her life being in a coma. She must have felt the same way Blair did. Waking up in a world she didn't recognize. A world that had moved on without them.

Cody parked and Blair practically jumped out of the car. The only reason she took any time at all was because she didn't want to dent Cody's car door. He'd gone through the trouble of buying something nice. Might as well not damage it.

"She's not here," Derek said when they all gathered under the tree.

"No shit." Blair looked around. All she'd seen was Olivia, the tree, and the capitol building. There were no time markers. No date markers. It could have happened already, or it could be an event that would happen. Or, and this was always a terrifying possibility, it was never going to happen. Blair could change the future, though not a lot. And only sometimes. Was this one of those times?

"Do you think she'll show up?" Cody asked.

"No idea." Blair noticed Mia standing a little further back. She'd wrapped herself in her arms, eyes a little glassed over. "Look, let's just wait a bit. Maybe we'll find evidence that she was here."

"Ah yes, because we have time for that," Cody said. "We should look for her again."

"I am not forcing myself into another vision." Cody could suck eggs for all Blair cared. She needed a break. "You and Derek search the tree."

"And where are you going?"

"Mia and I will look around the park."

Before Cody could argue more, Blair slipped her arm in Mia's and led her away from the boys. Mia didn't fight her. Once they were a good distance away, Blair let go of Mia and smiled at her.

"You've been quiet."

Mia looked at the ground. "Oh. Sorry. It's just…you all speak so fast."

Fast? They weren't speaking fast. Then again, if what Derek had said was true, Mia hadn't been speaking much English—if any—for five years. It took a lot to switch between languages.

"Right, uh, sorry." Blair laughed, though it was all nerves.

"It's fine." Her voice had the same accent as when they were kids. Back before she'd spent hours working on getting rid of it. "It's strange being here. Seeing everyone again. I never thought it would happen."

"Same." Blair looked around. She wanted to talk to Mia, but she also needed to help find Olivia. Or, at least a trace of Olivia. "But we're here. It's awkward, but we're here."

"Yeah." Mia sighed. "It's my fault it's awkward. Cody's mad at me."

"Because you slept with him?" Blair asked without thinking.

But Mia's cheeks brightened with a blush and she wrung her hands together. The wrong question, apparently. Before Blair could apologize, Mia shook her head. "No. It's not that. At least, he says it's not that."

"Oh. Did something happen?"

Mia breathed in, staring at the sky. "A lot has happened in the past five years. Hell, the last five *months*." There was a smile on her face that Blair had never seen before. "He's not handling those changes well."

"What changes?"

She was quiet for a minute. Contemplating, maybe? Deliberating something important. When she spoke again, her voice was very soft. "I'm not sure how to talk to you about this. I'm still not sure myself what's going on. Or maybe I am. I don't know."

"You're being cryptic, Mia."

A little laugh, then a shake of her head. "Sorry. It's nothing bad. I just met someone."

That was it? It'd been five years, of course Mia had met someone. Blair never expected her to stay single for long. It would explain why Cody was freaking out, but not why Mia felt like she couldn't talk to Blair about it. "What's his name?"

Mia grimaced. "*Her* name is Xue."

Oh. Well that made more sense. Not just about Cody, but *everything*. From Mia's hesitance to tell Blair to the fact that Mia had never paid any attention to boys when they were teens. Blair had always been happy not to talk about crushes—how did one explain to their best friend that she was in love with said best friend's twin brother?—but she had always found it strange that Mia didn't talk about it. Now she knew why. So much about Mia clicked into place.

"I see," Blair said, well aware that she'd been quiet for too long.

"Yeah." Mia looked at her feet, arms crossed.

"What's she like?" Blair was still trying to wrap her mind around the paradigm shift, but she didn't want to put that burden on Mia. Cody was making it into a big deal, but it wasn't one. Mia had a girlfriend. Okay. If she was happy, that's all that mattered.

The smile on Mia's face was the warmest Blair had ever seen.

"She's amazing. Strong willed, confident, kind, but gentle." Mia laughed. "Sometimes she reminds me of you, but like, different."

"Well, I can't wait to meet her. Though, if she's like me it might be too much cool for one room."

Mia's laugh caught the boys' attention. Blair smiled at them, then focused on Mia again.

"She's not part of the magical world," Mia said, "and she doesn't speak English yet. She wants to learn, but I've been too scared to teach her."

"You? Teach her?" Blair shuddered. "Mia, I love you, but you're a *terrible* teacher."

"Hey!" Mia shoved Blair, and Blair laughed. Before all of this drama, Mia shoving Blair would have resulted in Blair falling on her ass. Now, Mia didn't even make her budge. "I told her about the magical world, though. She took it really well. I just figured it wasn't a good idea to keep it from her, you know?"

"I get that," Blair said. "My mom tried to keep it from my dad for a long time. He found out the day Leo was born and it was a whole disaster."

"Oh no."

"But they worked it out." Blair smiled. "I'm glad you're happy."

"Me too." Mia yawned. She must have been exhausted. It was early in Colorado, but it had to be after midnight in China. "And I'm really happy that you're here. I didn't know how to live in a world without you."

Blair hesitated. How much pain had Mia been through the past five years? Derek had spoken about her like she'd lost her way. Blair had no doubt that she had, but now she'd found it again. Xue had helped her find it again. Blair knew that even if she hadn't come back, Mia would have been fine. She would have found a way to live in a world without Blair.

It stung, but Blair understood.

Wrapping an arm around Mia's shoulders, Blair said, "Well, you don't need to. I'm not going anywhere. Except back to the boys."

"Fair enough."

They headed over to the tree. Cody stood under it, looking up, and Derek was nowhere to be found.

"What's going on?" Blair asked.

Cody pointed up in the tree, only to stop when Derek practically fell out of it. In his hand was a plastic bag with a folded piece of paper and a black notebook. No, not a notebook.

A journal.

"Looks like Olivia was here," Derek said as he pushed himself to his feet. He held the bag out for Blair, and all of them looked at Mia. All of her previous joy was gone, replaced instead with fear.

Blair took the bag hesitantly. She reached in and pulled out the piece of paper before she offered the journal to Mia. Mia would know if it belonged to Jae.

Mia hesitated, but took the journal. As she opened it and flipped through the pages, Blair read the paper. The note.

I'm fine. Don't look for me. He wants them back.

That wasn't ominous at all. She passed the note to Derek, who passed it to Cody, who crumpled it up with one hand.

"Should we be worried?" Derek asked.

"No." Cody shrugged. "Olivia knows everything. She said she's fine, and I don't think she'd lie about it."

Mia closed the journal, but didn't offer it to anyone else. In fact, she held it against her chest, gripping it tightly. Blair grimaced. Mia didn't need to be part of this. Or, maybe she did. Because if anyone could negotiate with Jae it would be Mia. He wouldn't listen to any of them. He hated Cody. Couldn't stand Blair. Blamed Derek for everything.

Mia was his angel. He wanted his journals back.

"What does it say?" Blair asked.

"It's more of the same," Mia said. "But it's recent. He's talking about his regrets. About needing to escape from Enya."

"How did Olivia get his journal?" Cody asked.

"I don't know. I think she's the one who gave me the others, too." Mia closed her eyes. "Maybe she knew we'd need them."

"Need them for what?" Cody did not sound pleased. "They're the ramblings of an insane man."

"Well…." Mia sighed. "We need the knife, right?"

Blair was surprised Cody, of all people, hadn't put that together. It was fun to see his shocked expression as he understood the meaning behind Mia's words.

He scoffed. "You think that Jae will trade a knife that captures people's souls in return for some journals?"

Mia shrugged. "You never know."

"He's not an idiot."

"Even smart people do stupid things sometimes."

The four of them fell silent. Blair tensed. There was no way that didn't have a double meaning to it. But it wasn't her place to comment. Instead, she cleared her throat. "Right. So. The other journals?"

Mia's head hurt. She wasn't sure if it was the exhaustion or all the English. She'd forgotten how tiring it was to speak in her second language for this long. To be surrounded by only English. China called to her again, opening its arms with offers of a warm hug and her girlfriend to sleep next to. But she couldn't go back yet. Not until she'd done her part in helping destroy the knife.

"Where are the rest of the journals?" Mia asked. She clutched the most recent one. She didn't want them to read it. It wasn't like the others. It didn't have the insane ramblings of an unstable man, but it seemed to be a letter. To her. Asking for her forgiveness. Talking about her happiness and how he'd gone down the wrong path.

It was too personal. Too private. And she had a feeling that Jae would lose his cool if any of the others read some of the things he'd written. Or, if he didn't, then Derek absolutely would. Some of the things she'd seen were so protective and possessive of Mia that she'd felt sick to her stomach. It was clear that he was working through it all. Trying to process why he felt the way he did about his "angel," but there was no way Derek would let her help if he knew that Jae had considered taking her from China.

Cody shrugged. "Last I heard, the Iravata had them. Maybe Shubishi. Seems like something he'd like to *collect*."

Mia frowned at the harsh bitterness in his tone. Had something happened with Shubishi? What had she missed these past five years? Would Cody ever feel comfortable talking to her about it again?

She doubted he would. Things had changed so significantly between them. Maybe if she hadn't pulled away so strongly, and she'd let herself stay in his world, things would be different. They could have talked about the night before she left for China. She could have explained that she didn't want to be in a relationship with him, and they could have remained friends. Maybe she would have moved on sooner.

Maybe he would have too.

"Okay, I'm still not convinced Jae's going to trade a dangerous artifact that can steal people's souls for a couple of journals," Derek said.

"Maybe not," Blair said, "but at least it'll get him out of the woodwork."

"And then what? We fight him?" Derek laughed. "He was strong five years ago. Neither Cody nor I could fight him. Your grandmother didn't even try. You really think that we can take him?"

"Won't know unless we try."

"It's not worth risking our lives," Cody said.

"Well, it's either this or we wait until he finds *us*," Blair snapped.

Mia groaned. They were speaking so freaking fast. She opened the journal again as the three of them continued to argue. The handwriting had gotten neater. Less frantic. She ran a finger along the indented paper and closed her eyes. What would Jae want? Would he want these journals? If he had a chance to give up the knife, to repay his debts to society, would he? If the journals drew him out, then what would he do?

"You're crazy if you think this is going to work." Cody's voice broke through her thoughts.

"No, *you're* crazy if you think we can just sit by and do nothing." Blair.

"How about we stop calling each other crazy." Derek.

Mia opened her eyes. "If Shubishi has the journals, then we need to get them from him." The other three fell silent, looking at her. "This isn't just the best option, it's our *only* option. I'm done waiting for shit to hit the fan. Every time we've waited, life has kicked us until we were down. Let's stop waiting. Shubishi's probably keeping them in his house, right? Let's go."

Blair grinned, but the boys stared at her like *she* was the crazy one.

"Mia," Derek said, voice soft. "We don't have to do this. If he shows up—"

"I've dealt with him before." Mia held her head high, clutching the journal to her chest. "He won't hurt me. He wants to be free of his mother's grip. Let's help him."

"*Help?*" Cody asked incredulously. "Why the hell should we help

397

him?"

She knew they wouldn't understand. They'd never had a real conversation with him. They'd only ever seen him as the violent kidnapper and murderer. And he was. There was no excusing the pain he'd caused. But that didn't mean he wasn't worth helping.

"If you're not going to work with me, I'll go alone," Mia said. She took a step back.

"How? You don't have a way to travel to Florida," Cody said.

"I'll ask the Iravata for help." She wasn't playing. Derek's face paled. His gaze flickered to something over her shoulder, but then they were back on her.

Blair went to Mia's side. "I'm helping. You two going to just stand there?"

The pain on Derek's face was obvious. He didn't understand, and it was killing him that Mia was choosing to put herself in harm's way. Cody, on the other hand, just looked pissed.

"Fine," Derek eventually said. "I'll help too. But can we go back to the apartment for a few hours first?"

"Why?" Mia asked.

"Because it's late in China and you look like you're about to collapse."

At his words, the exhaustion returned. Mia swayed. How bad did she look? It couldn't be worse than Derek.

"Fine," she said. "Maybe sleep would be good for all of us."

Cody didn't look convinced about any of this, and he hadn't agreed to go along with her plot. She didn't care. They didn't need his participation.

The four of them headed back to Cody's car. Mia got in first, limbs turning to jelly. Blair got in next to her, rather than the front seat, and patted her shoulder. There was no way Mia was going to reject that offer. She leaned her head against Blair's shoulder and closed her eyes for a moment. A single, simple....

In her dream, Mia was wrapped in Xue's arms as Xue whispered to her that everything would be all right. Mia, snuggling closer, felt content and warm—safe in a way she never had been before. But then cold air replaced Xue's body, and Mia fell through nothingness. Somewhere in the back of her mind, she knew she should scream, but as the wind caressed her, it was impossible not to still feel safe. To still feel like she was where she belonged.

And when she landed on the ground, there was no pain. A gale cushioned her fall and laid her down as gently as a mother would with her newborn child.

She opened her eyes. She could see, but it was impossible to tell where the light was coming from. As she stood, she realized that a never-ending, glass lake held her afloat. Ripples from her feet extended out, accompanied by bells. They rang out in a simple, relaxing melody. One that tried to lull Mia back into false sleep.

Somehow, despite the exhaustion, she managed to move. To walk gently across the plane of water. Darkness encased her, and yet she could still see. How could she see? There was no sun here. No moon.

The bells dipped in volume. She pulled herself out of her thoughts and stared straight ahead where, out of nowhere, a glowing pedestal materialized. She should have been shocked. Honestly, this was the most abnormal dream she'd had in years. But for some reason, she decided that this was to be expected. Why shouldn't she find the pedestal? Why shouldn't she walk toward it? Toward the flower floating above it?

As a child, Mia had seen many lotus flowers. Her grandparents kept a garden with a lotus pond. In the spring, when they blossomed, she'd sit and stare at them. Sometimes, Derek would join her and ask what she was thinking about. Other times, her father would sit. One time, he explained to her that when they were deciding her name, all he could think about were the lotuses floating in this pond.

"There is an old Chinese proverb," he'd told her, *"that I couldn't get out of my head the day you were born. 'A broken lotus root is still connected by its strings.' When I saw you, I knew that you were not a new soul. That somewhere in your past, you had known heartbreak, but in this life, you will find happiness."*

She hadn't understood any of it at the time. Her father, as sweet as he was, had been talking nonsense. He wasn't one to believe in the spiritual, but for some reason her birth had given him a glance into something more than he was. She'd been too young to comprehend what he was saying. She wasn't broken. She was already happy.

But had she been happy? Or had she always felt like something was missing? A hole deep in her soul?

She reached out to touch the flower, to welcome the other half of herself back home, but it vanished as quickly as it'd appeared. In its place stood Derek. No, not Derek. A man who looked like Derek.

"Why are you here?" Mia asked.

Niran's gaze bore into her. His green eyes were an open window into his thoughts. Into his being. He'd been waiting for her.

"How?" he asked. He sounded like Derek. "How is it you?"

"Me?" Mia looked down at her hands. How could she see her hands?

Niran breathed in. "I want to be. But I don't know if I can. Not as long as you hold the key."

"What are you talking about?"

He reached out and touched her shoulder. "One day, when you've accepted yourself, you'll understand how important you are."

Mia frowned. "You're not making sense."

But Niran flickered into non-existence, leaving Mia to stand alone on the pond, only able to see herself. She tilted her head back to stare at the sky. The inky blackness threatened to consume her. It hovered there, waiting to swallow her whole. Yet, it didn't.

She reached a hand up and the blackness fled. It feared her. Why would it fear her? Or maybe it wasn't her that the darkness feared. Maybe it was the way she lit up the night.

The sound of arguing woke her. She opened her eyes, even though they didn't want to cooperate, and pushed herself to her knees. Blinking wearily and yawning, she listened in on the argument in an attempt to gain her bearings. She was in Derek's room. He was arguing with Cody. Somehow, she'd ended up in a bed—most likely Derek's bed, based on the messy room. What time was it? How long had she been asleep?

"Just let us go," Cody said.

She glanced at the door. Her head hurt, but this wasn't the time to think about that.

"Mia wants nothing to do with this and you look like death. Let me and Blair deal with it."

Derek laughed. "Not happening. We're not splitting up this time. Death seemed pretty clear that we had to work together."

"Death was not clear about anything," Cody snapped.

Mia sighed. Of course they were arguing about plans. She slipped out of bed and opened the door enough to keep listening without them noticing.

"Why would he have you bring Mia back if she wasn't supposed to be part of this?" Derek asked. "Why would he keep Blair alive? Why am *I* still alive?"

"Luck."

Cody's answer was quick enough that Derek didn't respond at first. Then, in a low voice, Derek asked, "What do you mean?"

"You're lucky, Derek. Do you think I haven't noticed you looking at someone who isn't there? Do you think I don't remember what you told us five years ago? Do you think I'm stupid enough not to realize that you're seeing Niran again?"

Mia tensed. Derek was seeing Niran? She'd seen Niran in her dream. Why hadn't Derek said anything about this?

"This has nothing to do with Niran."

"It has *everything* to do with Niran." Mia had never heard Cody snarl before. What was going on with him? "Don't you get it? We're in this because of Niran. He's the key to everything."

"Yet, you don't want me to come with."

"You need to spend your last living moments with your sister."

At this, Mia opened the door. She didn't want to hear about Derek having last living moments, and from the look on Blair's face when Mia entered the living room, neither did she. The boys fell silent, though neither one of them looked at her. Instead, they continued to glare at each other. Blair, meanwhile, mouthed at Mia, *Help.*

"We're all going," Mia said.

Derek looked at her for a second, and then to the floor. Cody shoved his hands in his pockets and scowled.

"This isn't up for debate. I'm going. Derek is too. We all need to be there. Derek's right. If Death wanted me here, then that means I have to be here. I don't think it had anything to do with Derek and Blair coming back from the Realm of Death. Let's just go ask Shubishi about the journals."

When had she become so confident? Why wasn't she running?

Holding her head high, she walked over to Derek. Blair hopped up from the couch and gave her a wry smile.

"Well," Blair said, "Mia has spoken. Let's go."

Mia placed a hand on Derek's arm. He gave her a look, one that held a million questions, and she shot one back with her own accusatory ones. Ones about how he'd kept so much a secret over the past five years. His expression turned to guilt.

Cody sighed. "Fine. Fine. We'll all go."

Five years ago, Mia would have sat down with him and asked him what was wrong. They would have gotten coffee or tea and sat together in downtown Willow Creek. He would have told her everything, and she would have helped him through it. If she offered help, would he take it? Or would he continue to let his anger at the world get in the way of moving on?

She closed her eyes. A familiar sensation tugged at her stomach. One she hated. One that told her they were traveling across the country in a matter of seconds. Breathing in, she tried to keep herself calm, but anxiety tugged at her heart. She was doing this. She was getting involved again. Going to the place where Lior had taken her five years ago. Where she'd learned about the Iravata. About Niran.

The tugging stopped. The sound of waves crashing against the shore tickled her ears. And when she opened her eyes, expecting the pristine house that Shubishi kept, she was shocked to discover that his study was completely and utterly destroyed.

Chapter Thirty-Four

Derek tensed, pushing Mia behind him. Jae had attacked Shubishi. It was the only explanation for the disaster zone they found themselves in. Mia's fear spiked, lathering his skin like foul smelling soap, and she grabbed his shirt, trembling. Apparently he wasn't the only one who'd come to the obvious conclusion. Next to him, Blair muttered a few choice swears, her fear raising his own. Derek resisted reaching out to calm the two girls, as he knew neither would appreciate it, when he realized that Cody hadn't reacted the same way. His emotions were steady and unamused.

"What the hell happened here?" Blair asked. "Did we miss a fight? Did Jae try and kill Shubishi for the journals?"

"Jae?" A familiar voice sounded from the doorway behind them. Derek spun around, making sure to keep Mia behind him. He wasn't sure which was more dangerous: the destroyed wall that revealed the outdoors, or the lovers standing in front of them.

He narrowed his eyes. Like always, Nina and Tori were touching each other. Nina leaned against Tori, while Tori had an arm around her wife's waist. Their emotions confused him. Entertainment with a mixture of pride. That, mixed with the girls' fear, and Cody's annoyance, made Derek sick to his stomach. It was too much. There were too many strong emotions.

"Where's Shubishi?" Blair asked. The first to collect herself. "What happened here? Did Jae come for the journals? Did he figure out we're trying to get him to show his stupid face?"

Tori laughed, while Nina shook her head. Tori whispered something to Nina and then let her go, stepping into the shattered room. "Jae wouldn't come here even if Shubishi did have the journals."

Derek clenched his fist. Why did they always have to be so cryptic?

"Then who did all of this?" Mia asked in a quiet voice from behind Derek.

Tori grinned. "Why don't you ask Cody?"

Cody? Derek glanced at his friend. He'd crossed his arms, glaring at the Iravata, but his emotions were still calm. Annoyed, but not panicked. Why wasn't he panicked? Had he really done all of this damage? Was that why he'd been covered in blood? Cody had never told them what he'd been through in the past twenty-four hours.

Blair snorted. "Cody did this? No way."

At this, Cody sighed, and then shrugged. "He pissed me off."

Tori howled with laughter. "I have to say, I'm impressed. I've never seen *anyone* rattle Shubishi the way you did. You should have heard the things he said after we found him. I gotta applaud you. He did *not* see your power coming."

Derek couldn't hold back his shudder. He knew that Cody was powerful, but not this powerful. He'd destroyed a building. He'd rattled not just an Iravata, but Shubishi. Freaking Shubishi. And instead of cowering, he was acting nonchalant about it.

"What happened?" Mia asked.

Cody ignored her. He stepped toward Tori, who continued to

grin. "We want the journals. If they're not here, then where are they?"

"Where do you think? With Shion."

"And where is Shion?"

Tori hesitated. "Look, I don't know what Death has been planning, but it might be best to go home and stay out of the fight. Shion has been doing her best to keep the four of you away from all of the drama for five years. She says that it's not your battle. You shouldn't have to sacrifice more than you already have."

Derek's brow furrowed. The Iravata were trying to keep them out of it? Why? They hadn't bothered to try before the fire.

"But, you humans do whatever you want," Tori said with a wave of her hand. "You're a silly group. Thinking you can control everything, no matter the consequences for everyone around you."

"Save your anti-human rant," Derek said. "Where are the journals?"

Nina frowned. "You're not staying out of the war? Even though we're trying to protect you?"

"The minute Death decided we were players, the decision was made for us," Cody said. "We don't have a choice."

"And besides," Mia said, voice quiet, "if you really wanted to protect us, you wouldn't have forced us to deal with Kathleen and Steven on our own. Or Jae. Or the mage clans. You haven't helped us."

Tori threw her head back and laughed. "Wow. Good to know you've completely ignored everything we've done. Not like Lior fought to protect your mind, Mia. Or Nina and I risked our safety to protect you two–" she gestured at Cody and Blair, "–when you went to Wyoming on your own. And what about you, Derek? Do you think that we haven't been trying to protect you all of these years? Jae's wanted you dead since you were a kid. Sending Kathleen and Steven was not his first attempt."

Derek's face went cold. He'd never realized that Jae had tried to harm him before that fateful fall. Still, even if the other Iravata tried to protect them, Shubishi had not. "Shubishi told me, when he gave me the knife, that I needed to learn to fight or I would die."

Tori didn't argue.

"He has his own plans," Derek continued. "He's pulling all the strings here, whether you like it or not. Shion might want us out of this war, but we're stuck in it. Either tell us where she is, or leave so we can figure it out."

There was a moment of silence while the lovers exchanged glances. Mia tugged at Derek's sleeve and he glanced at her, giving her a reassuring smile. Then his gaze went to Blair. Blair, whose unamused expression said more than words or textures against his skin ever could. He smiled. Even though Niran stood silently in the corner of the room, getting ever stronger, Derek didn't want to admit that this could be the last time he ever saw Blair look incredulous.

"Fine," Tori said. "We're not here to keep you from your mission. Only want to warn you. But if you're so insistent, Shion's in Flora's mountain home. You remember it?"

All too vividly. Derek bowed his head. "Thank you."

As he turned to help Mia travel across the country—again— Nina called out to them.

"I know what it's like for you," she said. Derek paused and looked at her. "I never wanted to be immortal. I never wanted to be kicked out of my home. I wanted nothing to do with the rebellion. All of my life, I have run from the difficult things." She breathed in. "What you're doing is brave. I would have run. I still might."

Tori took her hand, and their emotions mixed together. Love. Adoring endearment. Guilt.

"I wish you luck. Please, stay alive."

Derek had no idea where that came from. But he nodded. Staying alive was the plan, even if he was certain it wasn't in the cards for him. But, at least, he could make sure that the others survived and were able to thrive. Especially Mia. Especially his twin sister, who wanted nothing to do with all of this. She deserved to be happy with her girlfriend. She deserved to move on.

And then he wasn't in Florida anymore. He couldn't remember focusing on Flora's cabin. Maybe he hadn't. The Iravata had amazing powers. Maybe they had done something to transport the four of them to the Colorado wilderness. Because one second they were in Shubishi's destroyed home, and the next, Derek's lungs complained about the lack of oxygen.

He glanced up at the cabin. At the wooden walls. The glass windows. And he was back to that fall. When they knew nothing. The day that he'd thought he was never going to see his sister again. After he'd killed Steven and learned that there was more to this magic world than just fun tricks. He could remember, so clearly, feeling his sister's emotions. His own relief. He remembered hugging her with apologies tumbling out.

It wasn't Mia's emotions he felt from within the cabin this time. Without paying attention to his friends, his sister, or the phantom stalking him, he ran up the stairs and burst through the door. It took seconds. He could hear the footsteps of the others behind him. Blair even called out his name. He didn't listen.

Instead he strode into the beautiful living room. He stared at the woman—the Iravata—whose survival had changed the world.

Shion looked as beautiful as always. She wore a black dress that cut off at the knees, her bare feet nestled into the soft rug, her pitch black hair loose, hanging down to her waist. Like always, her red eyes sent chills down his spine, but he ignored them.

Next to him, Niran reached out a hand. Could she see him? If she could, wouldn't she stare at him, not at Derek? Or, maybe she saw Niran *in* Derek. He couldn't imagine what it was like to see the face of your lover and know that it wasn't him.

"You came," Shion said. She'd worked on her accent. She sounded almost completely American. "I knew, as soon as Shubishi told me about Ava and Cody, that you would come find me."

"Tell her I'm here." Niran's first words since the Realm of Death were so loud Derek almost lost his concentration. "Tell her I miss her."

Derek didn't acknowledge him. "We're looking for the journals. Tori said you had them. Where are they?"

At first, Shion didn't say anything. Her emotions, which had always been muted, trembled and scurried against his skin like a spider out for revenge. Without thinking, he tried to wipe them off. Get rid of the discomfort of her depression.

"You can feel my emotions." Shion gestured to Derek's hand.

"I'm not trying to," Derek said.

She nodded. "I know. But Niran could never feel emotions."

There was no time for this. Derek had never had many conversations with Shion. He didn't know if she was avoiding him or giving him space. Regardless, she'd always gone to Cody instead, and he'd made it clear that she was as cryptic as they came. Jumping from topic to topic as though being a statue for three thousand years had rattled her mind.

"I'm not Niran. We're here for the journals. We need to destroy the knife and we think they're the key. Where are they?"

Fear licked at Derek's skin. Shion's fear. Did she dread the reappearance of the knife?

When she stood, Derek flinched and took a step back. But she didn't reprimand him for his bluntness, nor did she walk toward him. Instead, she turned and practically floated out of the room. Not sure if he should follow or not, he remained where he was, aware that Cody, Blair, and Mia were watching him. Their emotions were quiet. Confusion, mostly. Concern? Why were they concerned?

After a few minutes, Shion reappeared with a stack of black notebooks. Derek tensed. She placed them on the coffee table and then settled back on the couch. When Derek didn't move, she gestured at them. Was she just giving them to him? He didn't have to argue? He didn't have to fight with her?

He stepped forward.

"I never wanted to involve you," Shion said quietly. Derek froze. "When I woke up, alive in a world I no longer recognized, I knew I needed to disappear. I ran from everything. From my friends, from my pain. But you called me back. You didn't mean to. I never should have come to see you, but you were so much like *him*. No matter how hard I tried, I couldn't see you for who you are. I could only see you as the man I once loved. The man who betrayed me. I can't explain what I felt seeing you as a scared teenager, living a different life in a different time. I needed you to be him."

She sighed. "Maybe it wouldn't have mattered if I'd disappeared. Death has plans, and Shubishi does as well. I cannot fight them, no matter how hard I try. Maybe it was fate that we met. Or maybe it is divine retribution. Punishment for the sins of my people."

Her sorrow threatened to drown him. He gasped for air. How could one person hold so much sadness?

She stood, waving at the journals. "Be careful, children. I'm sure I will see you again soon."

"Tell her I'm here!" Niran said. "Don't let her leave! Let me talk to her! Let me take away her pain!"

But she was gone. The journals sat on the table. Derek's chest finally let his lungs breathe and he leaned over, panting. Blair was at his side in a second, asking if he was okay. He was not okay. How could he be okay when Shion's sorrow had sunk into his skin? When next to him, Niran's fury was the only outside emotion he could feel? When Niran's fury was taking over his own emotions?

They didn't have long. He stood up straight. "We don't have

time. We need to figure out what to do with the journals."

Blair gripped his hand and he smiled at her. Soon. He'd be gone soon. But not until this was over. And who knew? Maybe everything would work out in the end. He had to hold onto hope that it would, otherwise he might lose himself completely.

Cody had never seen Shion look so gentle. Her conversation with Derek had chilled him to the bone. They spoke to each other like people who had known each other for a millennia. Shion had never spoken to Cody in that manner before. How much of Niran did she see in Derek? Was that going to make everything worse?

He clenched his fist. They'd gone on a fool's errand to Florida, but now they had the journals and could try and flush Jae out of hiding. But how were they going to do it? Cody wasn't exactly known for his bargaining skills, and he was the only one of the four who could fight against Jae's powers.

Derek, shaking more than before, picked up the top journal and turned it over in his hands. "Anyone have any suggestions?"

Cody prepared himself to speak and offer himself up, but he couldn't get the words out in time.

"I should do it."

Mia's voice was soft and trembling, but there was a strength there. Her mist, while fluctuating, still held the bright glow of confidence she'd gained at some point in the past five years. Cody's jaw dropped.

"Excuse me?" Blair asked.

Mia took a deep breath. "Look, I know that Jae won't hurt me. He's had the chance to do something for years and he hasn't. All he wants is for me to be happy. I don't know why. I don't know how

I caught his attention. But I'm his angel. If any of you are around, he's going to try and kill you. He hates all of you. He…loves me."

Cody clenched his fists. How could Jae love someone he kept hurting?

"I'll take the journals and call for him. I'm sure he knows we're here."

He'd mostly ignored Mia the past few hours. Hadn't even offered to bring her inside when she'd passed out in the car and wouldn't wake up despite Blair's jostling. He'd tried to let go. To make it clear to her, and to himself, that he didn't care anymore. But he *did* care, and he wasn't about to let Mia be alone with the man who had caused her nightmares.

"No," he said. "You can't talk to him alone. He's going to take you."

Mia shook her head. "He won't. I promise."

"How do you know?" Derek asked.

"He could have taken me from Willow Creek and he didn't."

The room fell silent. Cody tried to process the information Mia had dropped. Did she mean that he'd visited her in Willow Creek? Before the fire? He'd spoken to her? She'd seen him?

"What are you talking about?" Blair asked.

Mia wrung her hands together. "I didn't know how to tell you. But he visited me. A couple of times. He wanted his journals back, and he wanted to tell me that he wouldn't hurt me again."

Cody didn't like yelling. He especially didn't like yelling at Mia. In fact, he'd never yelled at her before. Why would he? She was the person who had saved him. She was the only person he'd ever loved. There was no reason to yell.

He yelled. "How could you not have told us that?"

"Cody…." Blair's warning was lost on him.

"This man kidnapped you, traumatized you, and tried to kill the rest of us. And you didn't bother to tell us that he was *visiting* you?"

He recognized the look on Mia's face. Her stubborn determination only came out when she was in the middle of a game and they were behind. When she was certain that if she worked just a little harder, she could save her team from certain defeat.

"No, Cody," she said, voice ice. "I didn't *bother* to tell any of you that Jae had visited me. How could I? You were all dealing with your own shit." She faced Blair. "You were obsessed with finding all the artifacts." Derek. "You were pouting because Blair and Cody didn't include you on their mission." Then Cody. "And *you*! You were upset that I was dating Chad and refused to look at me. So, no. I didn't tell you. And I'm not going to apologize for it."

Cody clenched his fists. So much had happened during that last year of high school. To all of them. None of them had been there for each other.

"Well," Cody said, "if you hadn't pulled away and tried to be normal, maybe things wouldn't have happened the way they did."

Had he just said that? He wanted to take back the words, but the fury on Mia's face told him it was too late.

"I'm sorry, but you're blaming *me* for your stupidity?" she asked.

"No, I–"

"I don't want to hear it!" The fight that had been brewing between Cody and Mia was finally raising its ugly head. Cody wanted to run. He wanted to hide. There was nowhere to hide. "You're angry because I pulled away? I pulled away because I was *scared*! I was traumatized! I was trying to recover! And what's your excuse? That I didn't want to date you? That I found happiness in Chad Rogers? Well I'm *sorry*, Cody, that I don't love you. I'm sorry that I'm not the woman you wanted me to be. I never have been, I never will be, and I never *wanted* to be! You have this picture of me that doesn't exist, and you need to burn it. I don't love you. I can't love you."

She grabbed the stack of journals and backed away from Cody. Her face was flushed and she was panting. "Now, I'm going to go

413

out in the woods and find Jae. If you have a problem with that, you can eat shit!"

She didn't wait for him to respond before she pushed through the small crowd and exited the room. The cabin. Cody tracked her mist down the stairs, unable to let go.

He closed his eyes. They were kids again. Him and Mia hiding under the slide. From the time he'd known what love was, he'd loved her. He'd imagined growing up with her. He'd imagined having a family with her. Getting old and watching the world change around them. He'd always thought she would be the most important person in his life.

He'd never been the most important person in hers.

A hand touched his arm and he opened his eyes. Tears spilled down his cheeks. Next to him, Blair breathed in deeply.

"It's time to let her go."

How could he? When she was so important to him? When she'd been the one who had saved him?

How could he accept the fact that she didn't need him anymore?

He brushed Blair's hand off and wiped the tears from his face. "What do we do now?"

Derek, who hadn't said a word for a while, crossed his arms. Cody hated the pity plastered on his expression. He wanted to snap at Derek. Piss him off so he would be angry at Cody instead of sad for him. But he didn't, and Derek spoke. "There's nothing we can do but wait and trust that Mia knows what she's doing."

Chapter Thirty-Five

Cody had been so angry. Mia didn't want to think about the fight, but she couldn't get it out of her mind. He'd gone too far when he'd blamed her for the events five years ago. She hadn't even been there when the mages had attacked. Lior had removed her from the situation. It wasn't her fault, and she refused to take responsibility for it. Especially not when Cody was the one blaming her.

She was outside in the woods when she sank to her knees. She held the journals tight against her body and tried to hold back a sob. Her emotions were getting the best of her. If she was going to face Jae, she needed to calm down. Even though she hadn't given the others a chance to respond, she knew they wouldn't come after her. If they were going to, they would have by now. She would have heard their feet breaking sticks or crunching leaves.

Good. She didn't want to talk to any of them. Derek would want to calm her fury. Blair would want to talk through it. Cody would want to apologize.

She refused to hear him apologize. He wouldn't let her go. He was pushing something that didn't need to be pushed. That shouldn't be pushed.

Her. He was pushing her. Forcing her to become someone she wasn't. His anger was a symptom. His anger was a mask. It let her know that he wasn't ready to move on. Why else would he be angry? People who had accepted reality didn't get so pissed.

Footsteps caught her attention. Had she misjudged her friends? Had they come after her? She stayed on the ground, squeezing her eyes tight. "Go away!"

The footsteps stopped. "I thought you wanted me to come."

Her head jerked up. The tears halted. He stood there, eyes soft, looking older, but also the same. A sad man with a sad story. A lost child desperate for love.

Jae crouched in front of her. He didn't touch her, but he was close enough that it wouldn't take much for him to. "This is one reason I hate him. I knew he would hurt you."

Hurt was part of life. Without hurt, there was no way to understand the joy. She never would have become the woman she was today if she'd never felt pain. Jae couldn't protect her from it. It wasn't his place to try.

"Why does it bother you if he hurts me?" Mia asked. "Why me?" She wasn't special. She didn't have magic or a special gift. She was a normal girl trying to live a normal life.

Jae reached forward and brushed her hair behind her ear. "You're my angel."

"But *why*?"

He stood and held out his hands for Mia to take. She dropped the journals and let him pull her to her feet. He stared down at her, and she up at him. If she hadn't known of all the things he'd done—if he hadn't hurt her and her friends—she might have seen him as a normal man. Someone trying to get along in a world that didn't want him.

She understood that.

"I've always been aware of Derek," Jae said, "but my mother hadn't told me about you. I'd thought it would be easy to do as she asked. To make sure that my father didn't get his way. But when I saw you, everything changed. I know it upset my mother. And I can't explain it. But your soul is unlike any I've ever seen."

Her soul? What did her soul have to do with any of this?

"I watched you from the time you were a kid," he continued. "I saw you grow up. I was in the shadows as you struggled and survived. You're strong. You're beautiful. You're kind. I don't love you in a romantic sense, but I do love you. I care about you very much. More than I have anyone in my life. And if I could explain why, I would. There's just something about you."

Mia looked at the ground. At the journals. "But I don't have magic. I'm not special."

"Magic isn't what makes a person special." Jae smiled. "You're special to me. To Cody. And most importantly, to Xue."

Mia gasped and stepped back. "You–"

"Don't worry," Jae said, holding up his hands. "I'm not going to do anything to her. Why would I? She brings you so much joy."

"But–"

"All I want is for you to be happy," Jae said. Then he looked at the forest floor. At the journals. "Why did you bring them?"

He didn't know? "We want the knife."

"Ah." He chuckled and reached into his coat. "And you want to bargain."

When he pulled out the sheathed knife, the world stopped existing. Mia's eyes trained to the beautiful artifact in his hands. Her pulse beat in her ears. A light whisper tried to break through, but it was inaudible. Still, she knew it was telling her to take the knife. She hadn't seen it since that night in the woods when she'd given it to Lior. Why had she ever given it to Lior? How could she have ever given up something that so clearly belonged to her?

She reached out to take it. Jae pulled it back and the spell broke. She blinked and stared up at him.

"I can't just give it to you," Jae said.

"Why not?" Mia asked. "What do you stand to gain by killing Lady Shion?"

Jae stared at the knife in his hands, then sighed. "I need to prove that I'm worth something."

Mia didn't understand. "You don't need to do anything to be worth something. You exist. You're worth something."

He laughed, bitter. "My parents would disagree."

"Screw them. They don't know anything. They're just idiot immortals who think they can do whatever they want with our lives. They don't define you. They don't get to dictate your life."

Jae smiled. A rare sight. He held out the knife, and it called to her, but she refrained from taking it. It was a trap. It had to be a trap.

"I've fought against her powers for years. My mother is a powerful woman. More powerful than I think the Iravata know. She wants this knife. She wants to manipulate you to use it, as it's useless to me now. It won't let me wield it. Already it senses you and wants to go home."

Mia frowned. "What are you—"

"I've kept it from her for five years. I've kept her away from you for five years. But I'm not strong enough to fight her forever. Unlike her, I'm mortal."

"You can," Mia said.

He shook his head. "I can't. But maybe you can stop me."

"What?"

He nudged the knife in her direction. The glowing writing on the blade was so bright it escaped the sheath. "Take it. Take it and end me."

Mia was certain her heart stopped. She stared into his beautiful, sad, gray eyes, and blinked back tears. "I...I...no...I...I can't...."

"You're right." He withdrew his hand. The knife. "I shouldn't have asked you to do that. I'm sorry. I wasn't thinking."

"This isn't the only option," Mia said. "You're not a bad person. You've done bad things, but you also housed all those Natara. No one asked you to do that. No one made you give them a safe place to live. You can go back to doing that. If we destroy the knife, Enya won't be able to use it and then you can be free."

He shook his head. "I'll never be free from her. As long as I live, I'll be stuck under her control. She can do that, you know. Control people."

A laugh, and then, "I will fight you if you take the knife from me. Maybe I was hoping you'd fight back. That you would end this without ever knowing that I have no choice. She gave me specific instructions. As long as I am alive, I must fight to kill the queen.

"But you're right. There is another option. One I hadn't thought of."

He smiled at her. "You're so kind. You look for the best in people. Even the people who hurt you. I always wanted to be as kind as you. But I'm not good."

He lifted the knife and unsheathed it.

Mia's eyes widened.

"Jae! Stop!"

"I hope one day you can forgive me for everything I've done. I'm sorry for hurting you."

She reached forward, desperate to take the knife, but she was too late. He thrust the knife into his stomach. A shock wave exploded through the forest, nearly knocking Mia off her feet.

Her vision went white for a moment. Just a moment.

And when it cleared again and the scenery of trees came back to her, she found the knife lying on the ground next to the journals, resting atop a fresh pile of ashes.

She screamed.

Derek felt his sister's grief moments before he heard her scream. He'd bolted from the room the moment the chilled liquid washed over his skin, leaving a confused Blair and Cody. But then Mia screamed. The footsteps behind him as he burst from the cabin let him know they were following. He didn't care about them, though. All he cared about was his sister.

He'd felt the moment Jae had arrived. He'd felt the moment Jae disappeared. What he didn't understand was why Mia had screamed.

The grief grew stronger, thickening to black tar on every inch of his skin. He nearly fell down the stairs he was running so fast, but he caught himself and spun into the forest. What had Jae done to her? Why, when he got close enough, did he hear her sobs?

"Mia!" he shouted between heavy breaths. He spotted her crouched over a pile of ashes and he skidded to a stop. Blair and Cody nearly crashed into him, and they shouted at him. But he couldn't move. The ashes. He'd seen ashes like that before. Except the last time he'd seen them, they'd blown away on the wind.

More than the ashes, another sight caused him to come to a grinding halt. Niran, standing over Mia. The ghost looked up at Derek, nodded, and then vanished.

What interest did Niran have in Mia? And why had he looked so sad?

Derek took a deep breath and walked over to his sister. She clutched something to her chest. Not a journal. Those were splayed in front of her, some covered in ash.

"Mia," Derek said. He touched her shoulder. "What happened?"

She unfurled, revealing a blue light. It shone through the evening forest, casting shadows and lighting up her face. The knife. She'd gotten the knife. But had she used it? Why did it shine so bright? It'd never done that when Derek or Jae had held it.

"You don't see it, do you?" Niran was back at Derek's side. "You don't see who she is."

Derek ignored him as Mia pushed herself to her feet, swaying. Derek caught her.

"He...." She breathed in with a hiccup. "He said it was the only way."

No. She couldn't have. "Did you–"

"No, he did." She faced him and held out the knife.

For the first time, Derek could see the knife's magic. He could see how it clung to Mia, pulsating. Thrilled. The souls inside were thrilled. How could he feel the souls' emotions?

"Destroy it. Free him. Free *them*. Let them find peace."

Could he do it? Obviously he had to try. They all had to try. But dread settled in his stomach as Niran's words finally registered in his mind. Who she is. His sister, the non-magical one in their group. The knife wanted her.

Mia was the true wielder of the knife. For the first time in six years, the knife was finally home. It's why she'd found it. It's why it'd protected her and not Derek. It's why Jae had been able to take it from Derek. Because Derek wasn't, and never had been, its wielder.

Derek reached forward, but he didn't take the knife. Instead, he curled Mia's fingers around it.

"What are you doing?" Mia asked. "Destroy it!"

Behind Derek, Cody gasped. He must have figured it out too.

"What?" Blair asked. "What's going on?"

"Do you understand now?" Niran asked.

Didn't he already know? Derek smiled at his sister. "You need to be sure, Mia. You're asking us to do the impossible, and we'll try. But I don't know what it'll do to you."

"Me? What are you talking about?"

"You're the wielder," Derek said.

Mia blinked, looking between Derek, Cody, and Blair. She opened her mouth, then closed it again as if trying to process what Derek had said. In times like this, he wished he could read her mind, not her emotions. Because her emotions were completely flat, condensed into shock, but it was clear she was processing *something*. The only question was, what?

"Oh," she breathed. "But, how? I don't have magic?"

Blair shrugged. "It's possible. It's not a real artifact. Maybe there's something about you that it likes. Cody, you always said that she's the only person in the world with a white mist."

All eyes turned on Cody, but he continued to stare at the knife, hands shoved deep in his pockets. He was trembling, Derek noticed. His emotions were a mix of frustration and confusion. Trying to understand the situation at hand.

"I want to figure out this mystery as much as the rest of you," he said slowly, "but I don't think we have time. There's no saying when Enya will realize what we're doing. If we're going to destroy the knife, we need to do it soon. Now, if possible."

Derek wanted to argue, even though Cody was right. If this went wrong, Mia could die. All of them could die.

Mia shoved the knife at him again. "Do it. I don't care what happens to me. Just do it so no one can ever be hurt by the knife again."

With a deep breath, Derek took the knife from her. The glow dimmed immediately, and its magic reached for Mia. If Mia had never found the knife, then would any of this had happened? Would she be in danger right now? Would any of them have been caught up in this war?

"We all need to try at the same time," Derek said. "Maybe, if we focus our magic into it, willing it to shatter, it'll overwhelm the knife. We're all powerful alone, but there's a reason we were brought together, and this might be it."

Shubishi and Death knew more than they were telling. Especially Shubishi. Had he known? All of these years, had he known that this day would come?

Mia backed away and Derek held out the knife. Its magic fluctuated. Fear crept up his arm, growing strong when Blair and Cody placed their hands on the weapon. Was that a good sign? That the knife was afraid? How could a knife be afraid?

Derek focused. Next to him, Niran waited with a somber expression, but Derek didn't care. Okay, he'd failed to find a way to save them both. And maybe this would kill Derek before Niran could take over. Maybe if Derek died, Niran would have free rein over his body. He didn't know. Everything was so uncertain. But it was too late to go back. He pushed his magic into the knife.

Golden magic flowed down his arm, mixing with Blair's blue and Cody's red. Hadn't Cody's been purple? No, it wasn't time to think of that. The magic mixed together as a cacophony of color and fought against the blue glow of the knife. It wasn't the same blue as Blair's. It was lighter. Almost white. How had he never noticed that before?

Sweat beaded on his forehead. His magic brightened. No, not his magic. Niran's magic. With each passing second, Niran grew more solid. More powerful. Derek was feeding into his own death, and there was nothing he could do to stop it. Even if he'd wanted to stop it.

This had to end. All of this needed to stop. He would become someone else, and it didn't matter. Because his sister would be free. Her ties to the magical world would end. That was worth all of this. He could protect her one last time.

The knife fought. It lashed out against the magic, but Cody's overpowered it in seconds. Blair's was next, consuming the blue-white glow with her sky-blue. And then Derek's. Niran's. Their magic swallowed the knife whole. Just when Derek thought he was going to pass out, the knife cracked. Mia gasped. The knife shattered. Mia collapsed to the ground.

Derek's first instinct was to grab her, but the knife, despite being in a million pieces, wouldn't let him go. It drained him, desperate to reform. He felt its pain. He felt its anger. Its sorrow. Its grief. A thousand souls screamed at him, confused and scared at the prospect of being free.

Then, Derek's magic snapped back into his hand. He stumbled away, temple pulsating, heart racing. The souls continued to scream, but this time they took shape. A gray hurricane that rose into the air, slowly regaining color. The souls separated, and Derek wondered if this is what Cody saw every day.

Collapsing to his knees, Derek looked at the pieces of the knife as they shimmered and then transformed. One second, they were metal and wood. The next, a man. He stood there, hair blond. Eyes gray. He looked at his hands, then at the sky where the souls danced together, lost but free.

A smile crossed his lips. And in words that Derek shouldn't have been able to understand, he whispered, "Thank you," before he vanished into a pure white soul that joined the others in the sky.

Chapter Thirty-Six

Cody stared, wide eyed, as the man transformed into a white soul and shot up to join the others. Who the hell was that?

He managed to stay standing, even as Derek and Blair both collapsed to their knees.

Mia lay unconscious, but alive, next to Derek. Her chest rose and fell, and her mist was a light gray. She would recover, he told himself. She had to recover.

He breathed in, and then out. They'd done it. Somehow, they'd destroyed the knife. All of them had lived through it, and they would recover. It was all going to be okay.

At least, that's what he thought until a new mist arrived. He didn't recognize it. Or maybe he did. It was one he'd felt before, but couldn't place. Someone who had lived in Willow Creek? But how was that possible? No one from Willow Creek knew about this place except the Iravata, and none of them had a purple mist.

Purple.

Cody's eyes widened and he looked up to find a woman standing over Jae's ashes. She had long locks of gorgeous red hair, and her blue eyes flickered with anger. She crouched down, silent, and ran her fingers through her son's ashes. Cody couldn't move. He wanted to. His mind screamed at him to grab Mia and run. To yell at the others to run as well. But he couldn't.

Why couldn't he run?

When Enya stood, she faced Mia. Bile rose in Cody's throat.

"No," he managed to get out. Derek and Blair couldn't speak. Enya's gaze snapped to him, and she sneered.

"You children are foolish. You were easy to play. Easy to manipulate. But now you've gone off script." She focused on Mia again, flames flickering between her fingertips. "My son was never supposed to die."

She raised her hand. Cody's eyes widened and he forced through whatever had trapped him. He was weak, and Enya was strong, but adrenaline overtook him and he pushed against the block. Enya must not have noticed. She was too focused on Mia. The flames grew stronger.

Cody reached out with his power. His red mist against her purple, and he grabbed her soul.

The flame went out. Enya gasped, but couldn't move. On either side of him, Blair and Derek gasped and moved. Not far. They were as weak as Cody.

"Let me go," Enya snarled.

Cody refused. But she fought him. The last time someone had fought him, they'd had power over souls. But this was different. There was another power layered beneath her wicked smile. One that blazed in her eyes as her face screwed up with contempt.

If Cody hadn't just destroyed a magical, soul stealing knife, he would have been able to hold her back. But his energy faltered and his mist shot back to his body. He stumbled as Derek managed to get to his feet. The fire grew stronger around Enya's fingers. She was going to kill Mia. Why would she kill Mia? Why, right as Mia

426

had found happiness, was Enya willing to take her from the world?

And why, after all of this, was Cody powerless to stop it?

Blair shouted something. Derek rushed forward. It was too late. They were all too late. Cody could only watch, helpless, as Enya prepared to kill Mia.

Then, the fire vanished. A hand clamped around Enya's wrist and yanked it up, turning her to face the man that Cody wanted nothing to do with.

Enya gasped and tried to pull away from Shubishi, but he wouldn't. His red mist layered over hers, calming her. Pushing her into submission.

"Enough," Shubishi said. "Leave the children alone. They've bested you."

Her vicious grin grew. "Bested me? No, they've merely set me back. All I have to do is start again. I have a white soul right here. I've made an artifact before, and I can do it again."

What the hell was she talking about?

As Enya and Shubishi glared at each other, Cody stumbled over to Mia's stirring body. She groaned, and he breathed out a sigh of relief. She was going to wake up. He crouched next to her and lifted her trembling body from the ground. He wasn't the strongest person in the world, but Mia was light, and he could do this for her.

"Cody?" she mumbled.

"It's okay," Cody said. "I'm here. You're okay. We're going to be okay."

Derek and Blair were at his side in a second, Blair urging them to get out of here. But they were too tired to run. All Cody could do was haul Mia to the side. Her eyes were still closed, but they flickered open every few seconds.

After he'd placed Mia back on the ground, leaning against a tree, he faced the immortals again. Enya had moved away from Shubishi, fire once more at her fingertips, and in the trees stood all of the

Iravata.

Were they going to fight? It wouldn't do anything. They were all immortal. The Iravata would have to talk Enya down from her rampage. But if they hadn't managed to talk her out of this before, how were they going to do it now?

"The girl is mine," Enya said. "Her soul will make a more magnificent knife. And this time, I'll be sure to do the honors of killing. No more pawns, Shubishi. It'll be just you and me. Me and Shion."

Shubishi, nonchalant as always, shrugged. "You can try. We've learned your tricks. We know of your other power."

Enya leaned her head back and howled. "Of course you have. It doesn't matter. In the end, I'll win. I am my people's protector and I will do everything I can to make sure they are safe."

"Safe? But who would they be in danger from?" Shubishi smiled as if he knew.

"From the last Seshen, of course." Enya pointed at the woods and Cody followed with his eyes. In all of the chaos, he hadn't noticed the black mist appear. He hadn't noticed Lady Shion melt from the shadows, walking toward Enya. Enya laughed again. "Look who finally decided to show her face. After all of these years of avoiding me. It would seem the queen has deigned to join the fight."

Enya bowed, but it was mocking. Her piercing laugh filled the woods.

Lady Shion stopped. "I am no threat to you or your people, Enya. I never have been, and I never will be. This conflict is in your head. All I want is to live out my immortality in peace."

"And what of my peace?" Enya asked.

No one spoke.

"How can I live a peaceful life knowing that I failed to kill all of my oppressors?"

The only one who wasn't overcome with shock was Shubishi.

He must have known all of these years, but for Cody, it came as a surprise. He should have seen it coming. Maybe all of them should have. But he hadn't. He hadn't considered that the perpetrator of the Seshen's downfall was the woman standing before them. Lady Shion took a step back, eyes widening.

Enya didn't stop to let her process. "You cannot die. I don't know how you convinced Death to give you immortality, but because of it you will pay. I will not rest until you have suffered the way my people suffered. The way *I* have suffered. And then, when I complete the new knife, I will finish what I started."

"You...you killed...my family." Lady Shion placed her face in her hands. "You are the reason I was forced into this. If you hadn't...that night...I'm here because of you. I would have lived a normal, happy life if it weren't for *you*."

"You don't deserve happiness," Enya said. Fire lighted in her palms. "Now, if you won't let me use the girl's soul, I will take my leave. I can wait. I will wait forever if I have to."

Lady Shion's head snapped up. "No."

"No?" Enya laughed. "You cannot control me, Shion. You are nothing. A coward."

Standing at her full height, Lady Shion didn't come across as intimidating. But when she spoke, it became clear who she was. "I cannot control you, Enya, but I am your queen. When I say you will harm no one ever again, it is your duty as a member of the council to obey!"

It was difficult to say what happened. One second, Lady Shion was speaking, and the next the world was white light, blinding Cody. Emotions flooded him. His? Hers? Enya's? He couldn't tell. Why couldn't he tell? But his mind went to war, fighting through the confusion and the anger.

And then, when the light cleared and the emotions disappeared, he found himself unable to stop staring at Lady Shion.

Blair gawked at Shion. Before the whiteness, Blair had felt herself growing more and more uncomfortable with the conversation. This wasn't about her and her friends anymore. This was about a conflict that was growing ever more confusing and complicated as Blair learned more information. It spanned thousands of years. Millions, maybe. It went back to the beginning of time itself, to a long history of pain for both Enya and Shion.

When the white light cleared, Blair found herself staring at a new woman. Not the Queen of the Iravata, but the Queen of the Vilaim. The woman from the stories, with her light brown hair and crystal blue eyes. Around her, the air shifted. A light pulsated from her skin. A signal to the world that everything had changed.

"We need to go," Blair said. Her skin crawled.

Derek grabbed her hand. "I can barely move."

She tore her gaze from the two women. Derek stood next to her, and next to him, Niran. Blair choked down a gasp. How could Niran be here already? How long had Derek been seeing him again? And why did Niran look so alive?

"Derek," she whispered.

He smiled at her, squeezing her hand. "It'll be okay."

No, it wouldn't. None of this would be okay. They needed to get out of there, and soon. If they didn't, then there was no saying what Enya would do to all of them. Though, when Blair looked back at the two women, she found Enya backing away. Her fire was gone and she was trembling.

Blair didn't blame her. Energy flowed out of Shion like water from a burst dam. The entire forest shuddered from her power. Birds flew into the air, calling out danger, and the trees seemed to withdraw from her. They respected her power. And what power it was.

"No!" Enya shouted. "I won't let you come back. We're happier without you. The Seshen destroyed us, and we've managed to rebuild. There is no queen. There is no obligation to bow down to a ruler who couldn't care less about us and our happiness. I will not let you ruin it!"

Lady Shion shook her head. "I want nothing to do with the Vilaim, Enya. That is not my home. This is my home, and I deserve to be happy here."

"No, you don't." Enya's hands lit up with flames again, the ground catching fire. Blair yelped. Her vision of fire. Had this been the cause? Was Enya about to burn more of Colorado to get her revenge?

At first, Blair didn't notice them. Not because they were hiding, but because she was too focused on the flickering flames to see their shadowy appearance. Their uncertain shape. Their murkiness. It wasn't until the world went silent and Enya collapsed to her knees, fire disappearing, that Blair took notice of the creature standing behind her.

Cody sucked in a deep breath. Next to him, Mia groaned and pushed herself to her feet. Derek muttered something in Chinese. And Blair stared as the figure took a humanesque form. No one spoke. Enya stared at her hands, flipping them back and forth. Her breaths increased. She scrambled to her feet, backing away from both the figure and Lady Shion—the latter of whom stared at the former with shock.

"What did you do to me?" Enya shrieked.

Death, in all of their glory, stood tall. "I have taken away your immortality."

They'd what now? Blair's jaw dropped. When had he learned to do that? Why had they done that? What was going on?

Enya shook her head, furious, and then she was gone. Death faced Lady Shion.

Mia stepped forward. Blair immediately grabbed for her, as did Derek and Cody, but Mia continued toward the deity who had caused all of this.

"You," she whispered. "I know you."

Death nodded at Mia, and Blair tried to wrap her mind around what was going on.

Chapter Thirty-Seven

Derek went after Mia. He had no idea what she was talking about, but it wasn't safe for her. Death was unpredictable. Unstable. He did things in his own time. At his own pace. Against all logic. Reality meant nothing to him. If he wanted to take Mia's soul, he could. Just like he'd made the immortals. Just like he'd taken away Enya's immortality.

Derek stumbled and Mia caught him. Niran stood not far away, watching everything in silence. Who could see him? Who couldn't? No one had acknowledged him, and he didn't try and speak. Even when he eyed Derek, and Derek glared at him.

Death eyed Shion before he focused on Mia. No, not just Mia. Mia and Derek. Derek's first instinct was to protect his sister, but how could he when he could barely stand.

"Don't disappear," Mia whispered to him.

He didn't plan on it, but when had anything gone to plan?

Neither of them moved. Death walked—well, glided—toward them. In the silence of the clearing, Derek could hear his own pounding heart. What was Death going to do to his sister?

"Don't you dare hurt her," Derek sputtered out. Mia hushed him, but how could he say nothing? Death was dangerous, and Mia didn't deserve any of this.

When Death reached out his hand, Derek made to smack it away, only to miss completely. Death's fingers trailed against Mia's forehead and she gasped. Panic settled in Derek's gut. Was Death making her immortal? Why would he do that? To protect her from Enya? She didn't want to be immortal. She just wanted to be *normal*.

Then Death reached for Derek. The deity's fingers were cold against Derek's forehead, and Derek prepared for the worst.

The world spun. Behind his vision, he saw his own memories. All of the times he'd used magic. Every moment he'd feared for his life. The joy, the hatred, the frustration, the love. Was this what it was like to die? Was his life literally flashing before his eyes?

But it wasn't that. Because he didn't grow weaker. His body regained physical strength, even as the magic left him. Mia's emotions dimmed. They didn't vanish, but they weren't as strong against his skin.

He sucked in a breath. A weight he hadn't realized was resting on his chest vanished. And when the world righted itself, he found himself unable to see magic. Unable to access magic. Unable to do anything but feel the dimmest emotions from his twin sister. Meanwhile, Niran stood before them, facing Shion. Shion stared at him, hand going to her heart.

"Holy shit," Cody muttered.

Derek glanced at him. He could move again. No stumbling. He didn't need to lean on Mia. "What?"

"Your mists," Cody whispered. "They've changed."

What did that mean?

Niran's voice caught Derek's attention. His whisper of Shion's name. Derek spun around. The man was fully formed, but not alive. He was a spirit of pure magic. White and gold.

He held out a hand to Shion. "I've missed you. I never could imagine how beautiful you would look with blue eyes."

Mia understood. While Derek pressed for answers, while Niran offered his hand to Lady Shion, while Cody muttered something under his breath and Blair looked between everyone, confused, Mia understood. The answer had been there all along. Why the knife had chosen her. Why she'd lit up the darkness. Even though she couldn't see her mist, she knew it was no longer white. An energy she'd always taken for granted was gone. Her soul was now her own.

"What is going on?" Derek snapped. It was good to hear him lively again.

"I have retrieved Niran's soul," Death said. How could she have never noticed him before? He'd always been in her periphery. A guardian angel—though she wasn't certain she would call him angelic. He was gaunt, hunched over, with a wrinkled face and his hands behind his back.

"But–"

"Derek," Cody interrupted. "Niran's soul was gold and white."

Derek fell silent. Did he understand now too? Did he understand that they were both Niran? He caught Mia's gaze. His eyes were no longer green, but a deep shade of brown. Almost identical to her own. That was going to take some getting used to.

Shubishi stepped forward, bowing his head at Death before he focused on the twins. "You are free from the magical world."

"But I–" Derek tried to say.

"You have been using Niran's magic for your entire life," Shubishi cut in. "Now it is back where it belongs. Both halves of the whole." He glanced at Mia with a raised brow. "You seem to be taking this quite well."

She was. Maybe she shouldn't, but everything had clicked into place. "Maybe I'm finally willing to believe that I was special too."

Shubishi's smile was something she hadn't expected. It wasn't malicious or all-knowing. It was gentle. Kind. Maybe a hint of the man he'd been before his immortality.

She had questions, but there would be time for questions later. Derek was going to live. Mia was free of the burden she'd carried. Blair was alive. Cody had sacrificed so much for this moment to happen. For the moment when Shion lifted her hand and placed it in Niran's. When Niran lifted it to his lips.

There would be time later. For now, all Mia could do was smile.

He watched the fruits of his labor, of all of his mistakes and all of his planning, and he found that it was satisfactory. The children were confused, but alive. The Iravata hesitant and watching from the shadows. The queen and the priest stood together, staring into each other's eyes as they should have done all of these years. They'd fought through so much. Separately. Together. Now, they were one.

She faced him, still holding on to her lover's hand.

He bowed his head. "I want you to live forever."

Her smile brought him joy. "I know. But it's not what I want. It's never what I wanted. Enya is right. There is no reason for my people to stay alive through me. Sometimes it's best to let the past be the past. It's time for my reign to end."

But she looked so much like Seshen. She was the last remaining remnant of his first memory of happiness. He never wanted to let go of the woman who had died without his permission. Who had passed on to the Realm of Death, and possibly beyond. She had been his first friend. The only one who had not wanted to use him. Who had treated him as an equal, even though he was her creator.

How could he move on?

To him, time had passed like nothing. One second he was creating Seshen, and the next he was here. He did not process time the way the mortals did. For him, it had been moments. For them, it had been lifetimes. They had lived through all of the pain and the frustration of life. They stood there, tall and strong. Waiting for him to decide to free them from the bonds he had forced upon them.

A hand touched his arm. He looked at the man who had given him the option to change the face of reality.

"It's time, old friend," Shubishi said.

It was time. He reached out. She looked so much like Seshen. He wanted to keep her forever. To keep her alive so he could relive the memories that were slowly disappearing. He couldn't.

He placed a hand on Shion's head.

And then, he let her go.

Epilogue

ven though Derek smiled, he felt wrong. Evening settled over the party, and he watched it from a safe distance away from the bonfire and dancing. Music blared through the air, matching the beat of his heart. Or maybe it was his heart that matched the rhythm of the drums. He couldn't tell, and it didn't matter.

He brought a cup of water to his lips. He wished for wine, but apparently it was forbidden at this party. Something about everyone needing to be clear-headed for the ceremony that would be taking place sometime soon. In his mind, he was back seven years ago, standing alone at his parents' museum opening with a glass of wine and a desire to escape. The wine might not have been there, but the desire certainly was.

Really, he was happy for Blair. This was the night when it would all come together for her. Once she reached the top of the plateau that waited for her in the distance, she'd become the leader of the Cokori Clan. The future she'd once run from was becoming her reality, and Derek was blessed to see it happen. At least, the party portion. The actual ceremony was for family members only.

Magical family members only.

Derek was neither.

Over the past month, he'd tried his best to get used to his new situation. To the fact that he wasn't the powerful mage he'd always thought he was. He still didn't understand it, but whatever Death had done to him and Mia, it'd changed him. Cody assured him that he was completely fine. He had a full soul. So did Mia. There would be no negative side effects to separating from Niran.

The problem was, Derek didn't believe it. Because a part of him was missing, and he didn't know how to get it back.

He spotted Blair. She looked beautiful, dressed in her clan's regalia. Colorful clothes that seemed to glow in the light of the bonfire. She danced with her brothers. The younger ones whooped, having the time of their lives, while Leo sat on the sidelines. He was still wheelchair bound, but healthier. All the doctors had said he was safe to leave the hospital.

Derek could still feel their emotions. They weren't as strong as they had been before, but they were still there. Glee overcame him. His and others'. The entire clan was celebrating, whether at the party or in their homes. But it wasn't just the clan. Derek's parents had come too, though they looked wildly uncomfortable sitting with the clan elders. They were sworn to secrecy, but Derek had a feeling that they were watching with fascination at the culture unfolding before them. And close by staring out at the dancing and listening to music, Mia sat with her girlfriend, while Cody, like Derek, stood alone.

"Derek!"

He'd been so focused on the others that he'd lost track of his girlfriend. Maybe his fiancée, if he got his way. Mrs. Arbour had cautioned him to wait until after the ceremony so as not to distract Blair from her duties, but Derek definitely planned to propose. To be part of her life forever.

His smile turned genuine as Blair bounded over to him.

"Come on," she said, "dance with us."

Her brothers whistled at the two of them, and Blair waved them off.

"I don't dance," Derek said.

"I've seen you dance."

"Okay, I don't dance *publicly*."

She laughed and tugged at his hands. He didn't move, but he did pull her closer. He might not have magic anymore, but he was still stronger than Blair. Not that she resisted. He cupped her cheek and kissed her, loving the way she wrapped her arms around his neck. Her emotions—still muted—fluctuated between excitement and a hint of lust. He couldn't stop the smile from spreading across his lips.

"Please?" she asked.

As much as it hurt to deny her plea, he shook his head. "It's almost time, isn't it?"

"I guess." She sighed and stepped back.

He still hadn't gotten used to how happy she was here in Sangota. How often she dragged him out into the city to learn about the place she loved more than anywhere else. Sure, people stared at them. Many didn't approve of their relationship, but what could they do? Blair was their leader, and she refused to let anyone kick Derek out of Sangota.

"Go talk to your sister," Blair said. "And Xue. Girl looks so confused."

Derek laughed. "Wouldn't you be? She barely speaks English and she's lived her whole life in China. This is *very* new to her."

"Exactly my point." Blair poked him in the chest.

"What do you think of her?" Derek really liked Xue. She was quiet in English, but when they switched to Chinese, it was clear as day that she was incredibly intelligent. Intira and Liang had welcomed her with open arms, Intira going on a long rant when she'd found out about Xue's relationship with her own parents.

"How could a mother ever disown her child?"

Then she'd insisted Xue come live with them and learn English. Derek had never seen someone so happy. Except maybe when Xue looked at Mia.

"I don't know her super well," Blair admitted. "But that'll come with time and language. You should pick up her tutoring. Mia's not great at teaching."

True. "I'll do my best."

"Blair!" Mrs. Arbour's voice rang out across the night and Blair jumped.

"Oh, it's time." She leaned up and kissed Derek. A quick peck. "I'll see you after the ceremony."

"Can't wait," he whispered. She kissed him again before she was off to join her family. Her mom, aunt, cousin, and brothers. They would find the elders at the top of the plateau and Blair would officially become the clan leader.

Once she was gone, he breathed out. His heart was still empty. But there was something there. A flickering of *something*. Without a word, he backed away from the bonfire and went to find someplace to think. He needed a moment alone to think about who he was. What he wanted. How he was going to get it.

The stars appeared faster in the sky, like paint splattered across an empty canvas. He stared up at them, willing them to have answers for him. If he wasn't Niran's reincarnation, then who was he? Was it okay to just be Derek?

They'd all told him he'd lost his magic. He would never get it back, they said. But he didn't believe that. He hadn't lost his empathy. Maybe, just maybe, that was a sign that Niran's magic hadn't been the only magic within him. After all, Niran hadn't picked him and Mia for no reason. For Mia, it was obvious why. But for Derek? Why had he chosen Derek? Could it be because of the power that had been repressed his entire life?

Holding out a hand, he focused. This used to come as easy as breathing for him. The magic would have flowed without any restraint. That had been Niran's magic, already primed and ready for use. Derek's magic was weak. He needed to retrain it. To focus.

He focused. A spark trickled down his arm. Warmth. It collected in his palm and a little orb of green light floated there for a second before it sparkled and vanished. Sweat dripped down his neck.

He wiped it away with a grin.

As the night wore on, Cody found himself unable to connect. The past month had been rough for him and his dad. The funeral had been quiet. They hadn't invited any of Ava's friends. They wouldn't have understood why, even if Cody had tried to explain.

He still didn't understand why.

Honestly, he didn't want to be here. The party raged on, even though Blair and her family had gone to the plateau. They would party until the sun rose and Blair returned, leader of the Cokori Clan. It wasn't that Cody wasn't happy for her. She'd found where she belonged. But sometimes, when he lay awake at night, staring at his bedroom ceiling, his jealousy got the best of him.

Where did he belong? It wasn't here, in Sangota. They wouldn't welcome him, even if he were the right kind of mage. Blair had offered a place for him and he'd declined. Derek was one thing. They would tolerate their leader's boyfriend. Cody, though? That would never happen.

Familiar laughter caught his attention. Xue had said something to Mia, and Mia was laughing into her shoulder. Cody didn't know what to make of Xue. She was quiet. A bit hesitant to speak around

Cody or Blair. Afraid of her limited English, he guessed. The two of them were living in D.C. with Mia's parents. Dr. Sòng had offered Cody a place with her too. That had been easier to turn down than Blair. The last thing he needed was to be around Mia and Xue every day.

So, what were his options? Denver pained him. Willow Creek didn't exist. Dylan wanted Cody to move in with him, to spend time together and figure out how to live in a world without Ava, but Cody couldn't do that. He needed to stop living in the past.

With a deep breath, he turned away from Mia and Xue to get some water. He'd come here to celebrate Blair, and here he was thinking only of himself. He didn't dance. He'd barely spoken to Blair. He'd barely spoken to anyone.

What was he even doing there?

"Cody."

He stiffened. He hadn't gone two feet before Mia's voice called out to him. He turned to face her.

"Are you okay?" Mia asked.

No. He was not okay. Mia knew that. "I'm fine."

"Getting water?"

"Yes."

"I'll come with you."

He grimaced, not wanting to spend time alone with her. Seeing her hurt him. Talking to her *hurt* him. But he couldn't say no to her, so he nodded, and the two headed off toward the table where someone was handing out water. On the way, they passed by Mia and Derek's parents. They waved at them, though Mia's mom was deep in conversation with an elder about the geopolitical ramifications of mage culture spilling out into the rest of the world, while her dad listened intently.

Mia rolled her eyes. "Typical."

Cody chuckled. The sound was foreign in his throat. When they reached the water, Mia stopped and faced him.

"What do you think of Xue?"

Great. He'd been hoping to avoid this conversation. "I don't know her well."

"She likes you," Mia said.

"Does she?"

"Yeah, but she thinks you hate her."

Cody flinched. It wasn't that he hated her. It was more that he hated that he couldn't *be* her. No matter how he tried, he would never be the person that Mia wanted. "I don't. Just don't know how to talk to her."

"Why not?"

"You know why not."

"Right."

Mia had changed. She wasn't the same girl he'd hidden under the slide with. Still, he loved her. He would always love her.

"It's…." He sighed. "It's never going to be me, is it?" He knew the answer, but he had to ask.

Mia shook her head. "No."

Cody grabbed a cup of water and handed it to Mia. She was beautiful. The most beautiful woman in the world. Her smile lit up everything. He wanted to be part of her life, but he wasn't sure he could be. "Go back to Xue. I need a moment."

Mia nodded and headed back to her girlfriend. Xue lit up the instant she noticed Mia coming back to her, and Mia sped up. Would anyone ever understand him enough to light up that way?

He ignored the offered water and headed away from the table, no longer thirsty. No one paid attention to him. He stood there, once again wondering what he was doing there. Wondering where he belonged.

A thought occurred to him. He pulled out his phone. There *were* people who understood him. Maybe not someone he'd ever love, but people who knew what he was going through.

Parker answered on the first ring. "Cody?"

Cody breathed in. "I'm in."

"In?"

"You wanted my help with the Natara kids, right? I'm in."

There was a minute of silence. No doubt Parker trying to wrap his mind around the change of attitude. "Oh. Great. Meet us now? We're in New York."

New York. Cody had always wanted to visit New York. "I'll be there soon." He hung up and glanced at Mia. She was laughing again, and Xue looked at her with the eyes of someone who had found the most precious gem in the world.

She *had* found the most precious gem in the world.

Maybe it was childish of him, but Cody needed to find a way to move on. He couldn't do that if he was in Mia's life. Maybe one day they could be friends. Maybe one day he'd know where he belonged. With a deep breath, he turned his back on Mia, on the party, on the life he'd clung to for the past five years. And then he walked away.

Blair wished that her grandmother could be here to see this. The last time Blair had climbed this plateau, it'd been a challenge. She hadn't been physically strong, and she hadn't been mentally ready. This time, she was both. There was no time limit, and no pressing reason for her to find the necklace and run for her life.

She'd never have to run from anything ever again.

As she climbed the plateau, her brothers staying quiet for the first time all night, she looked ahead. Not behind. All of her life, she'd fought this moment. Even though she was a seer, she'd never foreseen this moment. It had always been so out of her grasp. The future. Something that mocked her, always just out of her reach.

If she'd known that she'd one day walk up these steps to the vault that held her people's history, her people's magic, would she have run so hard? Knowing her, the answer was yes. This hadn't been a vision. This wasn't destiny dictating her life. This was her choice.

When they reached the top, she strode forward. Her mom was already there, beaming. Her aunt wiped away tears. Her brothers and cousin behind her stopped.

"Blair Demini," Esther said, "are you ready to take on the responsibility of leading your clan?"

"I am." Blair didn't hesitate. Her hands shook. Her stomach twisted itself in knots. Not because of nerves, but excitement. The past month, getting used to the living realm again, had shown her more than ever that she belonged in Sangota. She belonged here with her family. With Derek at her side.

She just wished Enola had lived to see this moment. As much of a pain in the ass as Enola had been, Blair knew that she'd done everything out of love. Fear, but also love. She'd loved Blair. And Blair loved her. Hopefully, her grandmother had made it to the Realm of Death and could work through her regrets until she passed on to whatever came next.

"Once I open these doors, there is no turning back," Esther continued. "Once the ceremony begins, you cannot take it back. Are you sure you're ready?"

Blair stared at the door. She could feel the necklace behind it, desperate to return to its rightful owner. It was a puzzle piece ready to find its place in the greater picture.

Just like Blair.

She nodded with a grin. There was no turning back, but she didn't want to turn back. There was no more running. No more hiding.

This was her birthright, and she was determined to take it.

"I'm ready."

Esther Demini-Arbour opened the vault door, and Blair straightened her back before she walked into the vault and let the new chapter of her life begin.

Mia had been aware of everyone all night. She'd noticed when Blair had gone off to the plateau. When Derek had disappeared to think. When Cody had vanished into the night. None of it worried her. She'd see them all again. Derek first, then Blair, then Cody. Even if it took time, she'd see Cody again. She had a feeling that fate wasn't done with them yet.

"This is amazing," Xue said. Mia smiled at her, then leaned in and kissed her cheek. Xue's grin was infectious. "I can't believe I'm here. This is nothing like you see in American television shows."

Mia couldn't help but laugh. "Surely by now you've realized that American TV isn't actually that accurate."

"Well, yeah, but this…." She waved a hand.

"It's magnificent." Mia breathed in the scent of burning firewood. In the past, it might have reminded her of Willow Creek burning to the ground, but tonight, it brought her nothing but good memories. Memories of school homecoming. Of s'mores and laughter with friends. Of warmth and comfort.

She glanced around. Her parents were sitting together, Intira's head on Liang's shoulder. It was good to see them. It was good to be back, living with them and reconnecting with the people who had raised her. She loved the way they'd accepted Xue. Even though her father was a little uncomfortable with the whole thing, he was trying. Intira didn't care that Xue was a woman. All she cared about was when the wedding would be.

Xue had blushed the first time Intira had brought it up. Mia had never seen Xue blush before, and she found she quite liked the sight.

Derek and Xue got along well too, and Mia knew that once Xue learned more English—or Blair bothered to learn Chinese—then the two of them would take over the world together. And maybe one day, Cody would be okay with it. He could come back and be part of her life once more.

It was amazing how much things had changed. The four of them had been so close, and now they were all going down their own paths. Mia was even applying to universities, though the idea of going when Xue couldn't bothered her. They'd work on that, though. Maybe she could convince Derek to help out. He'd always been better with languages than Mia. Of course, that would mean dragging him away from Blair and Sangota, but Mia figured she could manage that.

All of this, the happiness, the joy, reminded her so much of the time before the secrets had come out. Back in the days when Willow Creek was their prison, not a place in their past.

It had been her home.

Mia stood abruptly.

"You okay?" Xue asked.

"Yeah." She smiled down at her girlfriend and held out a hand. "You wanna see where I grew up?"

"Um…." Xue looked around. "I mean, yes, but I thought it burned to the ground. And is quite far."

Both true, but that was the thing about magic. It was possible to do anything. "I'll make it work." She grabbed her girlfriend's hands and pulled her to her feet. "Come on."

The party melted away as Mia led Xue somewhere quiet. The music and chatter quieted. The warmth from the bonfire faded. In her mind, Mia called for the one Iravata she knew would be listening.

Most of the others had given up their immortality, but Lior had decided he wanted to keep it for a while. Not forever, he'd said, but long enough.

He appeared, shaking his head. "If the mages find out I'm here, it'll cause trouble."

Xue jumped with a gasp. "He speaks Chinese?"

Lior bowed. "I do. It's a pleasure to meet you, Xue. I hope you're taking care of my favorite student."

"Of course," Xue said, though she sounded confused. Mia figured she'd explain later.

"Now then, what can I do for you, Poppet?"

Mia smiled and said, "Take me home."

In an instant, they were away from the party. From the fields of Sangota. All around them, burned trees stuck straight into the air, lonely without their foliage. Beneath them, in the charred ground, new, green life poked out from ashen soil. The mountain was healing. It would take time, and it would take effort, but eventually the scar would vanish. Maybe, one day, life would return.

Neither Mia nor Xue spoke as they walked together through the forest, through the destroyed town. Mia surveyed the damage. This place would never be the same, but that was okay. One day they'd rebuild, and this town would hold onto its history with pride.

Before long, Mia found herself on a familiar path. She'd walked it almost every day for ten years. A sidewalk leading to a cul-de-sac. And at the end of the cul-de-sac, the house she'd called home.

Mia let go of Xue's hand and walked up to the house. So much had happened over the past seven years. She'd never thought that life would bring her back here. She'd always thought she would escape from Willow Creek. From the small town vibe. The girls who had bullied her. The sheltered life that her parents had built for her. This place had become one of hatred. Of solitude.

Returning, she found it spoke of something different. It had been hell to grow up here, but it had been part of her journey. It had shaped her into the person she was now. Things would never be the same for Willow Creek. Things would never be the same between her and her friends. Her and her brother. They'd become their own people. But that was okay. That was the way life went. She'd found a way to spread her wings and fly.

As she stared into the heavens, wondering if Shion and Niran were there, tears streamed down her face. And for the first time in seven years, her heart was finally free.

The End

Acknowledgements

Thirty years ago, I came into this world. An hour later, my mother died.

There aren't enough words to describe the grief I feel from that loss. Even though no one blamed me, I still blamed myself for so many years. I fought against the voices of my friends and family reassuring me that it wasn't because of me and that she wanted me to live. Mothers have told me they know that she wouldn't have wanted me to hate myself for the way she died.

I still did.

And maybe I always will, just a little bit. Emotions are fickle beings. They're different for everyone. Grief is different for everyone. I don't claim to know what other people feel in my situation, only what I do. I'm no Derek. I'm not an empath. Maybe if I was, I wouldn't feel so alone.

When I set out to write this series, I was a foolish seventeen-year-old with no knowledge of how to write a book, how to write a series, or how to process the emotions eating me alive. I had an idea. An idea of darkness. Of pain. Of grief.

It wasn't until I was plotting out this book that I understood what it all meant.

For so many years, I thought this was just a series I was writing for fun. It meant nothing to me. But when I wrote the final lines, I knew it wasn't just that. It was me saying goodbye.

I could go on about how much this series means to me, and what writing these final words, saying "sayonara" to a series I've been working on for almost half of my life, makes me feel. These characters have been my comfort. They were always there in the back of my mind, waiting for me to finish their story and give them the closure I can never have.

Life is messy. Things don't go our way. Trauma lurks around every corner. Healing isn't guaranteed. It's something we have to fight for and look deep inside to find.

While Mia, Derek, Blair, and Cody's stories aren't complete, this tale is. They will continue on finding happiness, growing, and learning about themselves. So will I. But it's time for me to say goodbye to my mom and the pain I feel every year on my birthday when people tell me that they're so glad I'm in their life.

Thank you, everyone.

To my aunt, who has always told me to write about myself.

To Karen, who helped me so much with this entire series, from heavy revisions on *Lotus in the Mountain*, to final edits on *The Risen Queen*.

To Kathleen and Ashley, the other Crabby McStabbers who gave me so much input and helped me become the writer I needed to be to finish this story.

To Cas, helping me learn photoshop and listening to me vent about the state of publishing. Not to mention helping with my amazing website.

To Jules, who worked so hard to bring all these beautiful new cover into the world and managed to shift through my complicated explanations and moods and timelines to create something freaking beautiful!

To all my readers who gave me motivation when I just wanted to give up.

To my sister, who taught me to believe in myself.

To my brothers, who have both kept me sane, and driven me insane as I learned to be a better person.

To Grandma Helen. I wish you could have lived long enough to see this day.

And finally, to Mom. You gave me life, and I will never take it for granted. I may be letting you go, but I will always love you.

For anyone out there dealing with grief, keep going. Even if it's just one day at a time, you will make it through. Just remember: anything is possible with magic.

Linn Coldiron

About the Author

A Colorado native, Linn Coldiron spends her time reading, writing, and studying languages. Her love of language and culture has led her to live a peripatetic life filled with inspiration from all over the world.